Fuzzy Baseball

TRIPLE PLAY

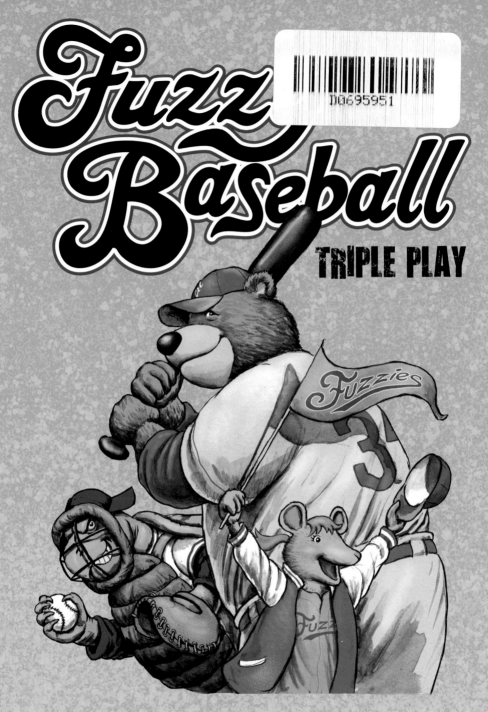

John Steven Gurney

PAPERCUTZ™

New York

MORE GREAT GRAPHIC NOVEL SERIES AVAILABLE FROM

PAPERCUTZ™

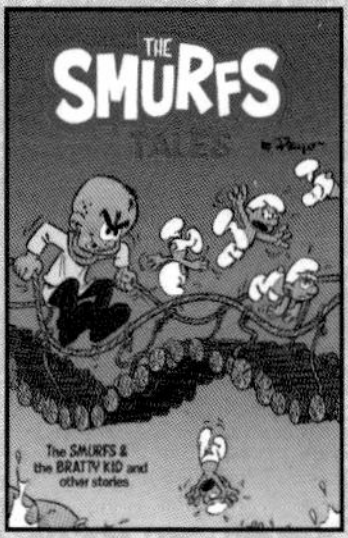
THE SMURFS
TALES
The SMURFS & the BRATTY KID and other stories
THE SMURFS TALES

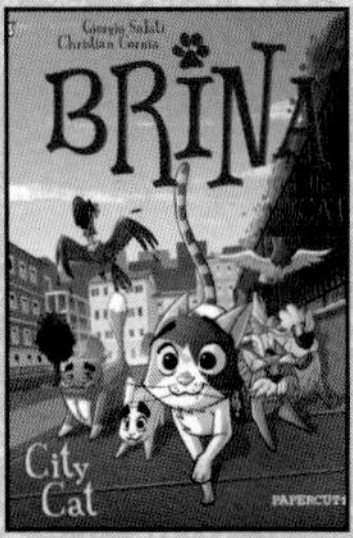
Giorgio Salati
Christian Cornia
BRINA
City Cat
BRINA THE CAT

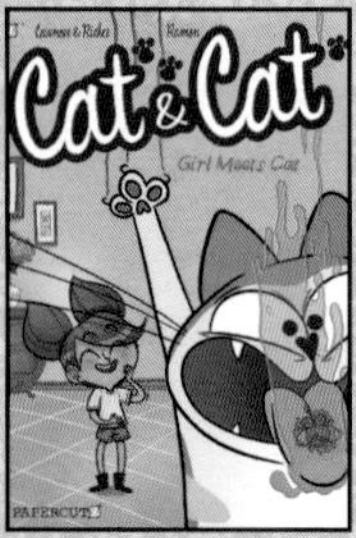
Cat & Cat
Girl Meets Cat
CAT & CAT

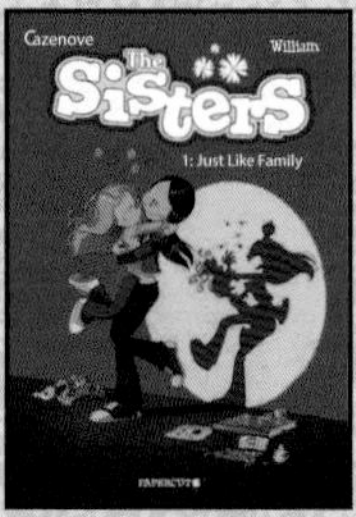
Cazenove
William
The Sisters
1: Just Like Family
THE SISTERS

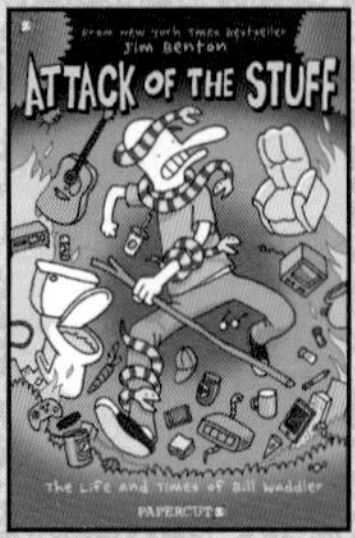
Jim Benton
ATTACK OF THE STUFF
The Life and Times of Bill Waddler
ATTACK OF THE STUFF

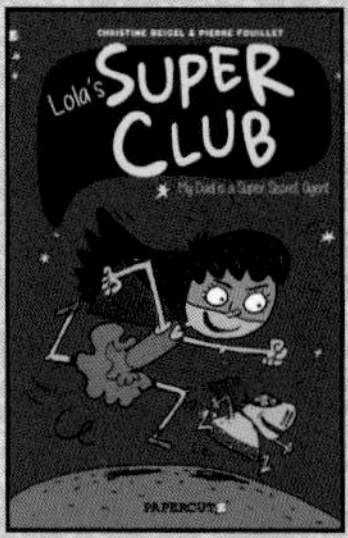
CHRISTINE BEIGEL & PIERRE FOUILLET
Lola's SUPER CLUB
LOLA'S SUPER CLUB

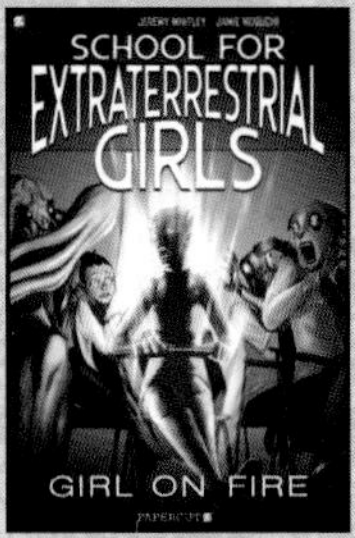
JEREMY WHITLEY
JAMIE NOGUCHI
SCHOOL FOR EXTRATERRESTRIAL GIRLS
GIRL ON FIRE
SCHOOL FOR EXTRATERRESTRIAL GIRLS

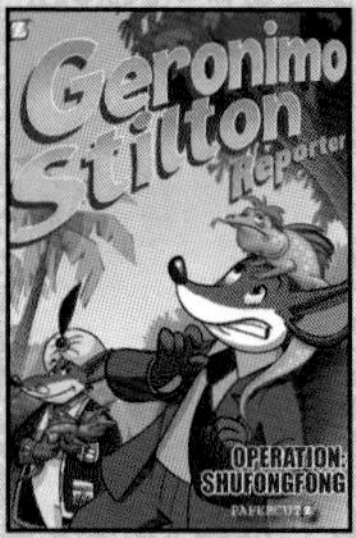
Geronimo Stilton
Reporter
OPERATION: SHUFONGFONG
GERONIMO STILTON REPORTER

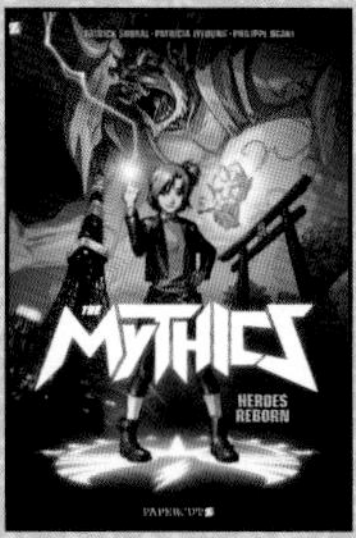
THE MYTHICS
HEROES REBORN
THE MYTHICS

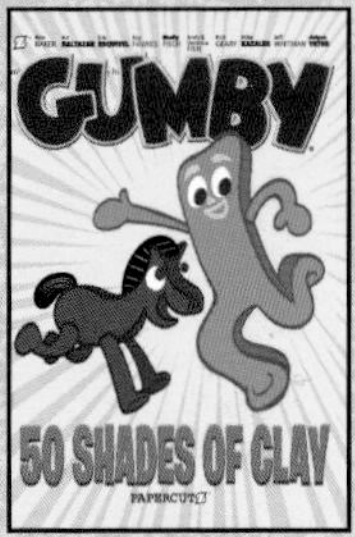
GUMBY
50 SHADES OF CLAY
GUMBY

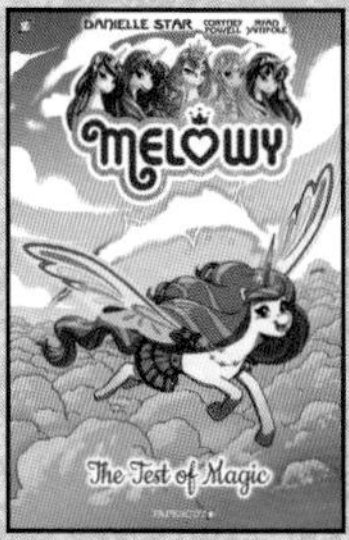
DANIELLE STAR
MELOWY
The Test of Magic
MELOWY

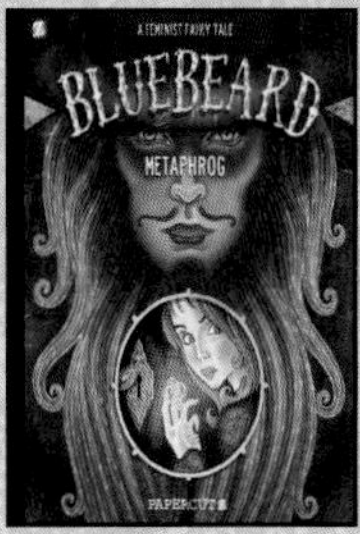
A FEMINIST FAIRY TALE
BLUEBEARD
METAPHROG
BLUEBEARD

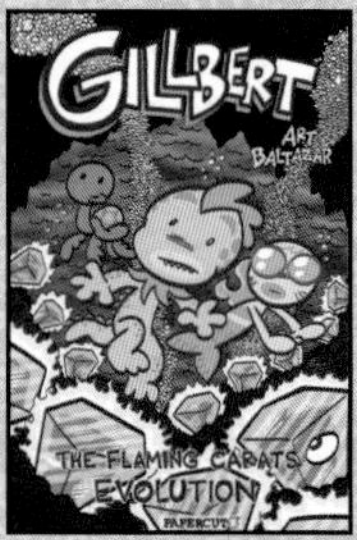
GILLBERT
ART BALTAZAR
THE FLAMING CARATS EVOLUTION
GILLBERT

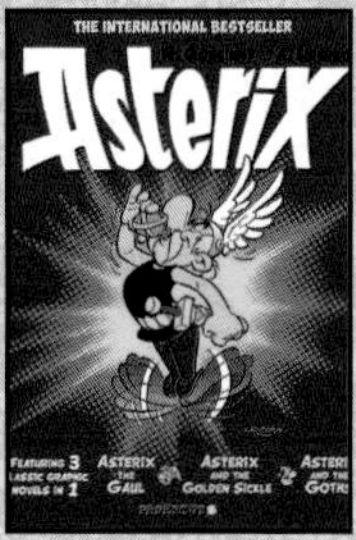
THE INTERNATIONAL BESTSELLER
Asterix
ASTERIX

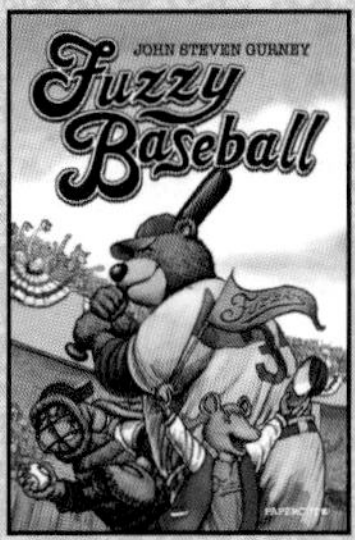
JOHN STEVEN GURNEY
Fuzzy Baseball
FUZZY BASEBALL

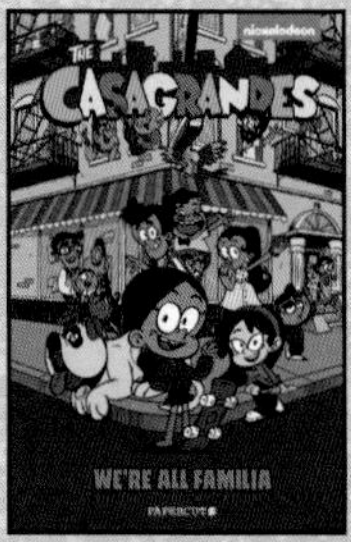
nickelodeon
THE CASAGRANDES
WE'RE ALL FAMILIA
THE CASAGRANDES

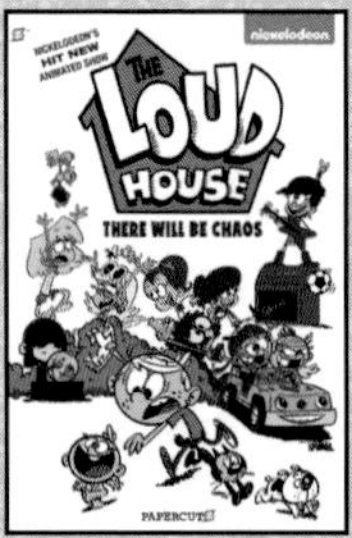
nickelodeon
THE LOUD HOUSE
THERE WILL BE CHAOS
THE LOUD HOUSE

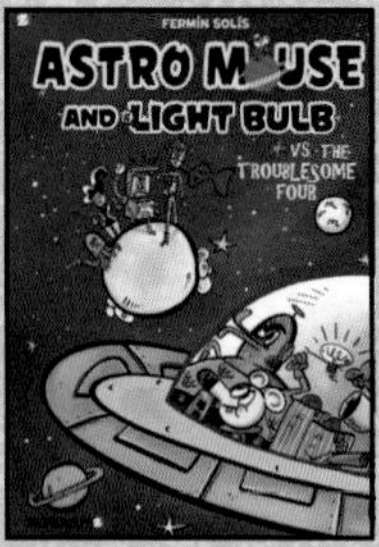
FERMÍN SOLÍS
ASTRO MOUSE AND LIGHT BULB
VS THE TROUBLESOME FOUR
ASTRO MOUSE AND LIGHT BULB

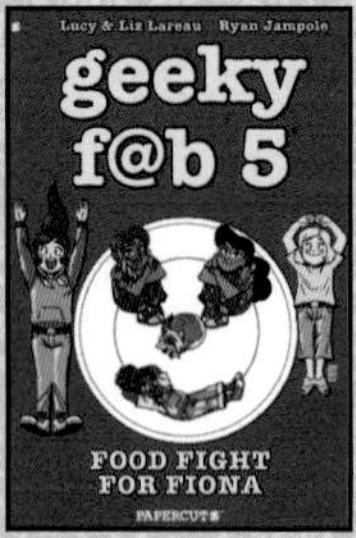
Lucy & Liz Lareau
Ryan Jampole
geeky f@b 5
FOOD FIGHT FOR FIONA
GEEKY F@B 5

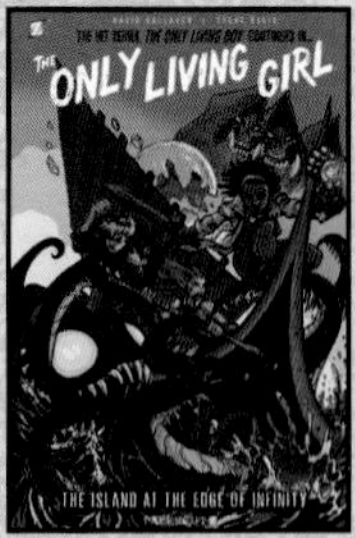
THE ONLY LIVING GIRL
THE ISLAND AT THE EDGE OF INFINITY
THE ONLY LIVING GIRL

papercutz.com

Also available where ebooks are sold.

Fuzzy Baseball
TRIPLE PLAY

Created by
JOHN STEVEN GURNEY

Collecting
FUZZY BASEBALL #1
FUZZY BASEBALL #2 "Ninja Baseball Blast"
FUZZY BASEBALL #3 "RBI Robots"

MARK McNABB – Production
JEFF WHITMAN – Managing Editor
JIM SALICRUP
Editor-in-Chief

Special thanks: DAWN GUZZO, MANOSAUR MARTIN,
SHANNON ERIC DENTON, KARLO ANTUNES, and BETHANY BRYAN

ISBN: 978-1-5458-0905-1

Printed in China
May 2022

Papercutz books may be purchased for business or promotional use.
For information on bulk purchases please contact Macmillan
Corporate and Premium Sales Department at
(800) 221-7945 x5442.

Distributed by Macmillan
First Printing

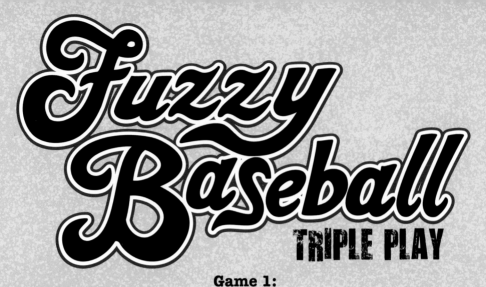

Fuzzy Baseball
TRIPLE PLAY

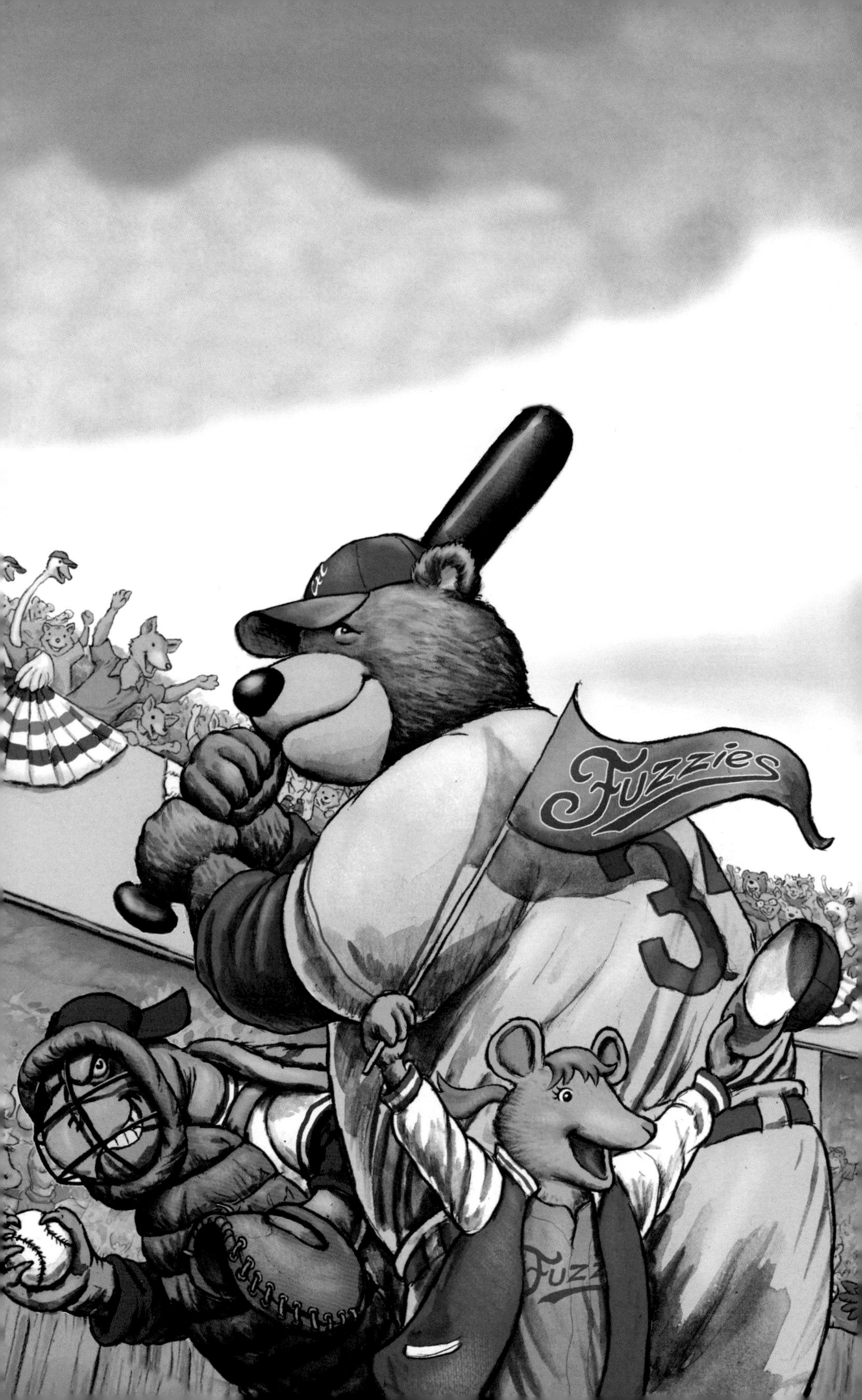
Fuzzies
3

THE FERNWOOD VALLEY FUZZIES

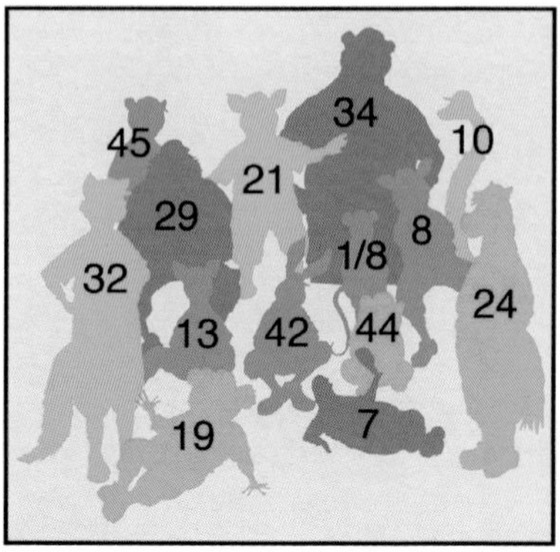

34
45
10
21
29
8
1/8
32
24
13
42
44
19
7

#1/8 Blossom Honey-Possom, Centerfield
#7 Percivale Penguino, Right Field
#8 Pam the Lamb, Left Field
#10 Larry Boa, Third Base
#13 Pepe Perrito, Shortstop
#19 Kazuki Koala, Right Field
#21 Hammy Sosa, Catcher
#24 Pony Perez, Shortstop
#29 Red Kowasaki, Pitcher
#32 Sandy Kofox, Pitcher
#34 Bo Grizzly, First Base & Manager
#42 Jackie Rabbitson, Second Base
#44 Walter Wombat, Outfield
#45 Kit Ocelot, Pitcher

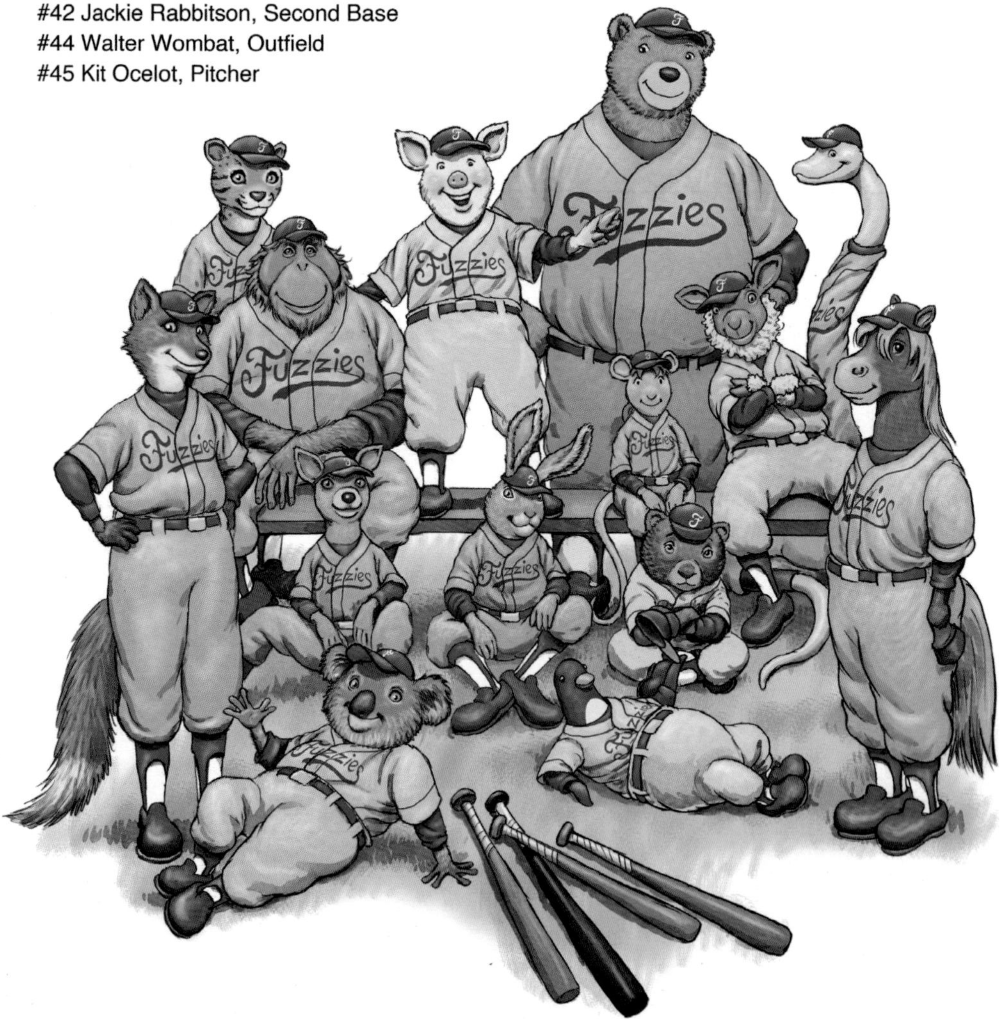

THE ROCKY RIDGE RED CLAWS

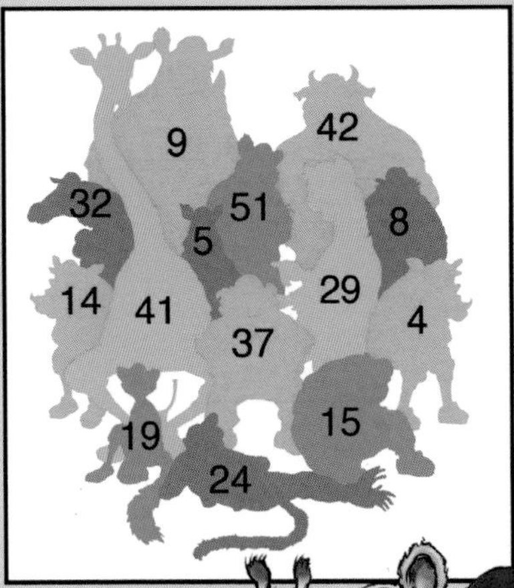
9
42
32
51
8
5
14
41
29
4
37
15
19
24

#4 Maude Hawg, First Base
#5 Jose Javelina, Second Base
#8 Bob Baboon, Starting Pitcher
#9 Reggie Rhino, Designated Hitter
#14 Ward Hawg, Third Base
#15 Snaps Tortelli, Catcher
#19 Liam Lemur, Left Field
#24 Monks McGillicuty, Right Field
#29 Spots Hathaway, Shortstop
#32 Gator Gibson, Starting Pitcher
#37 Mitsi McGraw, Manager
#41 Stretch Girafallo, Center Field
#42 Fernando Del Toro, Relief Pitcher
#51 Wolfy Wasabi, Relief Pitcher

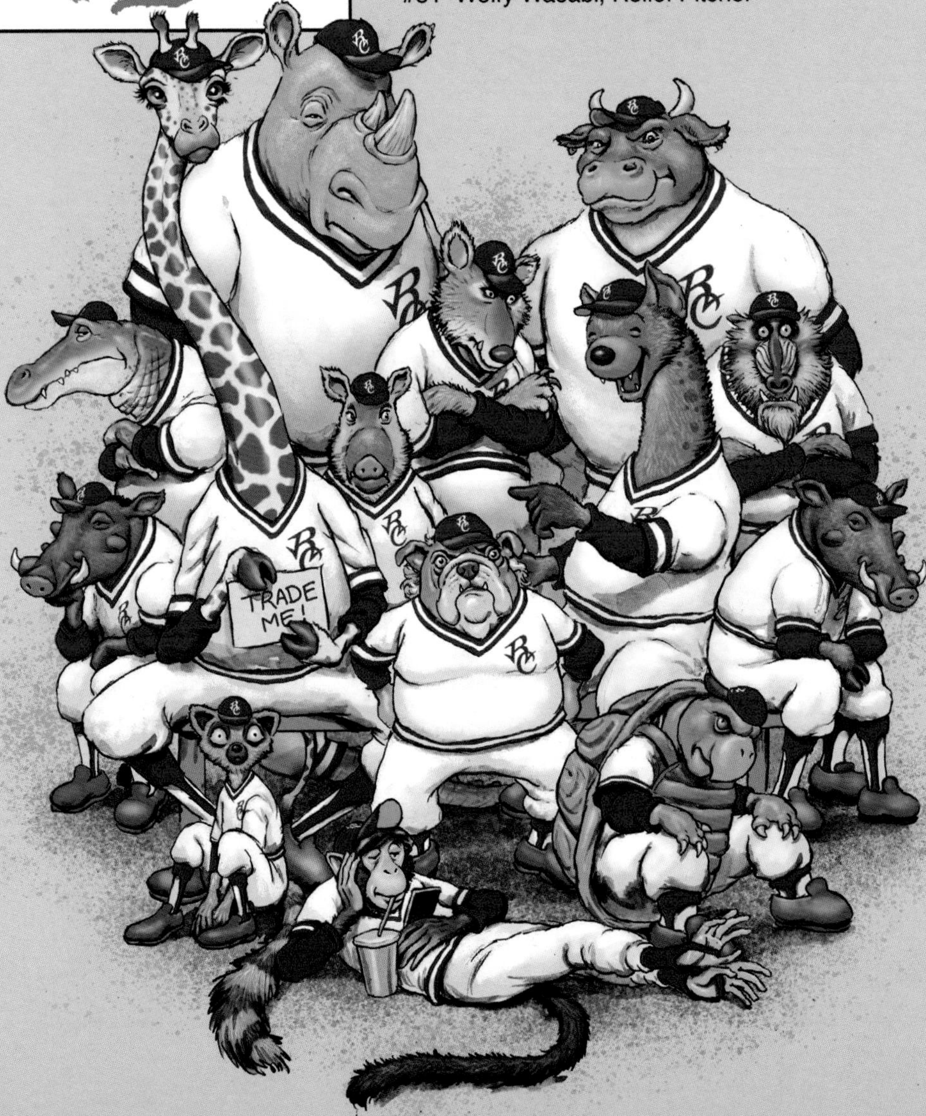
TRADE ME!

INTRODUCING THE FERNWOOD VALLEY

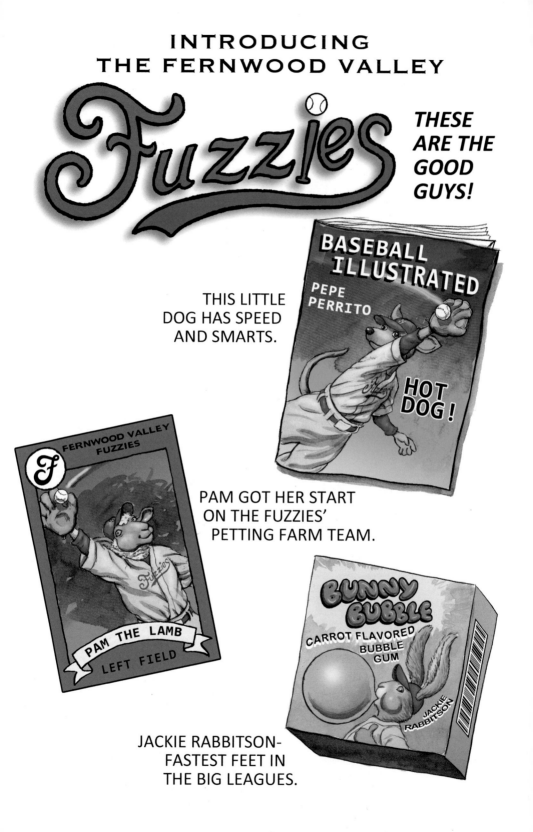

Fuzzies

THESE ARE THE GOOD GUYS!

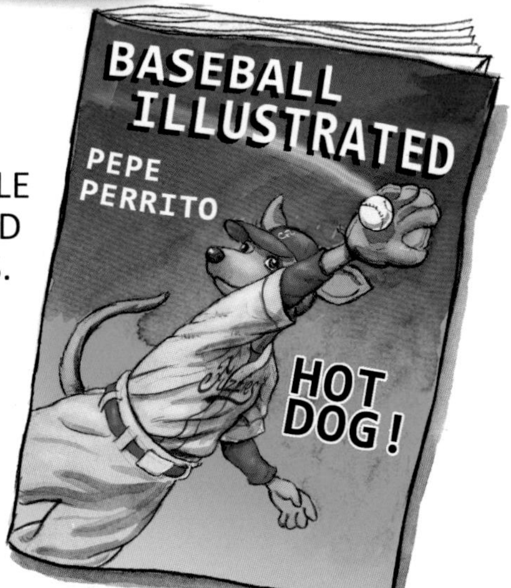

BASEBALL ILLUSTRATED
PEPE PERRITO
HOT DOG!

THIS LITTLE DOG HAS SPEED AND SMARTS.

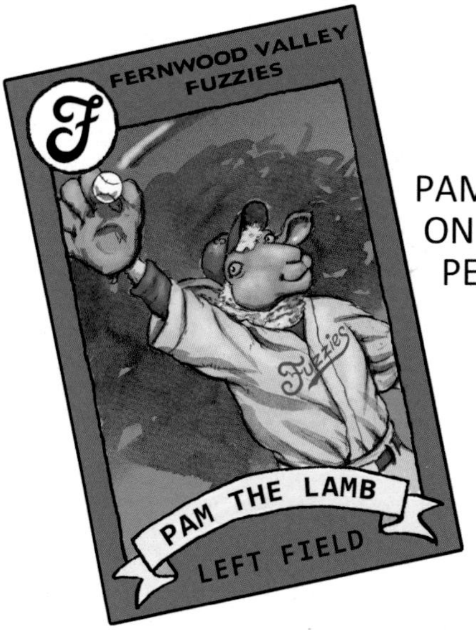

FERNWOOD VALLEY FUZZIES
F
Fuzzies
PAM THE LAMB
LEFT FIELD

PAM GOT HER START ON THE FUZZIES' PETTING FARM TEAM.

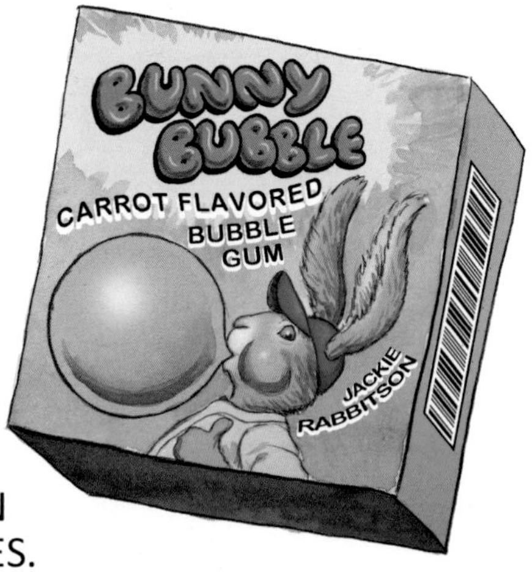

BUNNY BUBBLE
CARROT FLAVORED BUBBLE GUM
JACKIE RABBITSON

JACKIE RABBITSON- FASTEST FEET IN THE BIG LEAGUES.

BO “THE GRIZ” GRIZZLY-
ALL STAR SLUGGER
AND MANAGER.

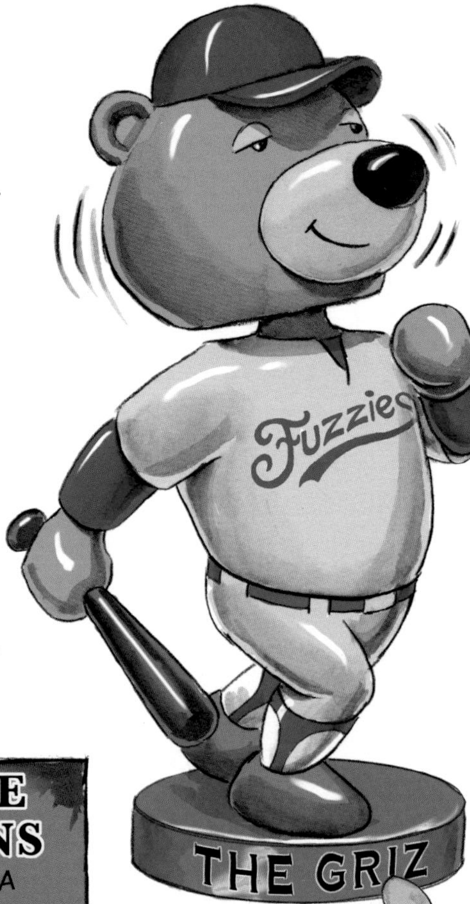
Fuzzies
THE GRIZ

HAMMY SOSA - THE FUZZIES’
CONFIDENT CATCHER

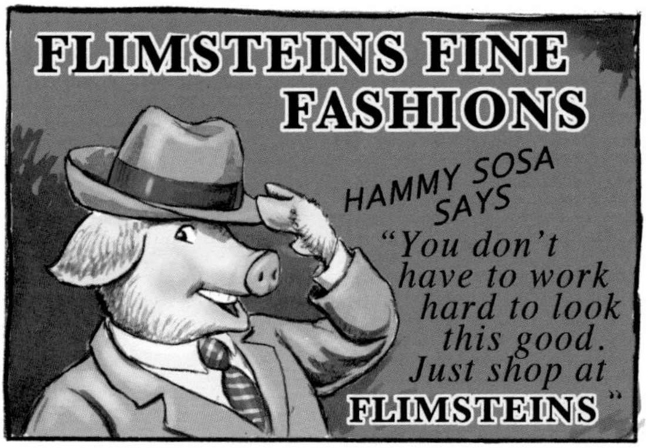
FLIMSTEINS FINE
FASHIONS
HAMMY SOSA
SAYS
“You don’t
have to work
hard to look
this good.
Just shop at
FLIMSTEINS”

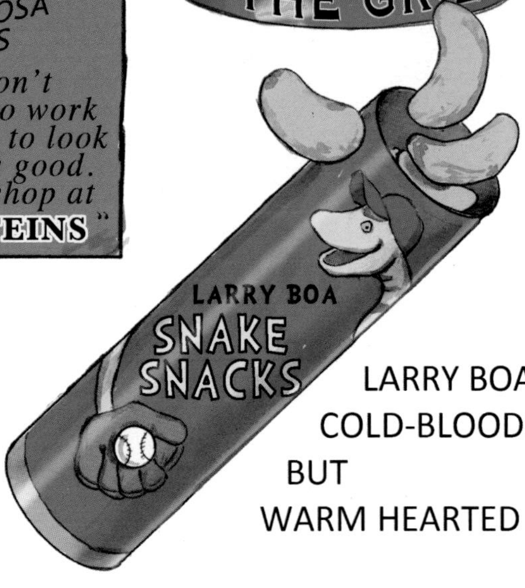
LARRY BOA
SNAKE
SNACKS

LARRY BOA-
COLD-BLOODED,
BUT
WARM HEARTED

YET, DESPITE ALL THIS TALENT, THE FUZZIES ALWAYS LOST TO THE ROCKY RIDGE RED CLAWS.

INTRODUCING
THE ROCKY RIDGE
RED CLAWS

*THESE ARE
THE BAD GUYS!*

THE THREE MAIN REASONS
THAT THE FUZZIES
CAN'T SCORE AGAINST
THE RED CLAWS

FIELDING

PITCHING

ROCKY RIDGE RED CLAWS

RC

MONKS McGILLICUTTY

RIGHT FIELD

ROCKY RIDGE RED CLAWS

RC

GATOR GIBSON

PITCHER

ROCKY RIDGE RED CLAWS

RC

FERNANDO DEL TORO

RELIEF PITCHER

MORE PITCHING

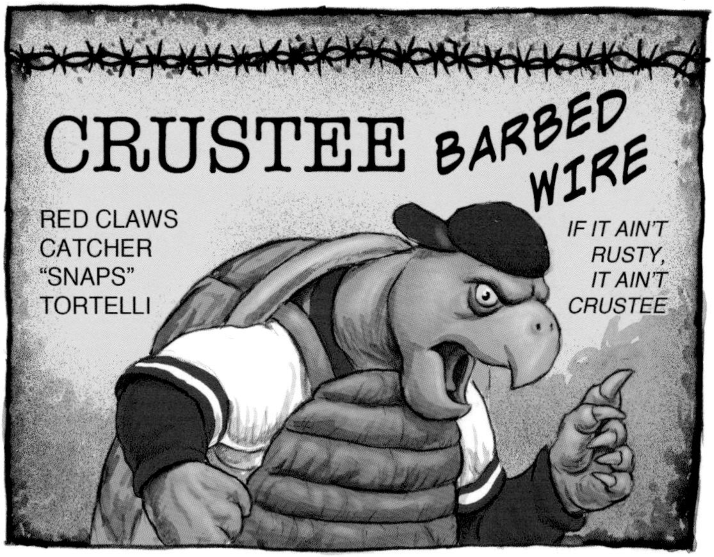
CRUSTEE
BARBED WIRE
RED CLAWS CATCHER "SNAPS" TORTELLI
IF IT AIN'T RUSTY, IT AIN'T CRUSTEE

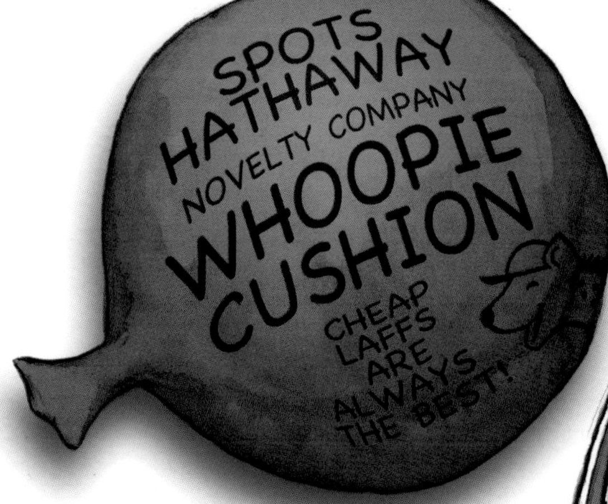
SPOTS HATHAWAY
NOVELTY COMPANY
WHOOPIE CUSHION
CHEAP LAFFS ARE ALWAYS THE BEST!

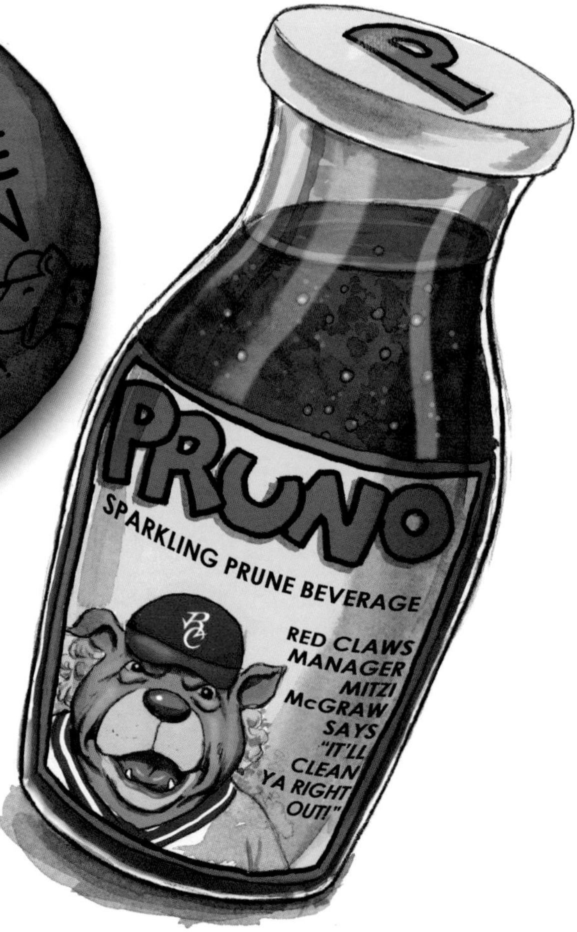
P
PRUNO
SPARKLING PRUNE BEVERAGE
RED CLAWS MANAGER MITZI McGRAW SAYS "IT'LL CLEAN YA RIGHT OUT!"

WAS THERE ANYONE OUT THERE WHO BELIEVED THAT THE FUZZIES COULD BEAT THE RED CLAWS?

INTRODUCING
BLOSSOM HONEY POSSUM
THE WORLD'S BIGGEST FERNWOOD VALLEY FUZZIES FAN

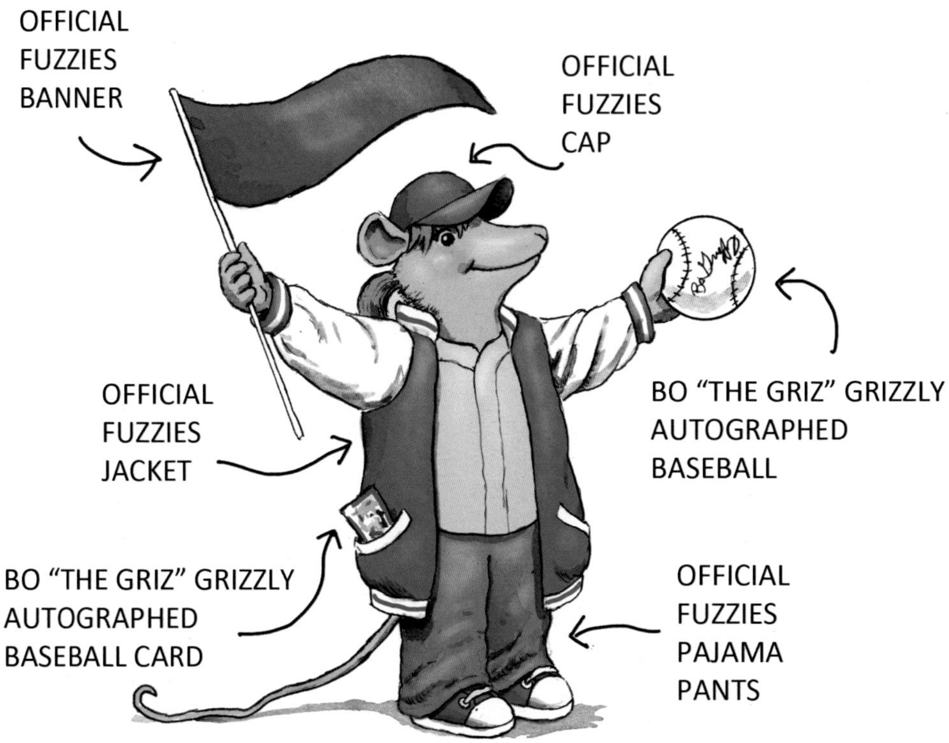
OFFICIAL FUZZIES BANNER
OFFICIAL FUZZIES CAP
OFFICIAL FUZZIES JACKET
BO "THE GRIZ" GRIZZLY AUTOGRAPHED BASEBALL
BO "THE GRIZ" GRIZZLY AUTOGRAPHED BASEBALL CARD
OFFICIAL FUZZIES PAJAMA PANTS

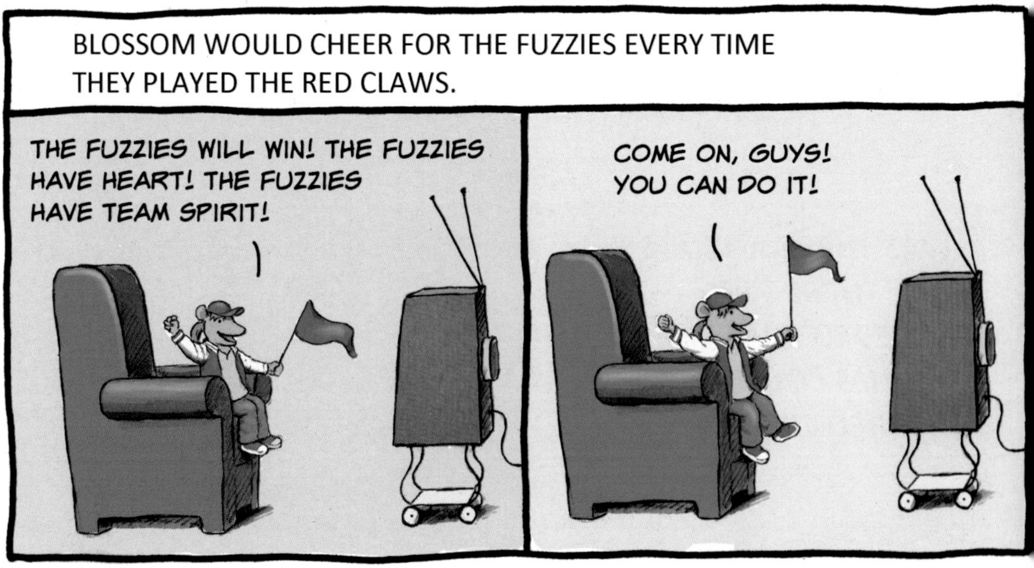
BLOSSOM WOULD CHEER FOR THE FUZZIES EVERY TIME THEY PLAYED THE RED CLAWS.
THE FUZZIES WILL WIN! THE FUZZIES HAVE HEART! THE FUZZIES HAVE TEAM SPIRIT!
COME ON, GUYS! YOU CAN DO IT!

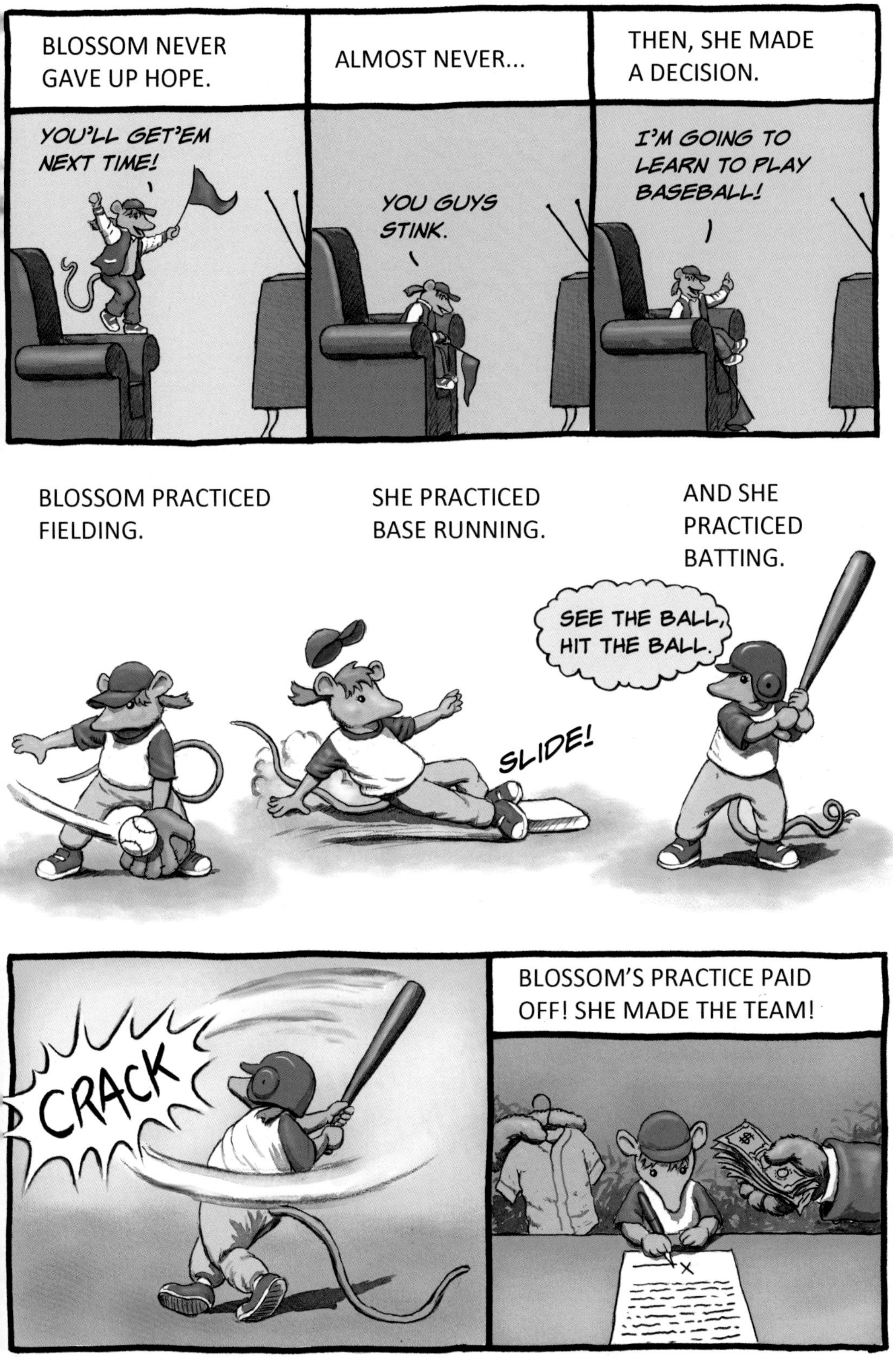
BLOSSOM NEVER GAVE UP HOPE.
YOU'LL GET'EM NEXT TIME!
ALMOST NEVER...
YOU GUYS STINK.
THEN, SHE MADE A DECISION.
I'M GOING TO LEARN TO PLAY BASEBALL!
BLOSSOM PRACTICED FIELDING.
SHE PRACTICED BASE RUNNING.
SLIDE!
AND SHE PRACTICED BATTING.
SEE THE BALL, HIT THE BALL.
CRACK
BLOSSOM'S PRACTICE PAID OFF! SHE MADE THE TEAM!
X

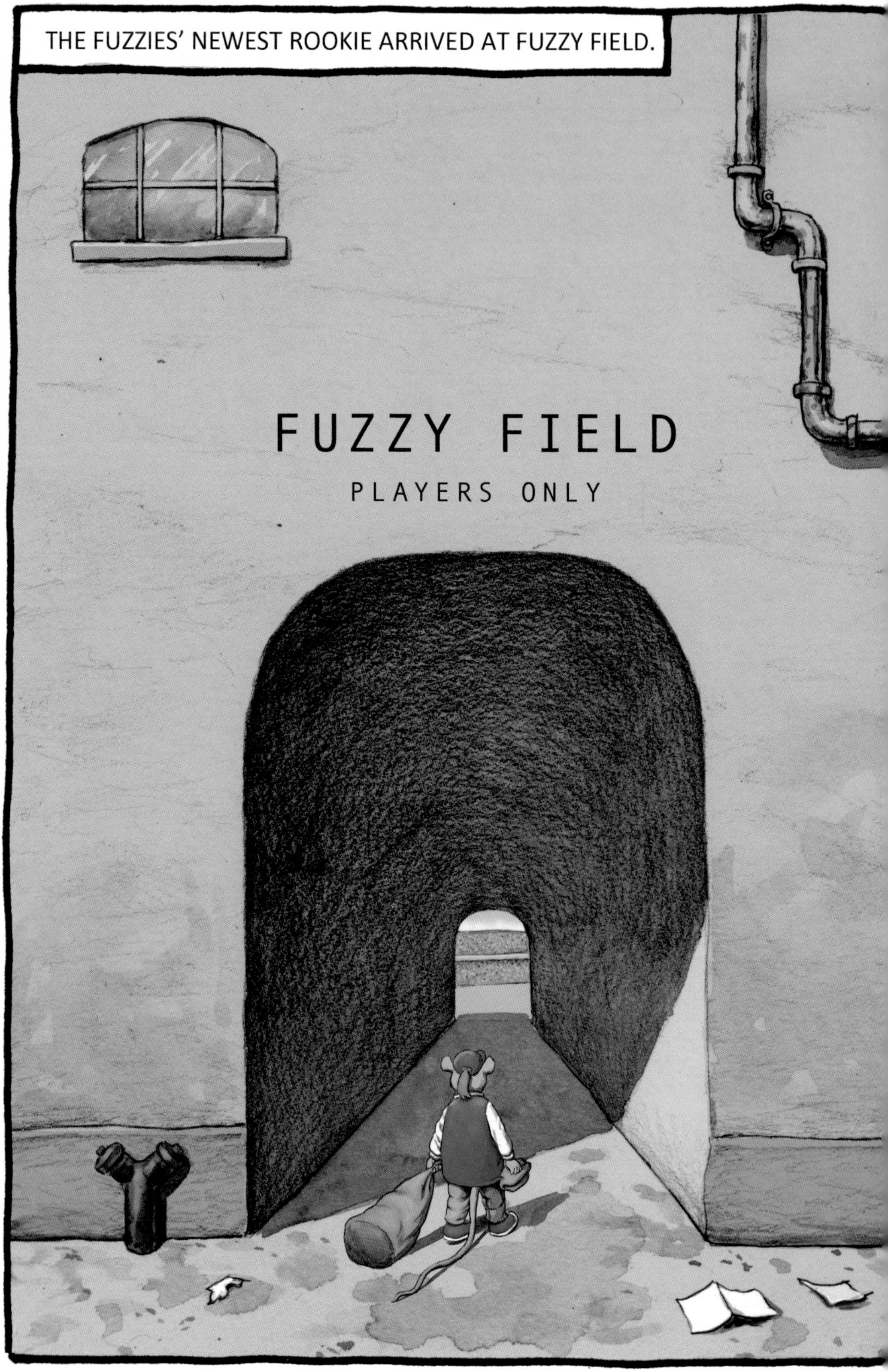
THE FUZZIES' NEWEST ROOKIE ARRIVED AT FUZZY FIELD.
FUZZY FIELD
PLAYERS ONLY

GAME DAY

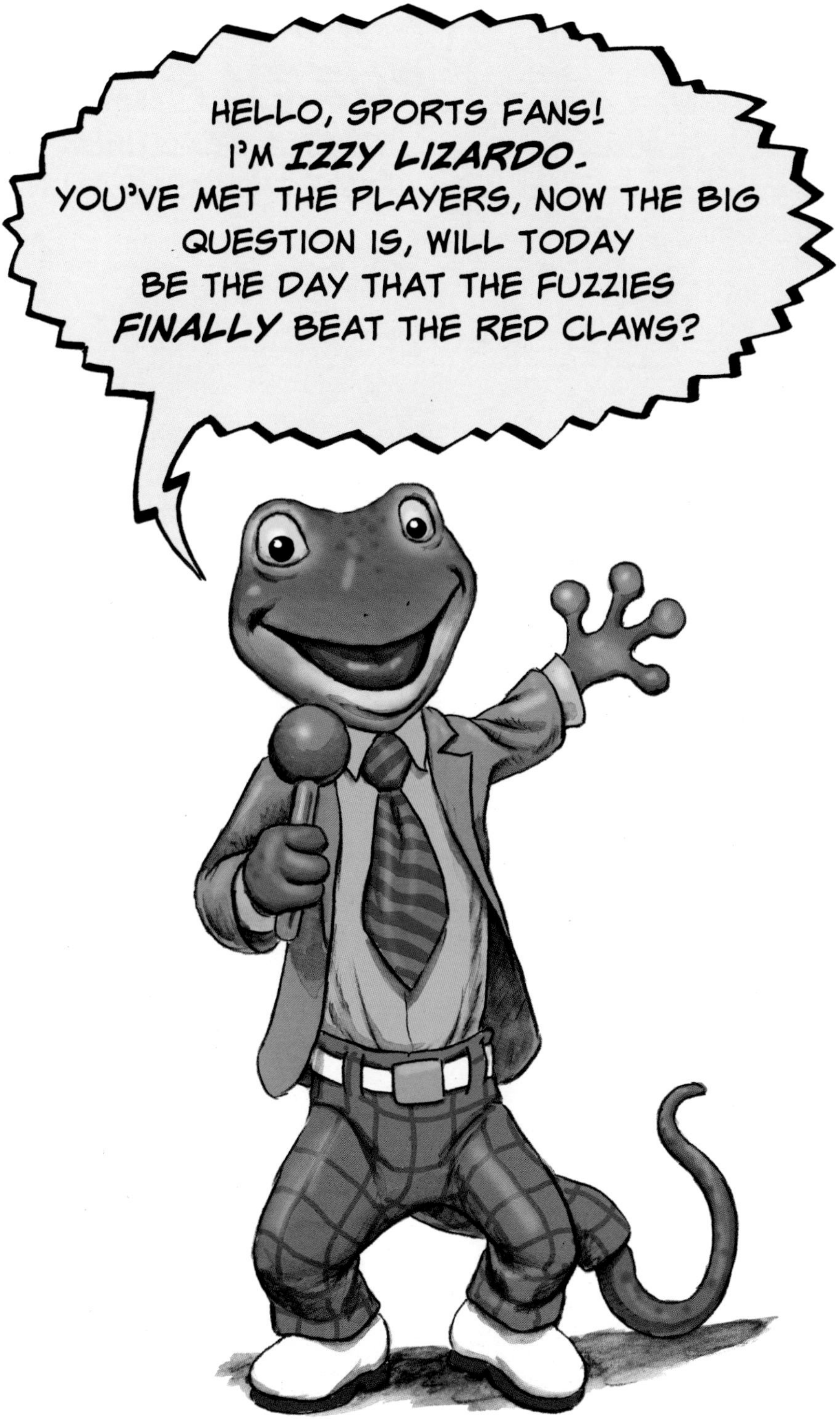
HELLO, SPORTS FANS!
I'M *IZZY LIZARDO*.
YOU'VE MET THE PLAYERS, NOW THE BIG QUESTION IS, WILL TODAY BE THE DAY THAT THE FUZZIES *FINALLY* BEAT THE RED CLAWS?

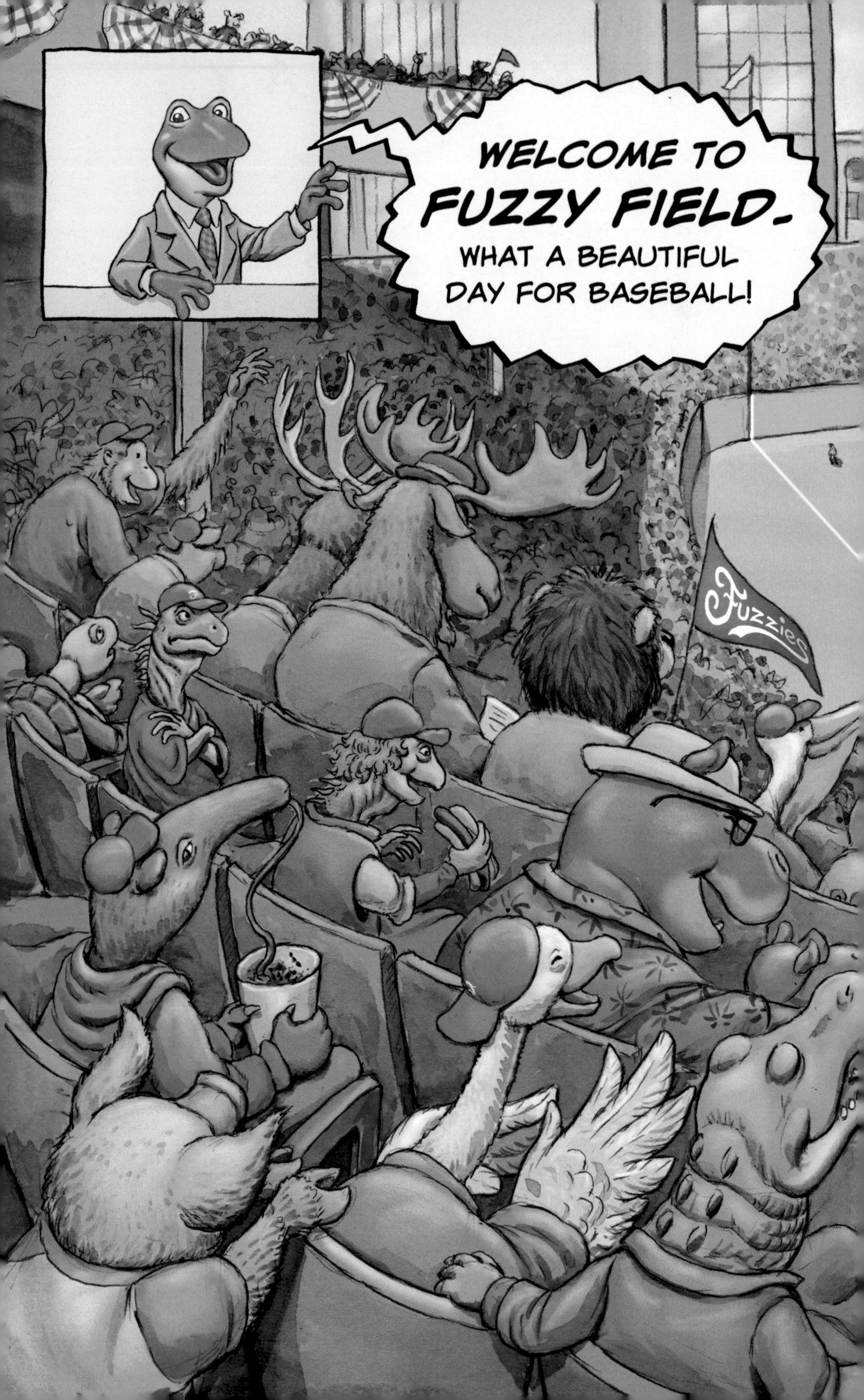
WELCOME TO FUZZY FIELD–
WHAT A BEAUTIFUL DAY FOR BASEBALL!
Fuzzies

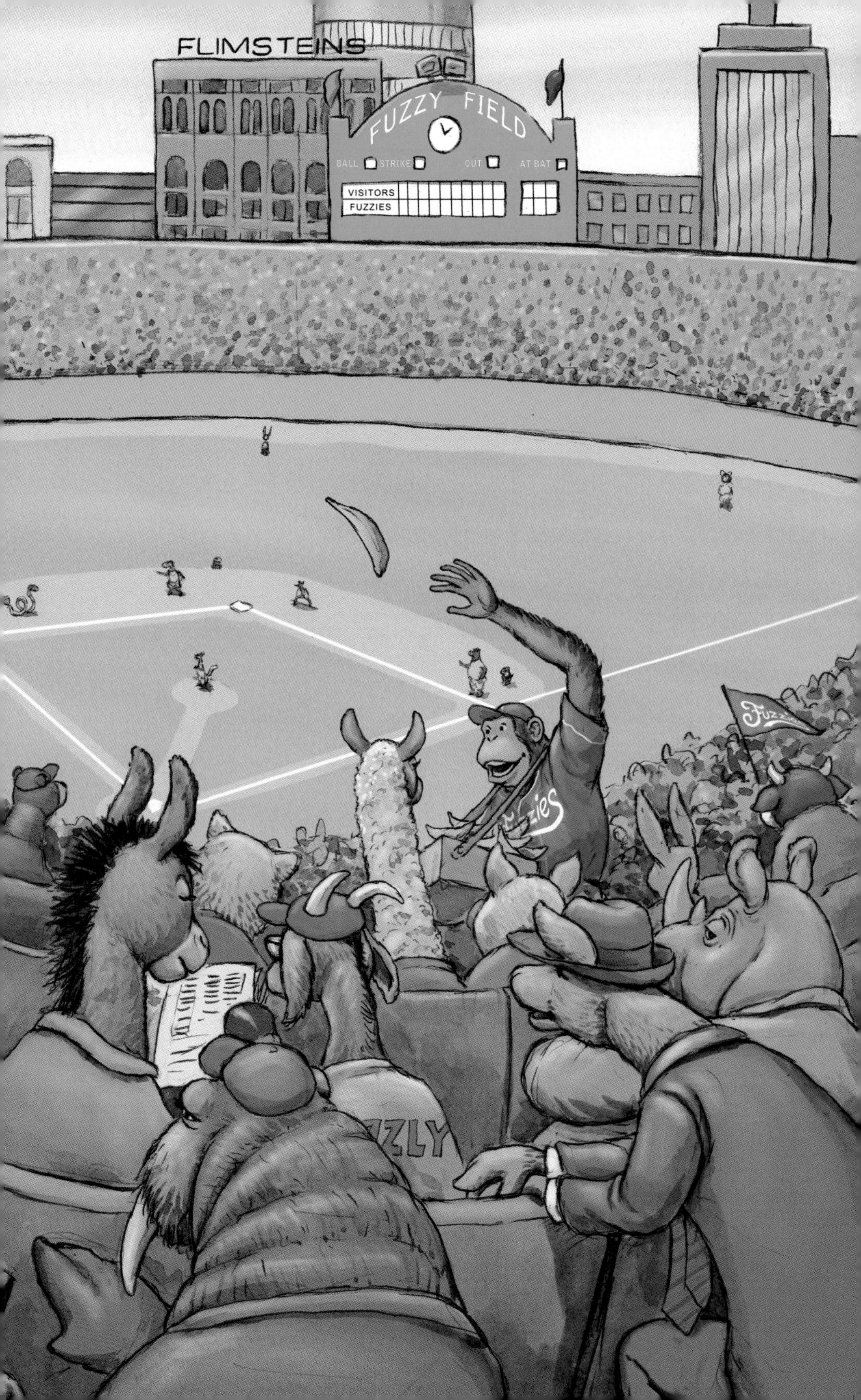

FLIMSTEINS
FUZZY FIELD
BALL
STRIKE
OUT
AT BAT
VISITORS
FUZZIES
Fuzzies
Fuzzies

THE FIRST EIGHT-AND-A-HALF INNINGS DID NOT GO WELL FOR THE FUZZIES.

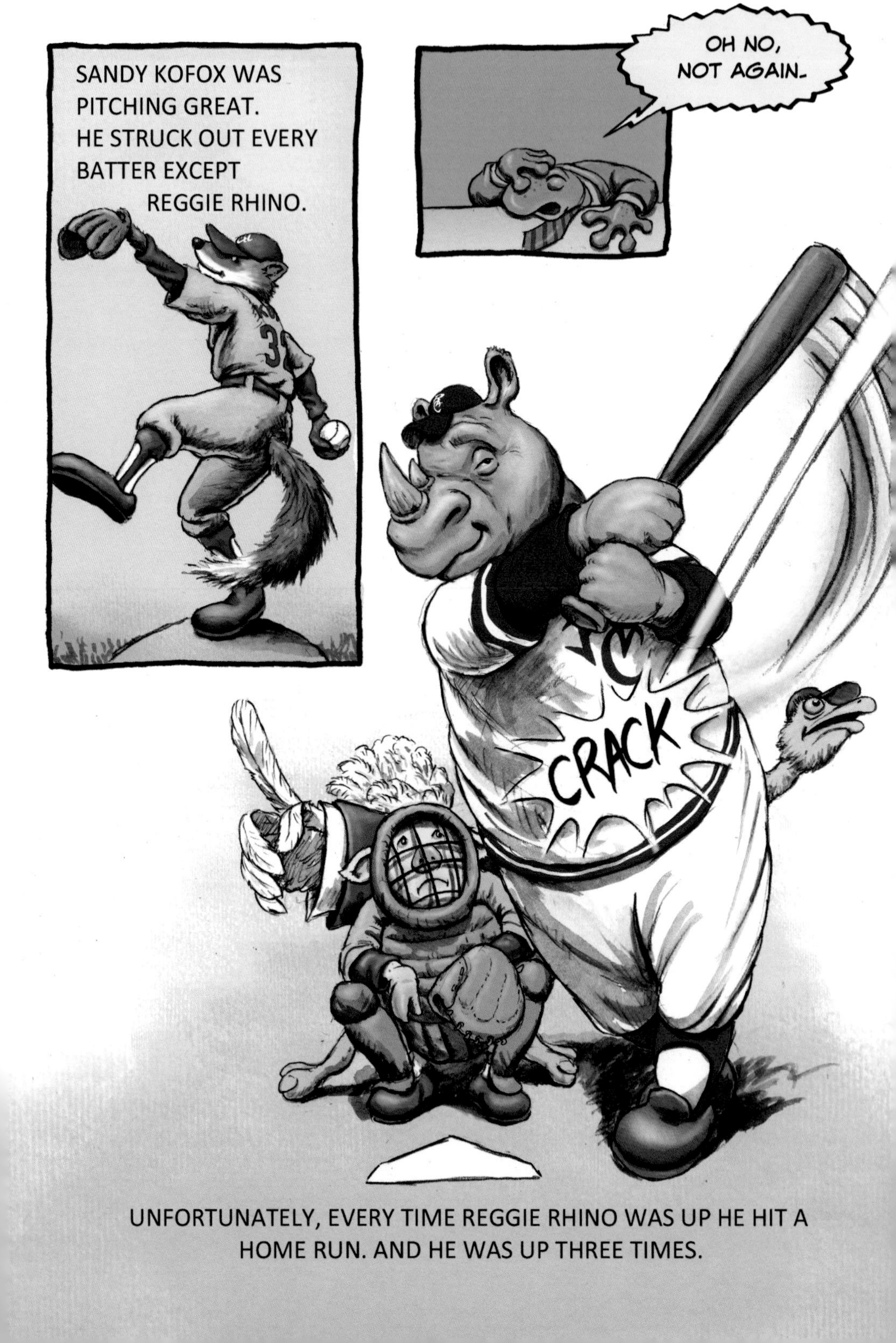
SANDY KOFOX WAS PITCHING GREAT. HE STRUCK OUT EVERY BATTER EXCEPT REGGIE RHINO.
OH NO, NOT AGAIN.
CRACK

UNFORTUNATELY, EVERY TIME REGGIE RHINO WAS UP HE HIT A HOME RUN. AND HE WAS UP THREE TIMES.

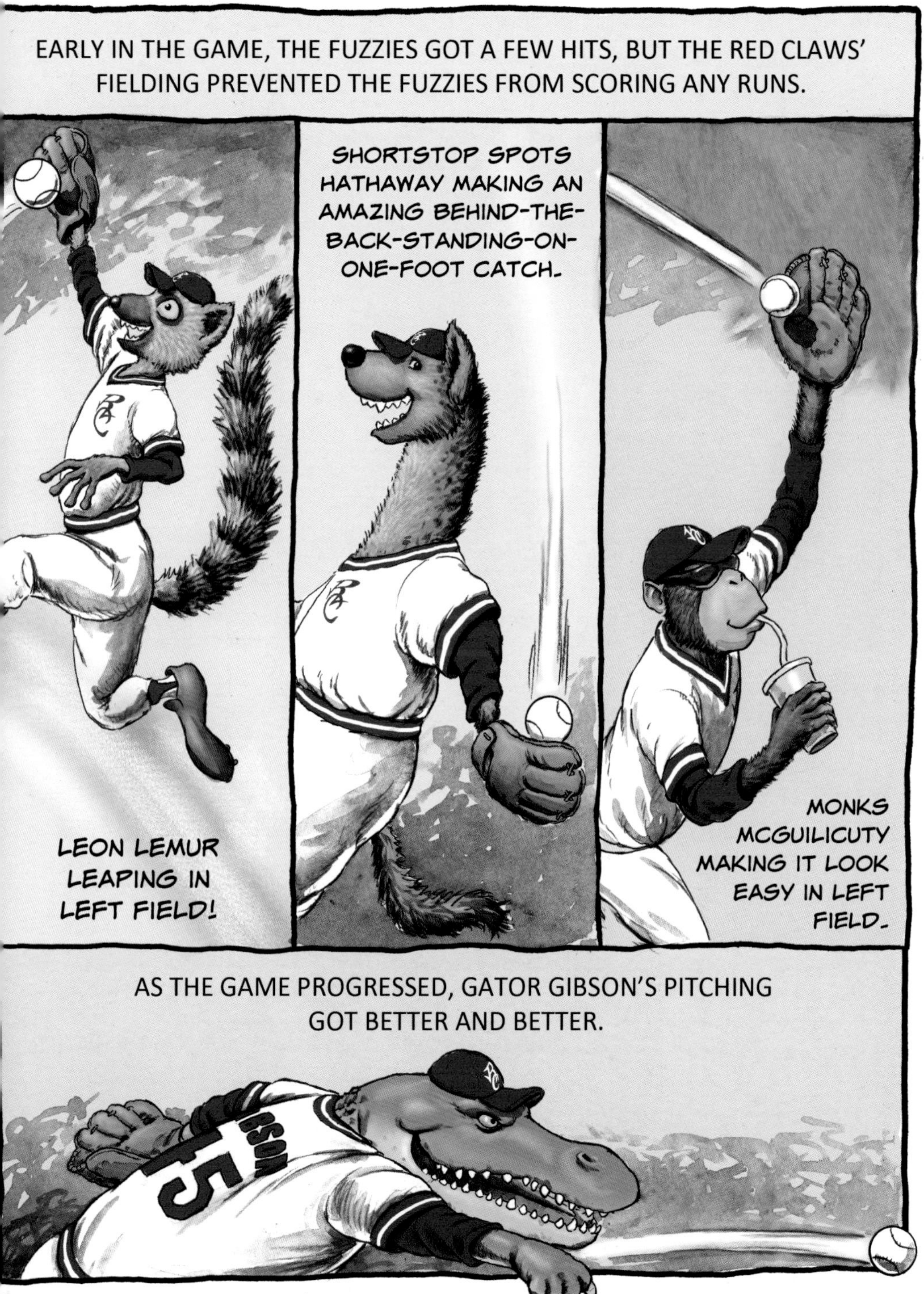
EARLY IN THE GAME, THE FUZZIES GOT A FEW HITS, BUT THE RED CLAWS' FIELDING PREVENTED THE FUZZIES FROM SCORING ANY RUNS.
LEON LEMUR LEAPING IN LEFT FIELD!
SHORTSTOP SPOTS HATHAWAY MAKING AN AMAZING BEHIND-THE-BACK-STANDING-ON-ONE-FOOT CATCH.
MONKS MCGUILICUTY MAKING IT LOOK EASY IN LEFT FIELD.
AS THE GAME PROGRESSED, GATOR GIBSON'S PITCHING GOT BETTER AND BETTER.

BY THE NINTH INNING HIS PITCHES WERE UNHITTABLE.

THE BOTTOM OF THE NINTH INNING. THE FUZZIES' LAST CHANCE.

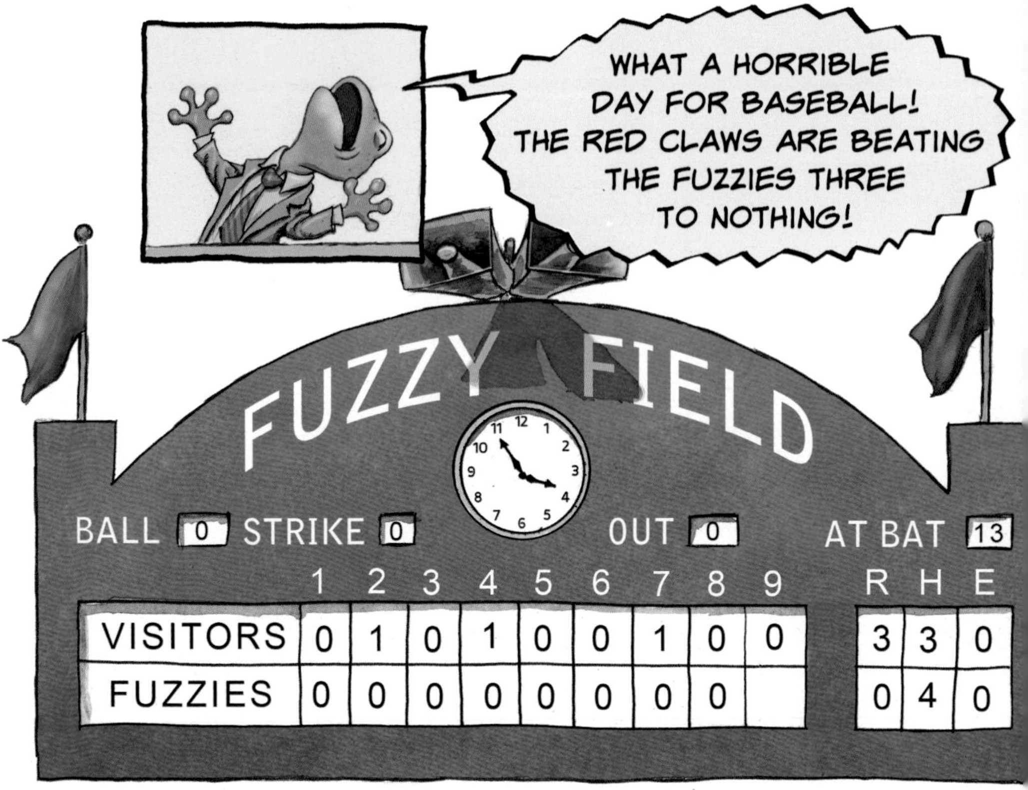
WHAT A HORRIBLE DAY FOR BASEBALL! THE RED CLAWS ARE BEATING THE FUZZIES THREE TO NOTHING!
FUZZY FIELD
BALL 0 STRIKE 0
OUT 0
AT BAT 13
1 2 3 4 5 6 7 8 9 R H E
VISITORS 0 1 0 1 0 0 1 0 0 3 3 0
FUZZIES 0 0 0 0 0 0 0 0 0 4 0

BLOSSOM WAS NOT SURPRISED THAT THE FUZZIES WERE LOSING. BUT SHE WAS SHOCKED AT HOW THEY WERE ACTING. THE FUZZIES DID NOT HAVE TEAM SPIRIT. THEY DID NOT HAVE HEART.

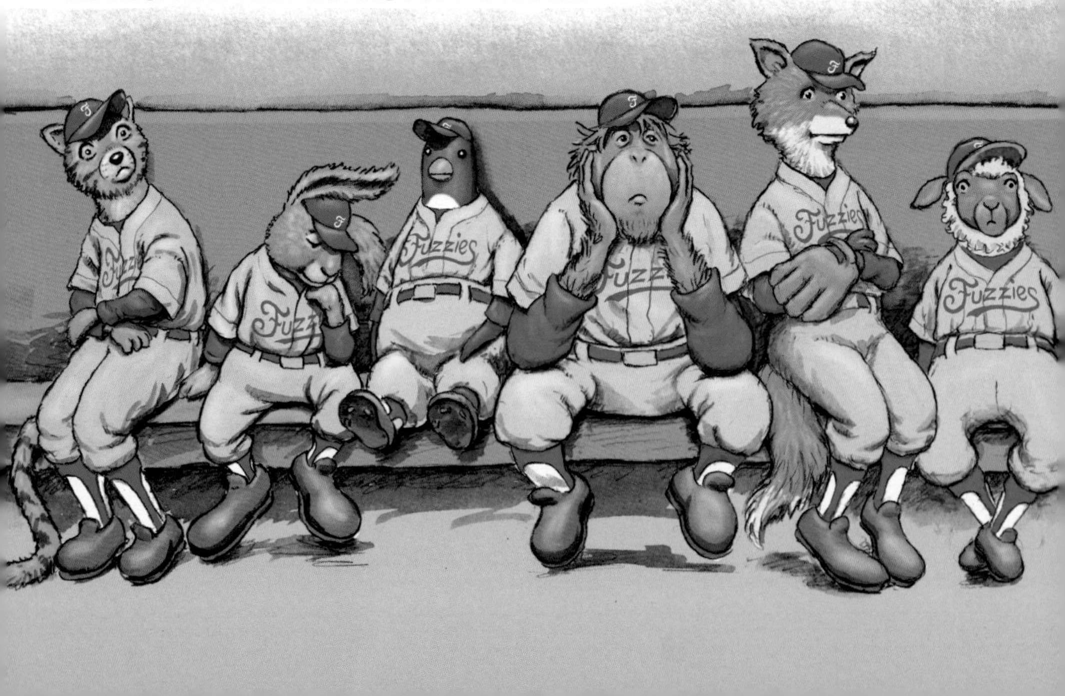
Fuzzies
Fuzzies
Fuzzies

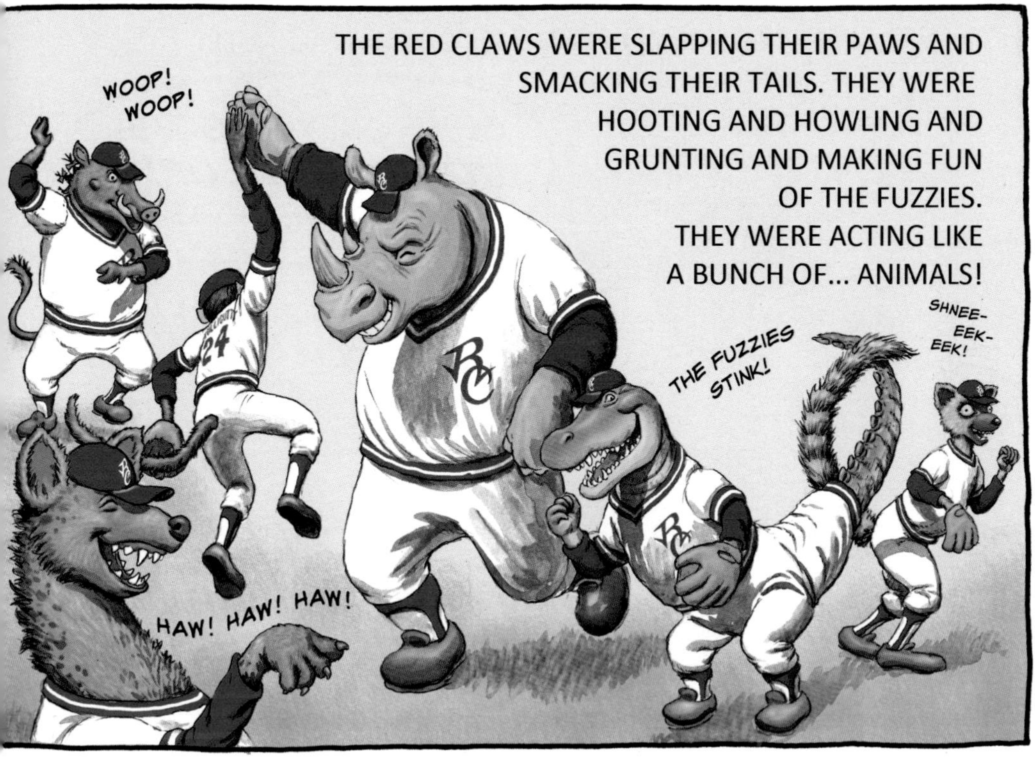
THE RED CLAWS WERE SLAPPING THEIR PAWS AND SMACKING THEIR TAILS. THEY WERE HOOTING AND HOWLING AND GRUNTING AND MAKING FUN OF THE FUZZIES.
THEY WERE ACTING LIKE A BUNCH OF... ANIMALS!
WOOP! WOOP!
24
HAW! HAW! HAW!
THE FUZZIES STINK!
SHNEE-EEK-EEK!

THE WORST PART WAS THAT THE FUZZIES WERE ACTING LIKE A BUNCH OF LOSERS.

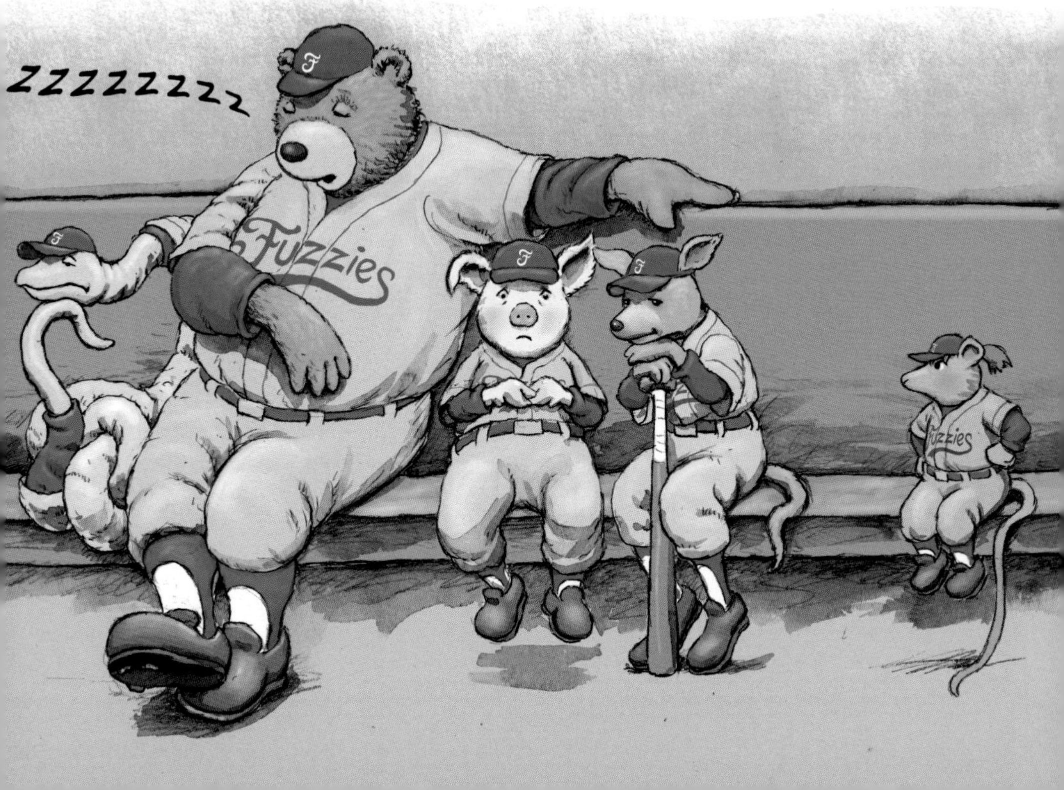
ZZZZZZZZz
Fuzzies

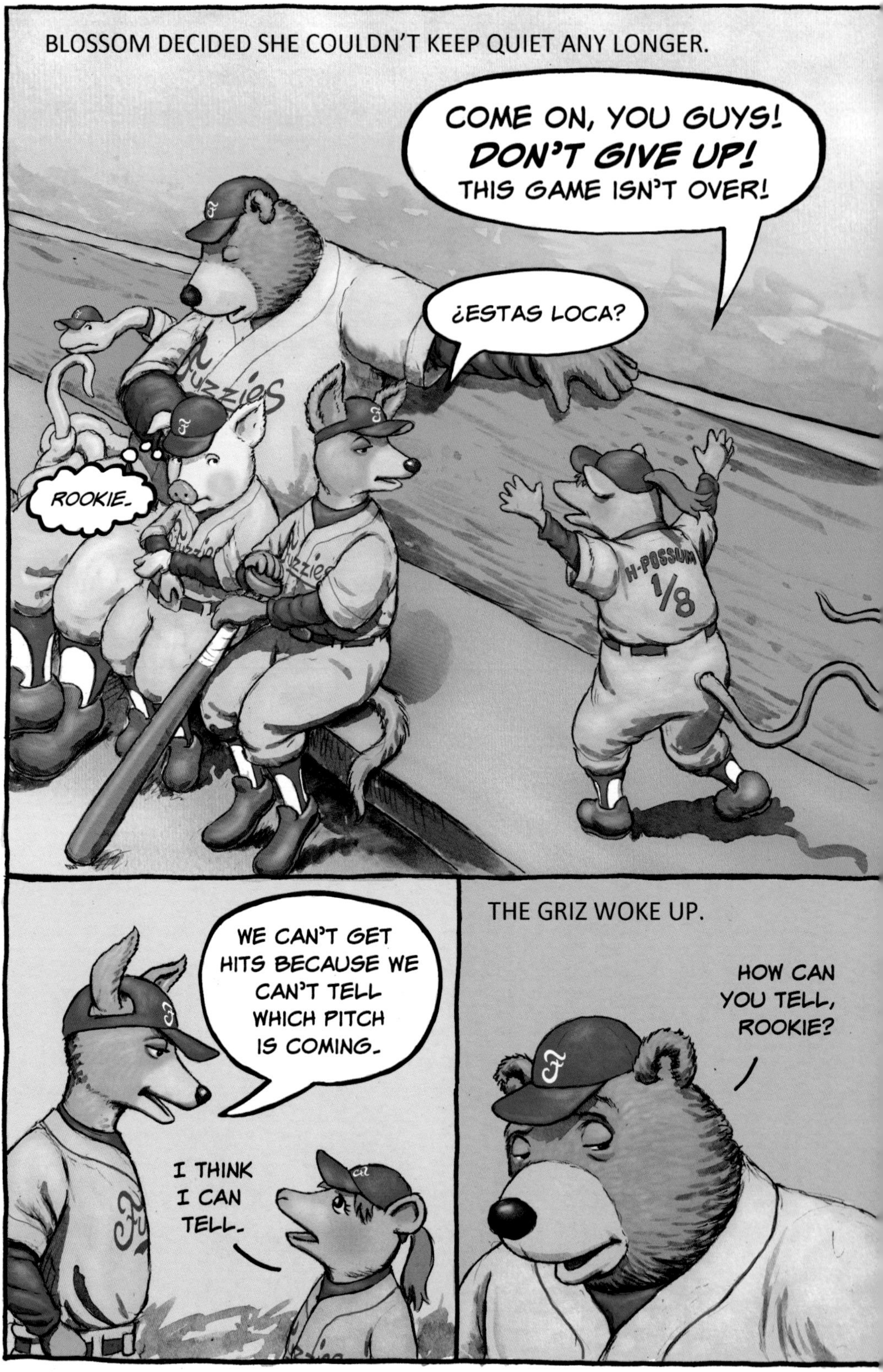
BLOSSOM DECIDED SHE COULDN'T KEEP QUIET ANY LONGER.
COME ON, YOU GUYS! DON'T GIVE UP! THIS GAME ISN'T OVER!
¿ESTAS LOCA?
ROOKIE.
H-POSSUM 1/8
WE CAN'T GET HITS BECAUSE WE CAN'T TELL WHICH PITCH IS COMING.
I THINK I CAN TELL.
THE GRIZ WOKE UP.
HOW CAN YOU TELL, ROOKIE?

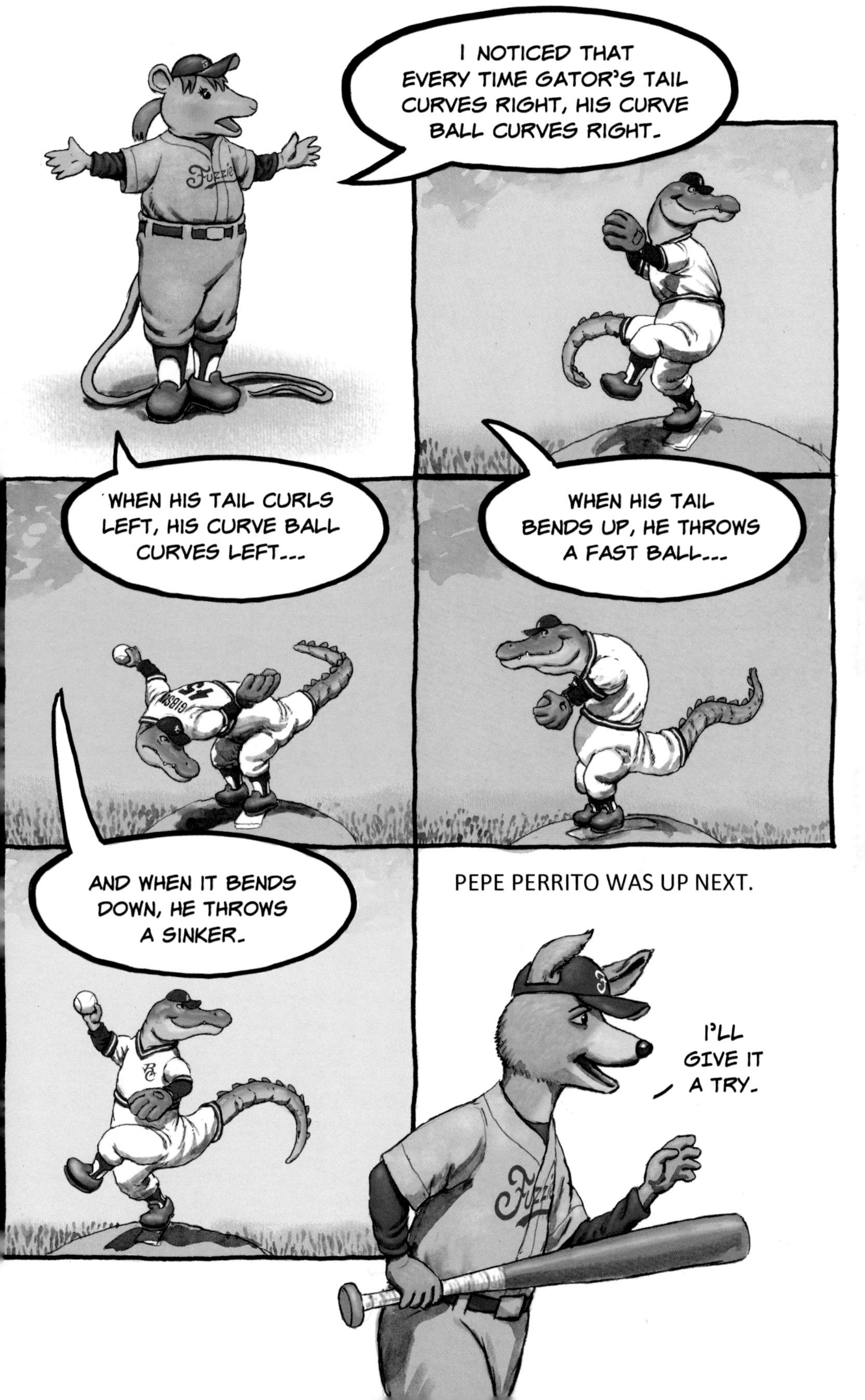
I NOTICED THAT EVERY TIME GATOR'S TAIL CURVES RIGHT, HIS CURVE BALL CURVES RIGHT.
WHEN HIS TAIL CURLS LEFT, HIS CURVE BALL CURVES LEFT...
WHEN HIS TAIL BENDS UP, HE THROWS A FAST BALL...
AND WHEN IT BENDS DOWN, HE THROWS A SINKER.
PEPE PERRITO WAS UP NEXT.
I'LL GIVE IT A TRY.

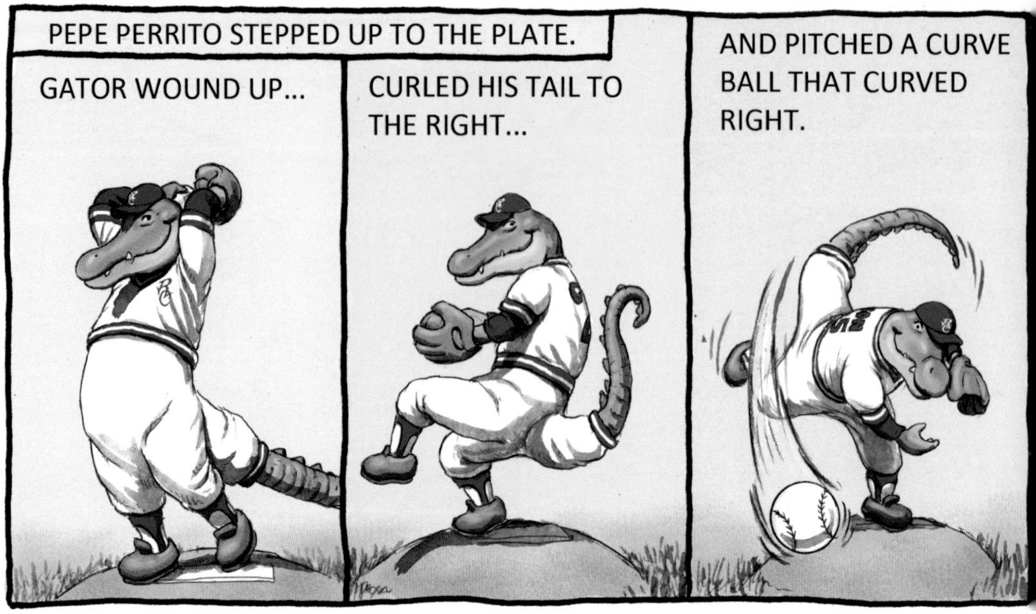
PEPE PERRITO STEPPED UP TO THE PLATE.
GATOR WOUND UP...
CURLED HIS TAIL TO THE RIGHT...
AND PITCHED A CURVE BALL THAT CURVED RIGHT.

PEPE KNEW JUST WHERE TO SWING AND...

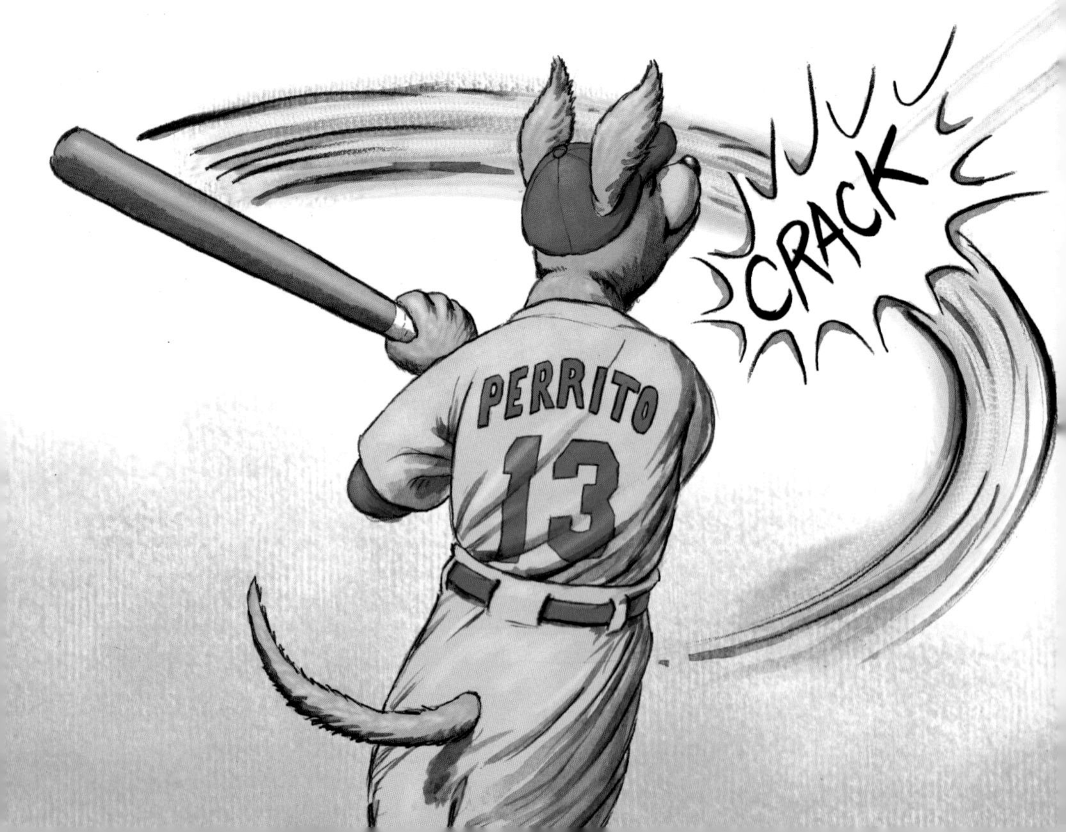
CRACK
PERRITO
13

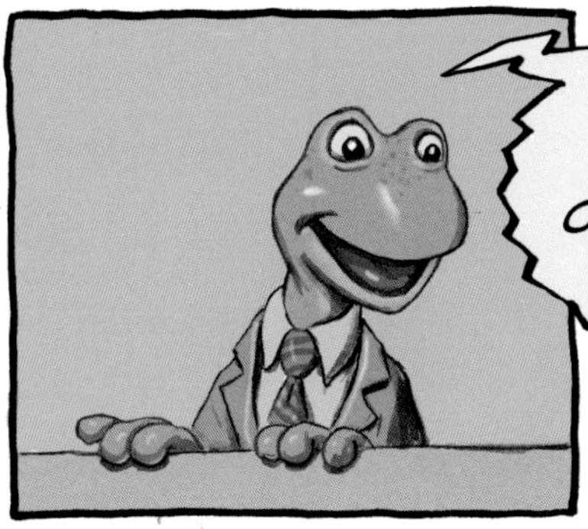
IT'S A LINE DRIVE TO CENTER FIELD!

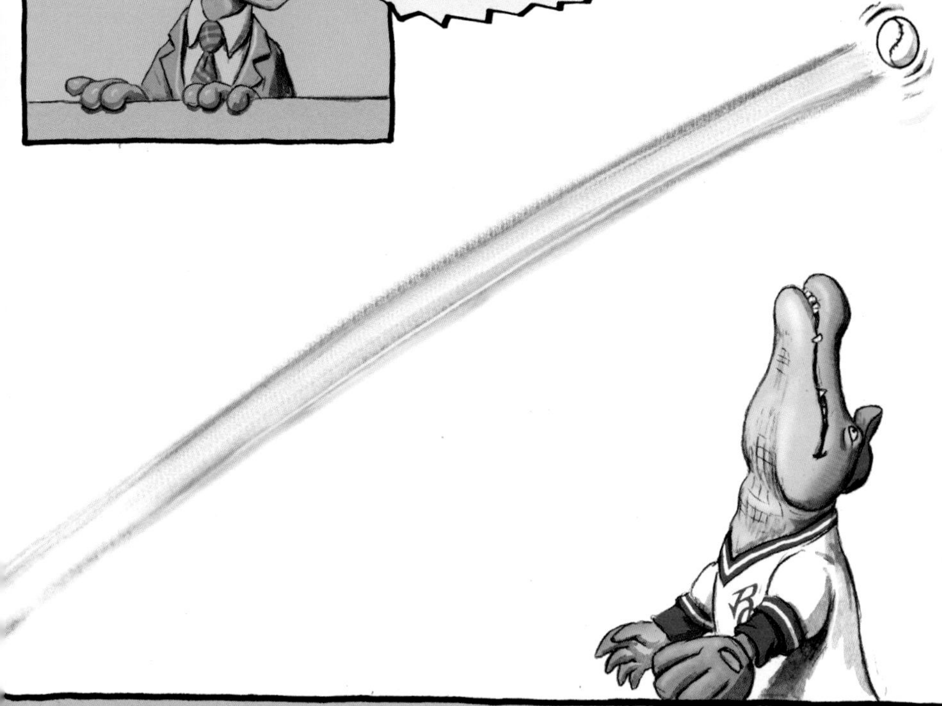

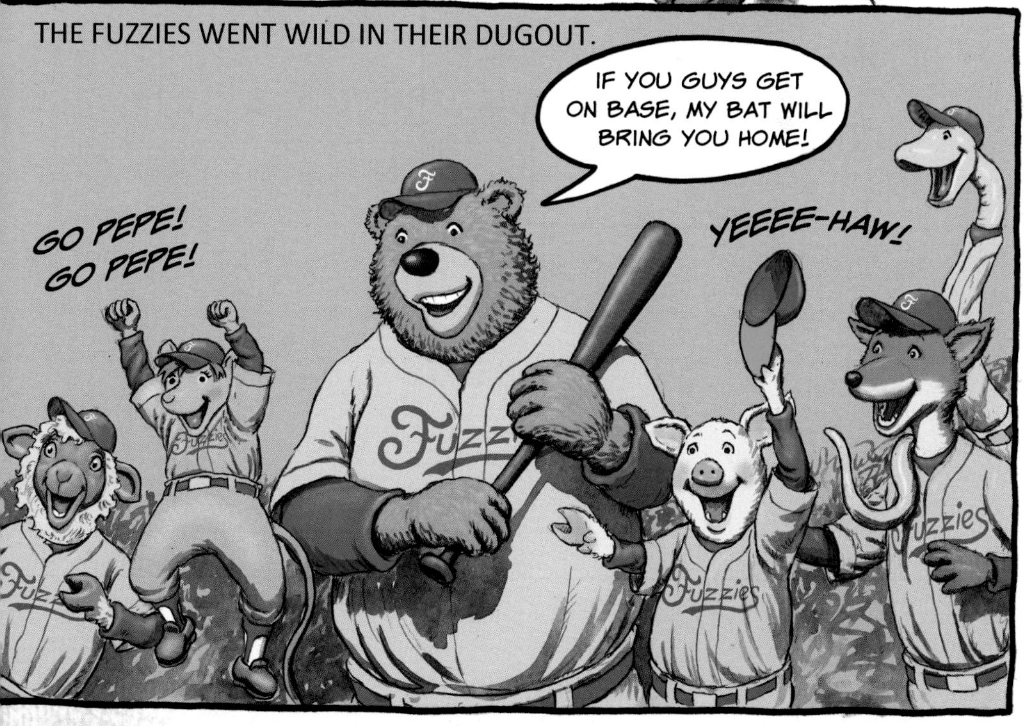
THE FUZZIES WENT WILD IN THEIR DUGOUT.
IF YOU GUYS GET ON BASE, MY BAT WILL BRING YOU HOME!
GO PEPE! GO PEPE!
YEEEE-HAW!

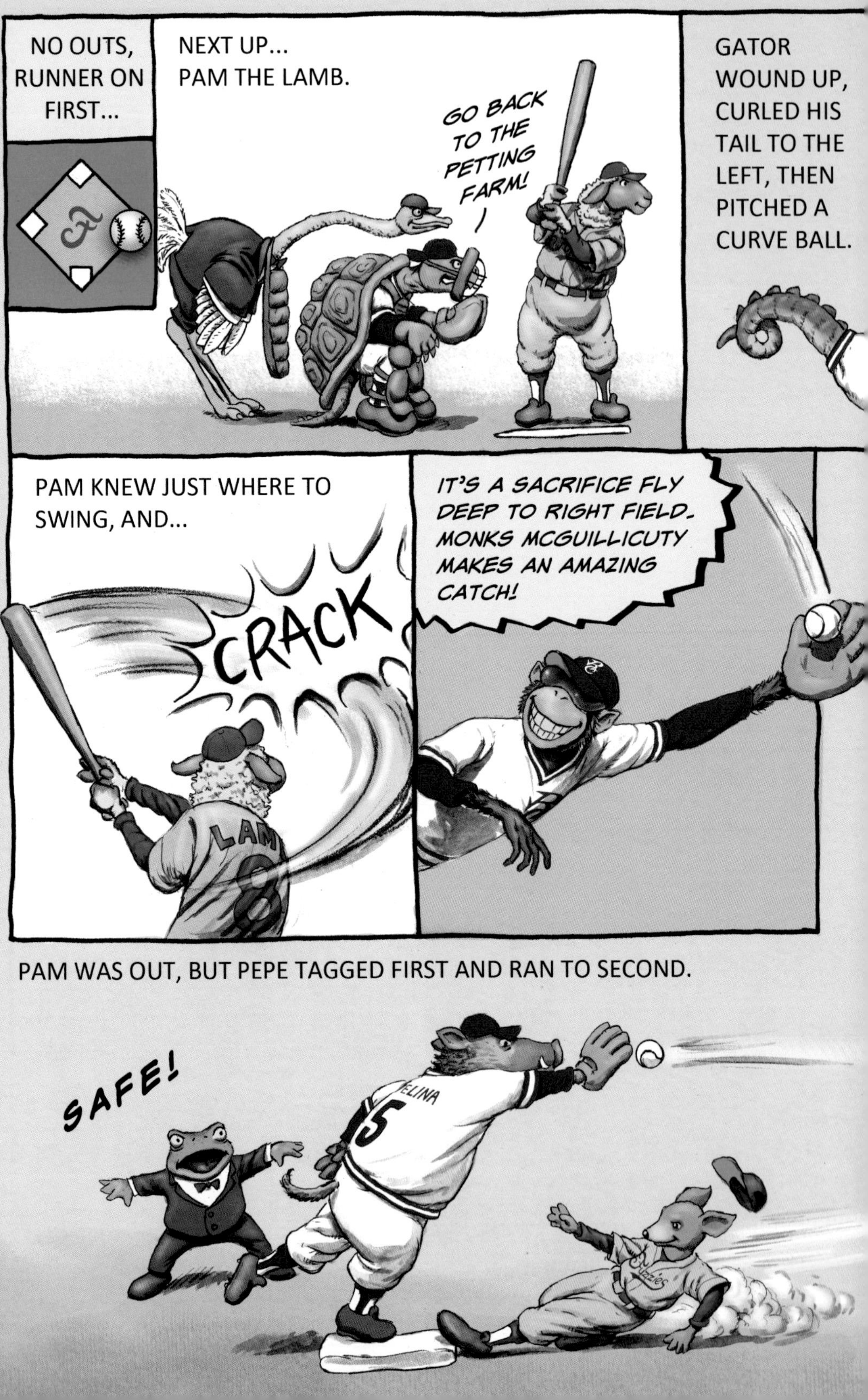
NO OUTS, RUNNER ON FIRST...
NEXT UP... PAM THE LAMB.
GO BACK TO THE PETTING FARM!
GATOR WOUND UP, CURLED HIS TAIL TO THE LEFT, THEN PITCHED A CURVE BALL.
PAM KNEW JUST WHERE TO SWING, AND...
CRACK
IT'S A SACRIFICE FLY DEEP TO RIGHT FIELD. MONKS MCGUILLICUTY MAKES AN AMAZING CATCH!
LAM
PAM WAS OUT, BUT PEPE TAGGED FIRST AND RAN TO SECOND.
SAFE!

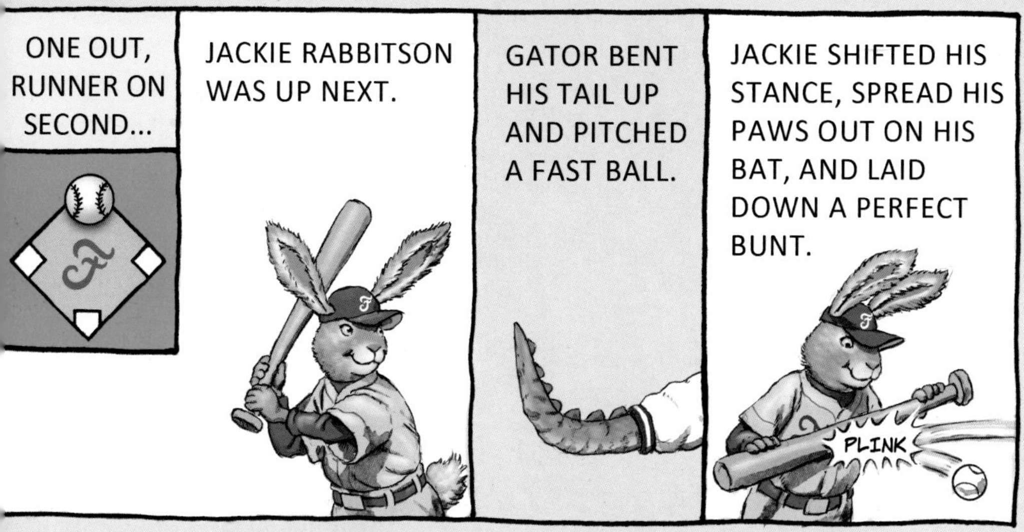
ONE OUT, RUNNER ON SECOND...
JACKIE RABBITSON WAS UP NEXT.
GATOR BENT HIS TAIL UP AND PITCHED A FAST BALL.
JACKIE SHIFTED HIS STANCE, SPREAD HIS PAWS OUT ON HIS BAT, AND LAID DOWN A PERFECT BUNT.
PLINK

RED CLAWS CATCHER "SNAPS" TORTELLI SCRAMBLED TO GET THE BALL AND THREW IT TO FIRST, BUT JACKIE WAS SAFE. AND PEPE RAN TO THIRD.

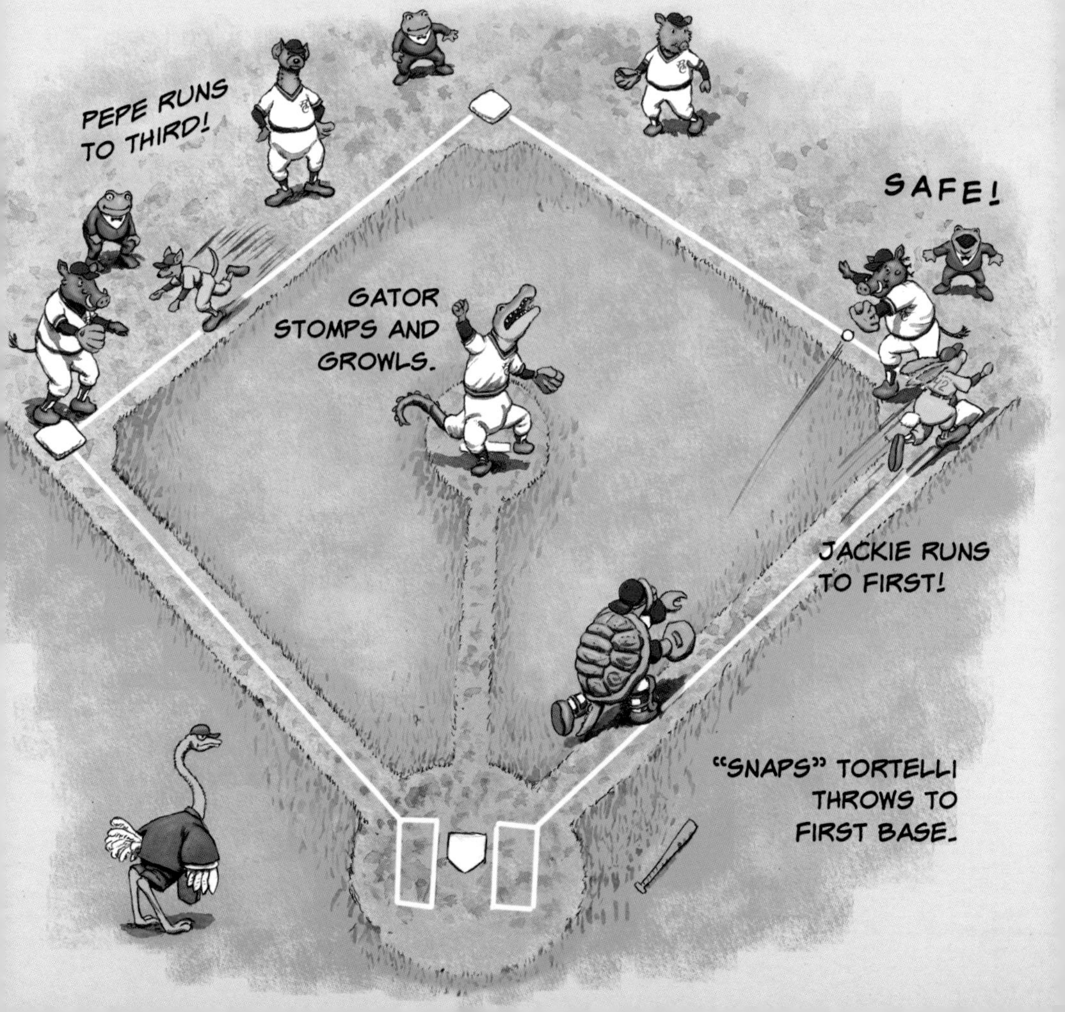
PEPE RUNS TO THIRD!
SAFE!
GATOR STOMPS AND GROWLS.
JACKIE RUNS TO FIRST!
"SNAPS" TORTELLI THROWS TO FIRST BASE.

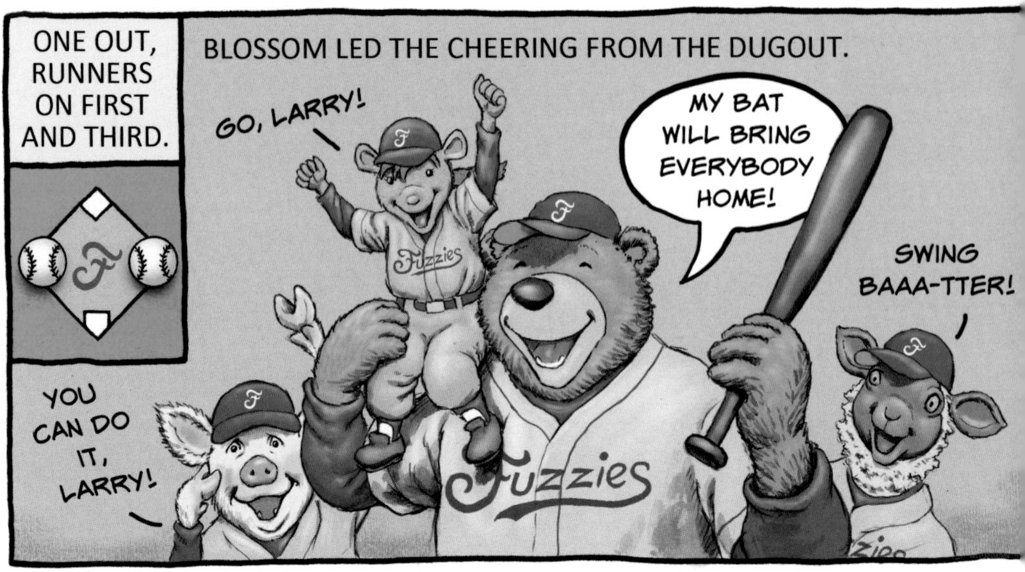
ONE OUT, RUNNERS ON FIRST AND THIRD.
BLOSSOM LED THE CHEERING FROM THE DUGOUT.
GO, LARRY!
MY BAT WILL BRING EVERYBODY HOME!
SWING BAAA-TTER!
YOU CAN DO IT, LARRY!
Fuzzies

LARRY BOA STEPPED UP TO THE PLATE. GATOR CURLED HIS TAIL TO THE LEFT AND PITCHED A CURVE BALL. LARRY DIDN'T SWING BUT...

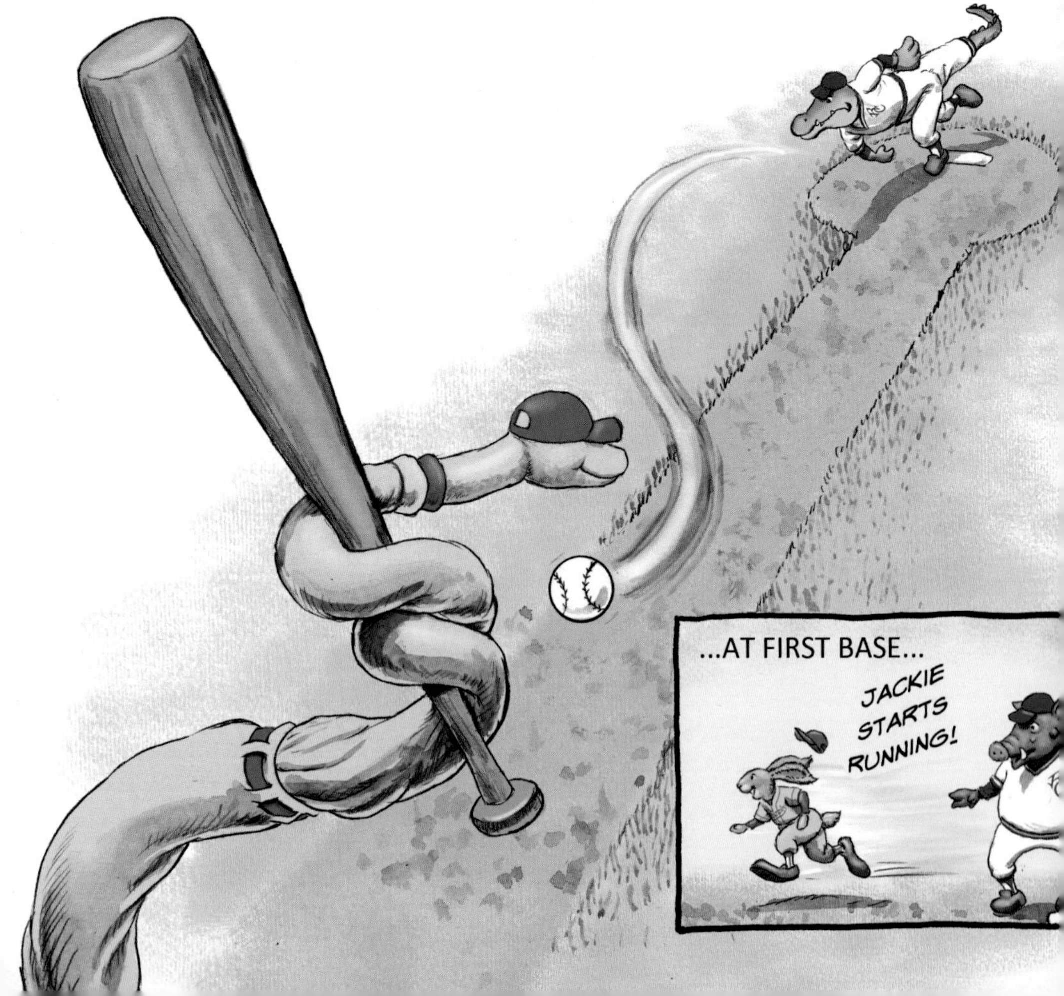
...AT FIRST BASE...
JACKIE STARTS RUNNING!

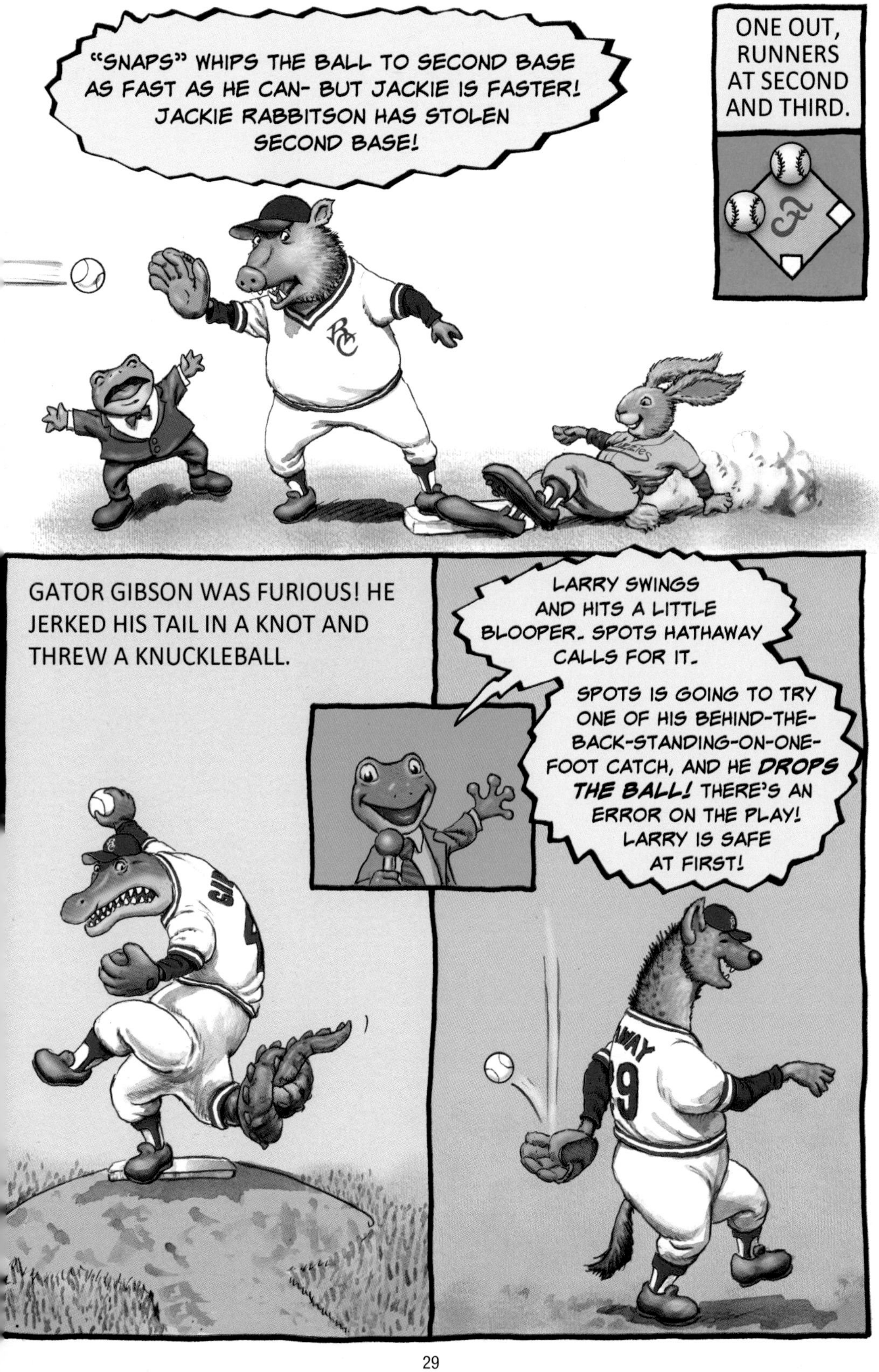
"SNAPS" WHIPS THE BALL TO SECOND BASE AS FAST AS HE CAN- BUT JACKIE IS FASTER! JACKIE RABBITSON HAS STOLEN SECOND BASE!
ONE OUT, RUNNERS AT SECOND AND THIRD.
GATOR GIBSON WAS FURIOUS! HE JERKED HIS TAIL IN A KNOT AND THREW A KNUCKLEBALL.
LARRY SWINGS AND HITS A LITTLE BLOOPER. SPOTS HATHAWAY CALLS FOR IT.
SPOTS IS GOING TO TRY ONE OF HIS BEHIND-THE-BACK-STANDING-ON-ONE-FOOT CATCH, AND HE DROPS THE BALL! THERE'S AN ERROR ON THE PLAY! LARRY IS SAFE AT FIRST!

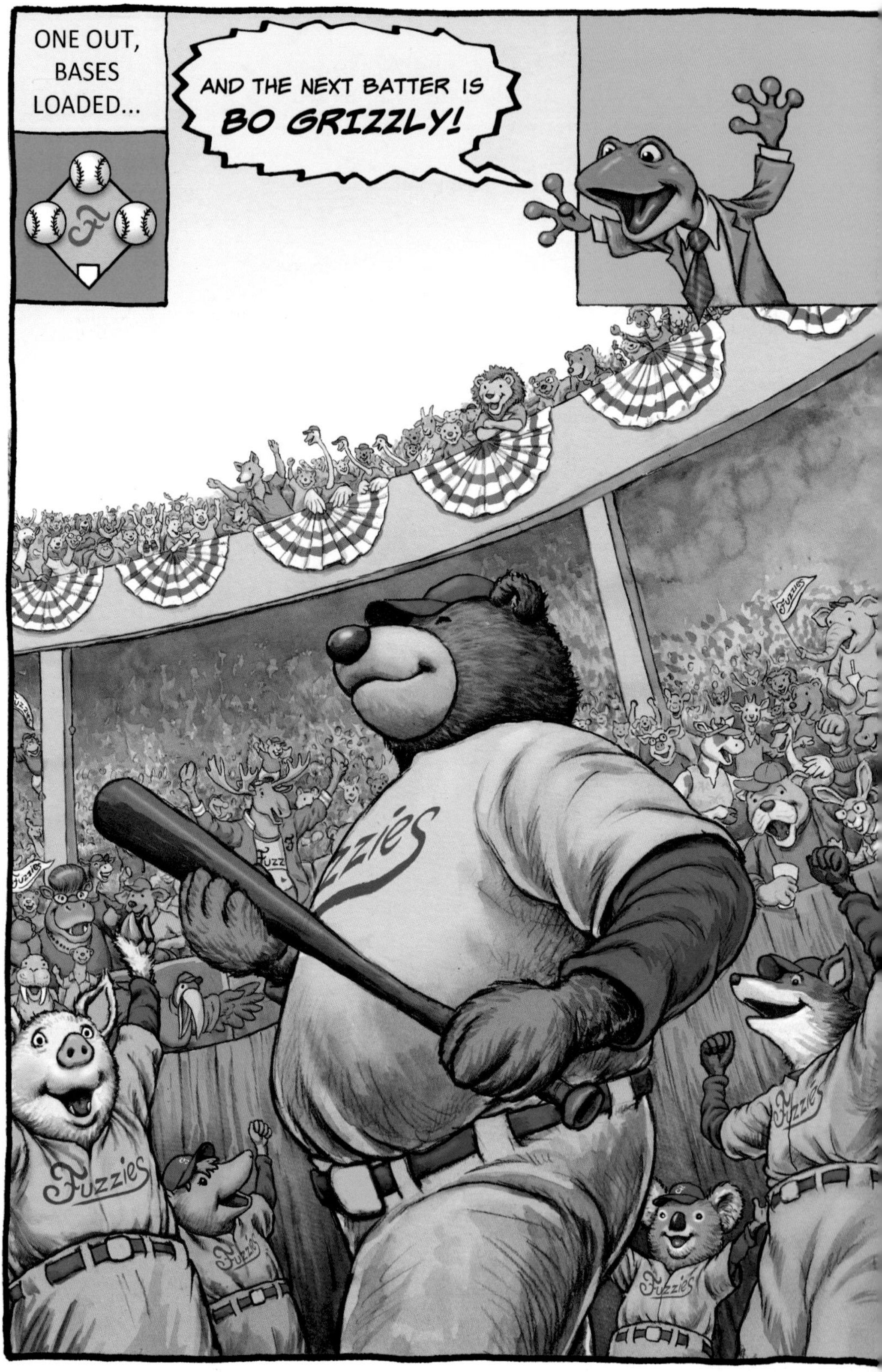
ONE OUT, BASES LOADED...
AND THE NEXT BATTER IS BO GRIZZLY!

RED CLAWS MANAGER MITZI McGRAW WALKED OUT TO THE MOUND.

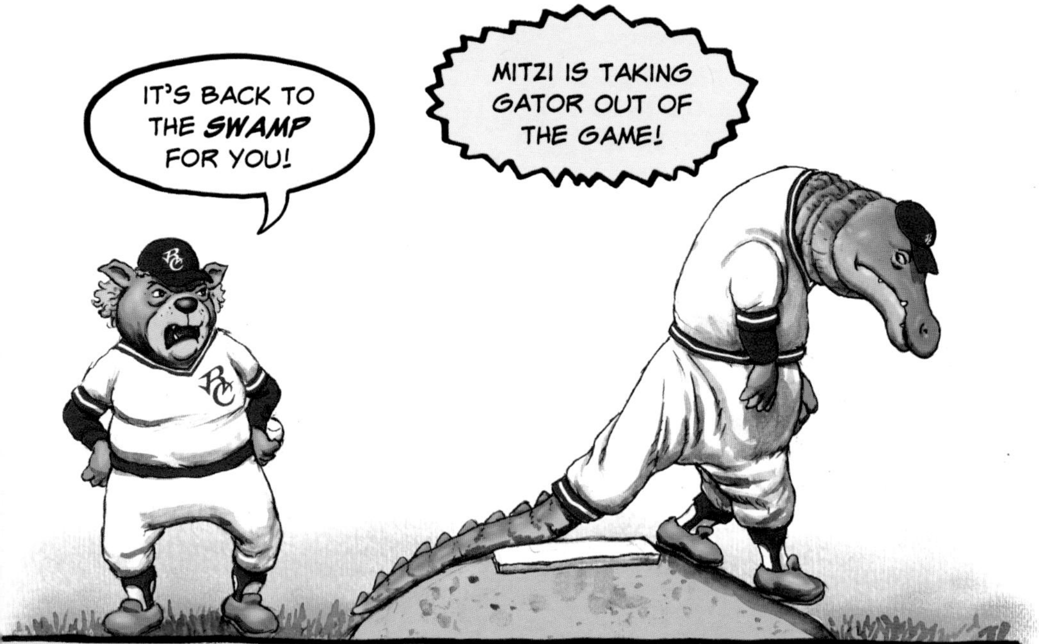
IT'S BACK TO THE *SWAMP* FOR YOU!
MITZI IS TAKING GATOR OUT OF THE GAME!

MITZI SIGNALED TO THE BULL PEN. RED CLAWS STAR RELIEF PITCHER, FERNANDO DEL TORO, CHARGED TO THE MOUND.

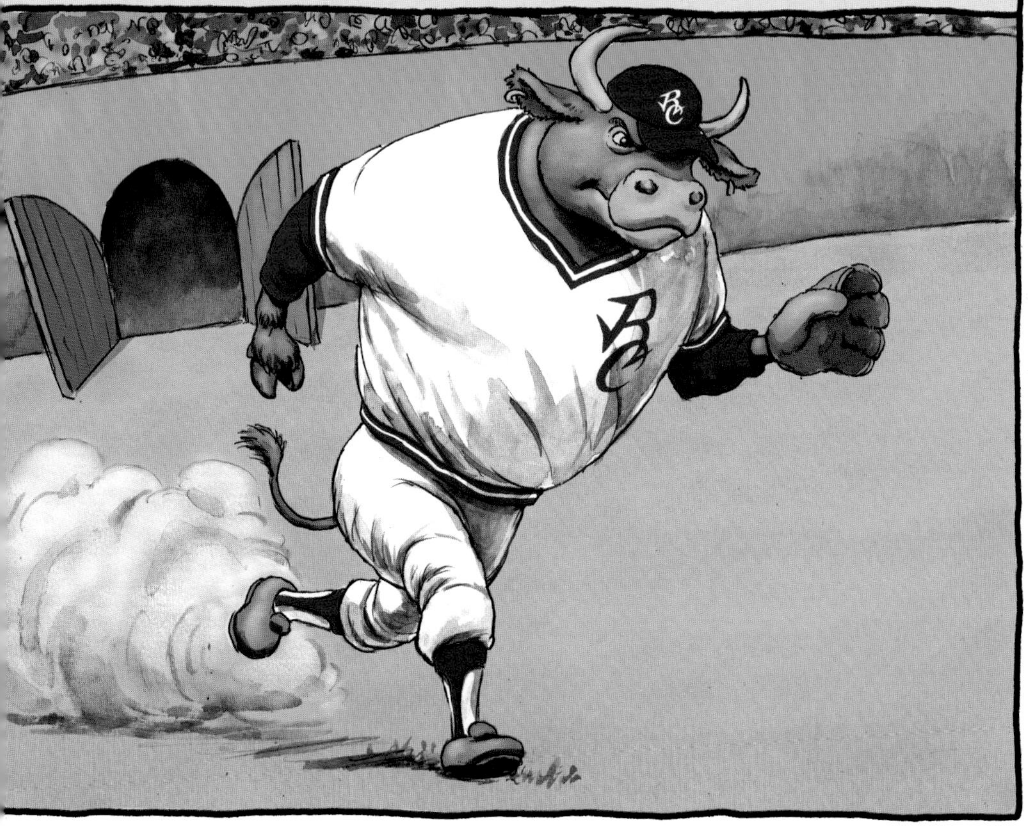

THE FUZZY'S DUGOUT WAS SUDDENLY SILENT AGAIN.

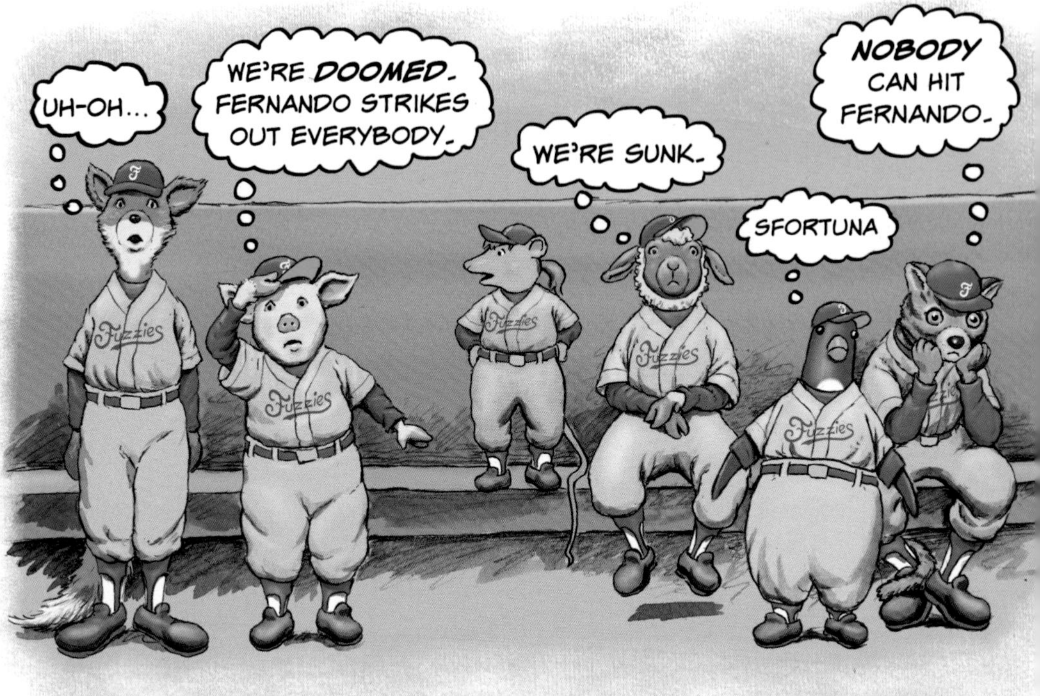
UH-OH...
WE'RE DOOMED. FERNANDO STRIKES OUT EVERYBODY.
WE'RE SUNK.
SFORTUNA
NOBODY CAN HIT FERNANDO.
Fuzzies

BLOSSOM COULD NOT STAY QUIET... AND NEITHER COULD ANYBODY ELSE!

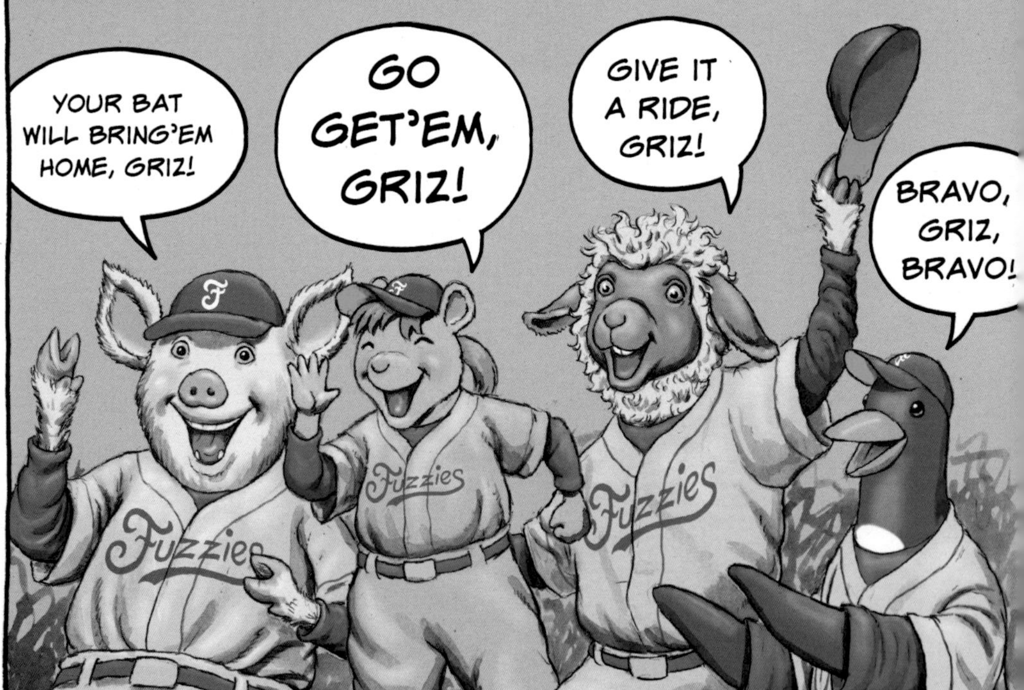
YOUR BAT WILL BRING'EM HOME, GRIZ!
GO GET'EM, GRIZ!
GIVE IT A RIDE, GRIZ!
BRAVO, GRIZ, BRAVO!
Fuzzies

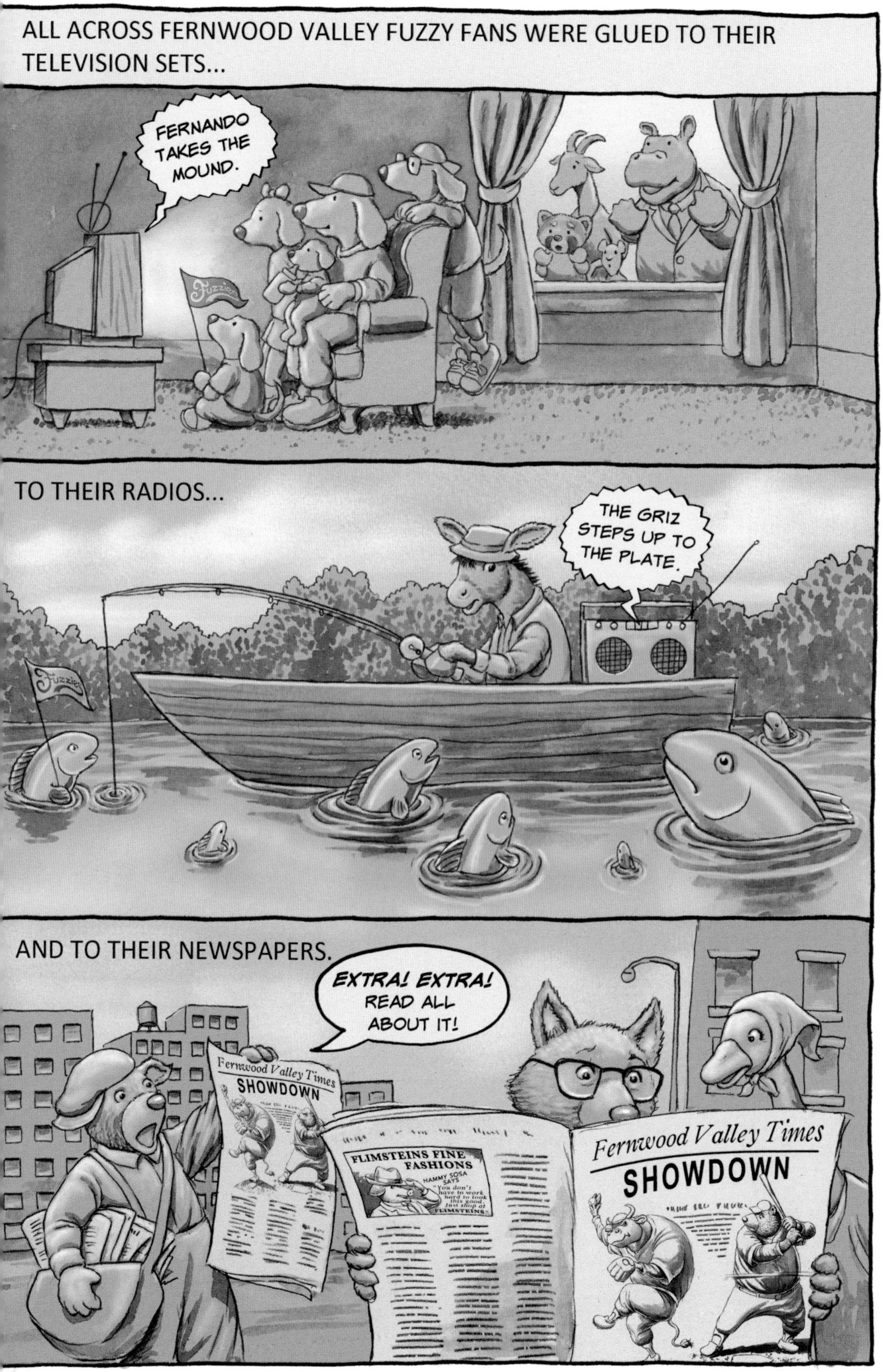
ALL ACROSS FERNWOOD VALLEY FUZZY FANS WERE GLUED TO THEIR TELEVISION SETS...
FERNANDO TAKES THE MOUND.
Fuzzies
TO THEIR RADIOS...
THE GRIZ STEPS UP TO THE PLATE.
Fuzzies
AND TO THEIR NEWSPAPERS.
EXTRA! EXTRA! READ ALL ABOUT IT!
Fernwood Valley Times
SHOWDOWN
FLIMSTEINS FINE FASHIONS
HAMMY SOSA SAYS
"You don't have to work hard to look this good. Just shop at FLIMSTEINS"
Fernwood Valley Times
SHOWDOWN

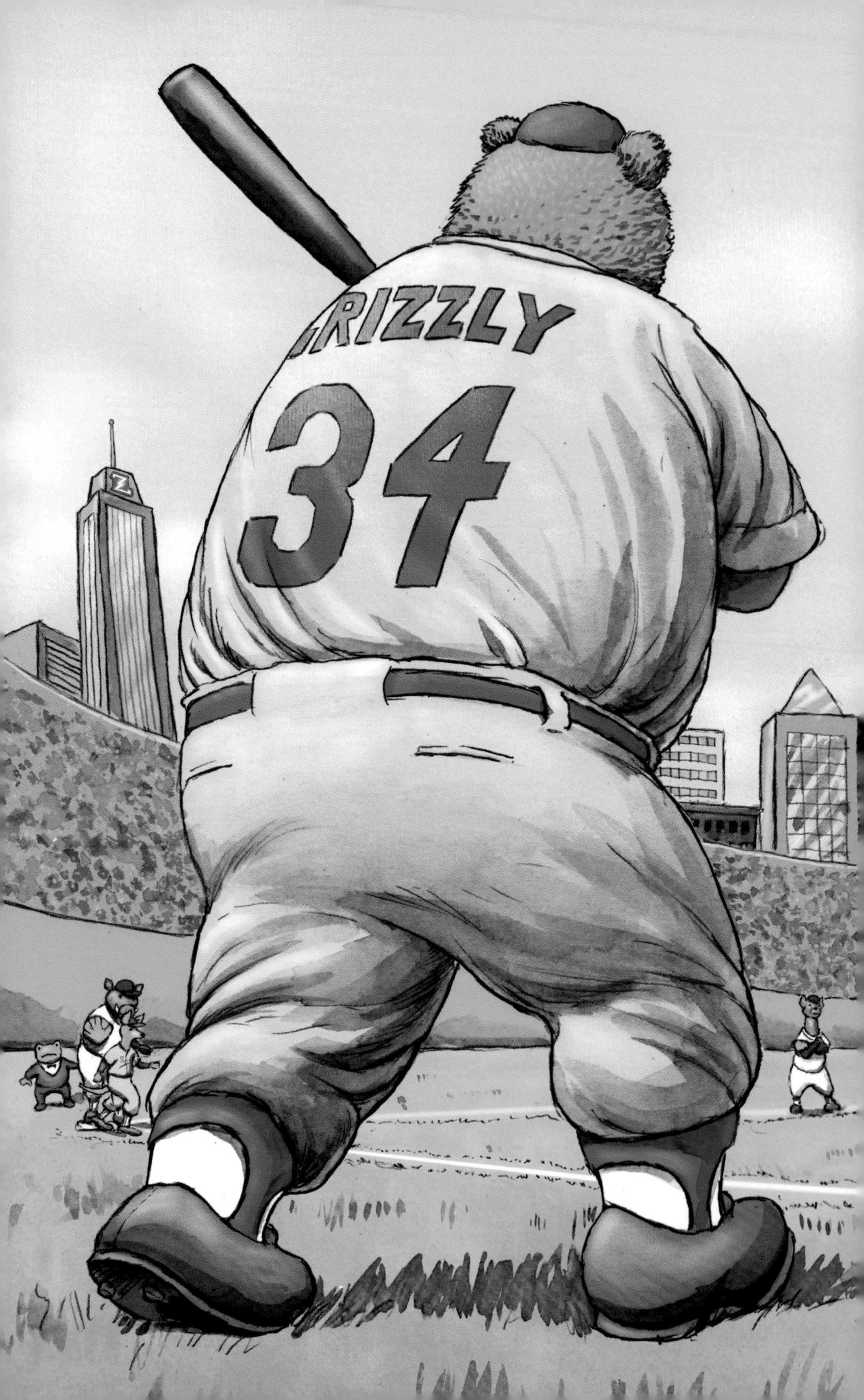
RIZZLY
34
Z

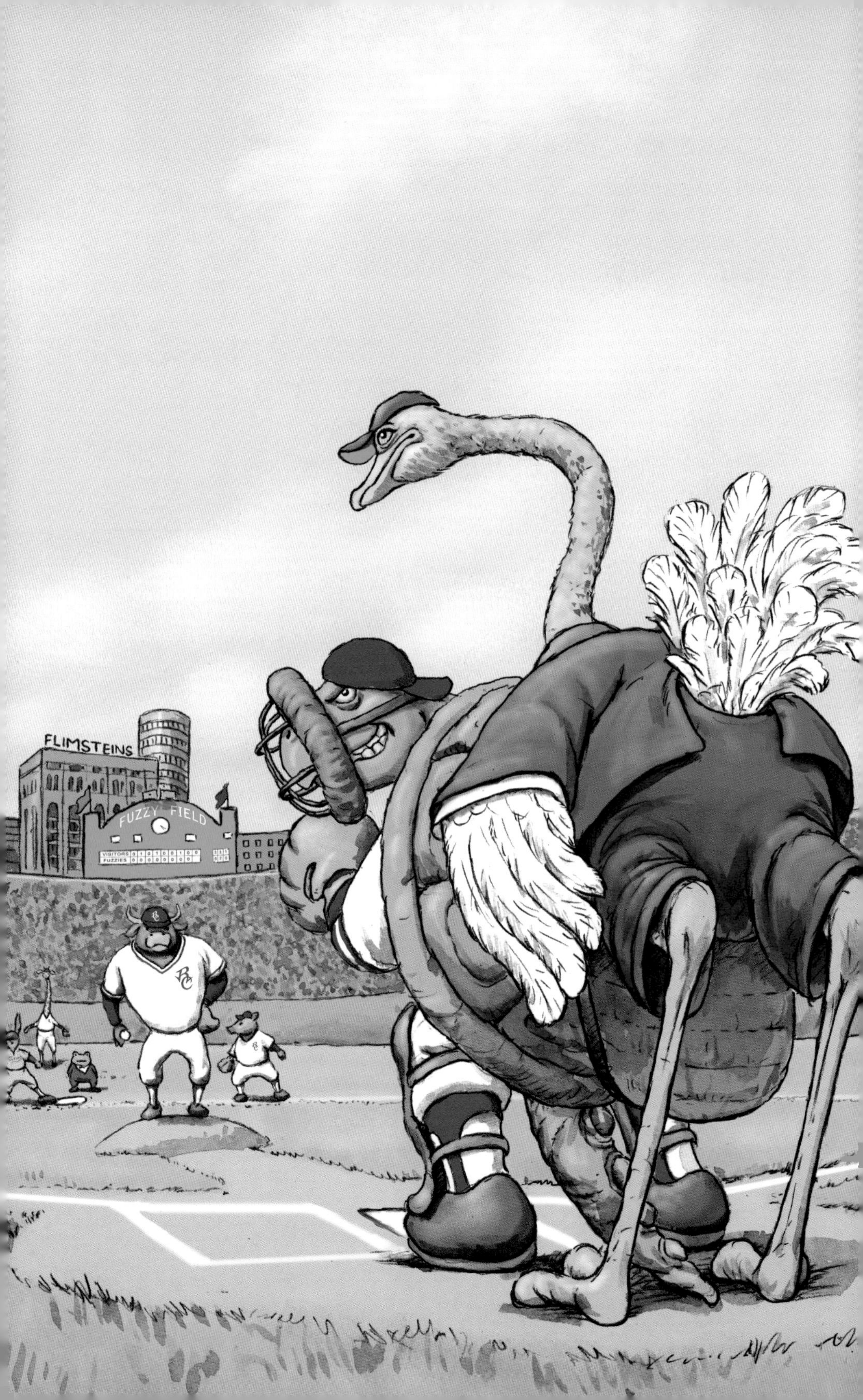

FLIMSTEINS
FUZZY FIELD
VISITORS
FUZZIES

FOUR TIMES FERNANDO SNORTED, STOMPED HIS FOOT, WOUND UP, AND THREW A LIGHTNING FAST PITCH.

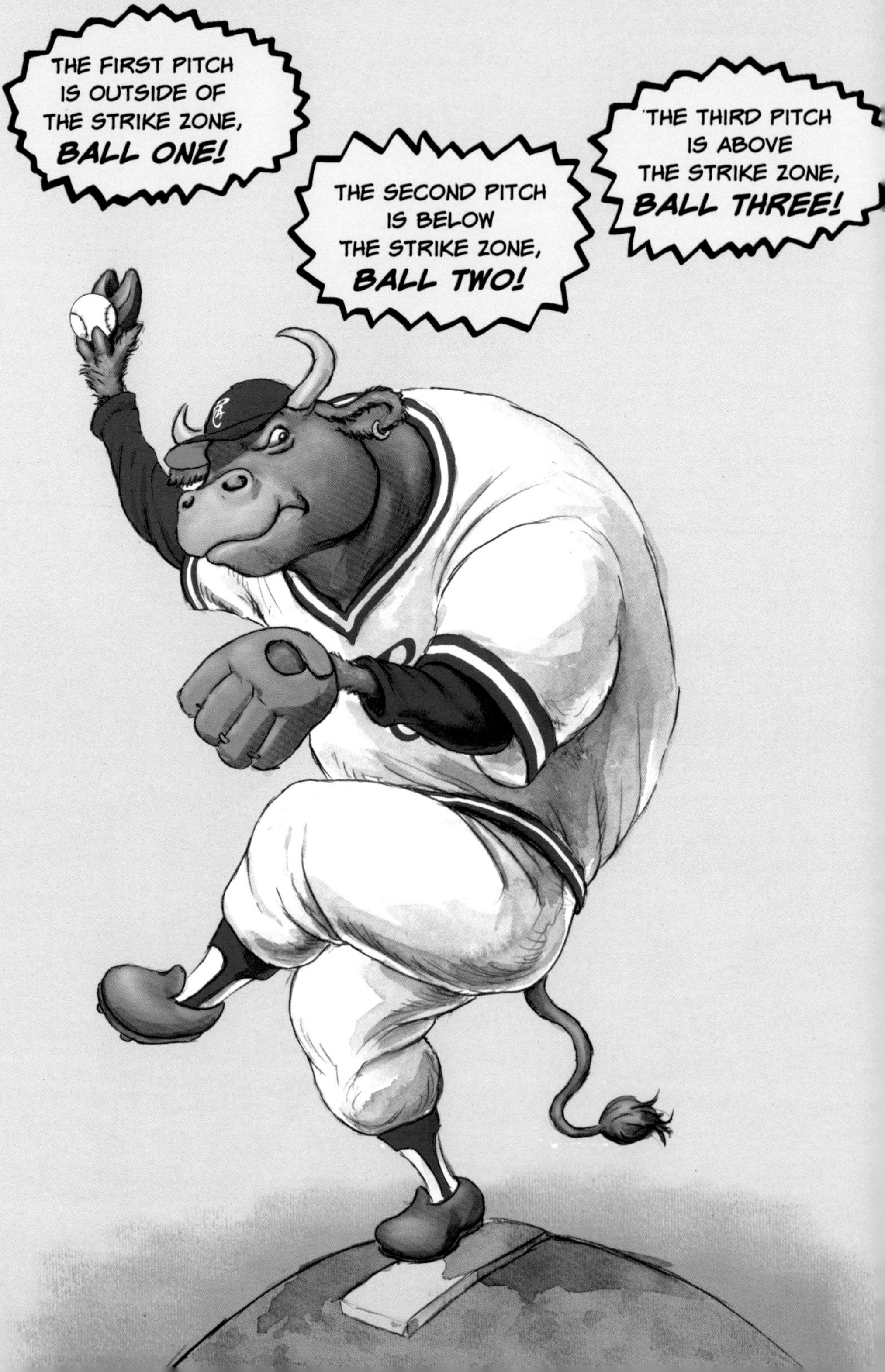
THE FIRST PITCH IS OUTSIDE OF THE STRIKE ZONE, BALL ONE!
THE SECOND PITCH IS BELOW THE STRIKE ZONE, BALL TWO!
THE THIRD PITCH IS ABOVE THE STRIKE ZONE, BALL THREE!

AND FOUR TIMES THE GRIZ DID NOT SWING. HE DID NOT TWITCH. HE DID NOT EVEN BLINK.

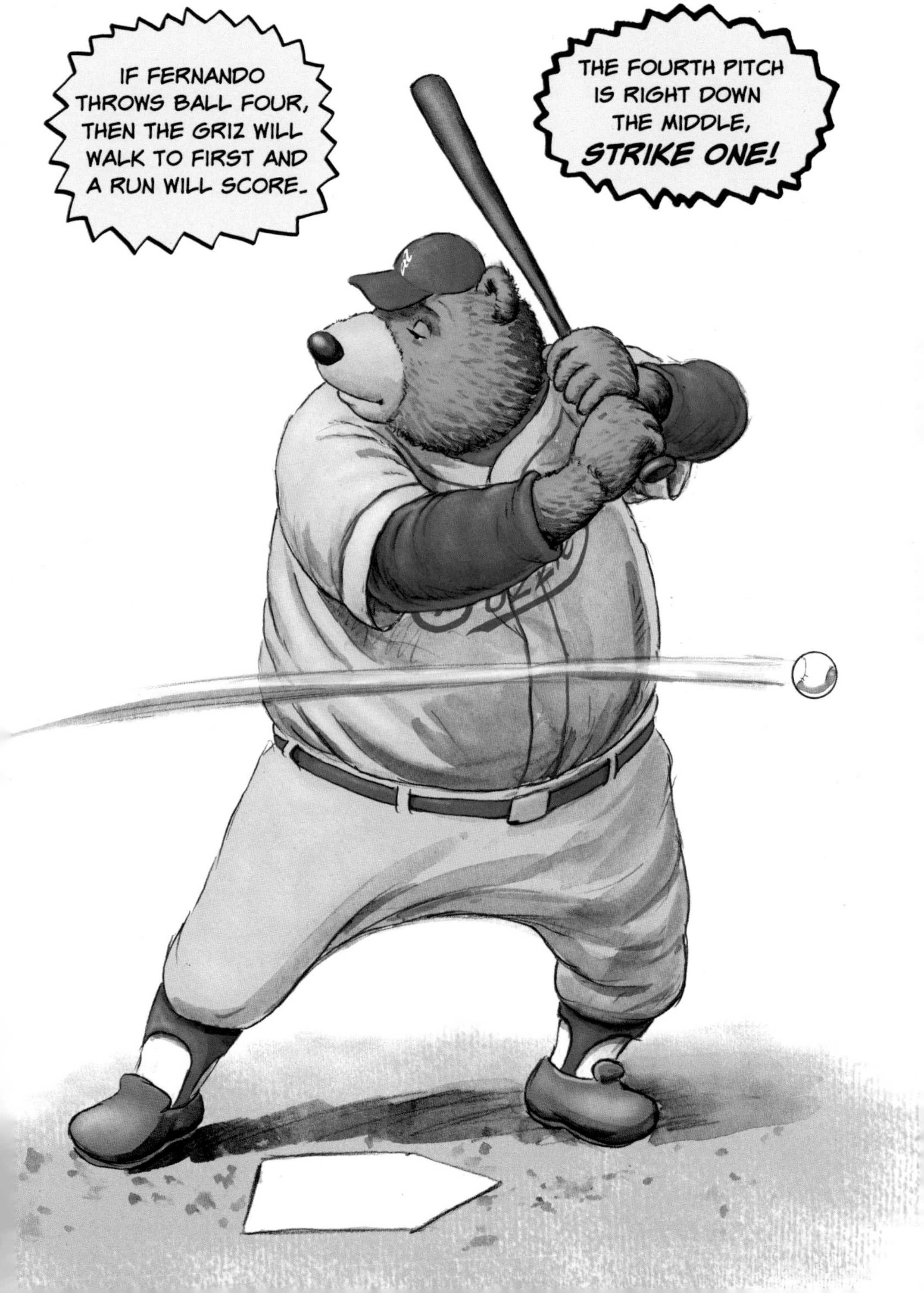
IF FERNANDO THROWS BALL FOUR, THEN THE GRIZ WILL WALK TO FIRST AND A RUN WILL SCORE.
THE FOURTH PITCH IS RIGHT DOWN THE MIDDLE, ***STRIKE ONE!***

THREE BALLS AND ONE STRIKE. FERNANDO WOUND UP AND THREW A FASTBA
DOWN THE MIDDLE OF THE PLATE. THE GRIZ TOOK A BIG SWING AND...

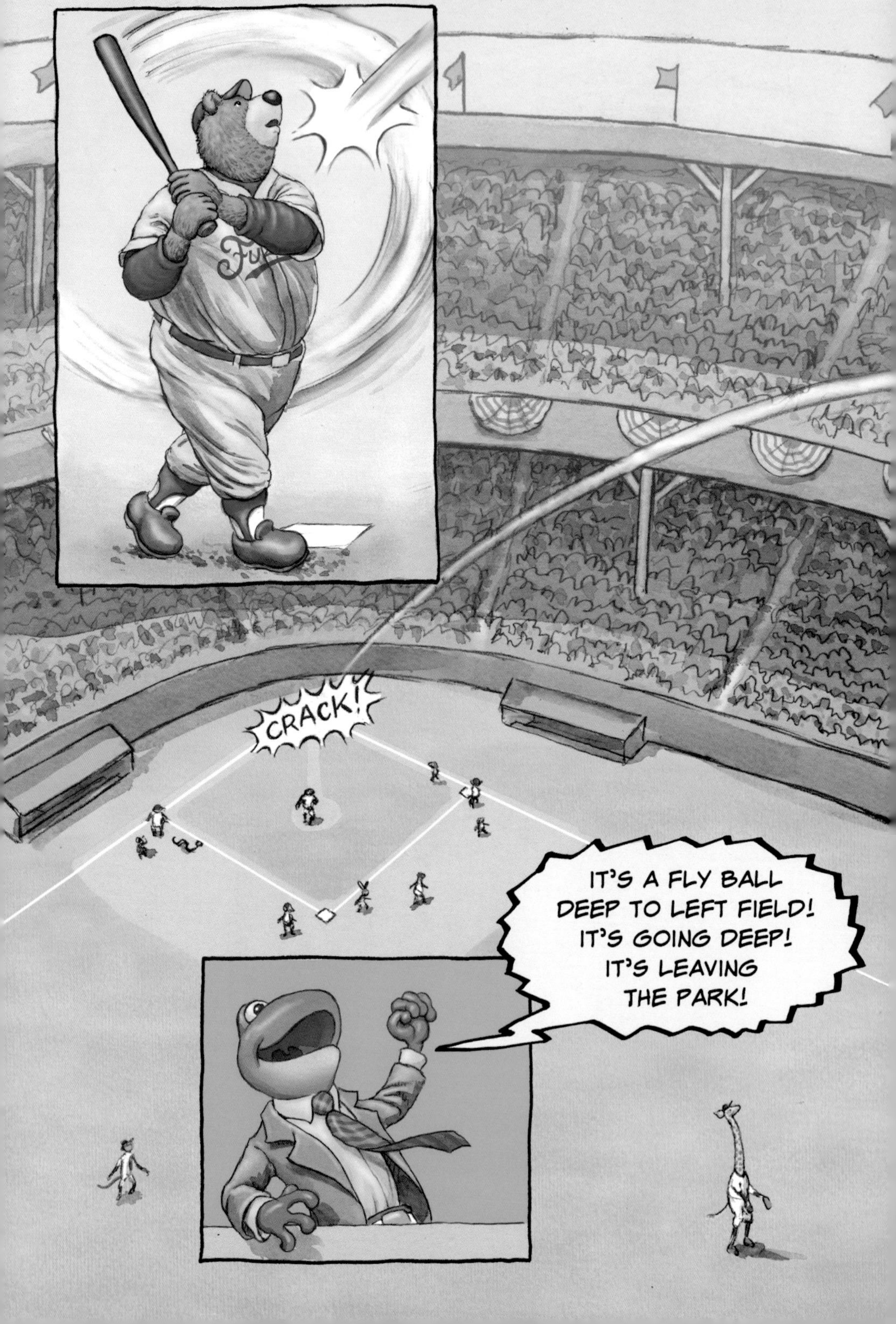
CRACK!
IT'S A FLY BALL DEEP TO LEFT FIELD! IT'S GOING DEEP! IT'S LEAVING THE PARK!

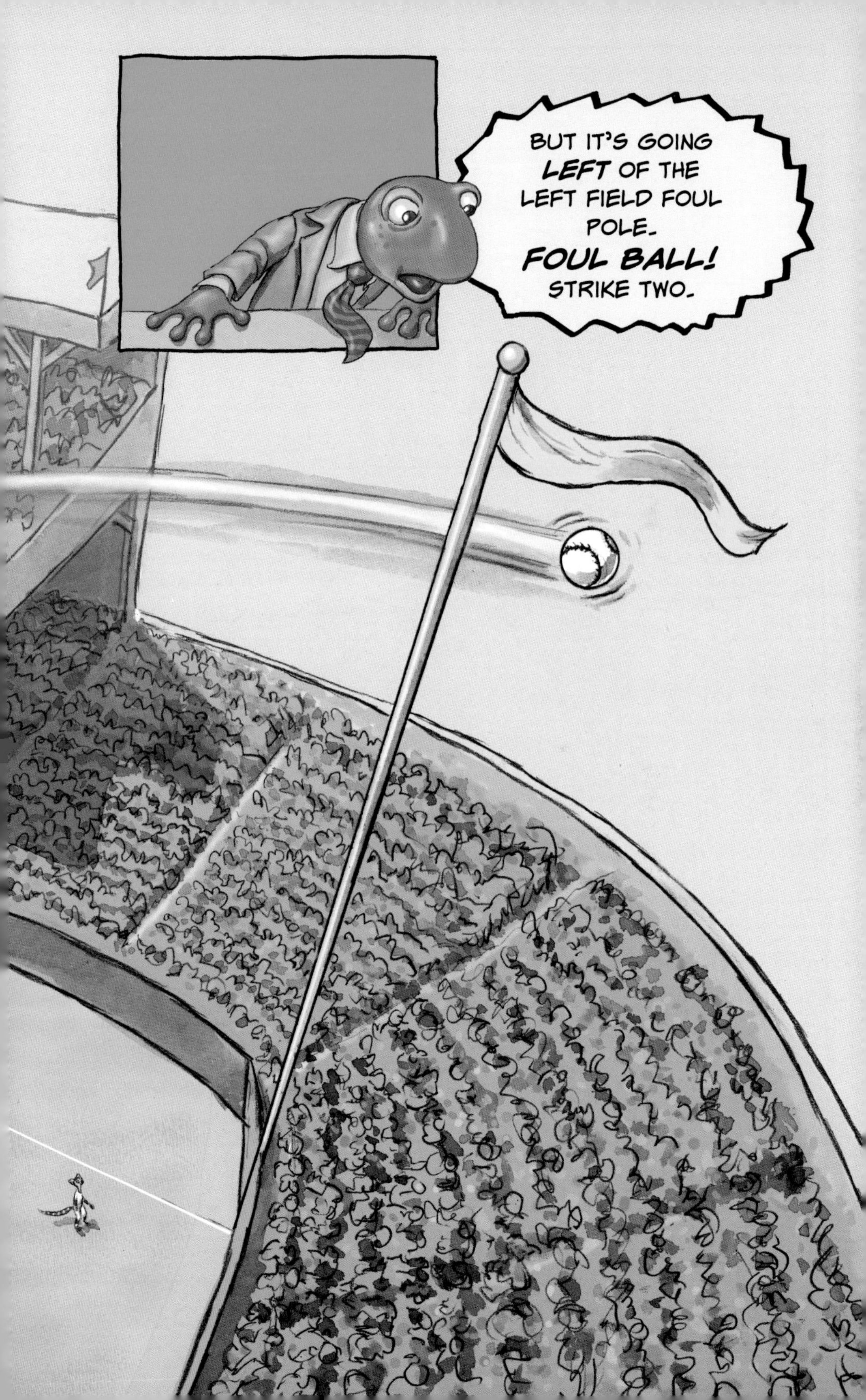
BUT IT'S GOING LEFT OF THE LEFT FIELD FOUL POLE. FOUL BALL! STRIKE TWO.

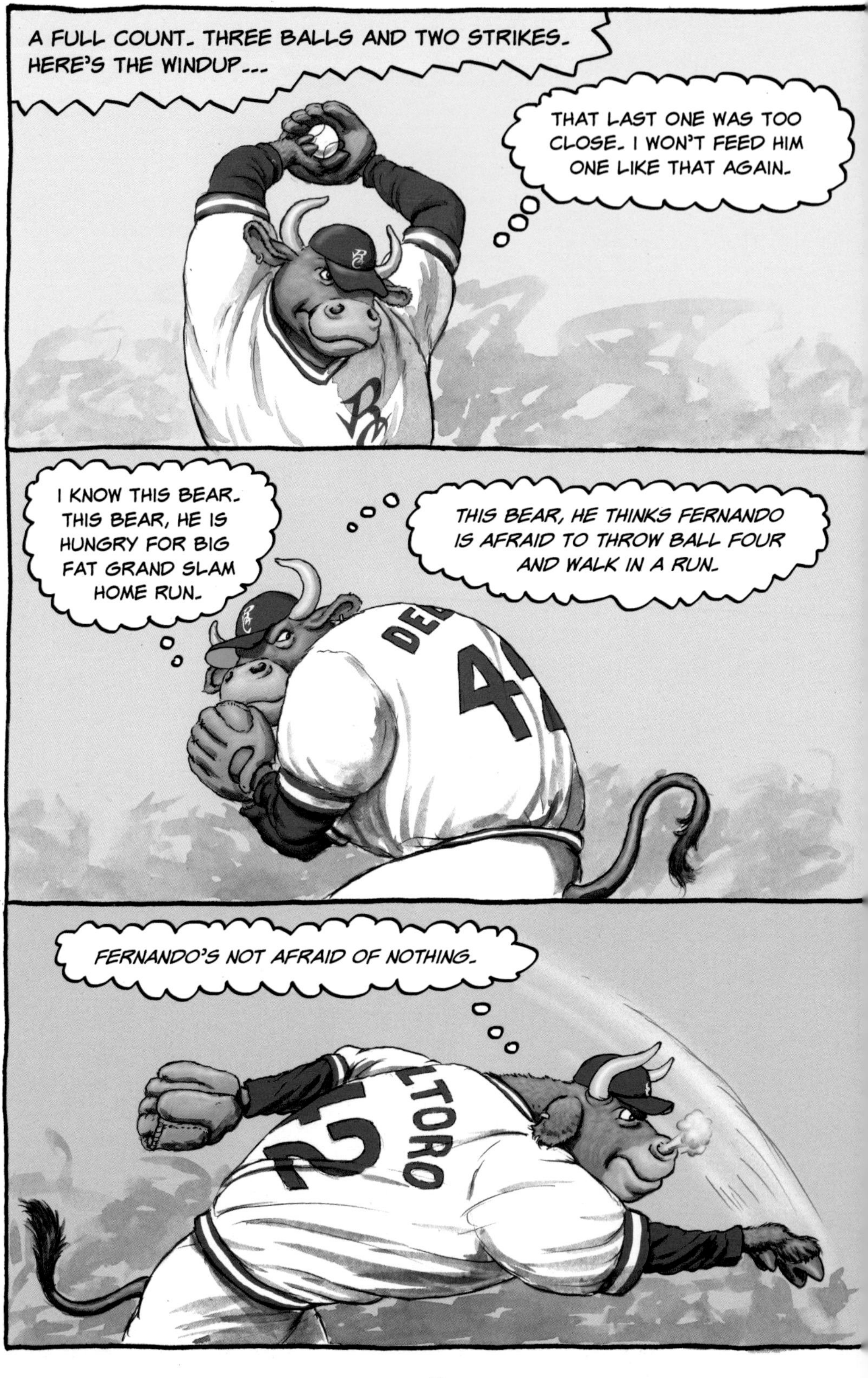
A FULL COUNT. THREE BALLS AND TWO STRIKES. HERE'S THE WINDUP...
THAT LAST ONE WAS TOO CLOSE. I WON'T FEED HIM ONE LIKE THAT AGAIN.
I KNOW THIS BEAR. THIS BEAR, HE IS HUNGRY FOR BIG FAT GRAND SLAM HOME RUN.
THIS BEAR, HE THINKS FERNANDO IS AFRAID TO THROW BALL FOUR AND WALK IN A RUN.
FERNANDO'S NOT AFRAID OF NOTHING.

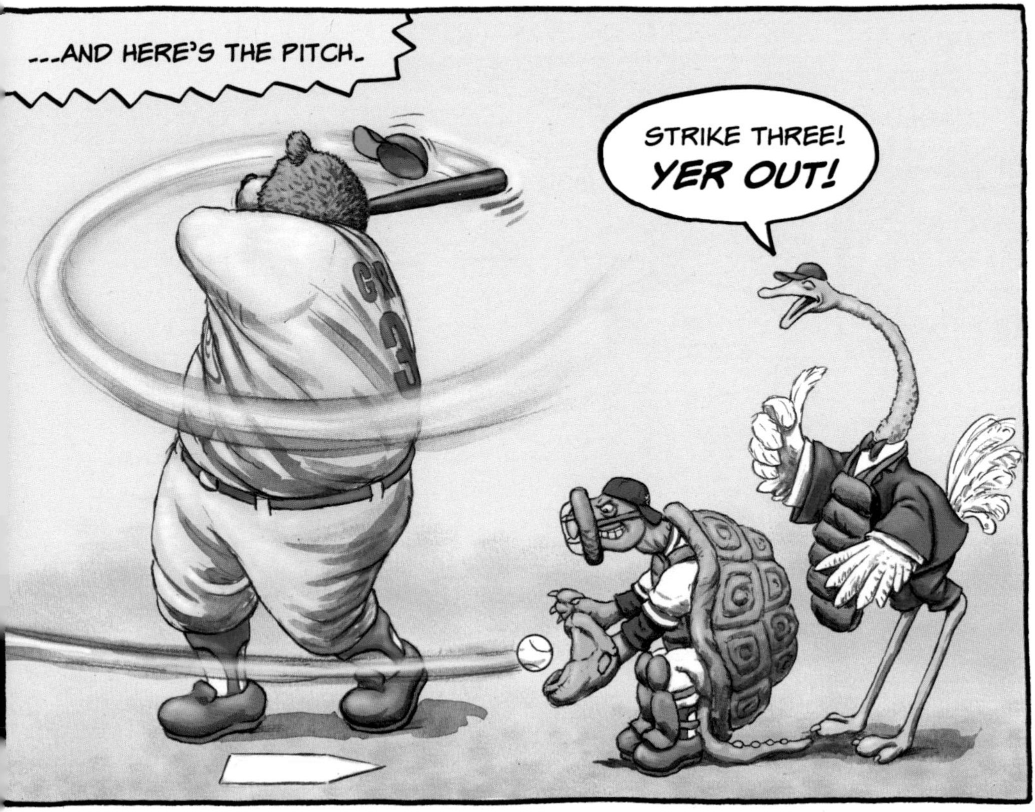
...AND HERE'S THE PITCH.
STRIKE THREE! YER OUT!

THERE WAS NO JOY IN FERNWOOD VALLEY.

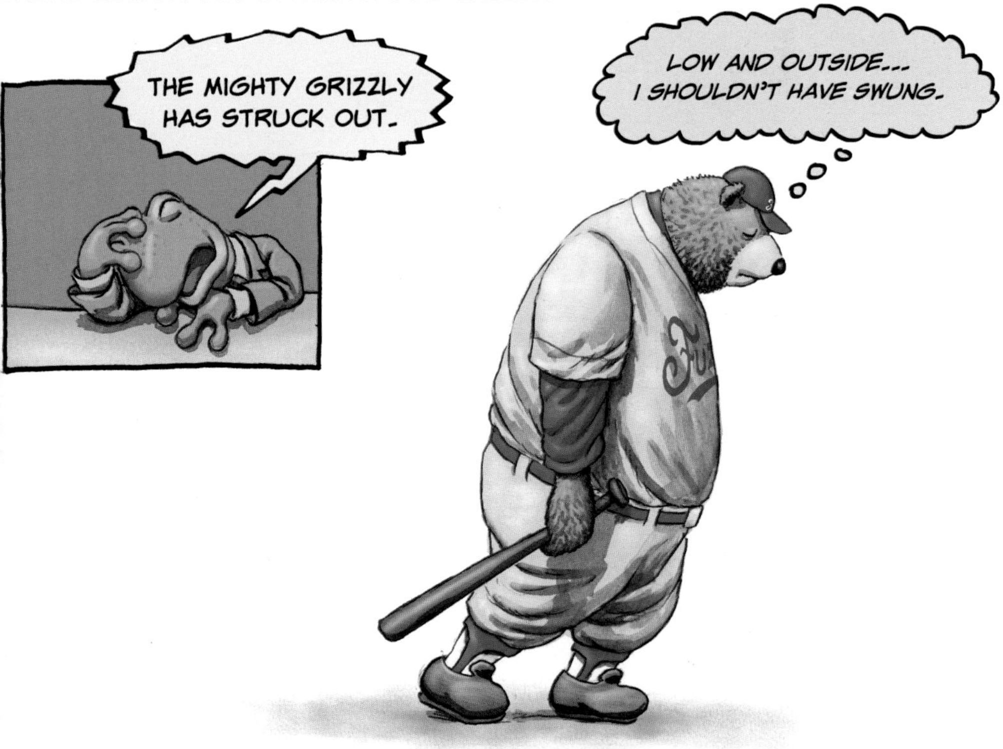
THE MIGHTY GRIZZLY HAS STRUCK OUT.
LOW AND OUTSIDE... I SHOULDN'T HAVE SWUNG.

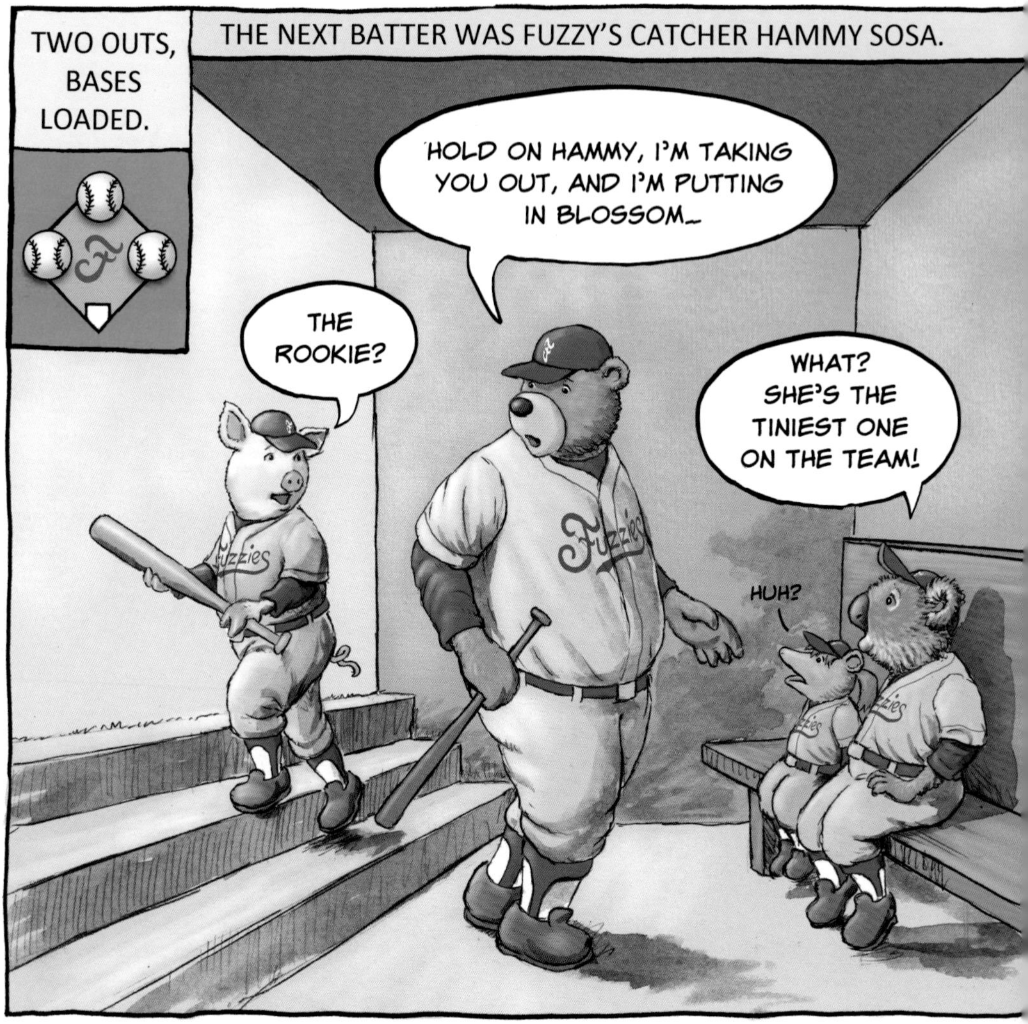
TWO OUTS, BASES LOADED.
THE NEXT BATTER WAS FUZZY'S CATCHER HAMMY SOSA.
HOLD ON HAMMY, I'M TAKING YOU OUT, AND I'M PUTTING IN BLOSSOM.
THE ROOKIE?
WHAT? SHE'S THE TINIEST ONE ON THE TEAM!
HUH?

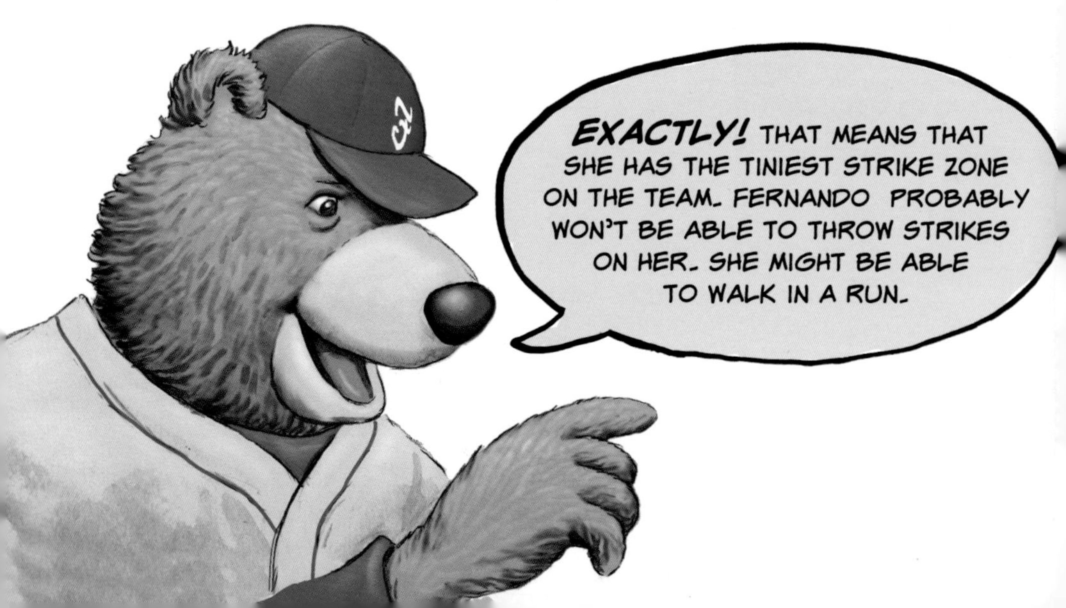
EXACTLY! THAT MEANS THAT SHE HAS THE TINIEST STRIKE ZONE ON THE TEAM. FERNANDO PROBABLY WON'T BE ABLE TO THROW STRIKES ON HER. SHE MIGHT BE ABLE TO WALK IN A RUN.

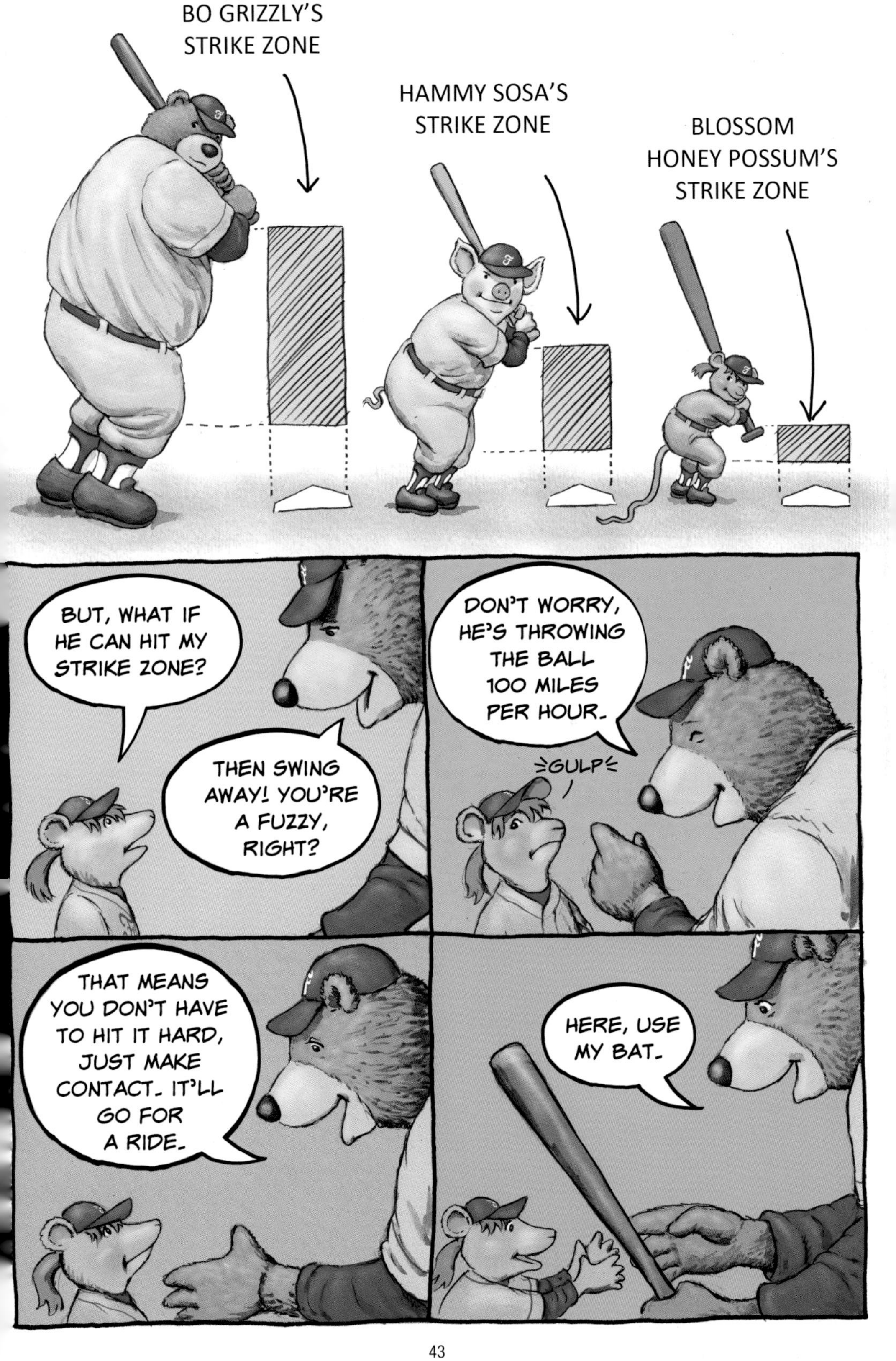
BO GRIZZLY'S STRIKE ZONE
HAMMY SOSA'S STRIKE ZONE
BLOSSOM HONEY POSSUM'S STRIKE ZONE
BUT, WHAT IF HE CAN HIT MY STRIKE ZONE?
THEN SWING AWAY! YOU'RE A FUZZY, RIGHT?
DON'T WORRY, HE'S THROWING THE BALL 100 MILES PER HOUR.
GULP
THAT MEANS YOU DON'T HAVE TO HIT IT HARD, JUST MAKE CONTACT. IT'LL GO FOR A RIDE.
HERE, USE MY BAT.

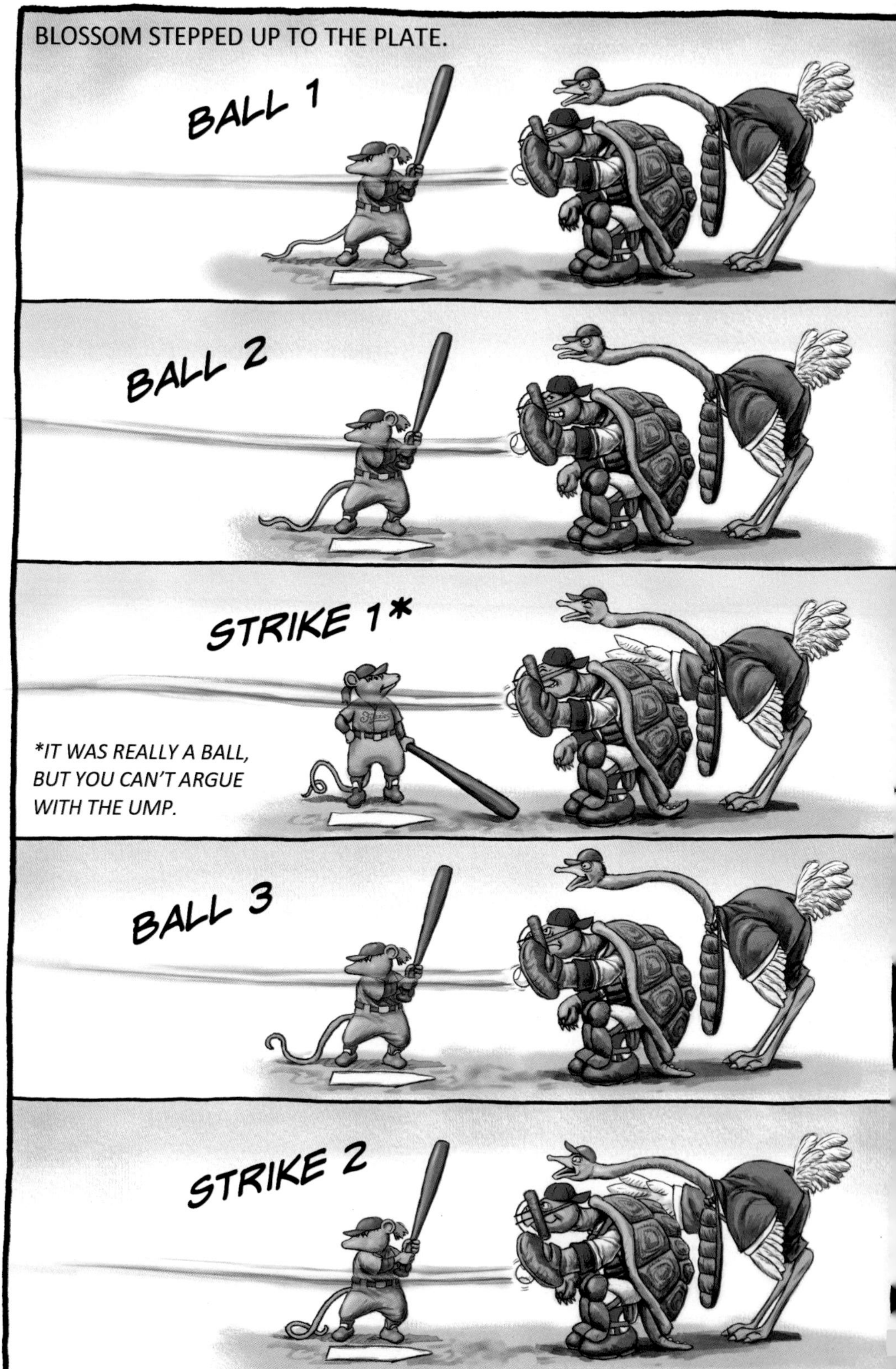
BLOSSOM STEPPED UP TO THE PLATE.
BALL 1
BALL 2
STRIKE 1*
*IT WAS REALLY A BALL, BUT YOU CAN'T ARGUE WITH THE UMP.
BALL 3
STRIKE 2

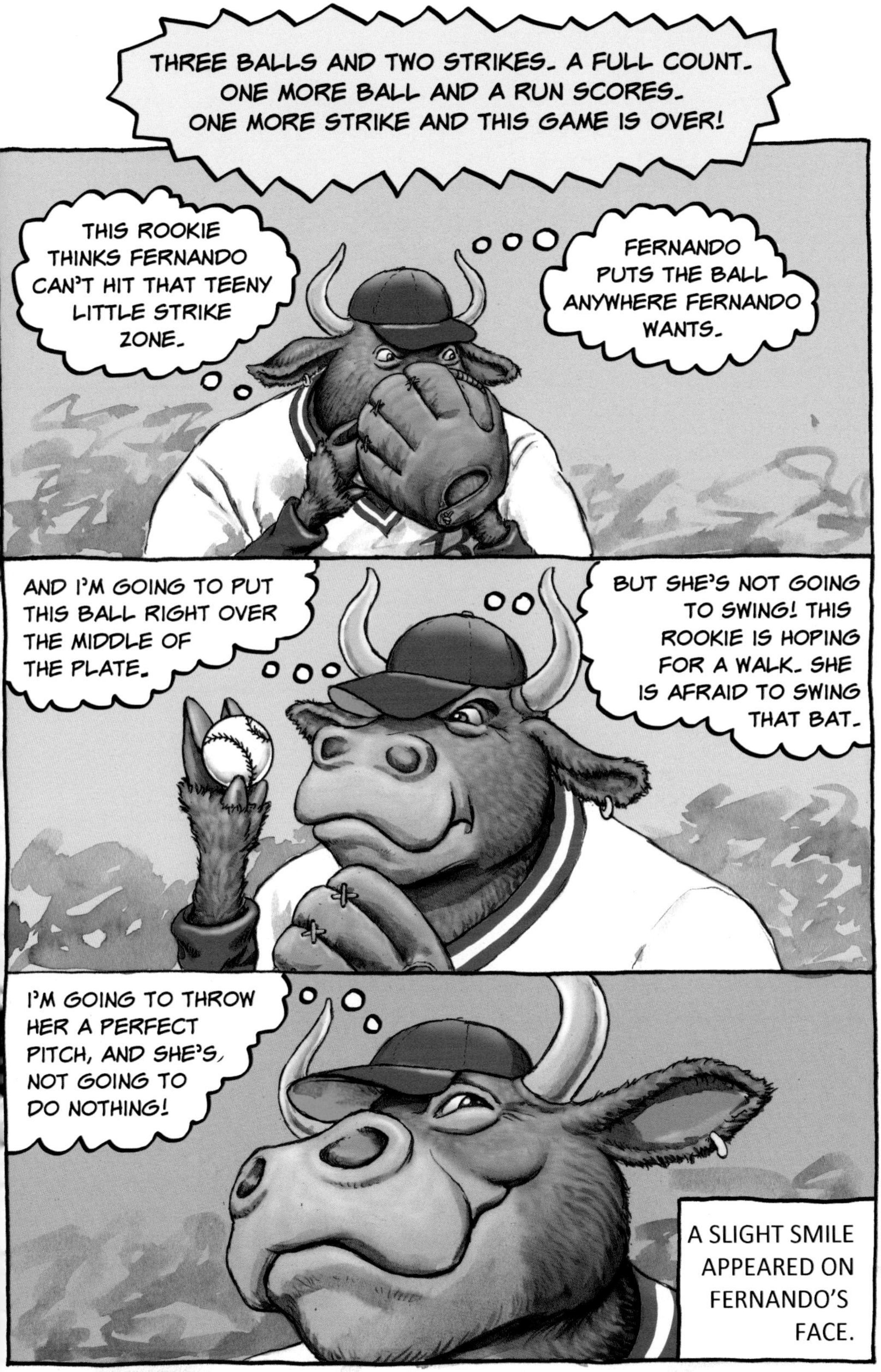
THREE BALLS AND TWO STRIKES. A FULL COUNT. ONE MORE BALL AND A RUN SCORES. ONE MORE STRIKE AND THIS GAME IS OVER!
THIS ROOKIE THINKS FERNANDO CAN'T HIT THAT TEENY LITTLE STRIKE ZONE.
FERNANDO PUTS THE BALL ANYWHERE FERNANDO WANTS.
AND I'M GOING TO PUT THIS BALL RIGHT OVER THE MIDDLE OF THE PLATE.
BUT SHE'S NOT GOING TO SWING! THIS ROOKIE IS HOPING FOR A WALK. SHE IS AFRAID TO SWING THAT BAT.
I'M GOING TO THROW HER A PERFECT PITCH, AND SHE'S, NOT GOING TO DO NOTHING!
A SLIGHT SMILE APPEARED ON FERNANDO'S FACE.

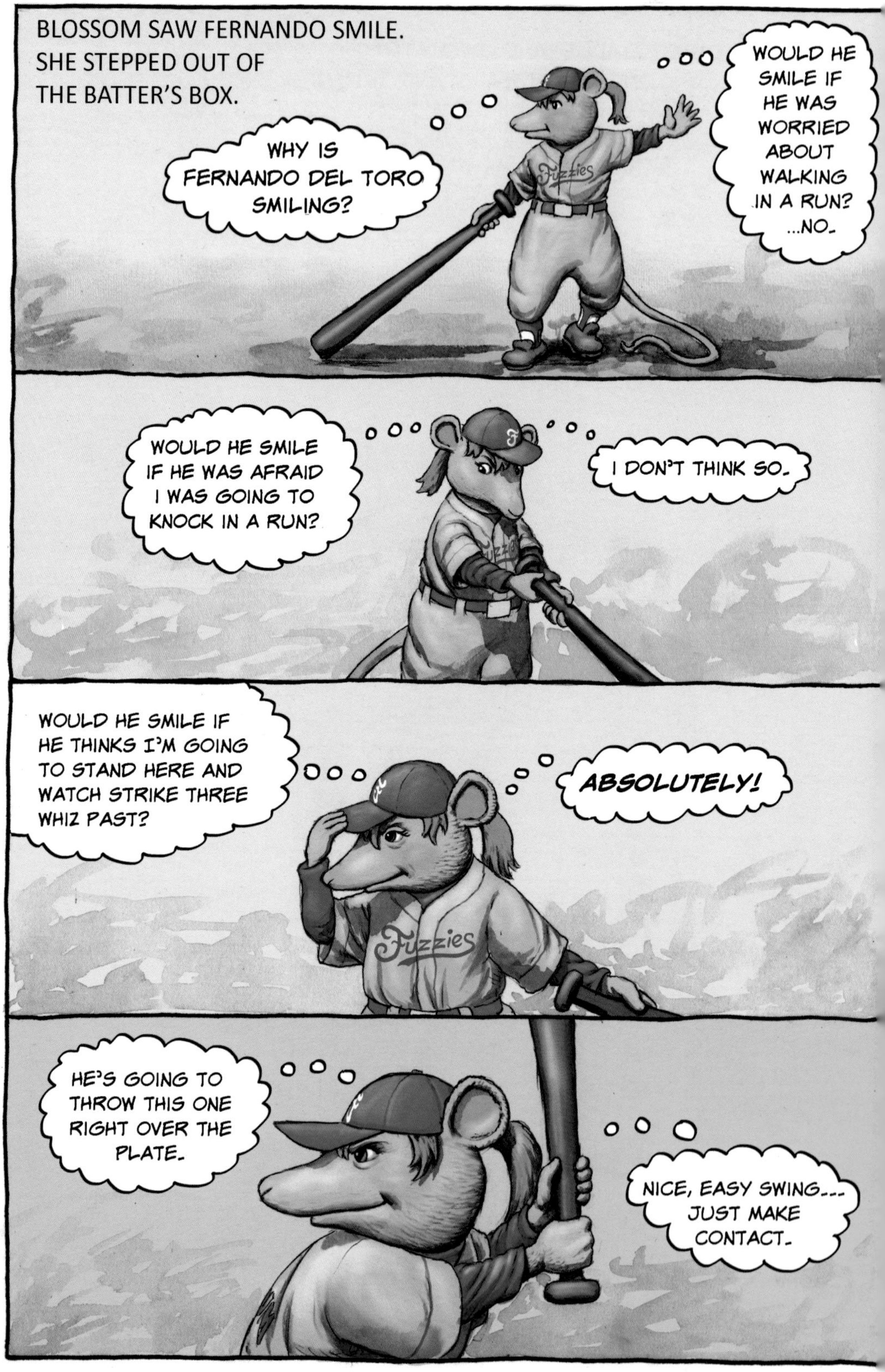
BLOSSOM SAW FERNANDO SMILE. SHE STEPPED OUT OF THE BATTER'S BOX.
WHY IS FERNANDO DEL TORO SMILING?
WOULD HE SMILE IF HE WAS WORRIED ABOUT WALKING IN A RUN? ...NO.
WOULD HE SMILE IF HE WAS AFRAID I WAS GOING TO KNOCK IN A RUN?
I DON'T THINK SO.
WOULD HE SMILE IF HE THINKS I'M GOING TO STAND HERE AND WATCH STRIKE THREE WHIZ PAST?
ABSOLUTELY!
HE'S GOING TO THROW THIS ONE RIGHT OVER THE PLATE.
NICE, EASY SWING... JUST MAKE CONTACT.

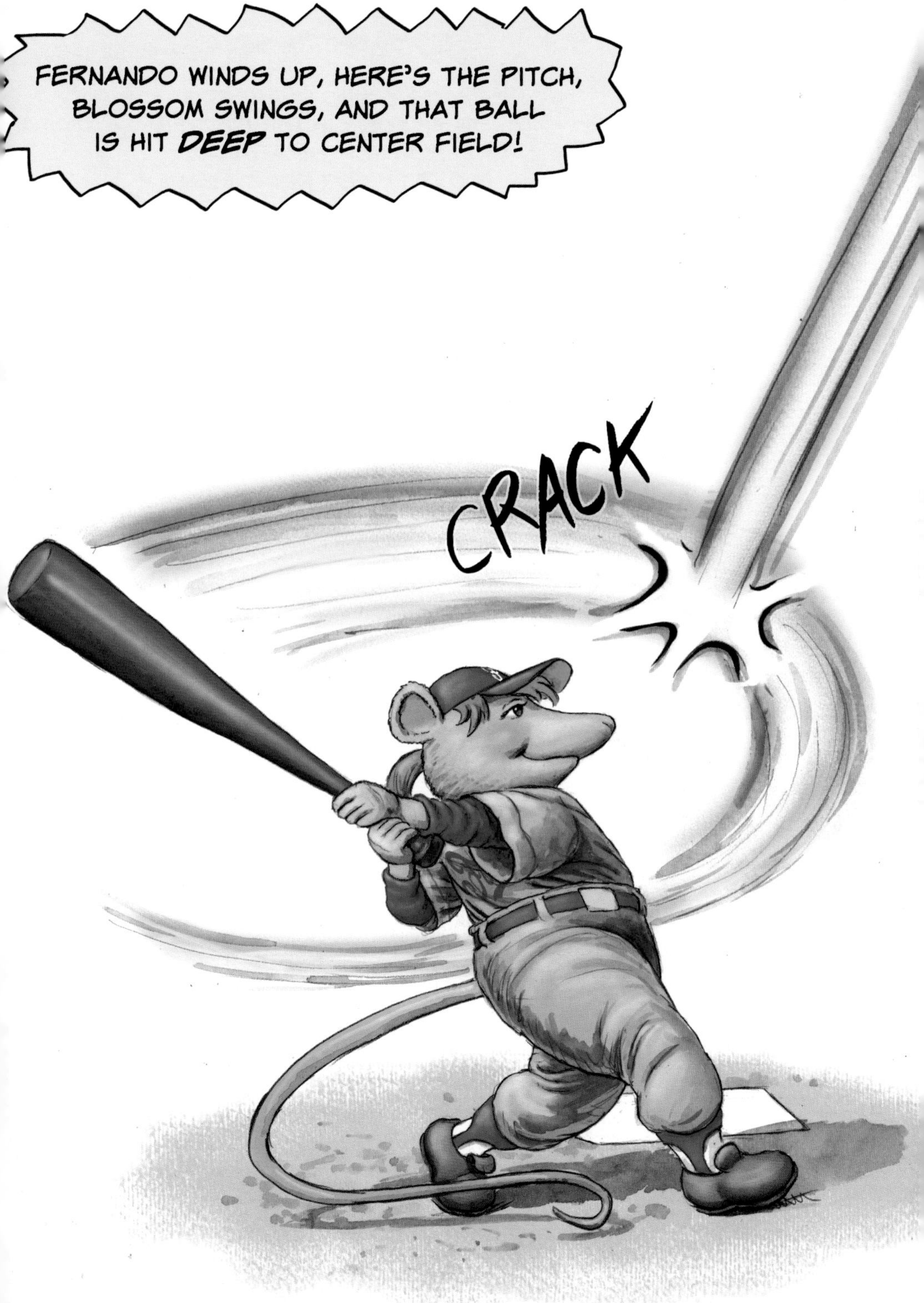
FERNANDO WINDS UP, HERE'S THE PITCH, BLOSSOM SWINGS, AND THAT BALL IS HIT *DEEP* TO CENTER FIELD!
CRACK

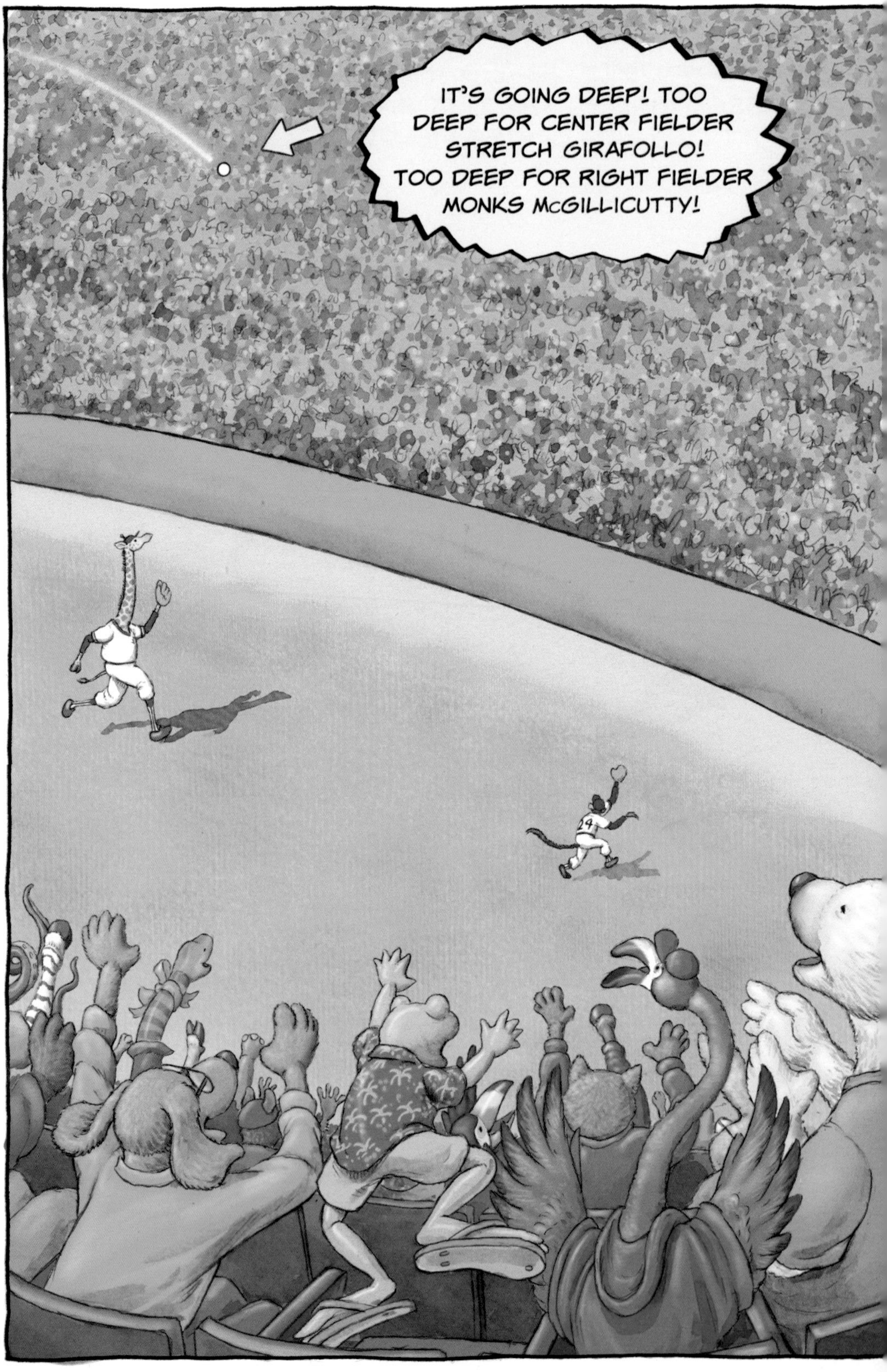
IT'S GOING DEEP! TOO DEEP FOR CENTER FIELDER STRETCH GIRAFOLLO! TOO DEEP FOR RIGHT FIELDER MONKS McGILLICUTTY!

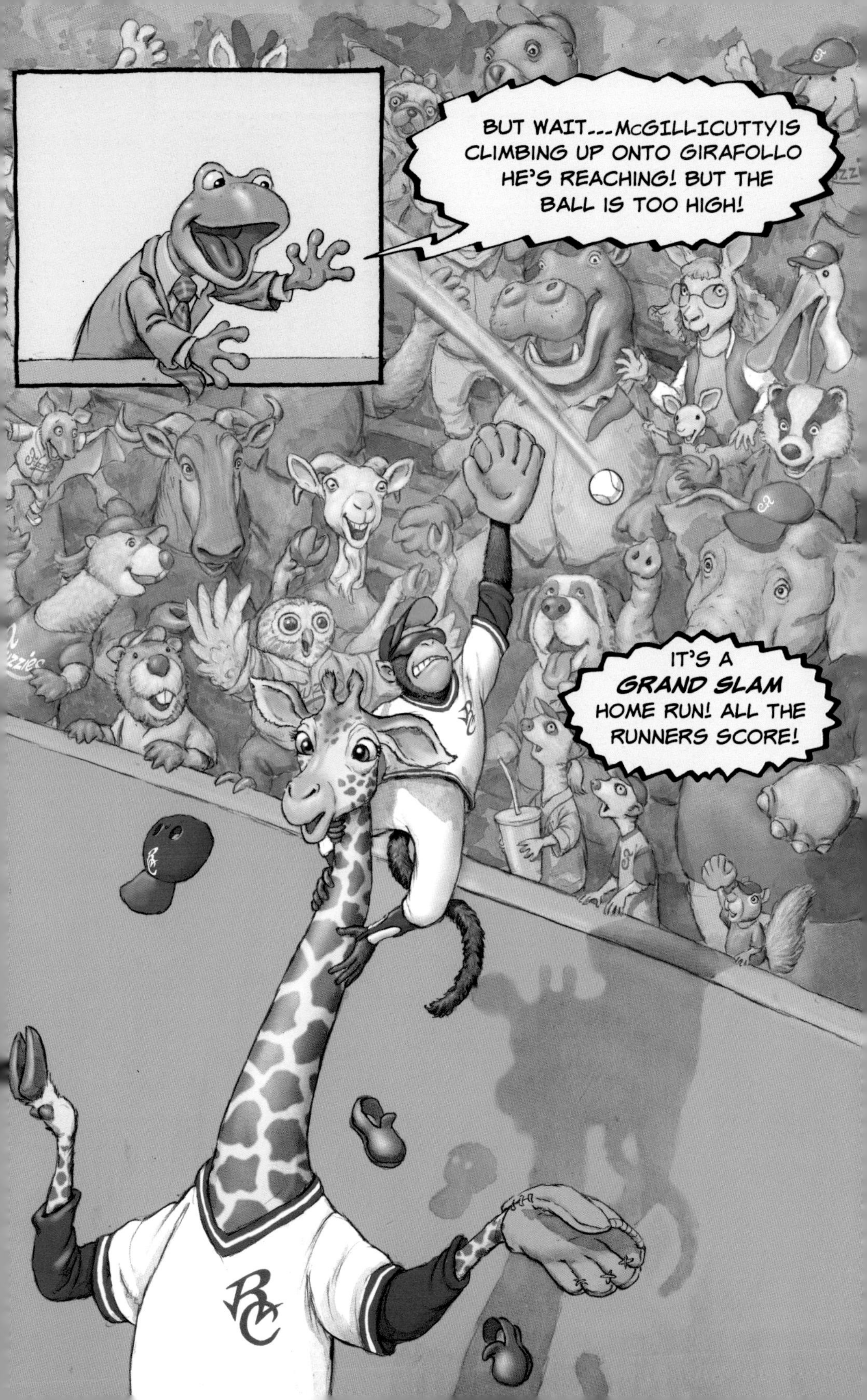

BUT WAIT... McGILLICUTTY IS CLIMBING UP ONTO GIRAFOLLO HE'S REACHING! BUT THE BALL IS TOO HIGH!
IT'S A GRAND SLAM HOME RUN! ALL THE RUNNERS SCORE!

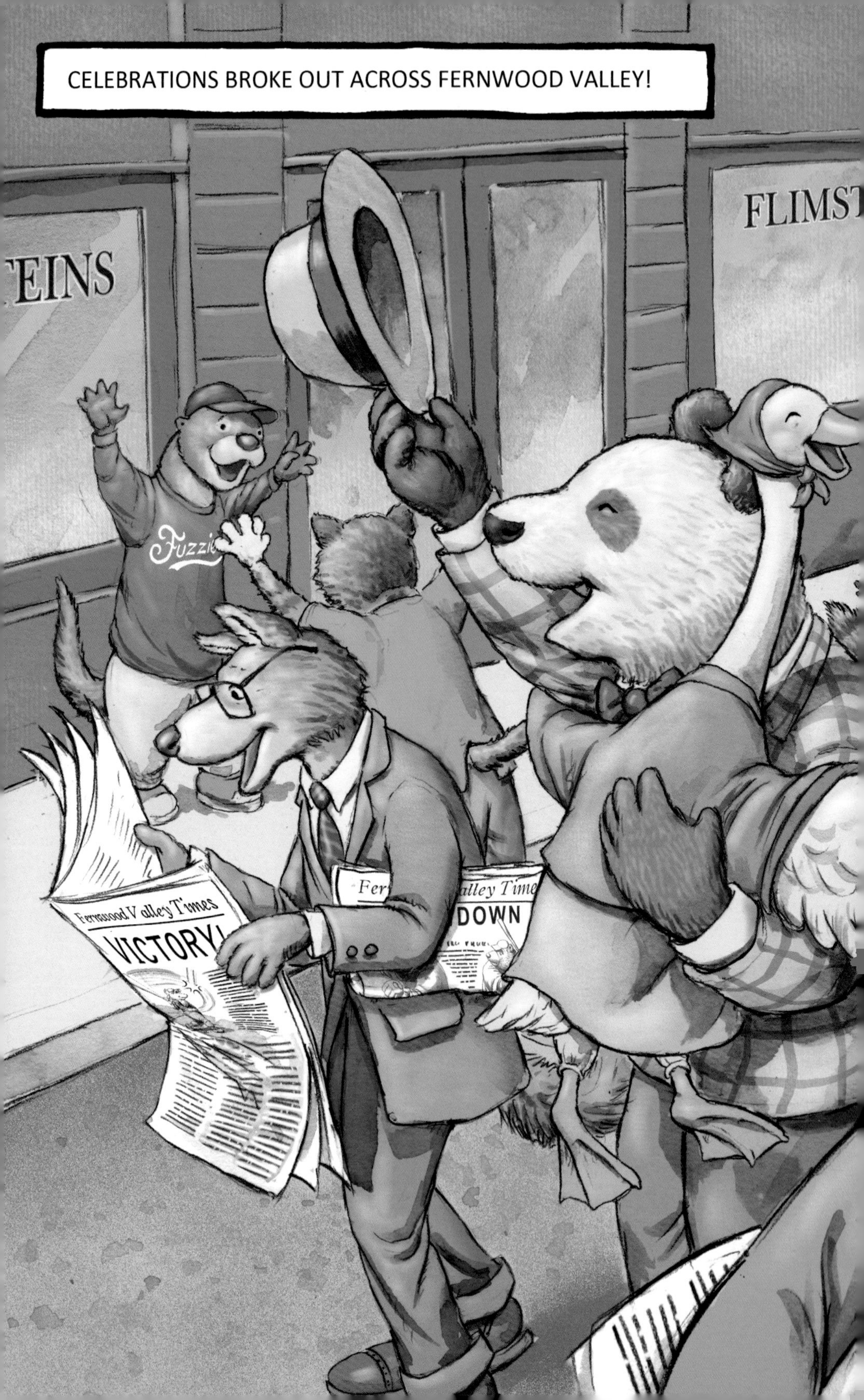
CELEBRATIONS BROKE OUT ACROSS FERNWOOD VALLEY!
Fernwood Valley Times
VICTORY!

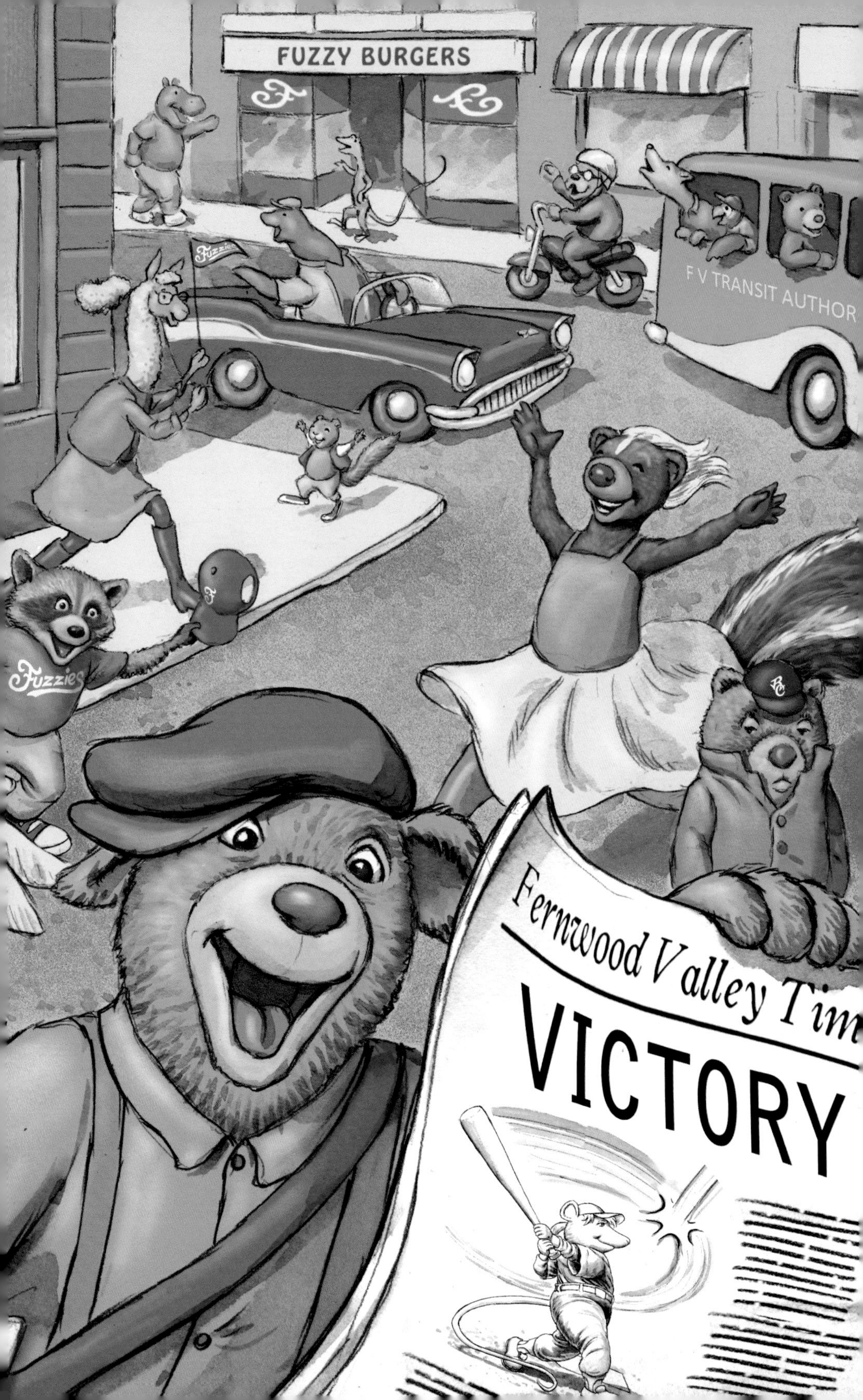
FUZZY BURGERS
Fuzzies
F V TRANSIT AUTHOR
Fuzzies
Fernwood Valley Tim
VICTORY

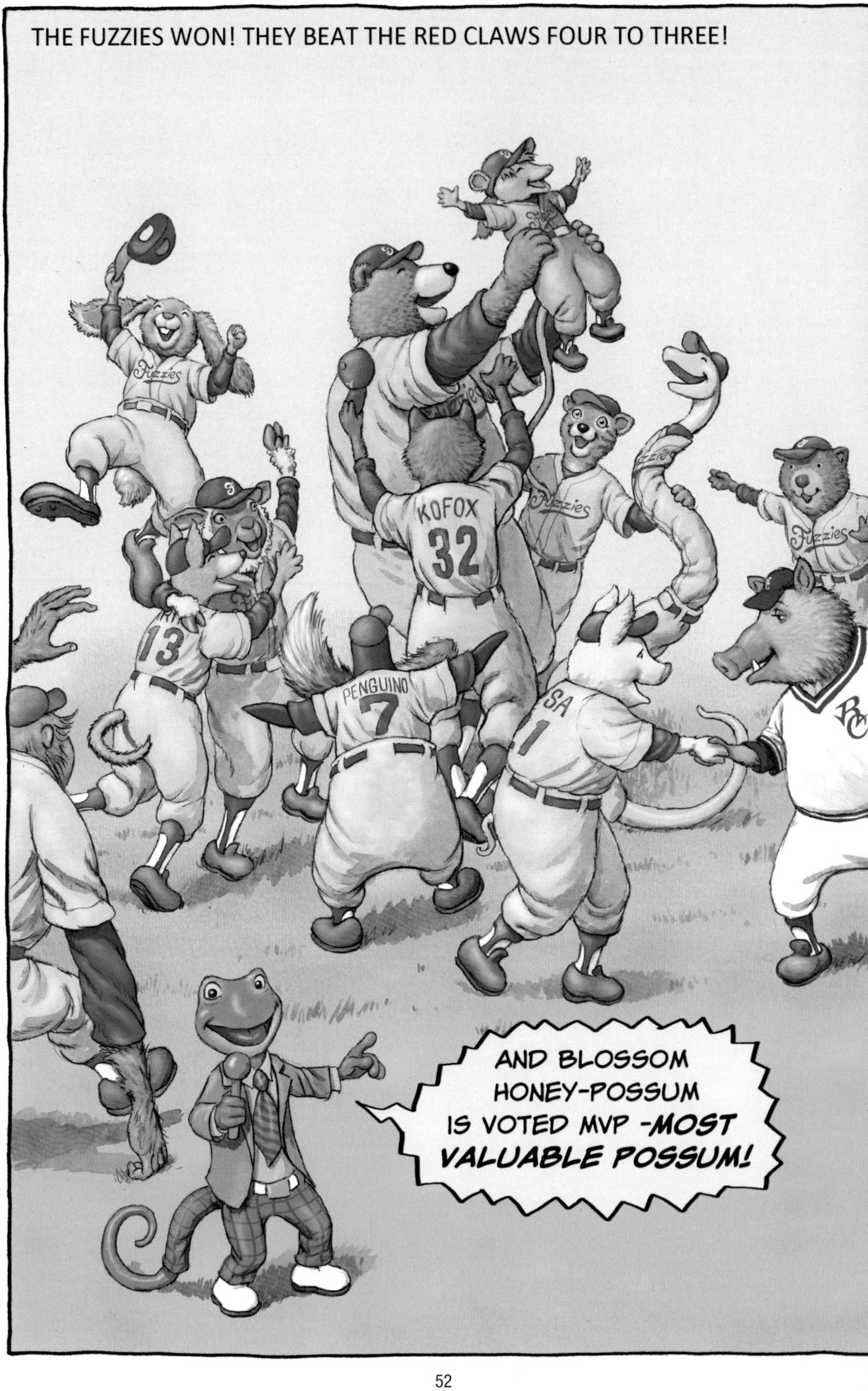
THE FUZZIES WON! THEY BEAT THE RED CLAWS FOUR TO THREE!
AND BLOSSOM HONEY-POSSUM IS VOTED MVP -*MOST VALUABLE POSSUM!*

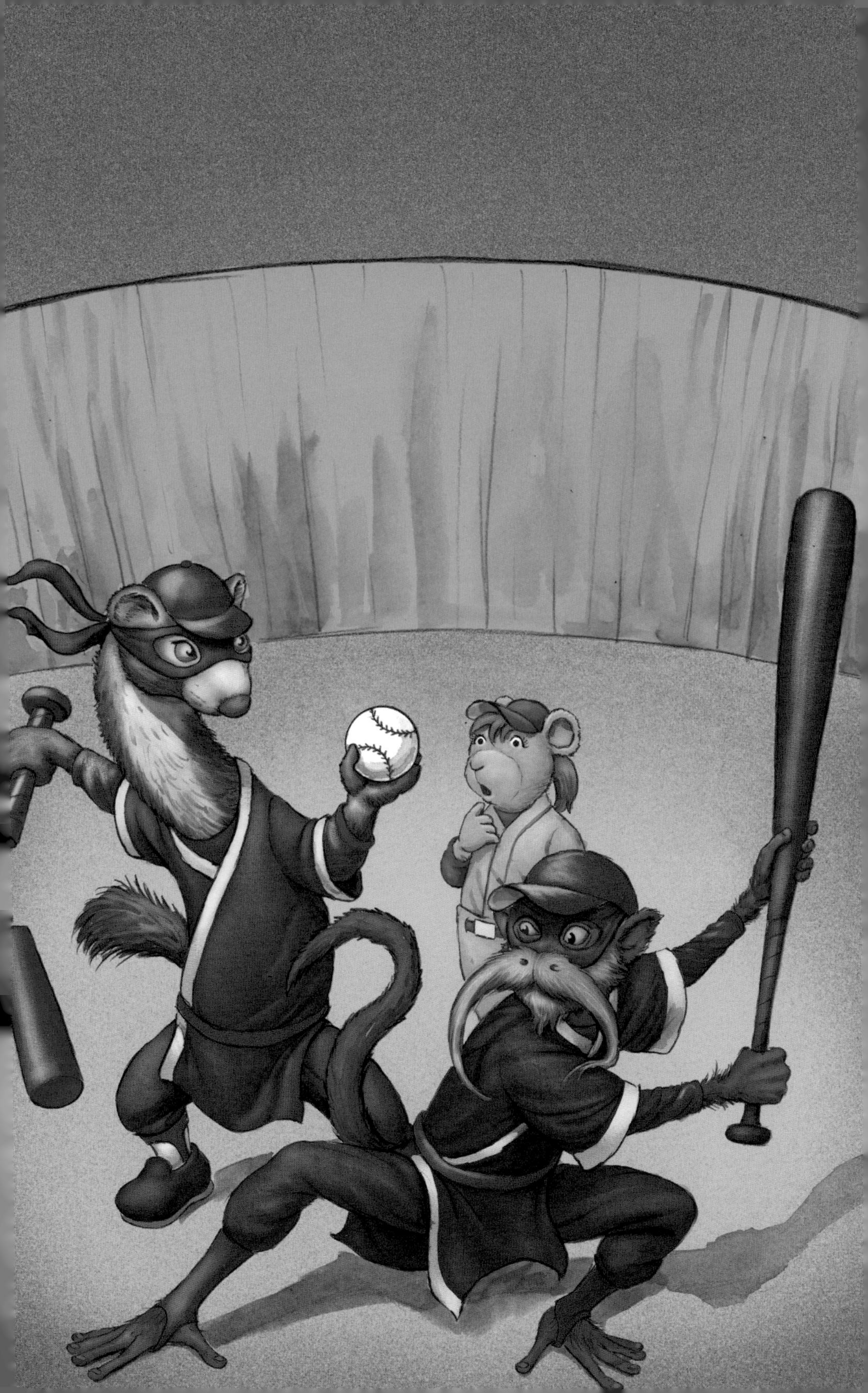

Fuzzy Baseball

NINJA BASEBALL BLAST

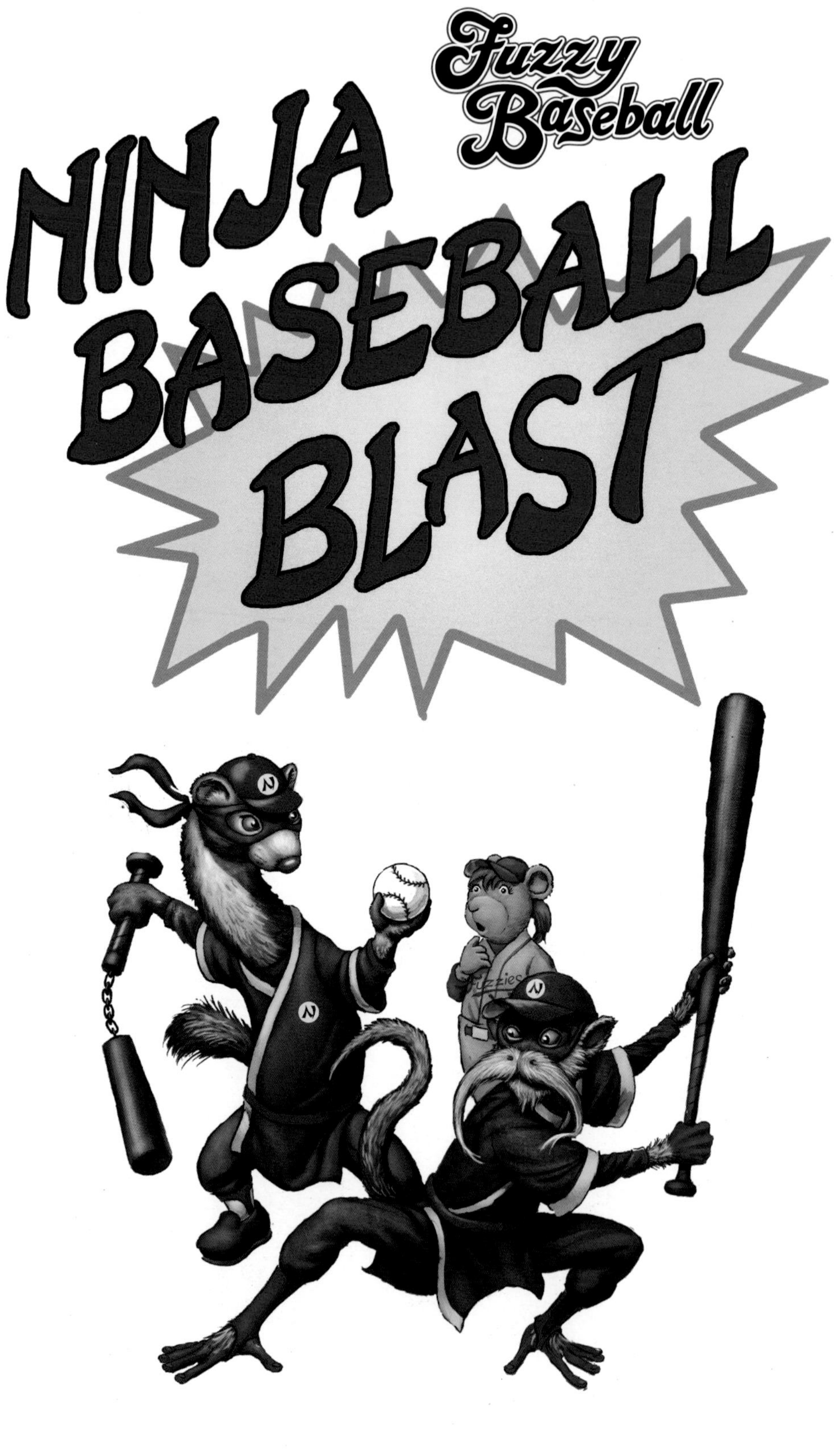

THE SASHIMI CITY NINJAS

#1 KENNY KOMODO, MANAGER
#14 ANDRES GALAGO, RIGHT FIELD
#5 MELVIN OTTER, SECOND BASE
#55 NICO MAEKI, PITCHER
#27 HIDEKI HEDGEHOG, THIRD BASE
#32 HIROSHI HOP, FIRST BASE
#11 PUG RODRIGUEZ, CATCHER
#7 SATOSHI SQUID, THIRD BASE
#4 MUTSUMI MUTT, OUTFIELD
#43 AYANO ANOLE, INFIELD
#8 IGNACIO IGUANA, LEFT FIELD
#9 ICHIRO IGGLE, CENTER FIELD
#15 TOMIKO TAMARIN, PITCHER
#62 YUKI SKIRL, SHORTSTOP

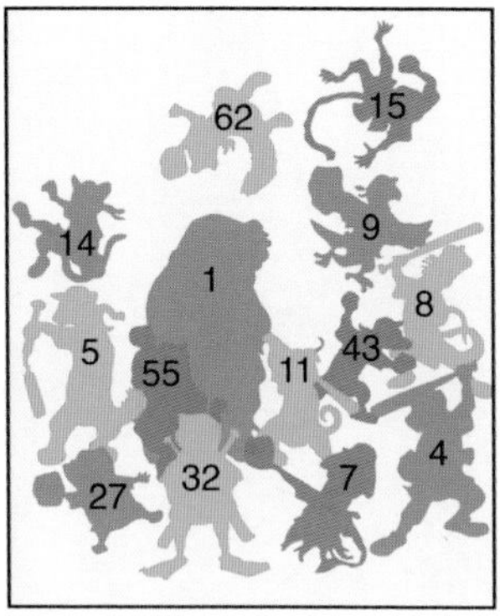
62
15
14
9
1
8
5
55
11
43
4
27
32
7

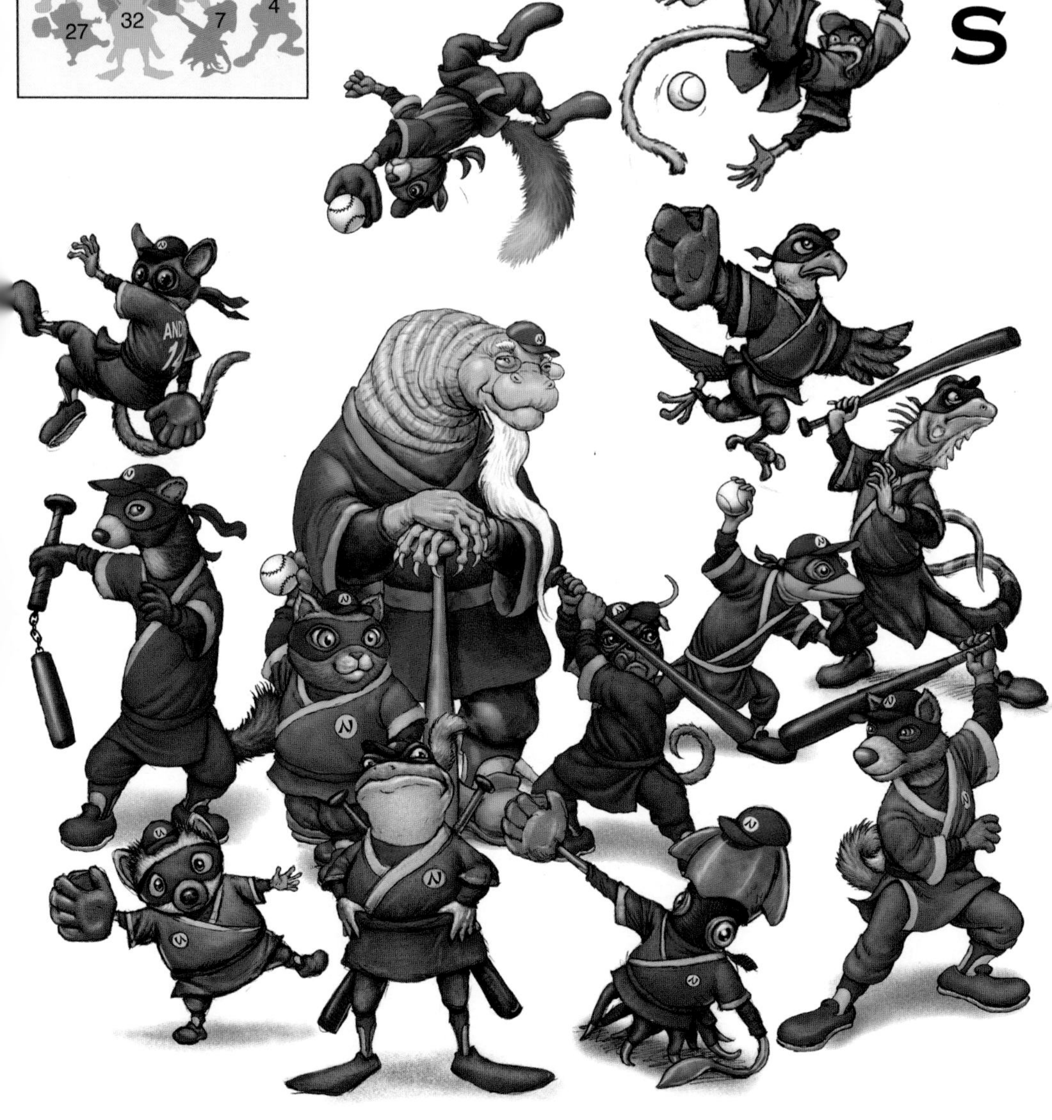

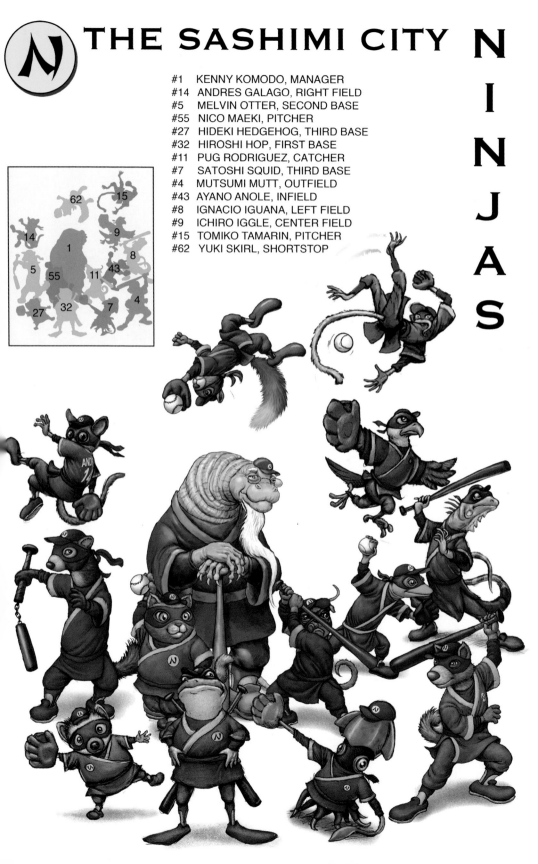

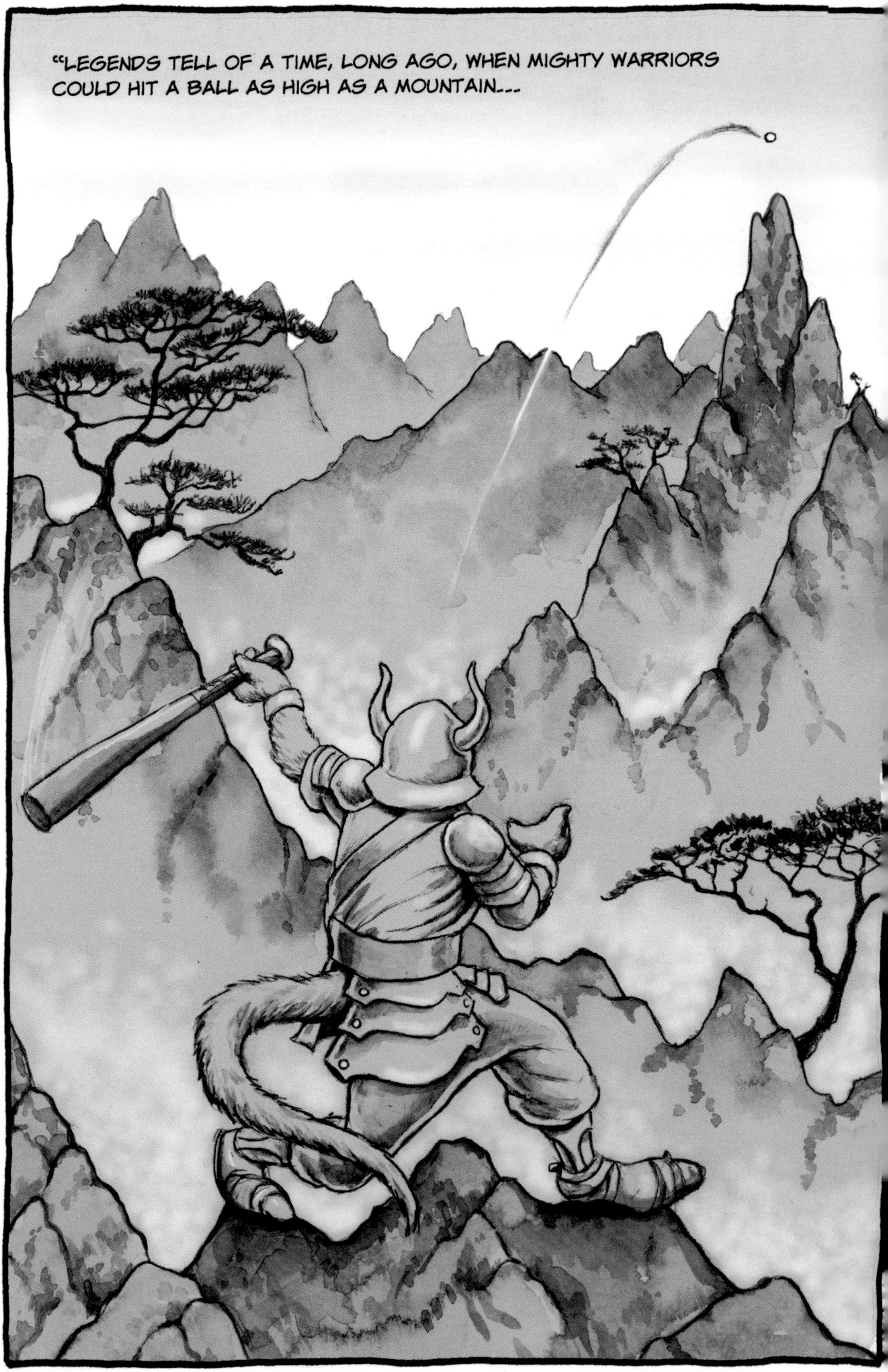
"LEGENDS TELL OF A TIME, LONG AGO, WHEN MIGHTY WARRIORS COULD HIT A BALL AS HIGH AS A MOUNTAIN...

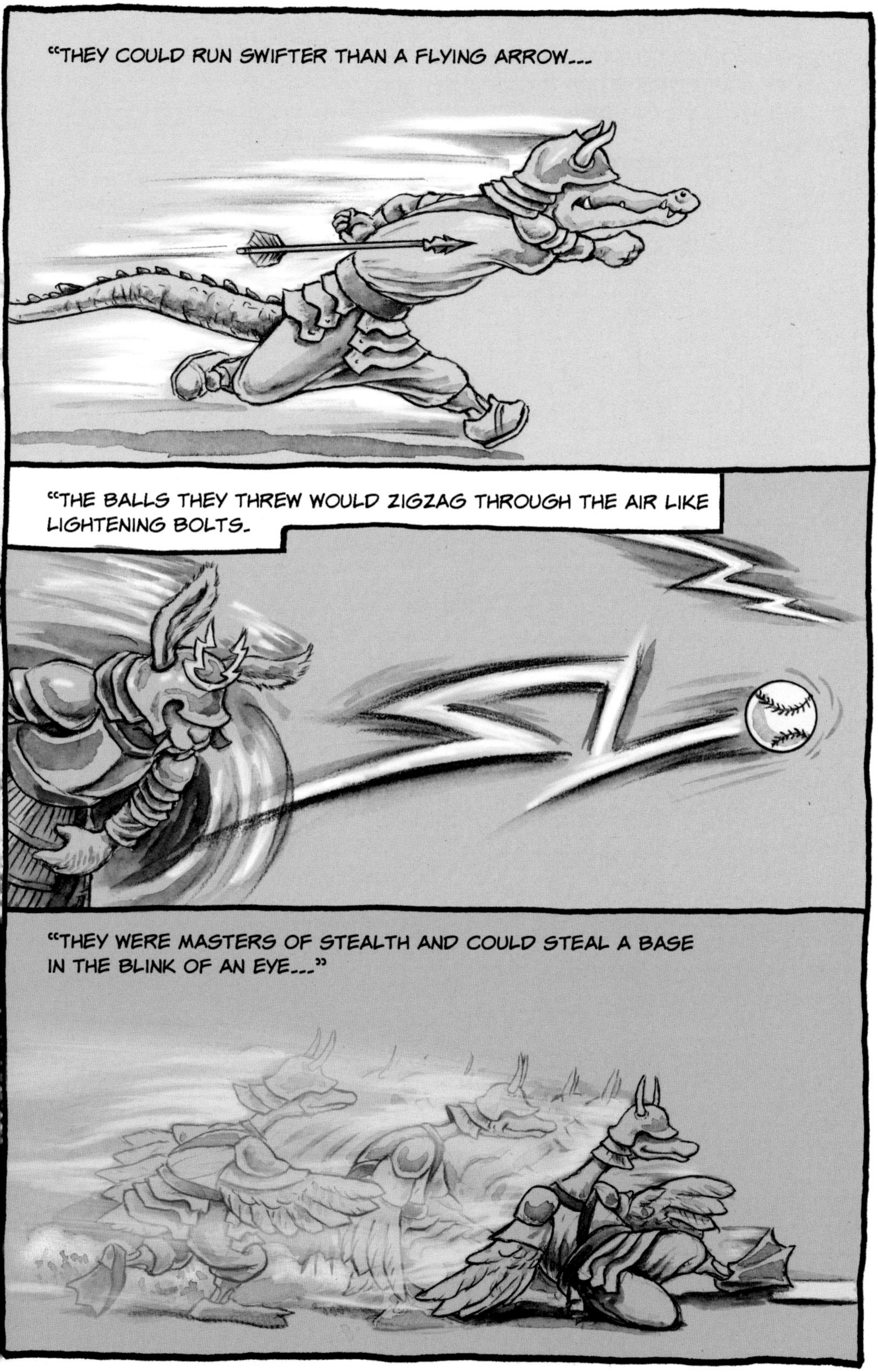
"THEY COULD RUN SWIFTER THAN A FLYING ARROW...
"THE BALLS THEY THREW WOULD ZIGZAG THROUGH THE AIR LIKE LIGHTENING BOLTS.
"THEY WERE MASTERS OF STEALTH AND COULD STEAL A BASE IN THE BLINK OF AN EYE..."

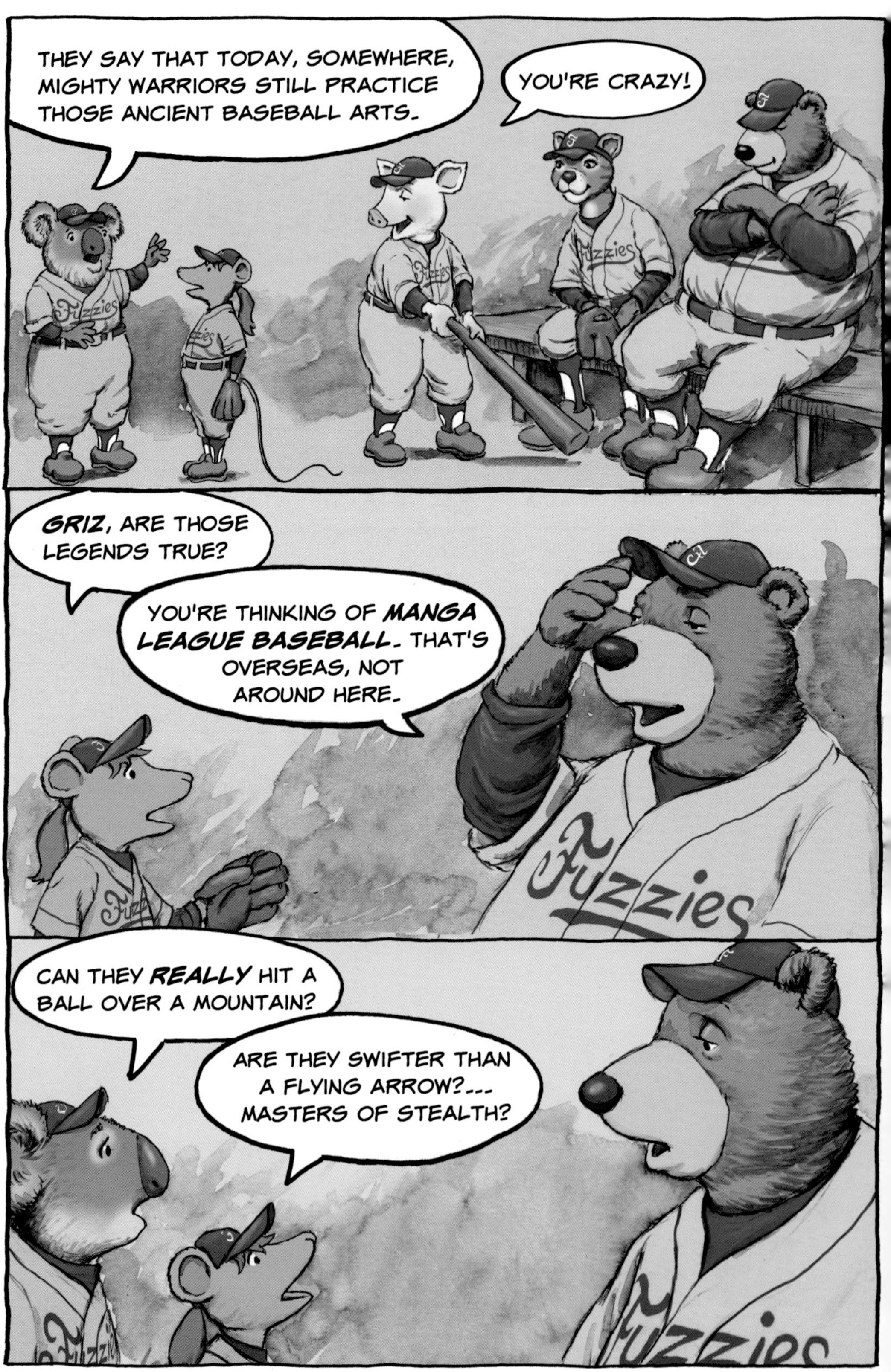
THEY SAY THAT TODAY, SOMEWHERE, MIGHTY WARRIORS STILL PRACTICE THOSE ANCIENT BASEBALL ARTS.
YOU'RE CRAZY!
GRIZ, ARE THOSE LEGENDS TRUE?
YOU'RE THINKING OF MANGA LEAGUE BASEBALL. THAT'S OVERSEAS, NOT AROUND HERE.
CAN THEY REALLY HIT A BALL OVER A MOUNTAIN?
ARE THEY SWIFTER THAN A FLYING ARROW?... MASTERS OF STEALTH?

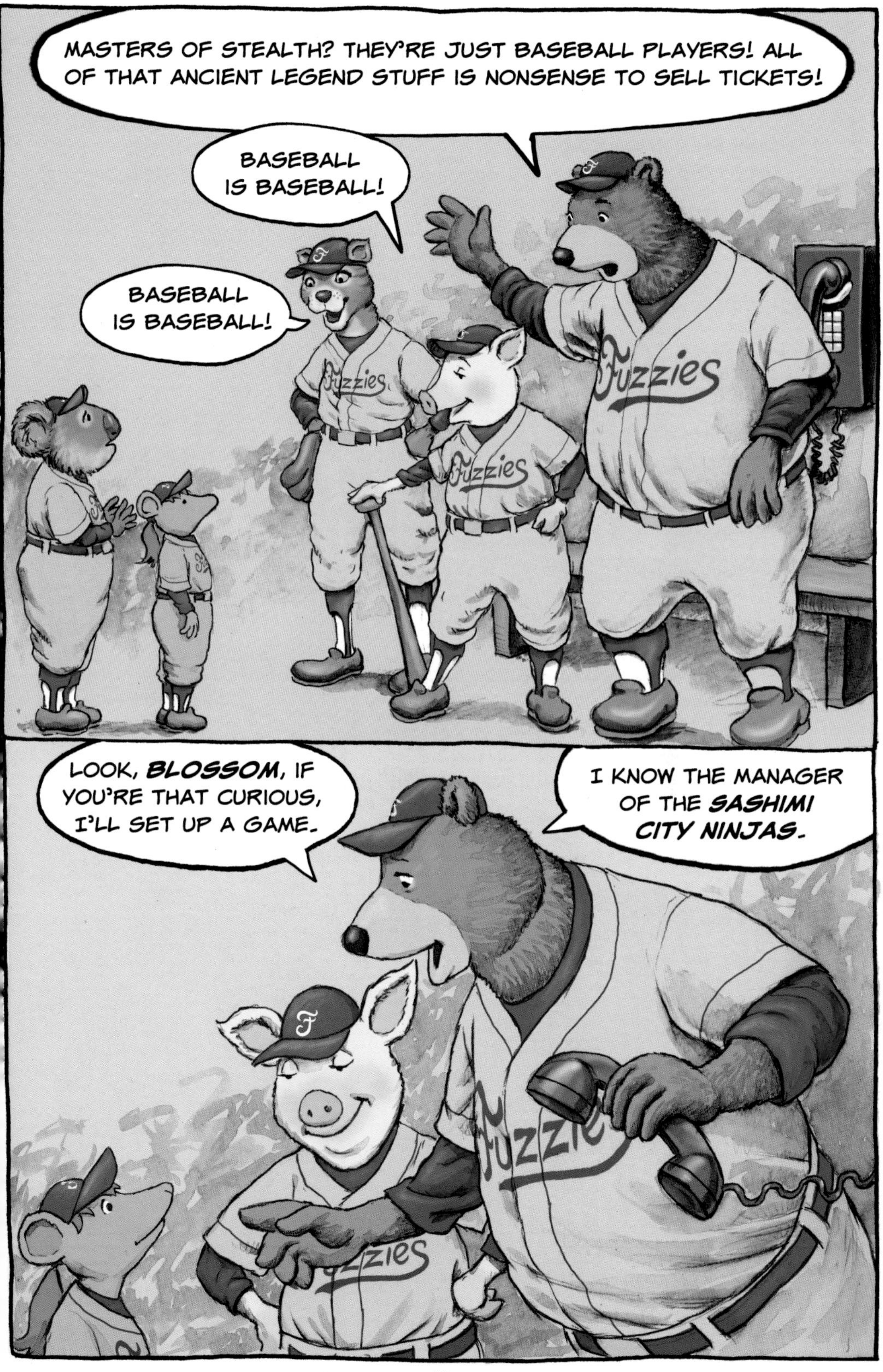
MASTERS OF STEALTH? THEY'RE JUST BASEBALL PLAYERS! ALL OF THAT ANCIENT LEGEND STUFF IS NONSENSE TO SELL TICKETS!
BASEBALL IS BASEBALL!
BASEBALL IS BASEBALL!
LOOK, BLOSSOM, IF YOU'RE THAT CURIOUS, I'LL SET UP A GAME.
I KNOW THE MANAGER OF THE SASHIMI CITY NINJAS.

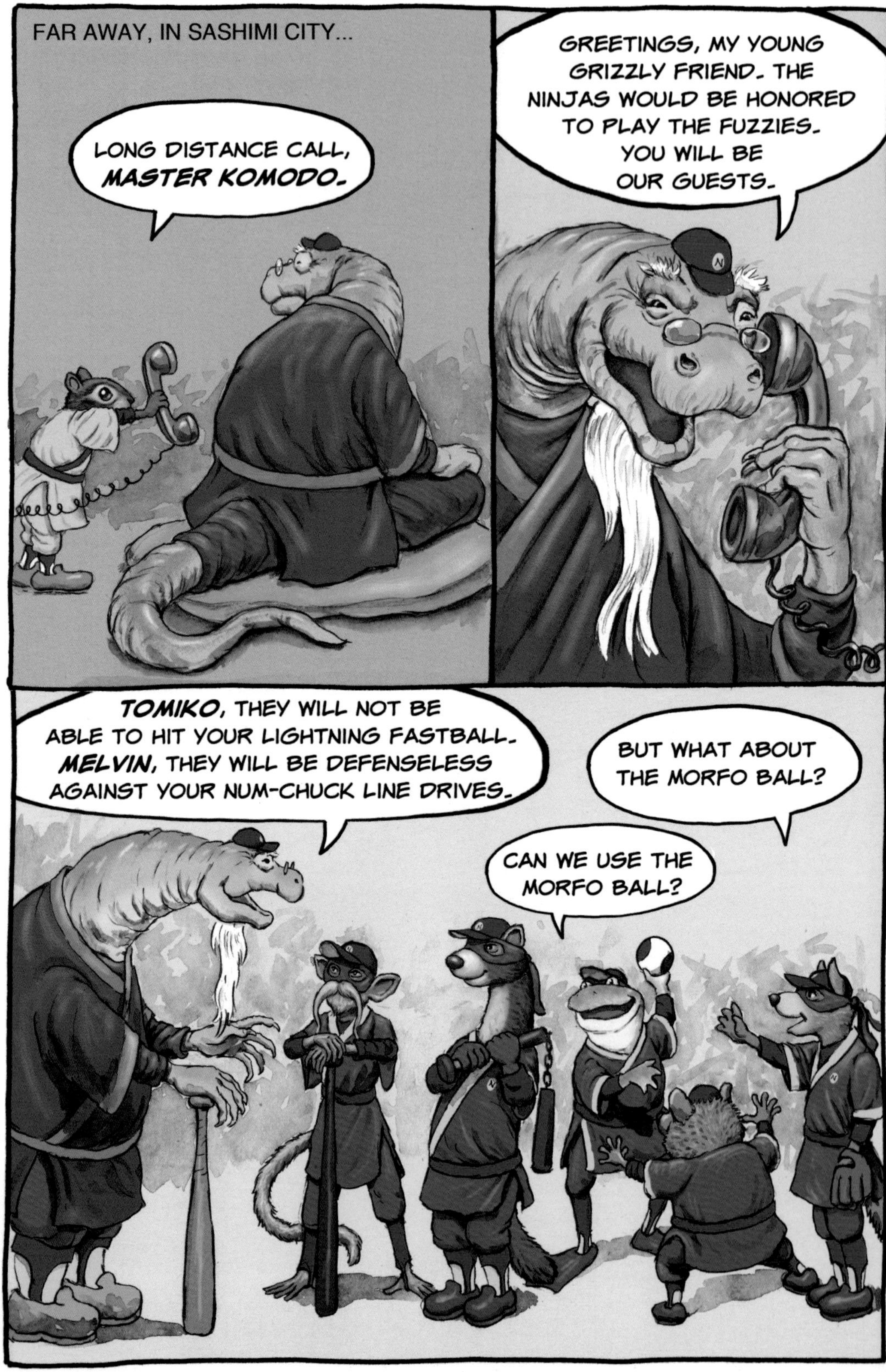
FAR AWAY, IN SASHIMI CITY...
LONG DISTANCE CALL, MASTER KOMODO.
GREETINGS, MY YOUNG GRIZZLY FRIEND. THE NINJAS WOULD BE HONORED TO PLAY THE FUZZIES. YOU WILL BE OUR GUESTS.
TOMIKO, THEY WILL NOT BE ABLE TO HIT YOUR LIGHTNING FASTBALL. MELVIN, THEY WILL BE DEFENSELESS AGAINST YOUR NUM-CHUCK LINE DRIVES.
BUT WHAT ABOUT THE MORFO BALL?
CAN WE USE THE MORFO BALL?

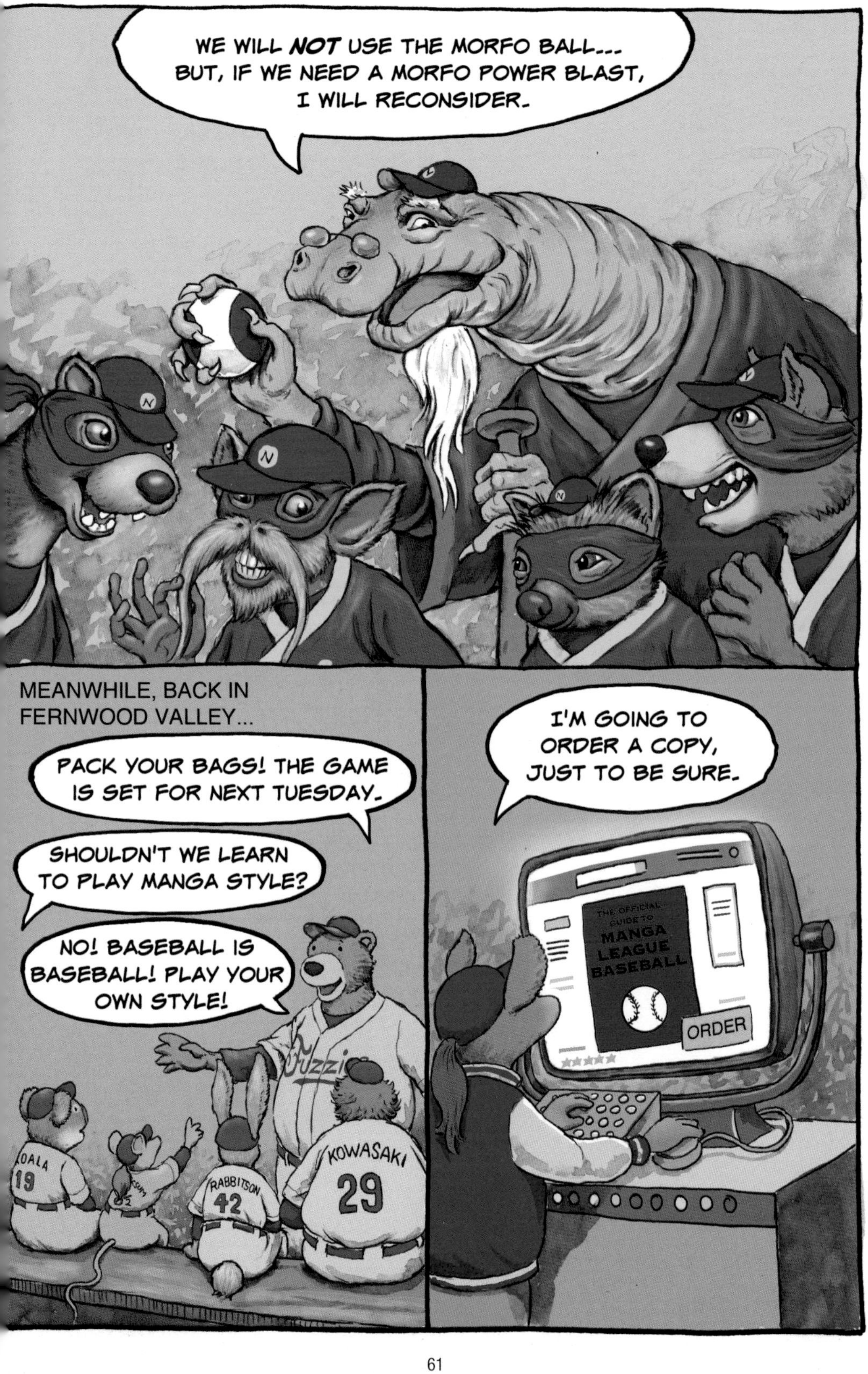
WE WILL ***NOT*** USE THE MORFO BALL... BUT, IF WE NEED A MORFO POWER BLAST, I WILL RECONSIDER.
MEANWHILE, BACK IN FERNWOOD VALLEY...
PACK YOUR BAGS! THE GAME IS SET FOR NEXT TUESDAY.
SHOULDN'T WE LEARN TO PLAY MANGA STYLE?
NO! BASEBALL IS BASEBALL! PLAY YOUR OWN STYLE!
RABBITSON
42
KOWASAKI
29
I'M GOING TO ORDER A COPY, JUST TO BE SURE.
THE OFFICIAL GUIDE TO MANGA LEAGUE BASEBALL
ORDER

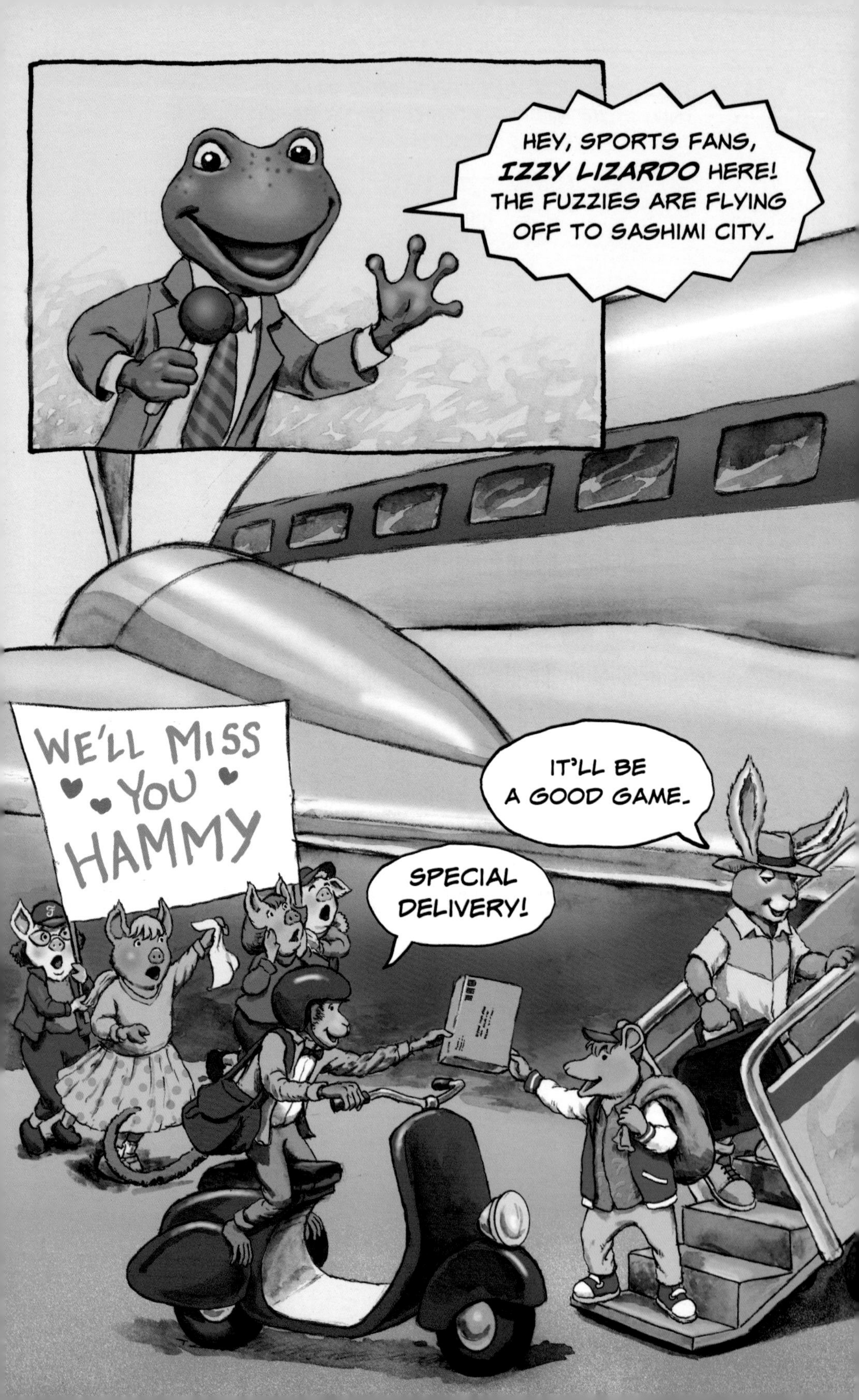
HEY, SPORTS FANS, IZZY LIZARDO HERE! THE FUZZIES ARE FLYING OFF TO SASHIMI CITY.
WE'LL MISS YOU HAMMY
IT'LL BE A GOOD GAME.
SPECIAL DELIVERY!

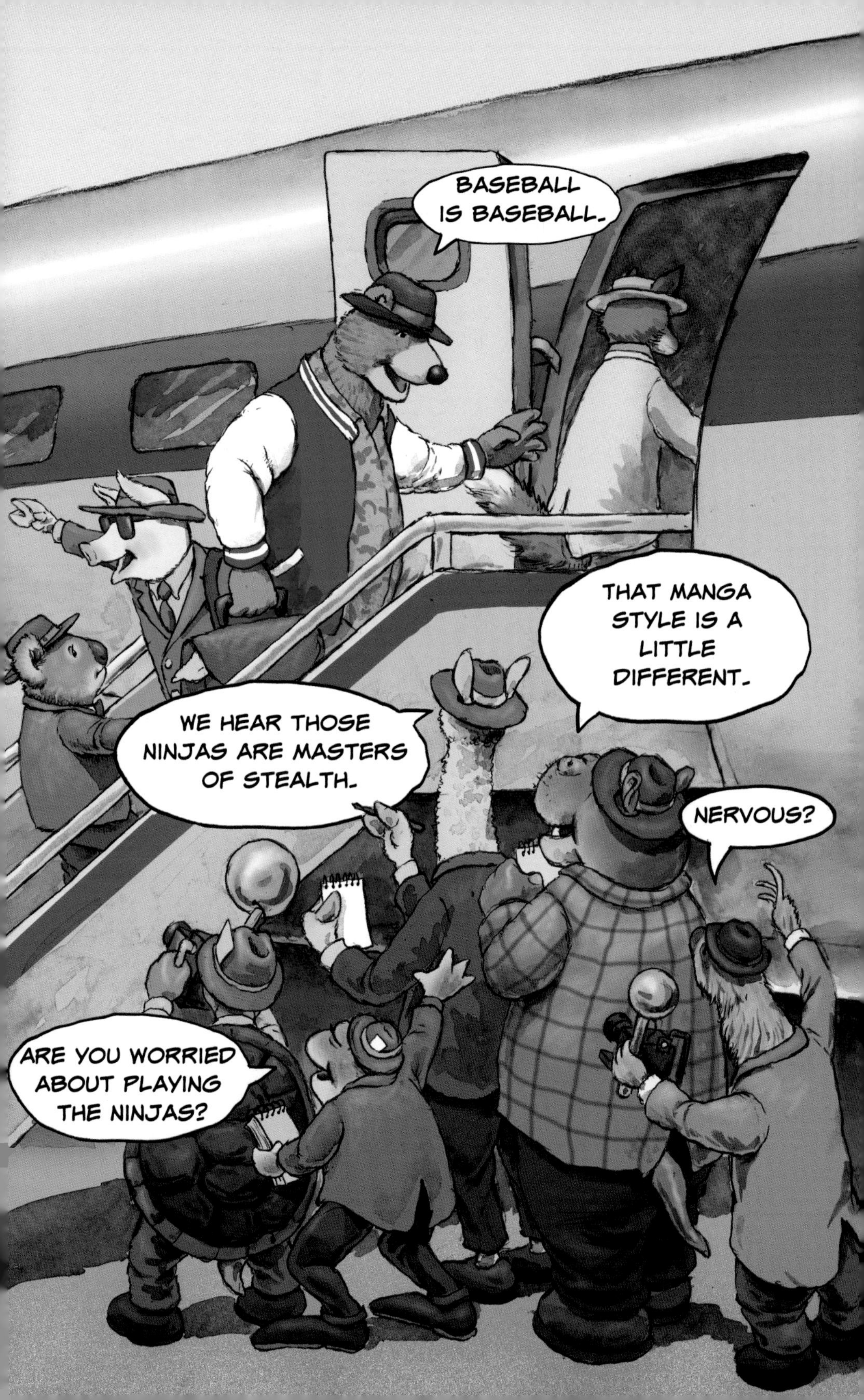
BASEBALL IS BASEBALL.
THAT MANGA STYLE IS A LITTLE DIFFERENT.
WE HEAR THOSE NINJAS ARE MASTERS OF STEALTH.
NERVOUS?
ARE YOU WORRIED ABOUT PLAYING THE NINJAS?

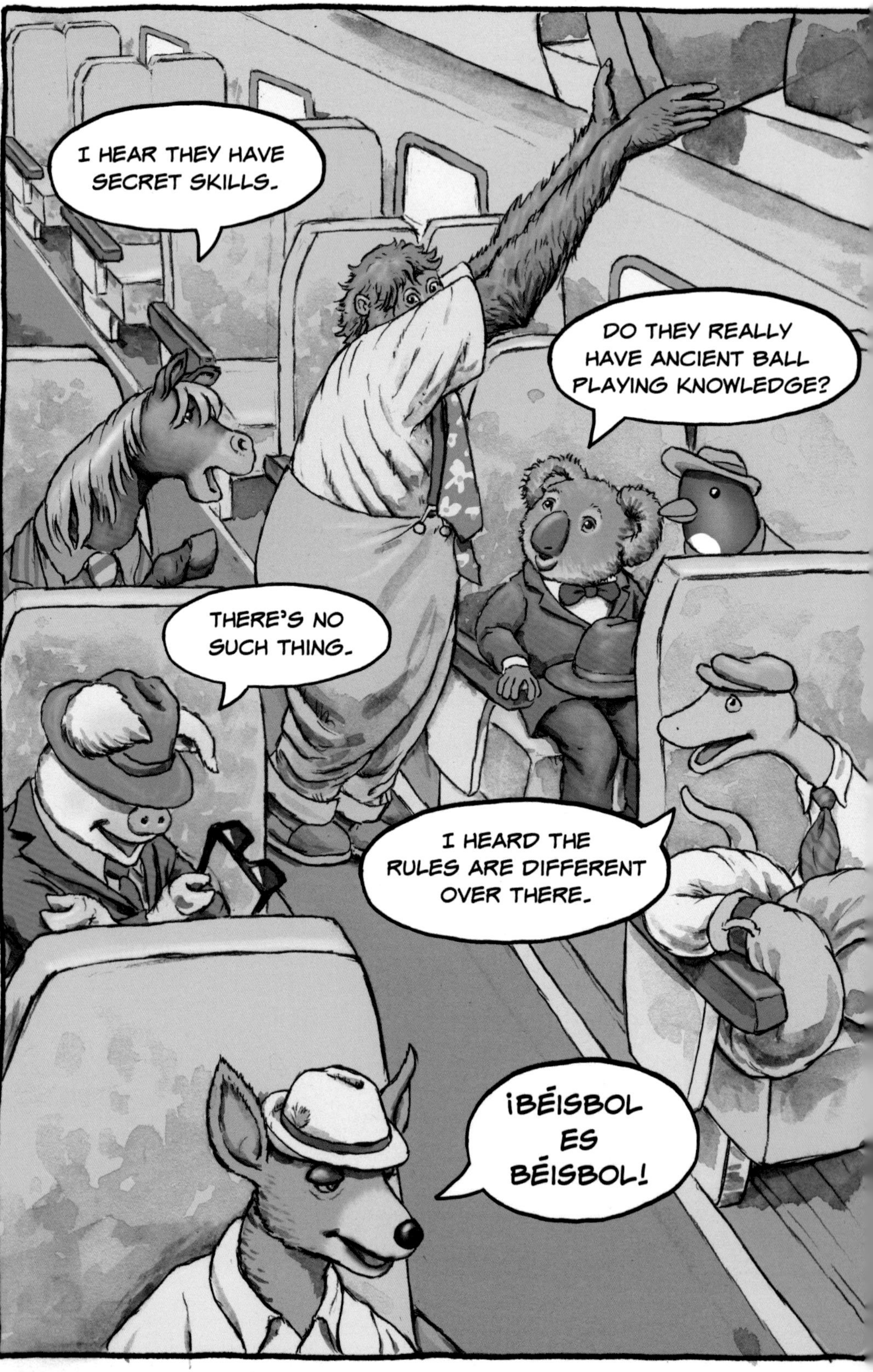
I HEAR THEY HAVE SECRET SKILLS.
DO THEY REALLY HAVE ANCIENT BALL PLAYING KNOWLEDGE?
THERE'S NO SUCH THING.
I HEARD THE RULES ARE DIFFERENT OVER THERE.
¡BÉISBOL ES BÉISBOL!

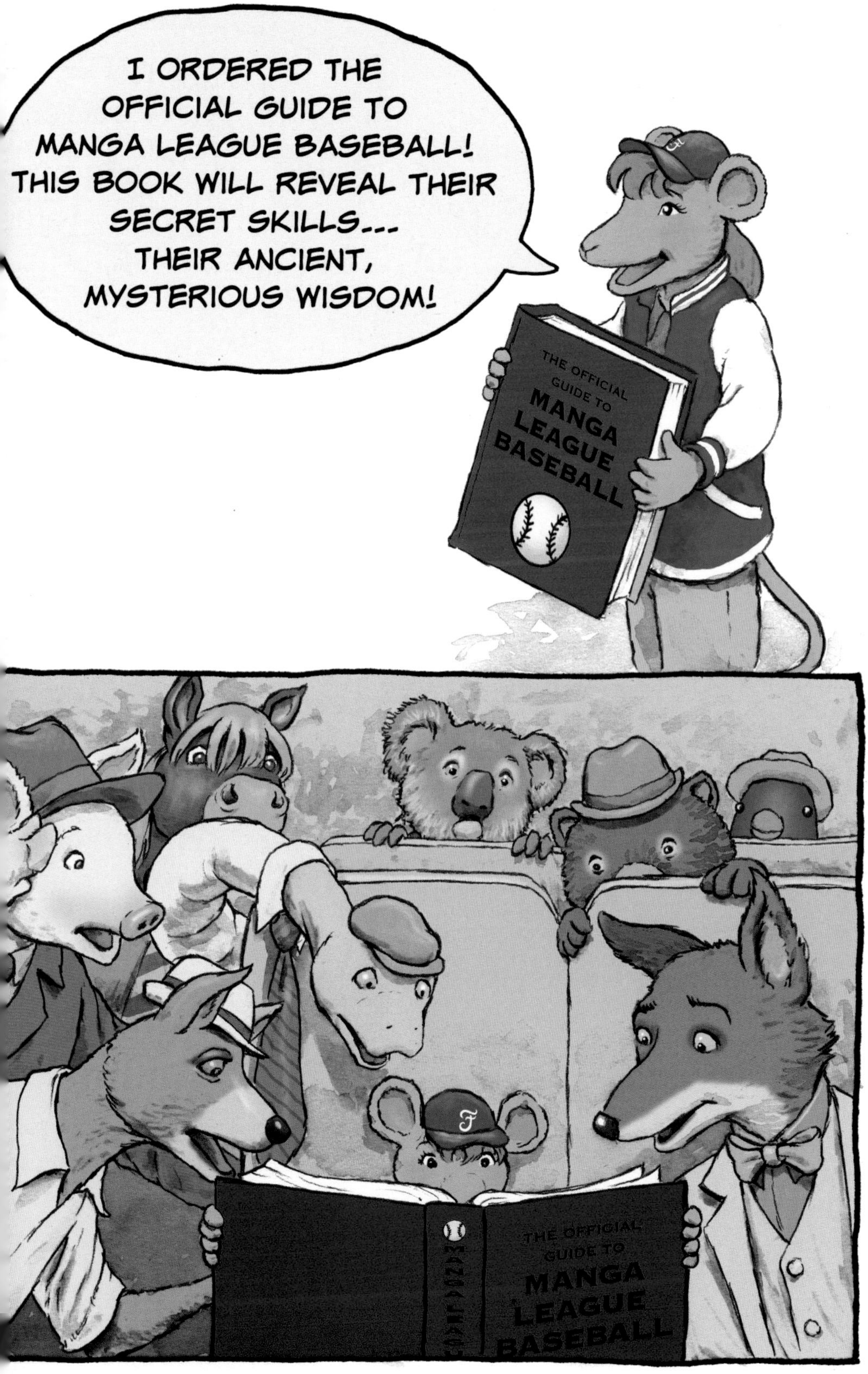
I ORDERED THE OFFICIAL GUIDE TO MANGA LEAGUE BASEBALL! THIS BOOK WILL REVEAL THEIR SECRET SKILLS... THEIR ANCIENT, MYSTERIOUS WISDOM!
THE OFFICIAL GUIDE TO MANGA LEAGUE BASEBALL
THE OFFICIAL GUIDE TO MANGA LEAGUE BASEBALL

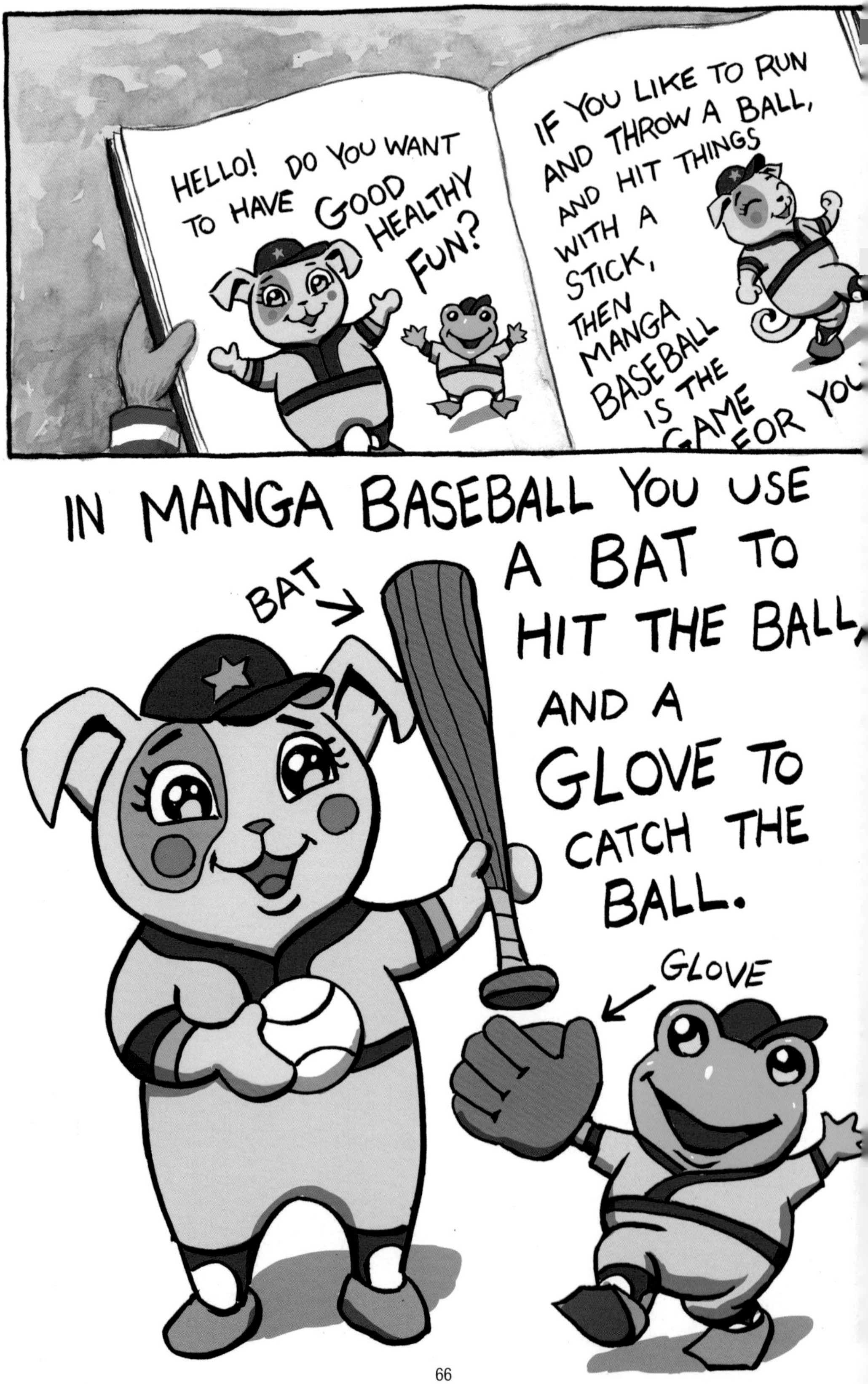
HELLO! DO YOU WANT TO HAVE GOOD HEALTHY FUN?
IF YOU LIKE TO RUN AND THROW A BALL, AND HIT THINGS WITH A STICK, THEN MANGA BASEBALL IS THE GAME FOR YOU
IN MANGA BASEBALL YOU USE A BAT TO HIT THE BALL, AND A GLOVE TO CATCH THE BALL.
BAT
GLOVE

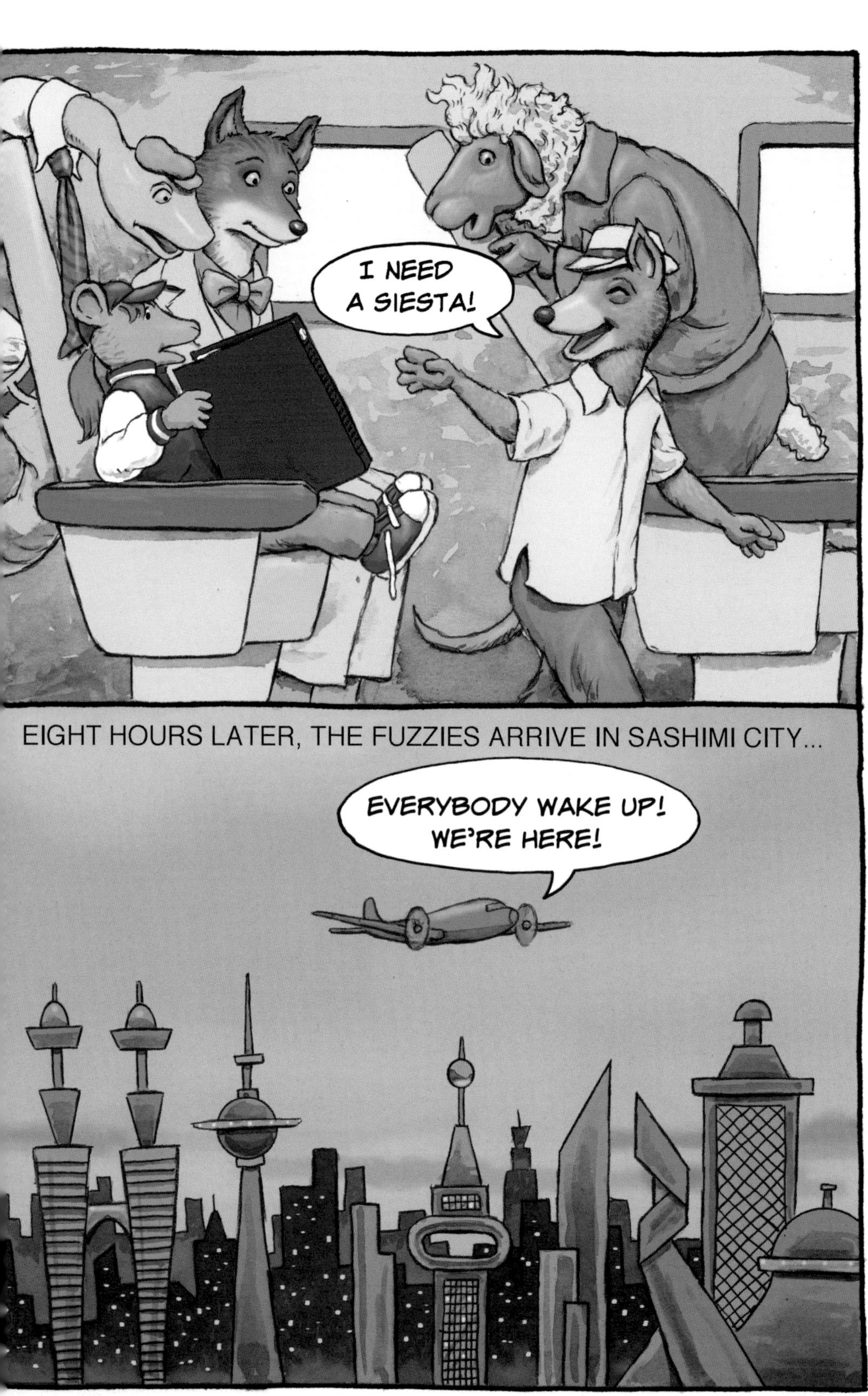
I NEED A SIESTA!
EIGHT HOURS LATER, THE FUZZIES ARRIVE IN SASHIMI CITY...
EVERYBODY WAKE UP! WE'RE HERE!

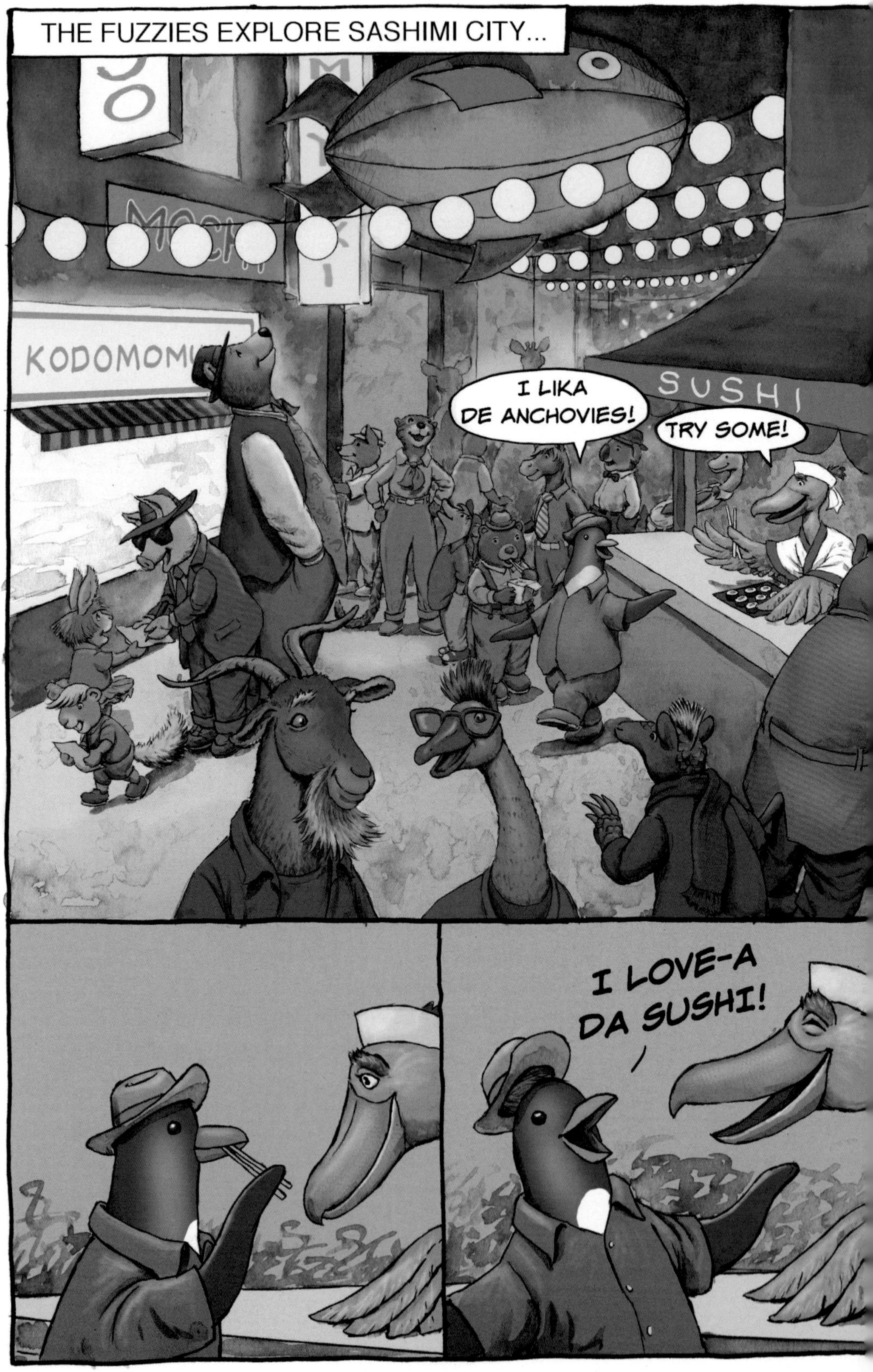
THE FUZZIES EXPLORE SASHIMI CITY...
KODOMOMU
SUSHI
I LIKA DE ANCHOVIES!
TRY SOME!
I LOVE-A DA SUSHI!

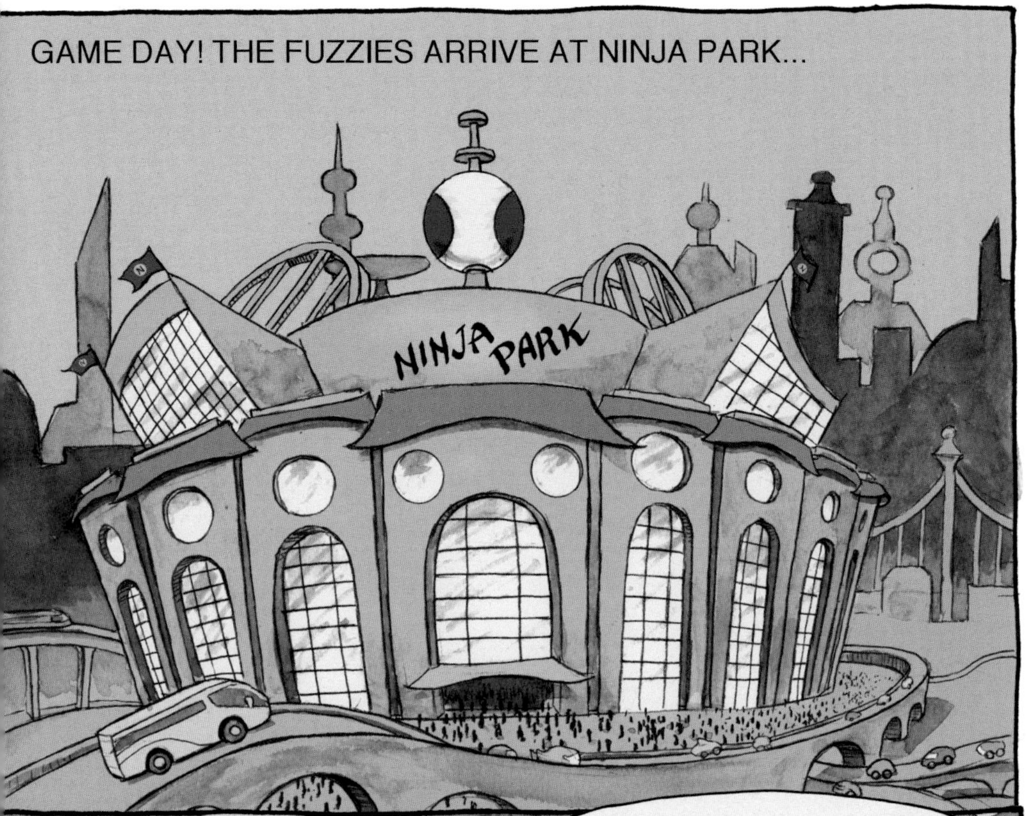
GAME DAY! THE FUZZIES ARRIVE AT NINJA PARK...
NINJA PARK

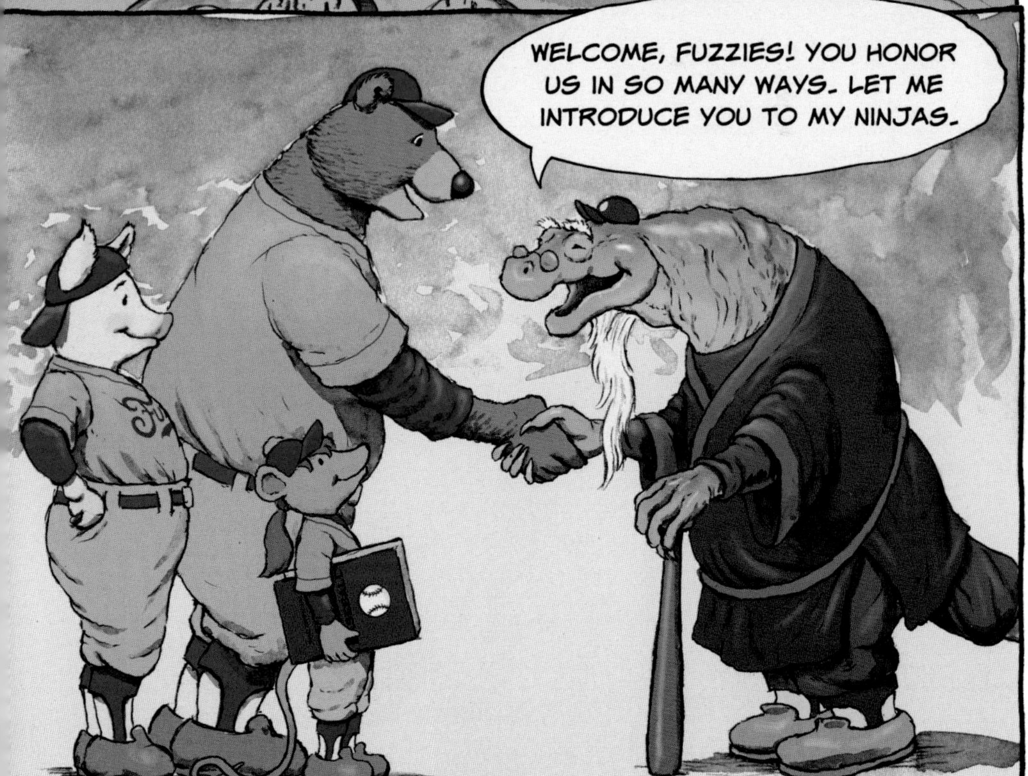
WELCOME, FUZZIES! YOU HONOR US IN SO MANY WAYS. LET ME INTRODUCE YOU TO MY NINJAS.

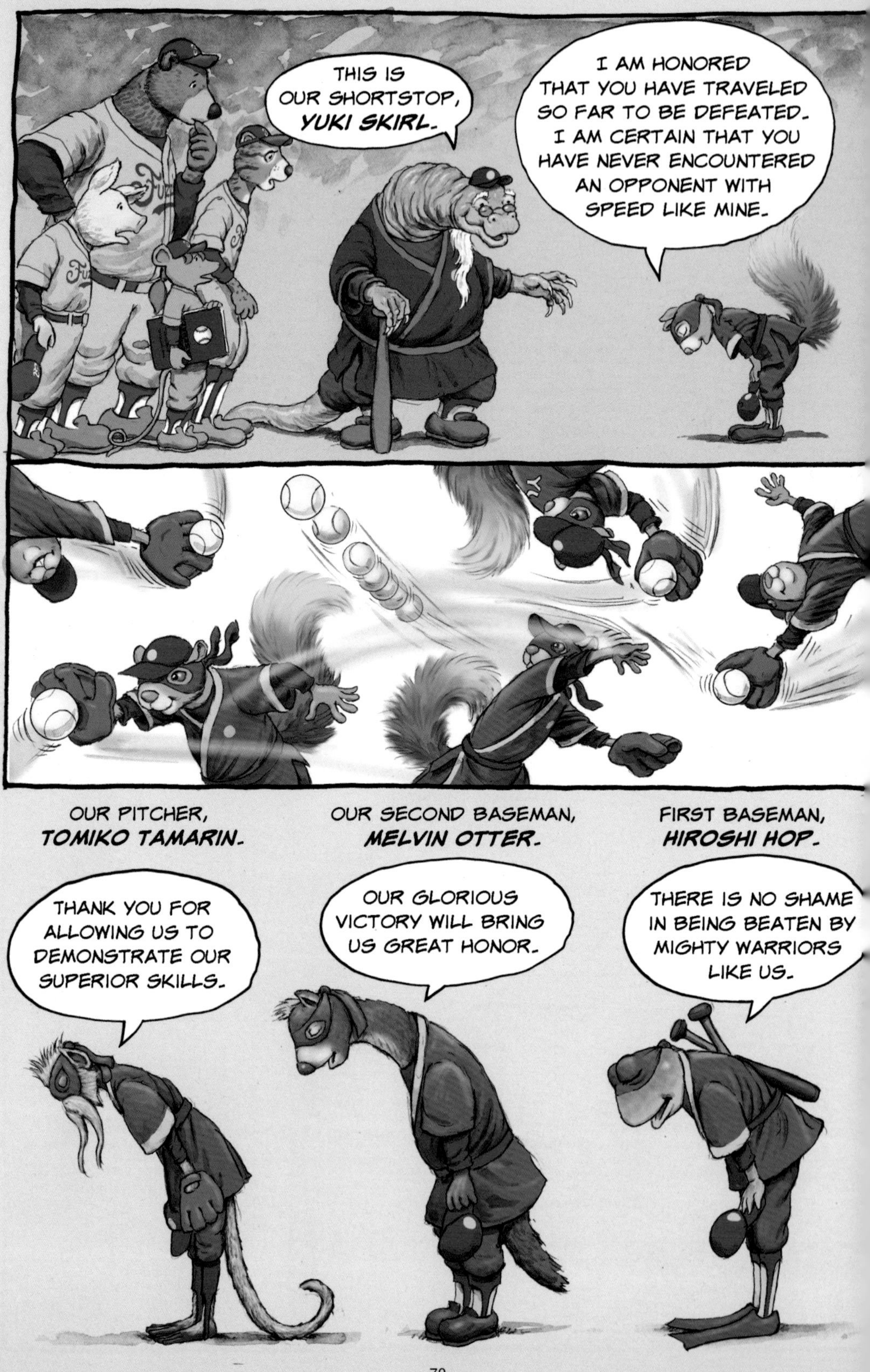
THIS IS OUR SHORTSTOP, YUKI SKIRL.
I AM HONORED THAT YOU HAVE TRAVELED SO FAR TO BE DEFEATED. I AM CERTAIN THAT YOU HAVE NEVER ENCOUNTERED AN OPPONENT WITH SPEED LIKE MINE.
OUR PITCHER, TOMIKO TAMARIN.
OUR SECOND BASEMAN, MELVIN OTTER.
FIRST BASEMAN, HIROSHI HOP.
THANK YOU FOR ALLOWING US TO DEMONSTRATE OUR SUPERIOR SKILLS.
OUR GLORIOUS VICTORY WILL BRING US GREAT HONOR.
THERE IS NO SHAME IN BEING BEATEN BY MIGHTY WARRIORS LIKE US.

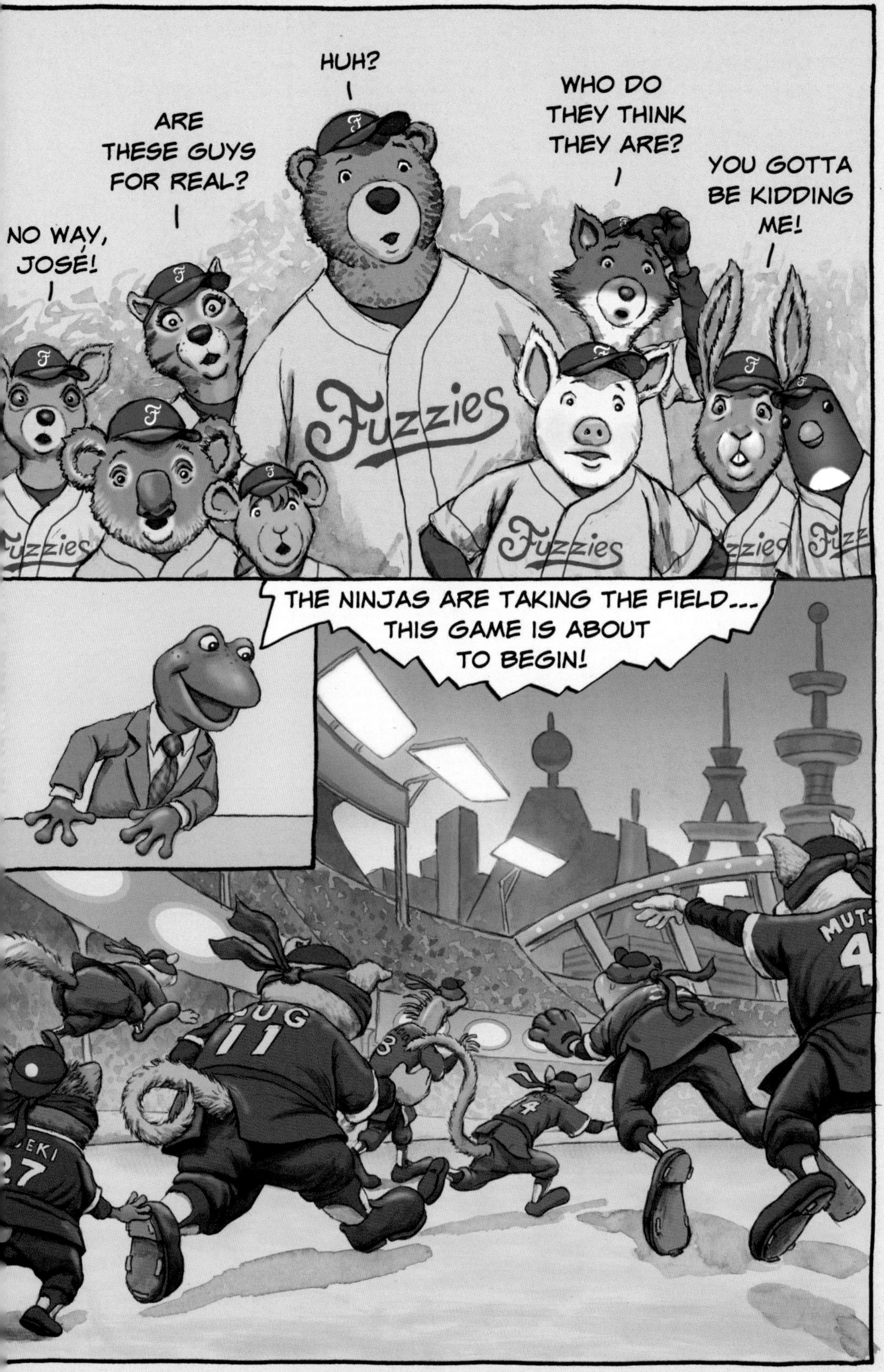
NO WAY, JOSÉ!
ARE THESE GUYS FOR REAL?
HUH?
WHO DO THEY THINK THEY ARE?
YOU GOTTA BE KIDDING ME!
THE NINJAS ARE TAKING THE FIELD... THIS GAME IS ABOUT TO BEGIN!

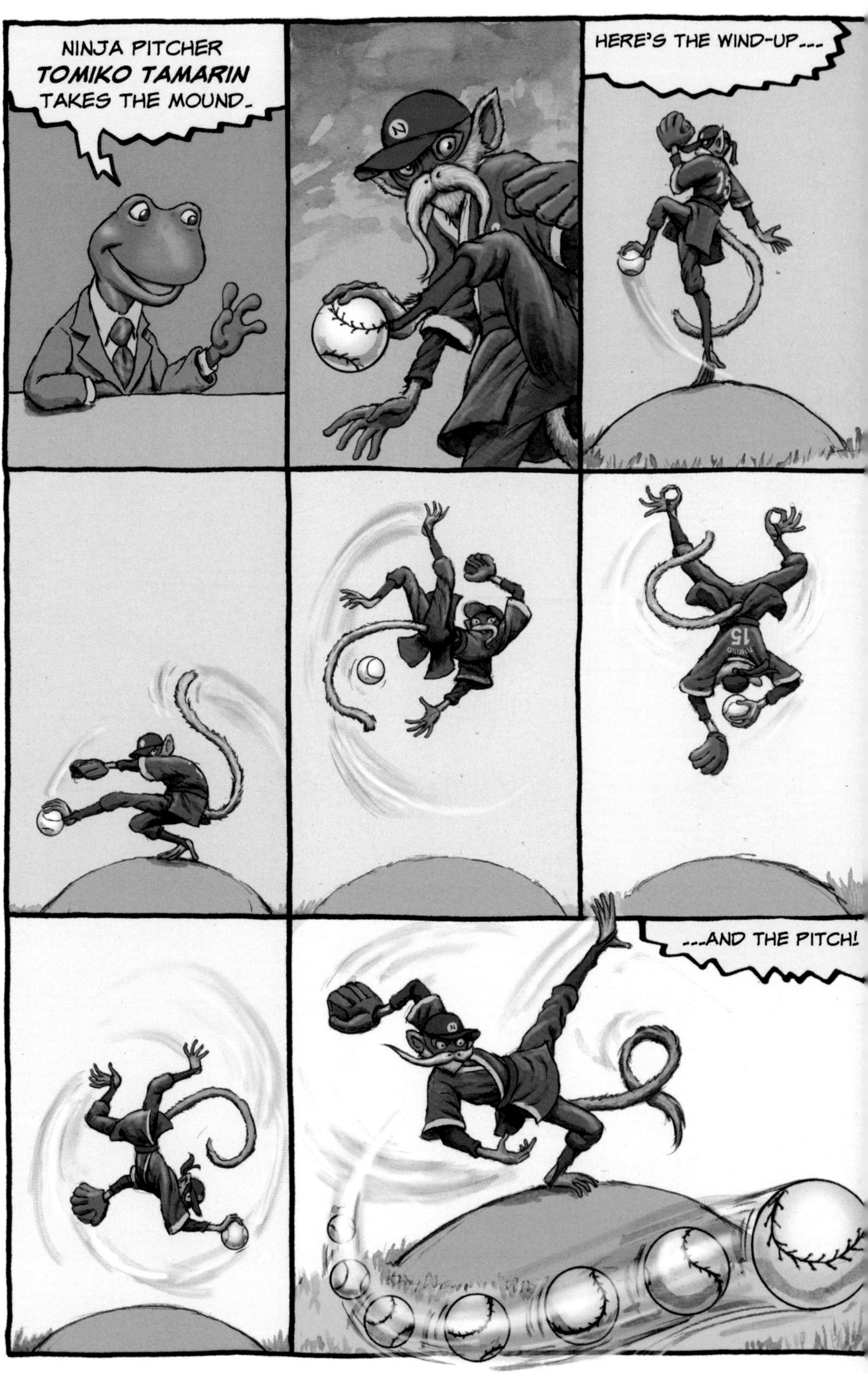
NINJA PITCHER TOMIKO TAMARIN TAKES THE MOUND...
HERE'S THE WIND-UP...
...AND THE PITCH!

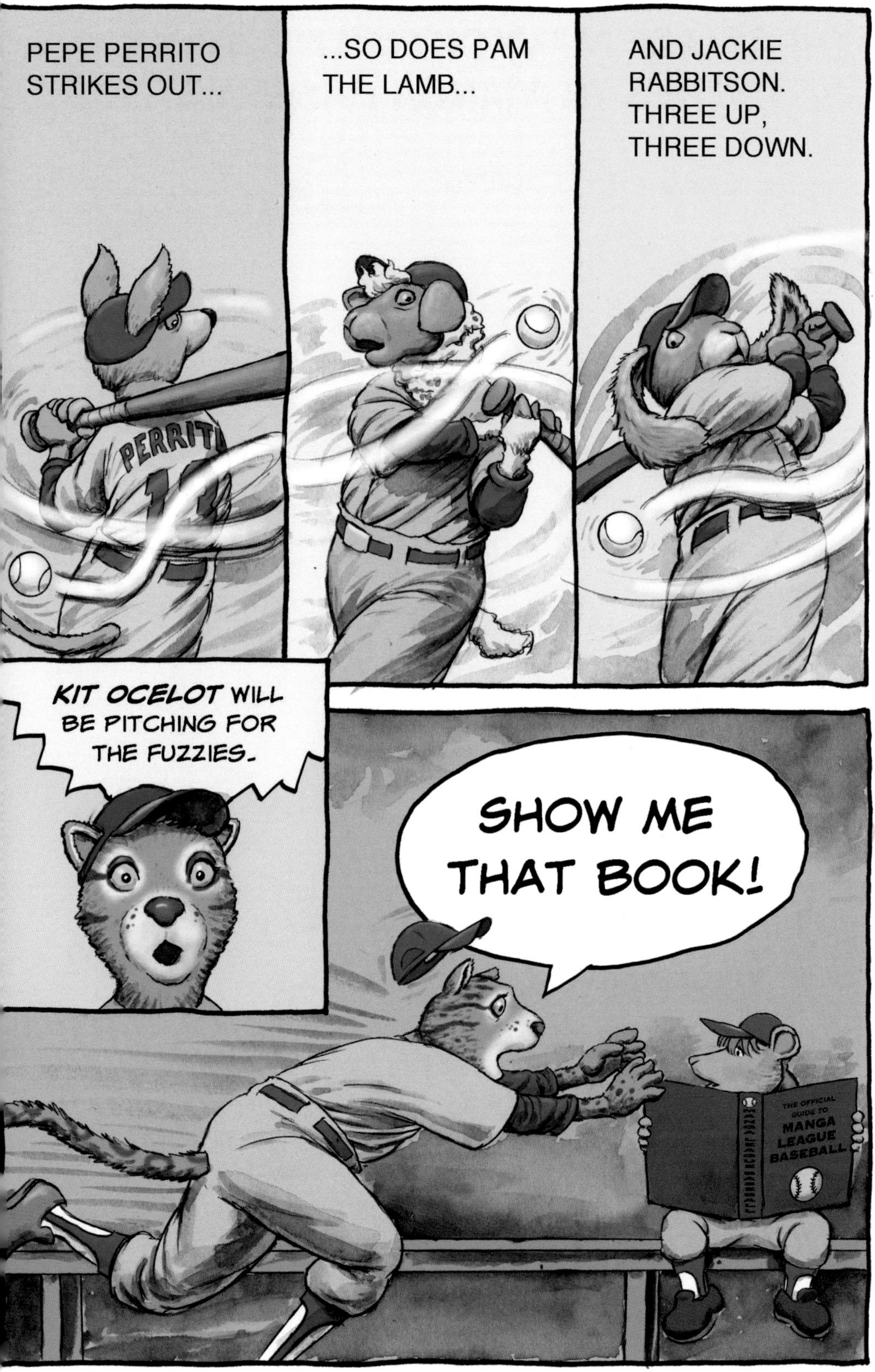
PEPE PERRITO STRIKES OUT...
PERRITO
...SO DOES PAM THE LAMB...
AND JACKIE RABBITSON. THREE UP, THREE DOWN.
KIT OCELOT WILL BE PITCHING FOR THE FUZZIES.
SHOW ME THAT BOOK!
THE OFFICIAL GUIDE TO MANGA LEAGUE BASEBALL

THERE ARE MANY DIFFERENT TYPES OF PITCHES IN MANGA BASEBALL.

THE CRISS-CROSS TURTLE

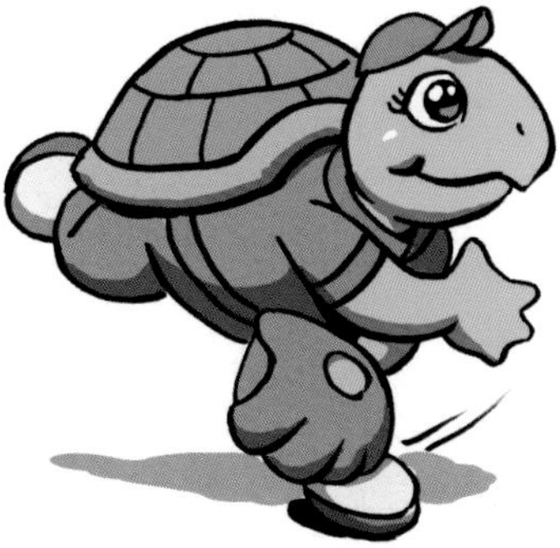

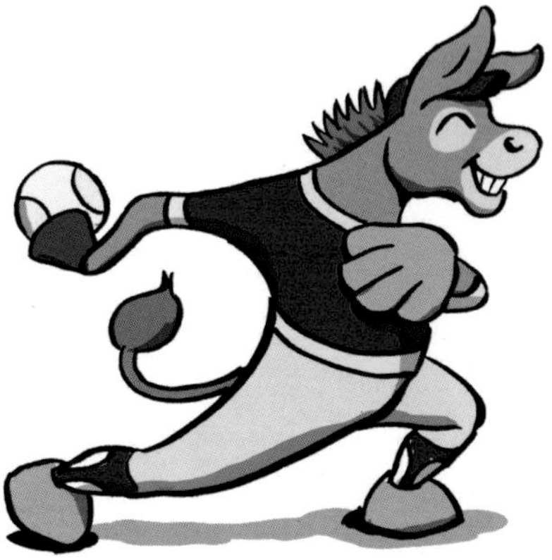

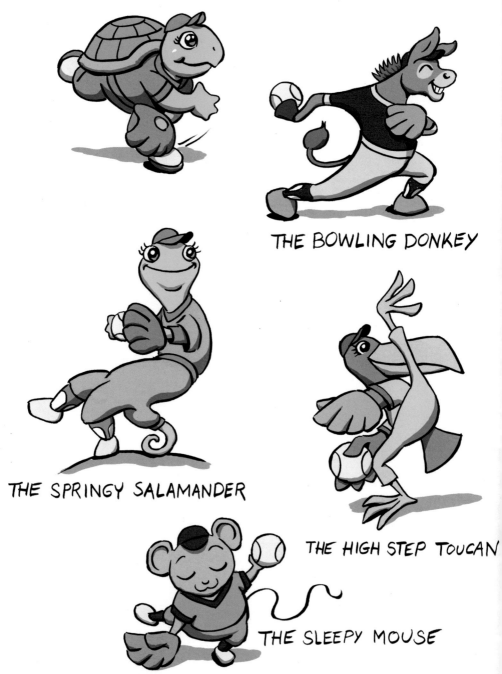

THE BOWLING DONKEY

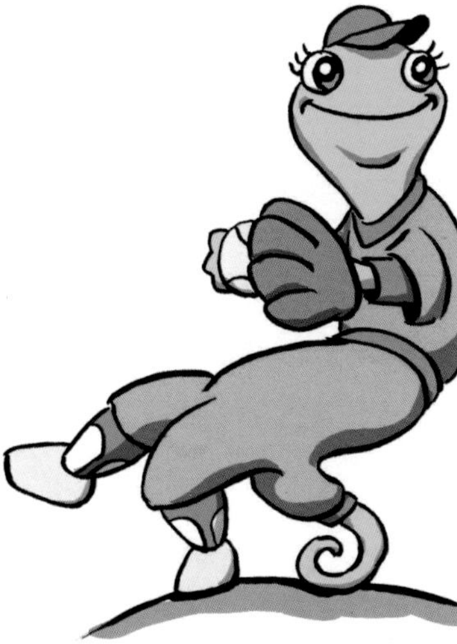

THE SPRINGY SALAMANDER

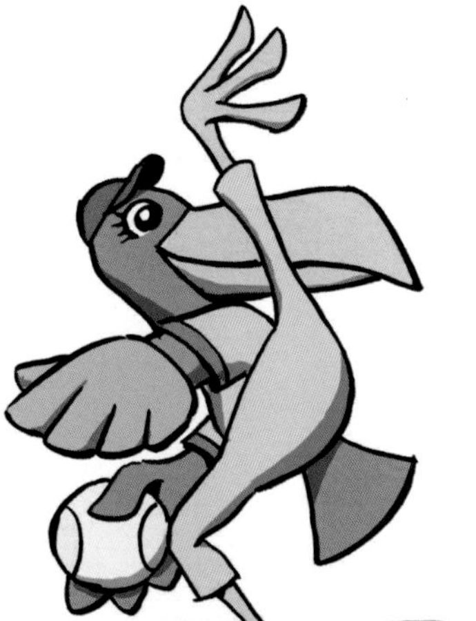

THE HIGH STEP TOUCAN

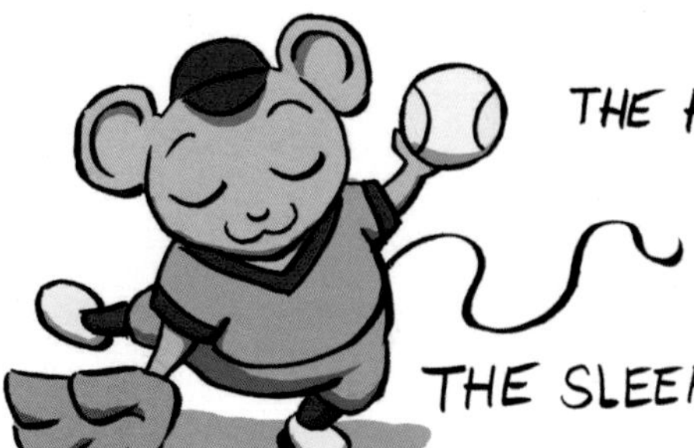

THE SLEEPY MOUSE

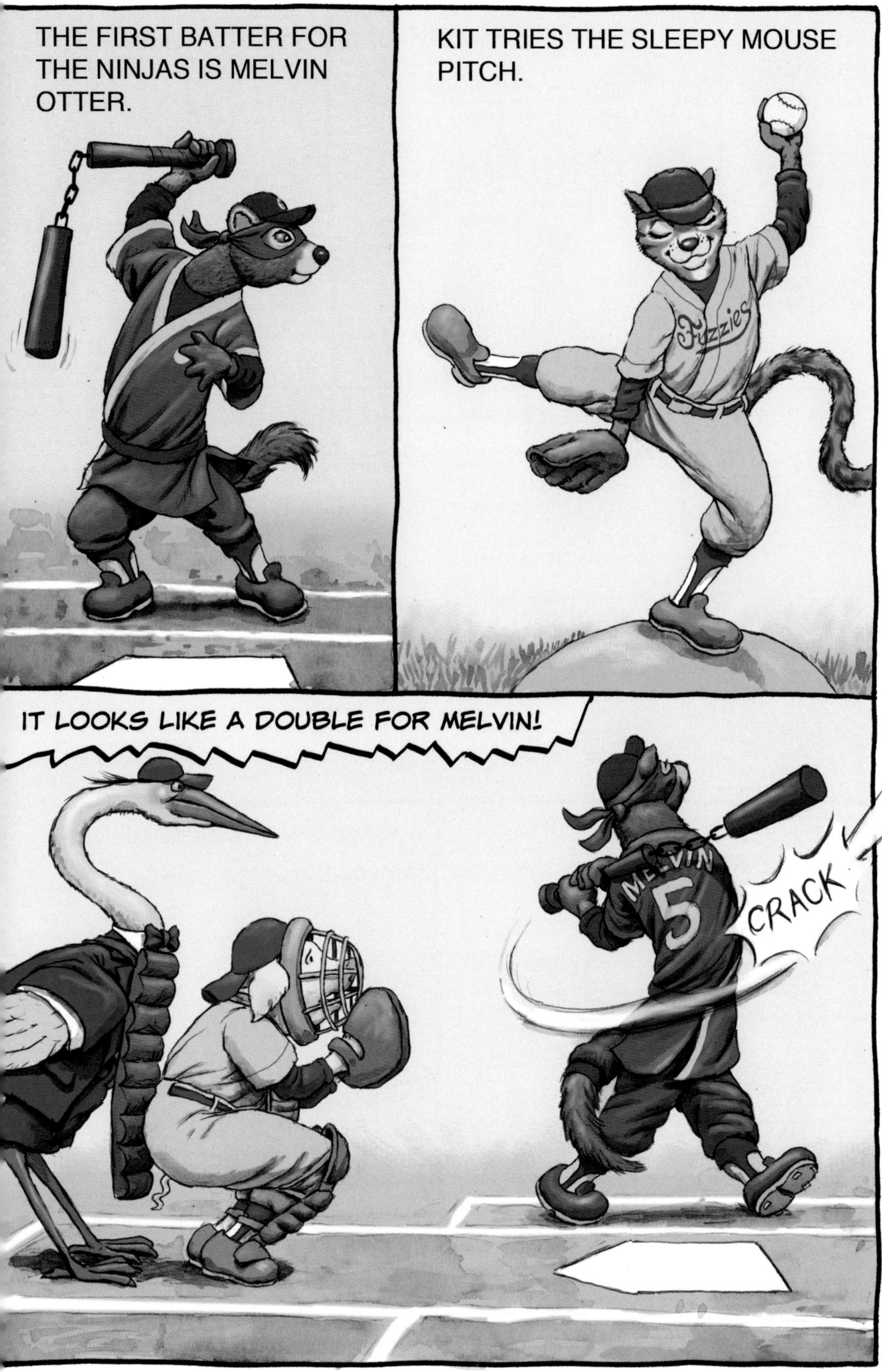
THE FIRST BATTER FOR THE NINJAS IS MELVIN OTTER.
KIT TRIES THE SLEEPY MOUSE PITCH.
Fuzzies
IT LOOKS LIKE A DOUBLE FOR MELVIN!
MELVIN 5
CRACK

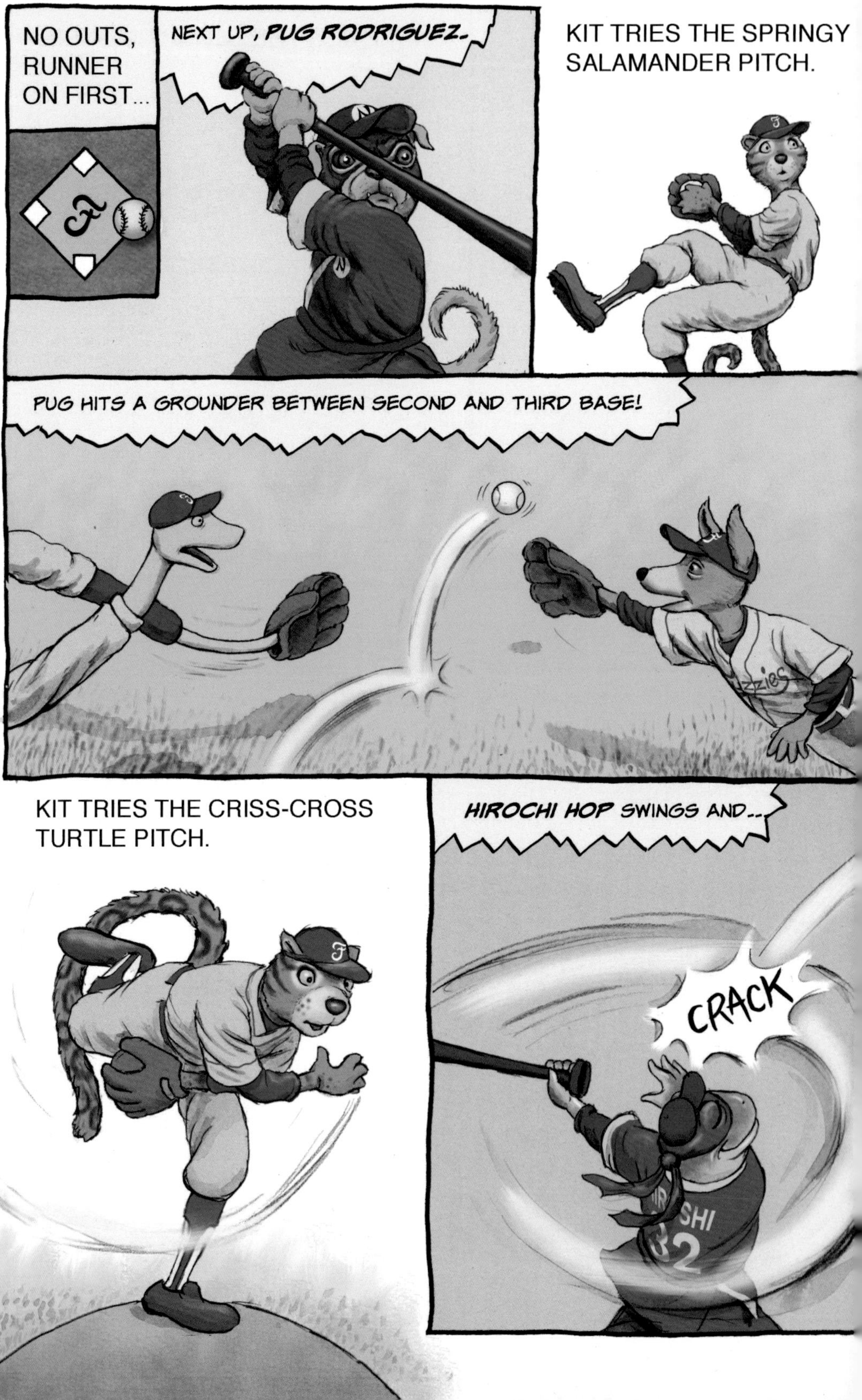
NO OUTS, RUNNER ON FIRST...
NEXT UP, PUG RODRIGUEZ.
KIT TRIES THE SPRINGY SALAMANDER PITCH.
PUG HITS A GROUNDER BETWEEN SECOND AND THIRD BASE!
KIT TRIES THE CRISS-CROSS TURTLE PITCH.
HIROCHI HOP SWINGS AND...
CRACK

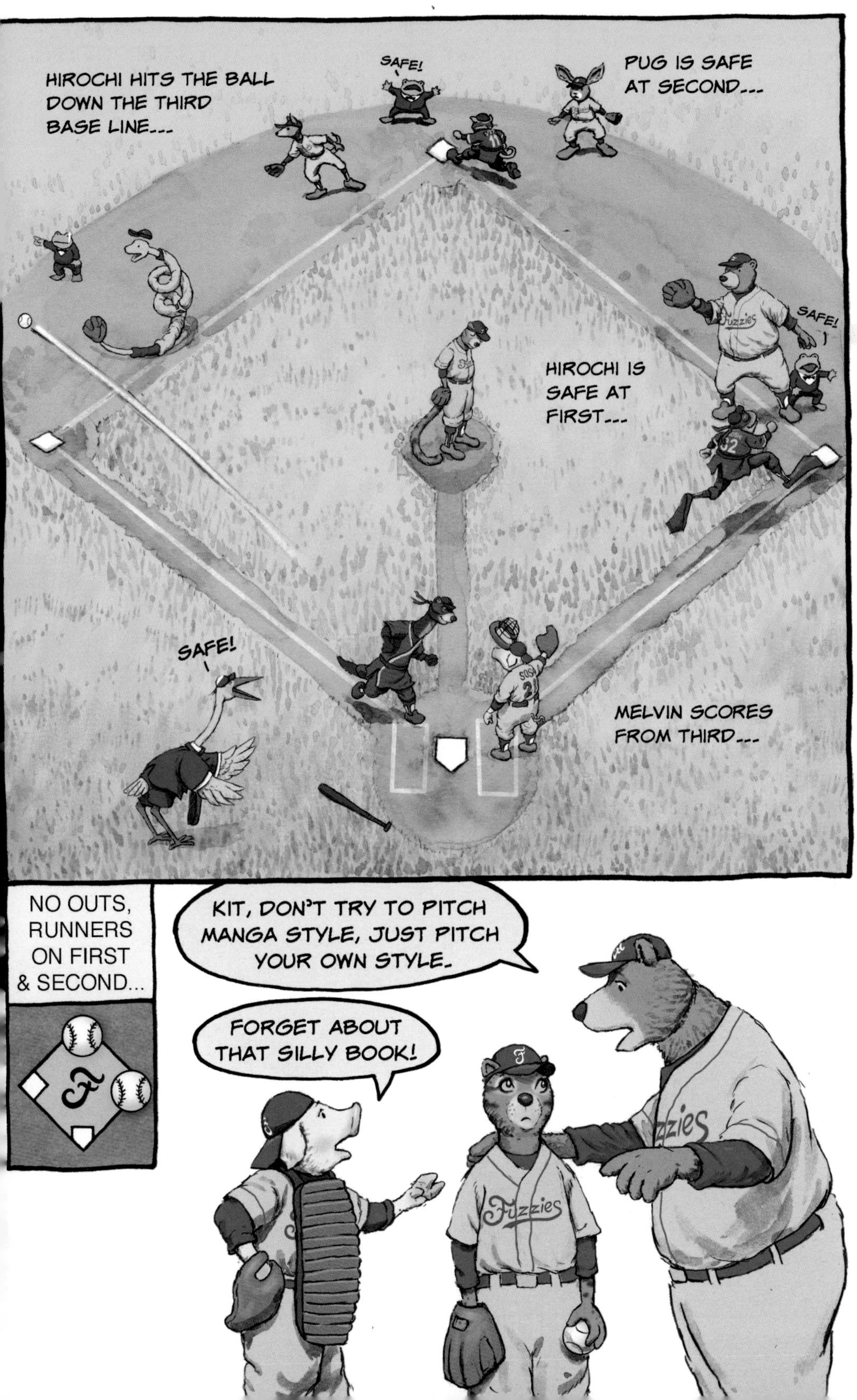
HIROCHI HITS THE BALL DOWN THE THIRD BASE LINE...
SAFE!
PUG IS SAFE AT SECOND...
SAFE!
HIROCHI IS SAFE AT FIRST...
SAFE!
MELVIN SCORES FROM THIRD...
NO OUTS, RUNNERS ON FIRST & SECOND...
KIT, DON'T TRY TO PITCH MANGA STYLE, JUST PITCH YOUR OWN STYLE.
FORGET ABOUT THAT SILLY BOOK!

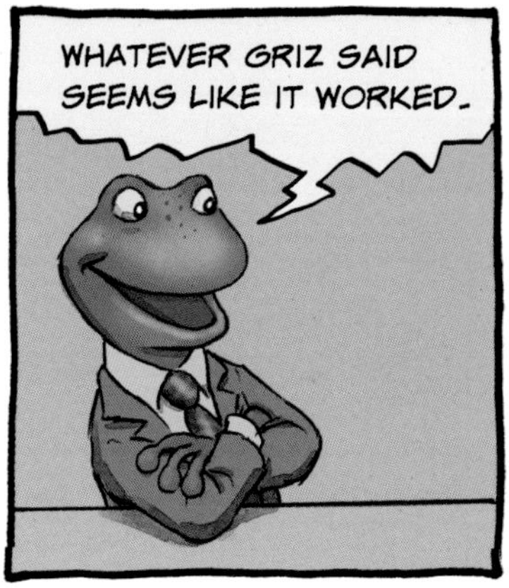
WHATEVER GRIZ SAID SEEMS LIKE IT WORKED.

KIT STOPS THINKING ABOUT PITCHING MANGA STYLE. SHE FOCUSES ON PITCHING HER OWN STYLE...

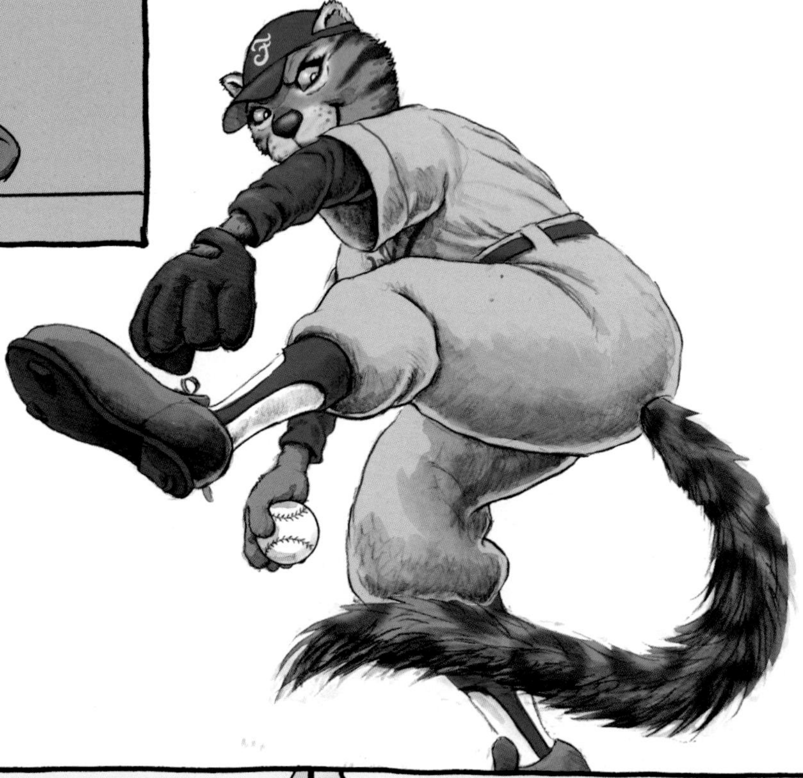

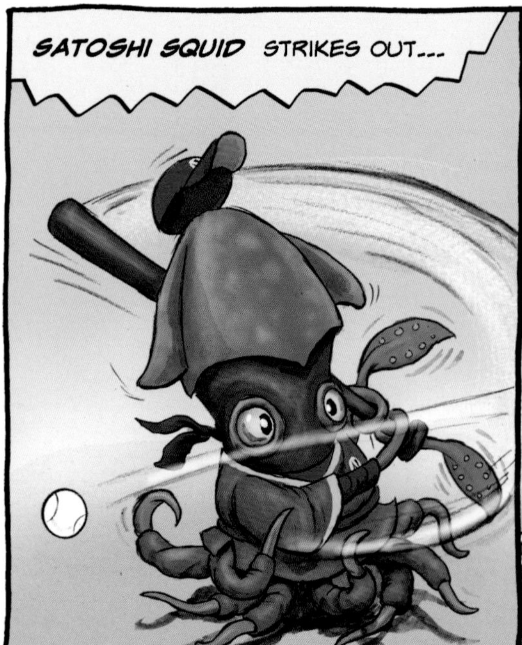
SATOSHI SQUID STRIKES OUT...

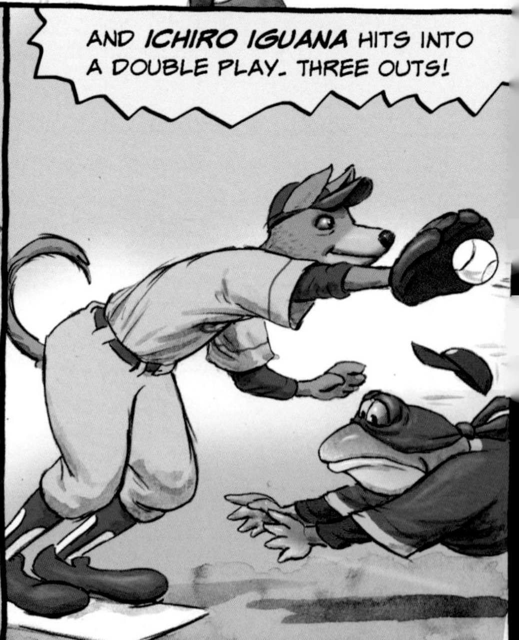
AND ICHIRO IGUANA HITS INTO A DOUBLE PLAY. THREE OUTS!

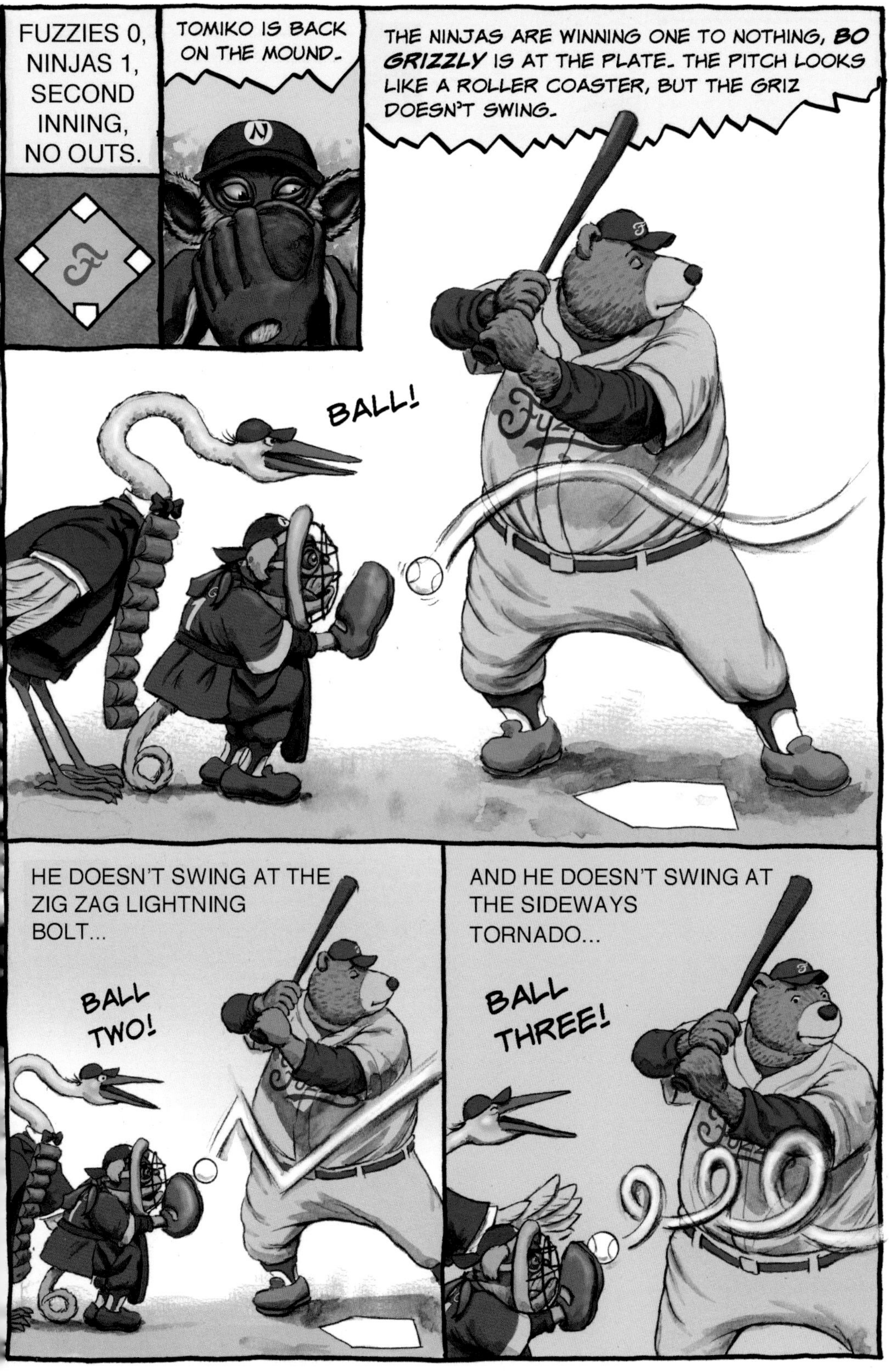
FUZZIES 0, NINJAS 1, SECOND INNING, NO OUTS.
TOMIKO IS BACK ON THE MOUND.
THE NINJAS ARE WINNING ONE TO NOTHING, BO GRIZZLY IS AT THE PLATE. THE PITCH LOOKS LIKE A ROLLER COASTER, BUT THE GRIZ DOESN'T SWING.
BALL!
HE DOESN'T SWING AT THE ZIG ZAG LIGHTNING BOLT...
BALL TWO!
AND HE DOESN'T SWING AT THE SIDEWAYS TORNADO...
BALL THREE!

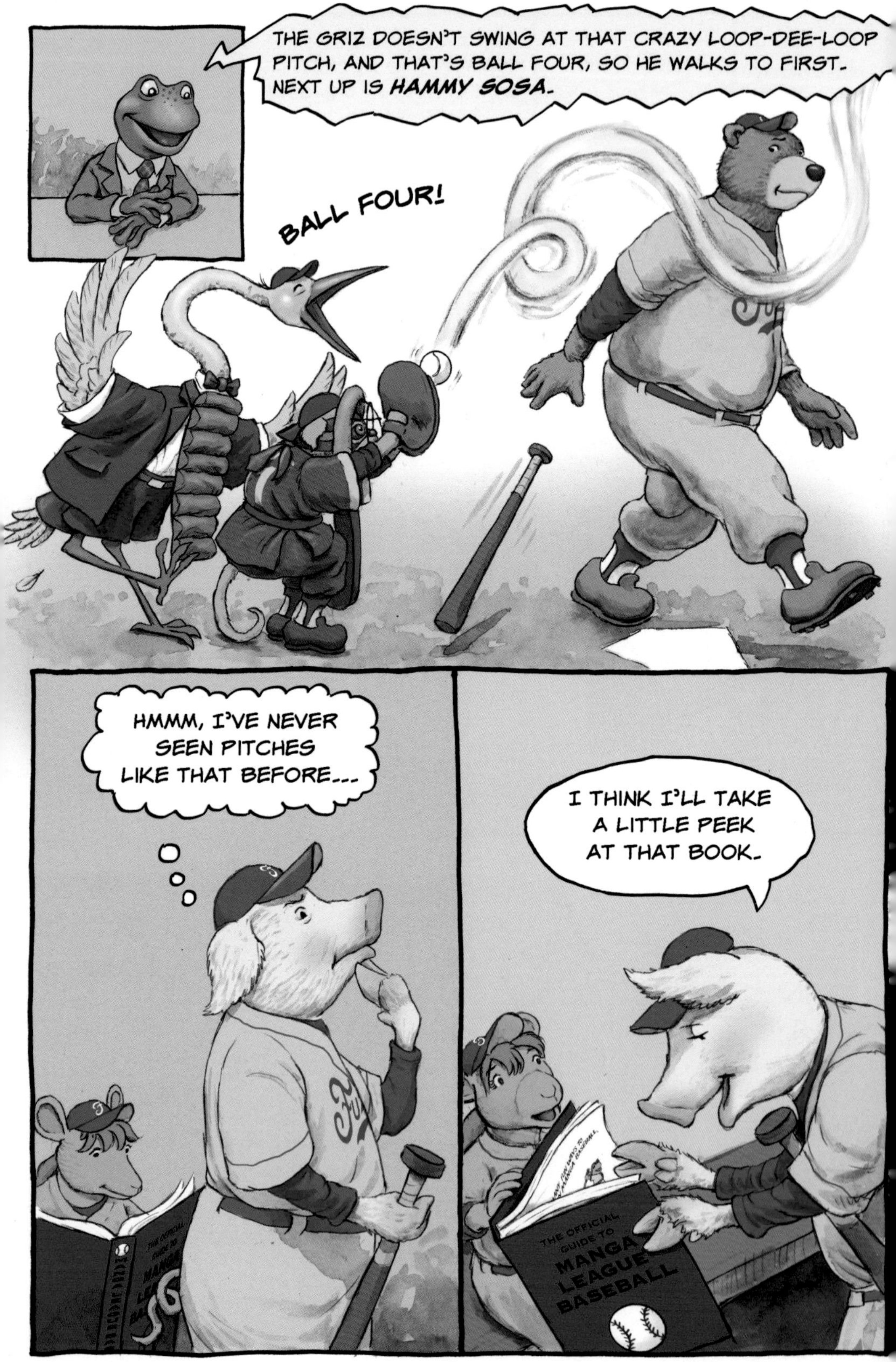
THE GRIZ DOESN'T SWING AT THAT CRAZY LOOP-DEE-LOOP PITCH, AND THAT'S BALL FOUR, SO HE WALKS TO FIRST. NEXT UP IS HAMMY SOSA.
BALL FOUR!
HMMM, I'VE NEVER SEEN PITCHES LIKE THAT BEFORE...
I THINK I'LL TAKE A LITTLE PEEK AT THAT BOOK.
THE OFFICIAL GUIDE TO MANGA LEAGUE BASEBALL

THERE ARE MANY FUN WAYS TO HOLD THE BAT IN MANGA BASEBALL.

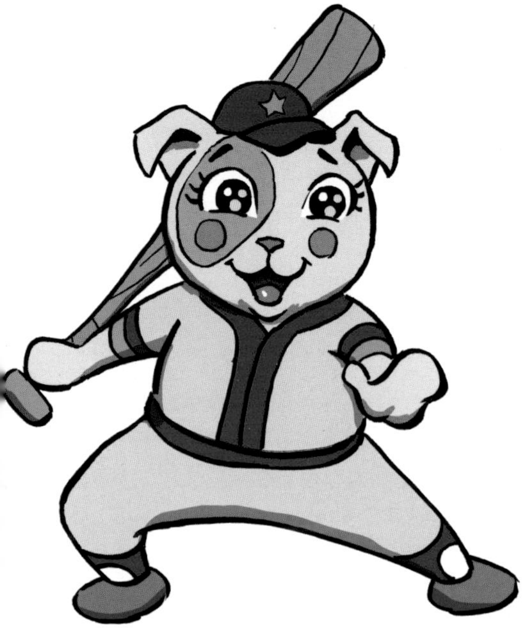

JAZZY SWING

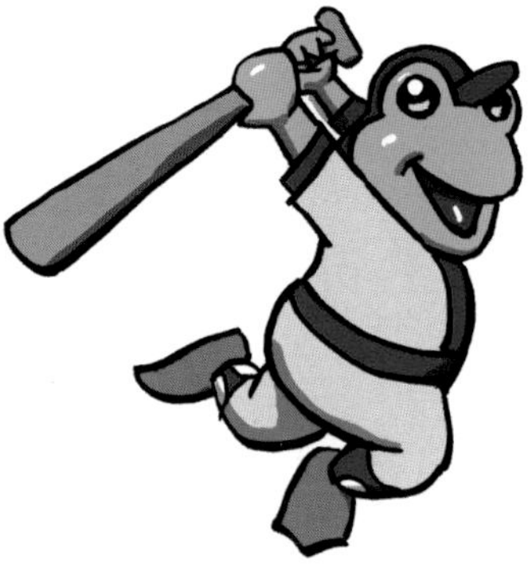

CHOP-CHOP SWING

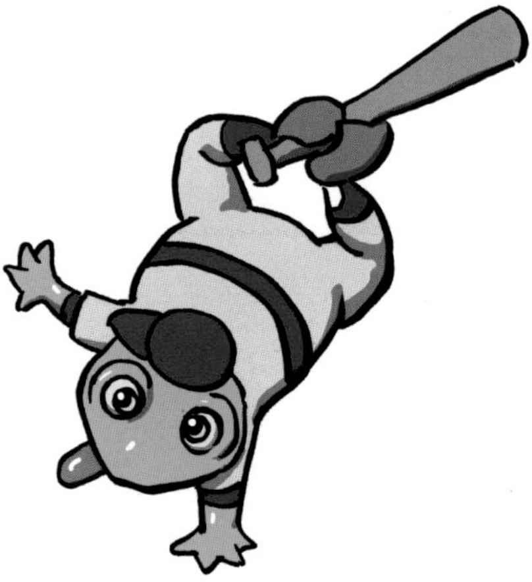

BUTTS UP SWING

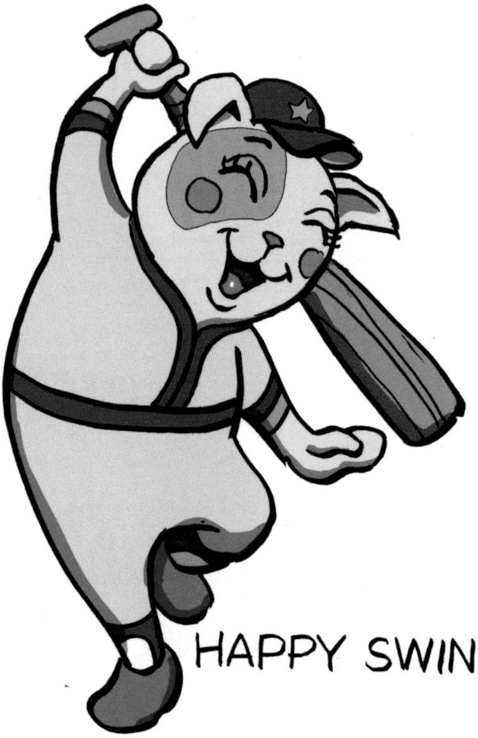

HAPPY SWING

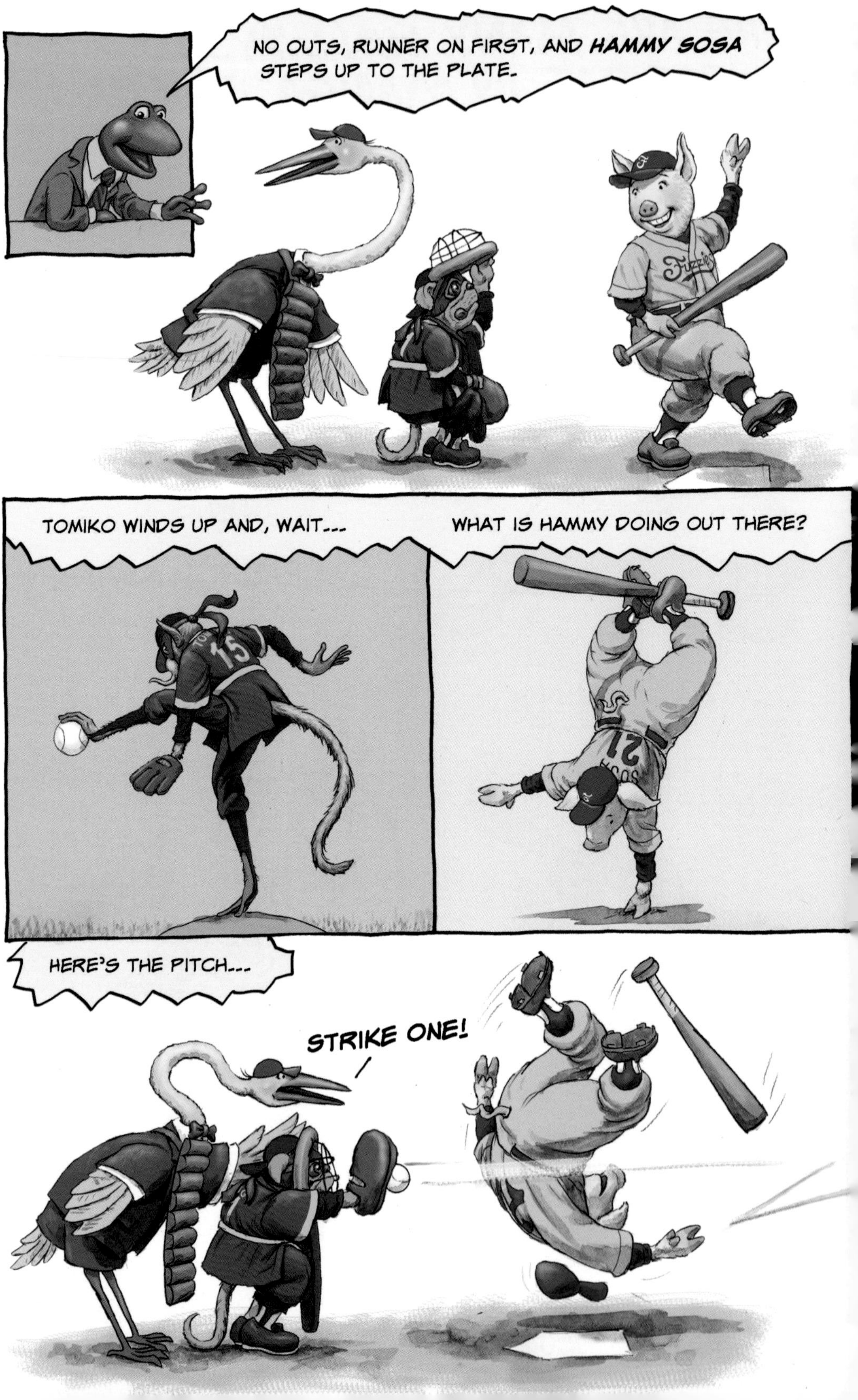
NO OUTS, RUNNER ON FIRST, AND HAMMY SOSA STEPS UP TO THE PLATE.
TOMIKO WINDS UP AND, WAIT...
WHAT IS HAMMY DOING OUT THERE?
HERE'S THE PITCH...
STRIKE ONE!

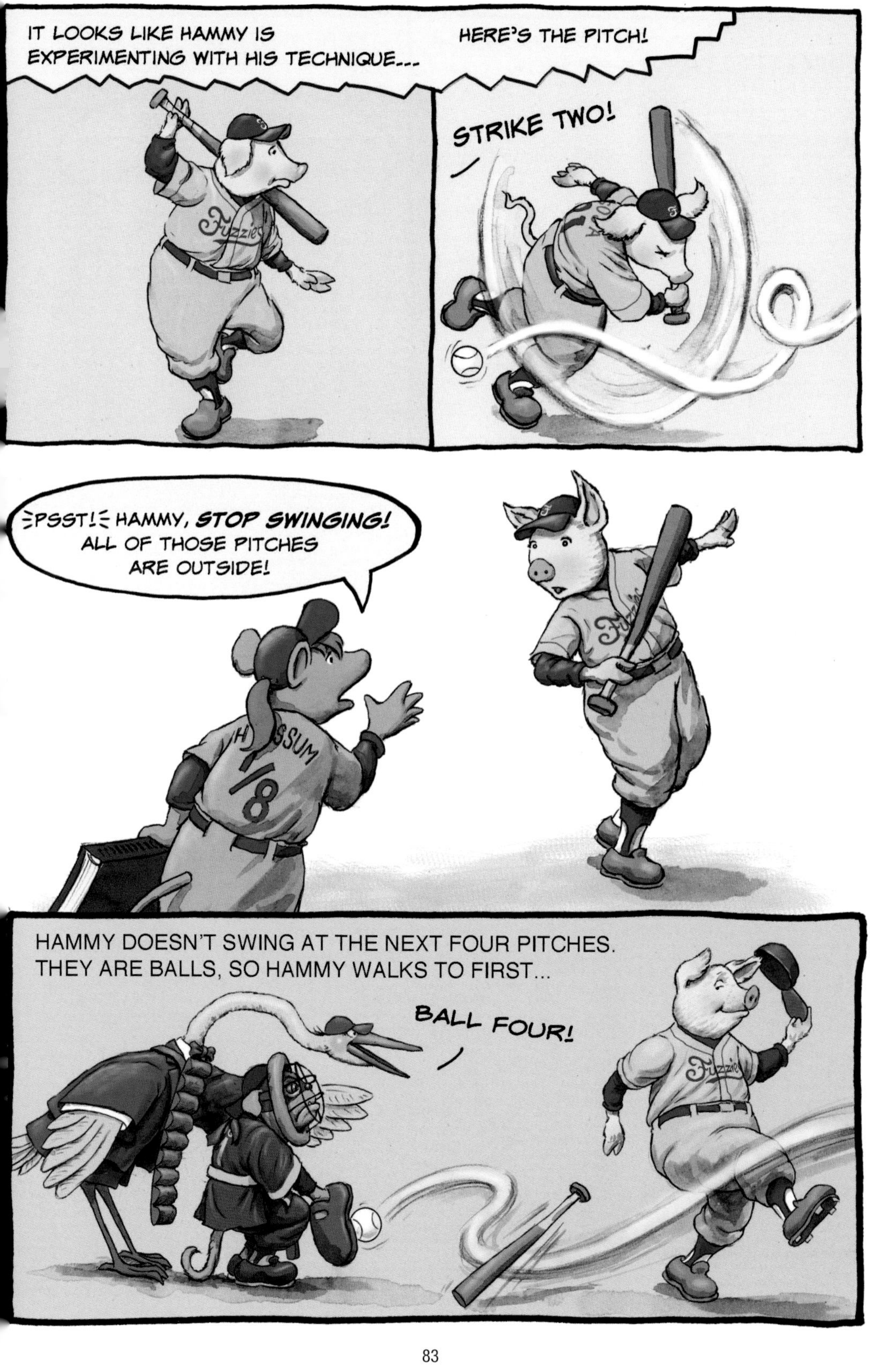
IT LOOKS LIKE HAMMY IS EXPERIMENTING WITH HIS TECHNIQUE...
HERE'S THE PITCH!
STRIKE TWO!
PSST! HAMMY, *STOP SWINGING!* ALL OF THOSE PITCHES ARE OUTSIDE!
HAMMY DOESN'T SWING AT THE NEXT FOUR PITCHES. THEY ARE BALLS, SO HAMMY WALKS TO FIRST...
BALL FOUR!

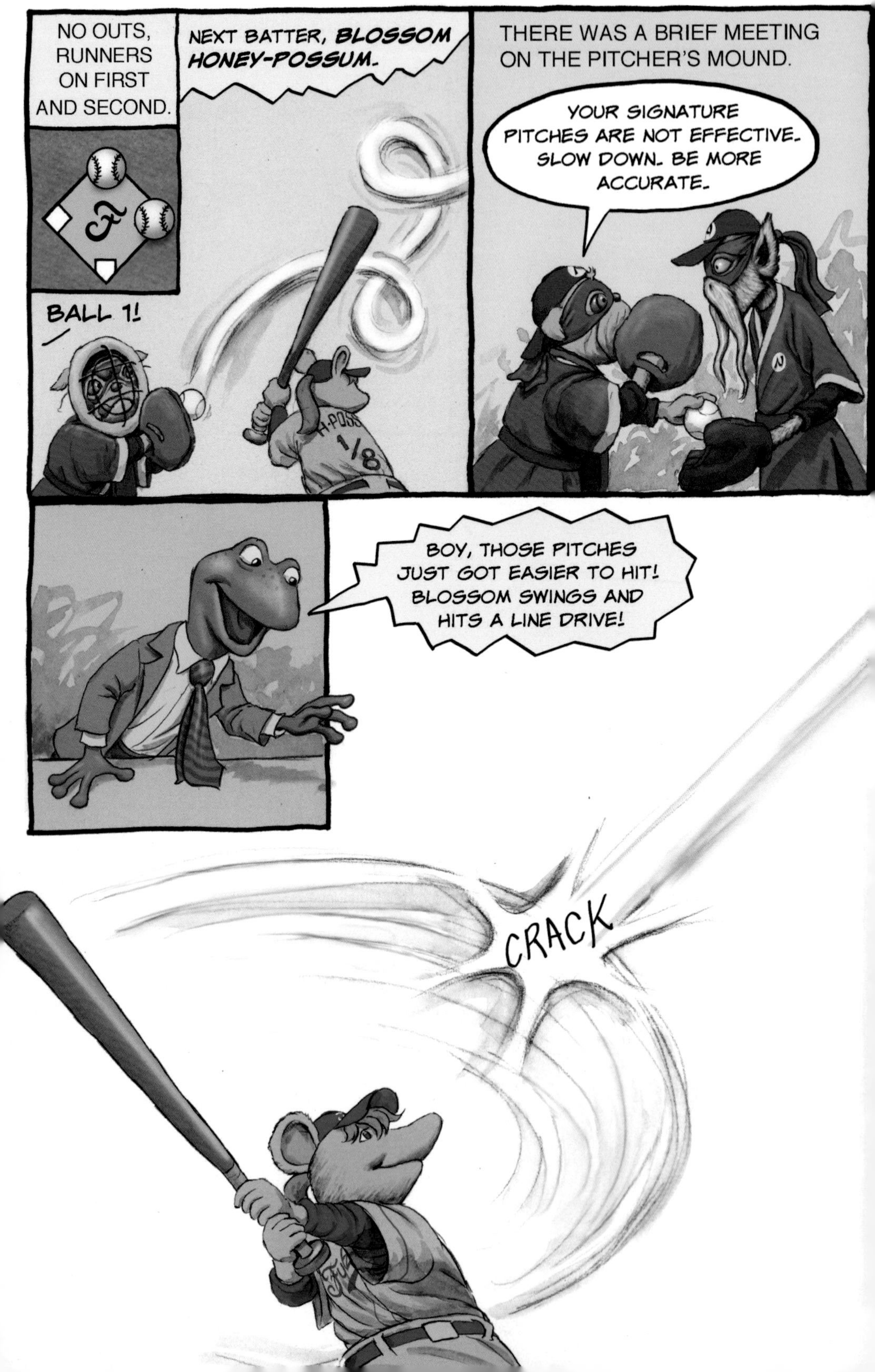
NO OUTS, RUNNERS ON FIRST AND SECOND.
NEXT BATTER, BLOSSOM HONEY-POSSUM.
BALL 1!
H-POSS 1/8
THERE WAS A BRIEF MEETING ON THE PITCHER'S MOUND.
YOUR SIGNATURE PITCHES ARE NOT EFFECTIVE. SLOW DOWN. BE MORE ACCURATE.
BOY, THOSE PITCHES JUST GOT EASIER TO HIT! BLOSSOM SWINGS AND HITS A LINE DRIVE!
CRACK

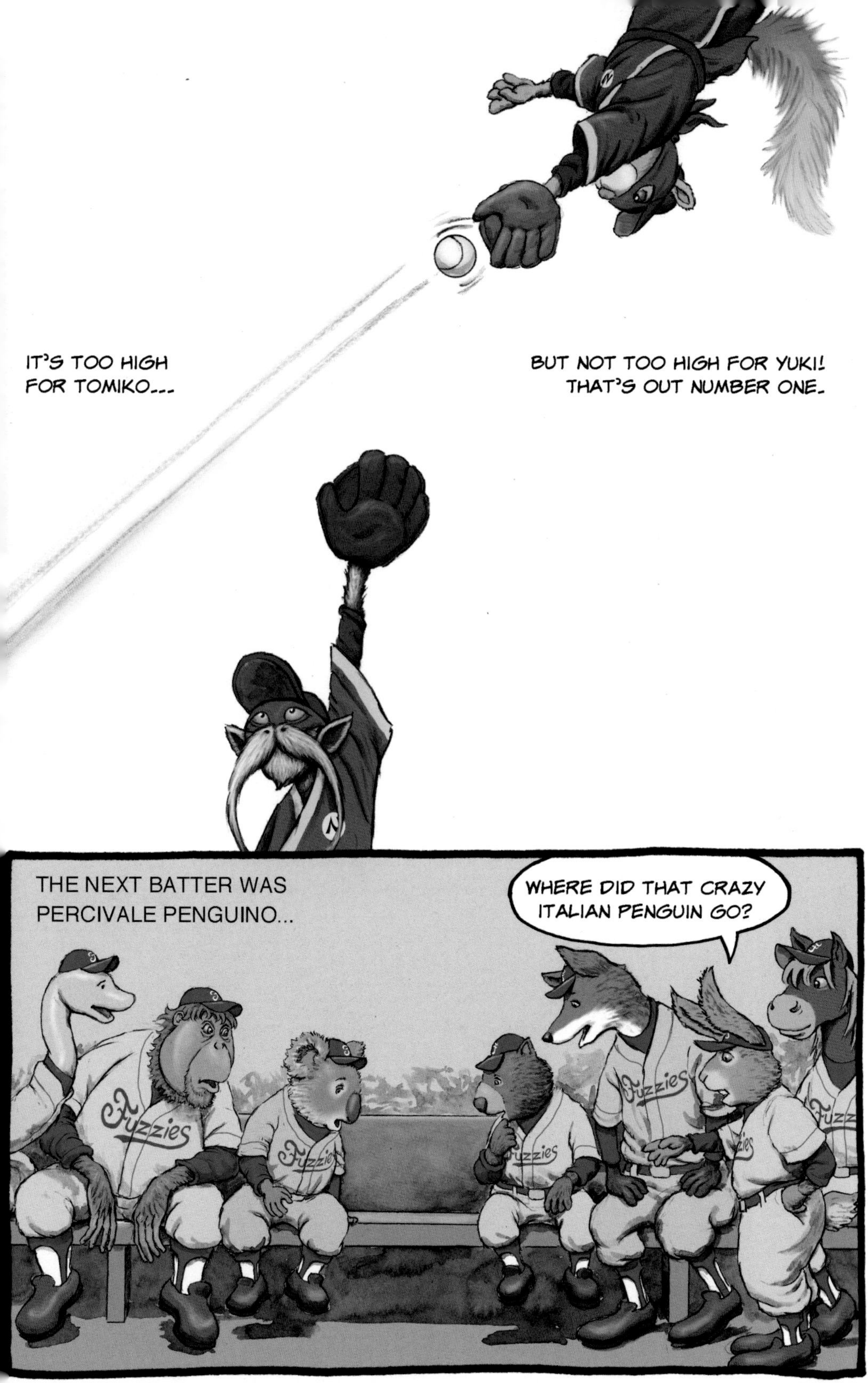
IT'S TOO HIGH FOR TOMIKO...
BUT NOT TOO HIGH FOR YUKI! THAT'S OUT NUMBER ONE.
THE NEXT BATTER WAS PERCIVALE PENGUINO...
WHERE DID THAT CRAZY ITALIAN PENGUIN GO?
Fuzzies

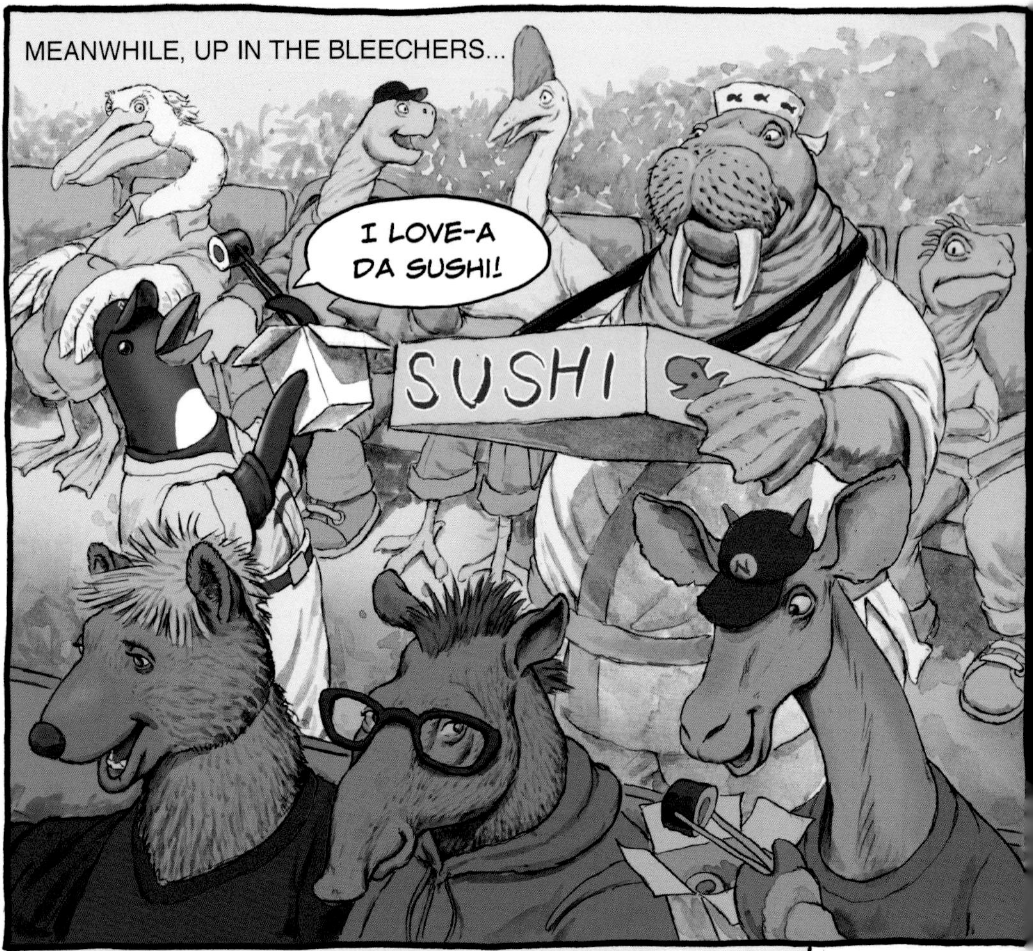
MEANWHILE, UP IN THE BLEECHERS...
I LOVE-A DA SUSHI!
SUSHI

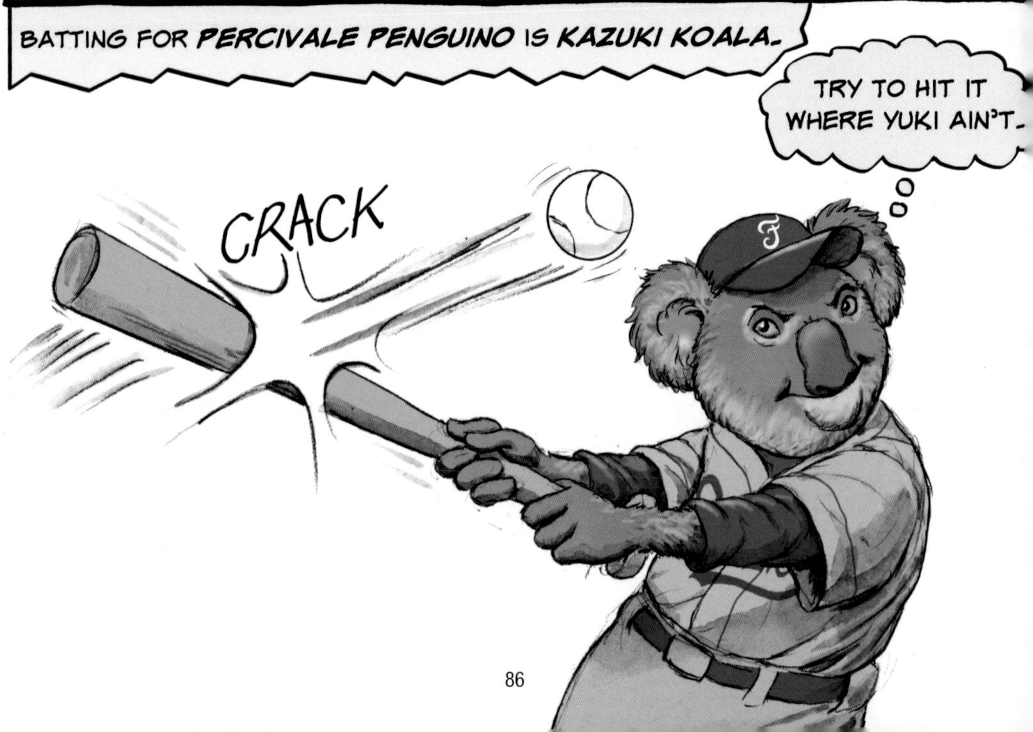
BATTING FOR PERCIVALE PENGUINO IS KAZUKI KOALA.
TRY TO HIT IT WHERE YUKI AIN'T.
CRACK

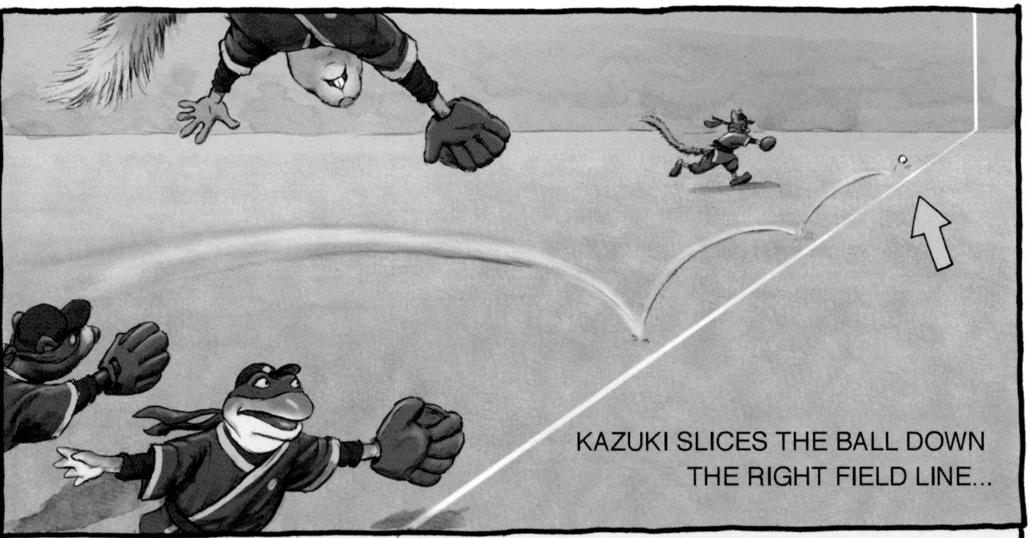
KAZUKI SLICES THE BALL DOWN THE RIGHT FIELD LINE...

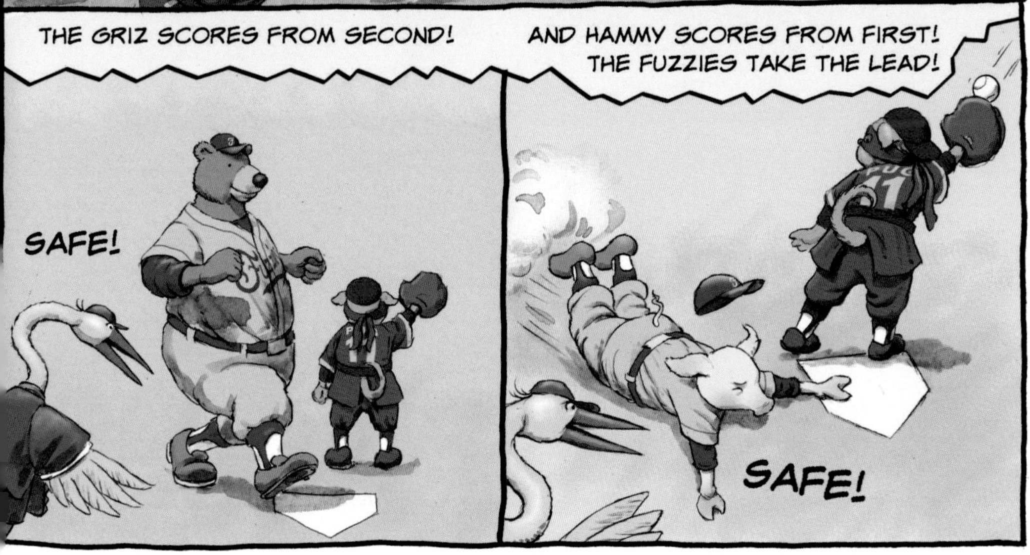
THE GRIZ SCORES FROM SECOND!
AND HAMMY SCORES FROM FIRST! THE FUZZIES TAKE THE LEAD!
SAFE!
SAFE!

KAZUKI IS SAFE AT THIRD. NEXT UP: LARRY BOA...

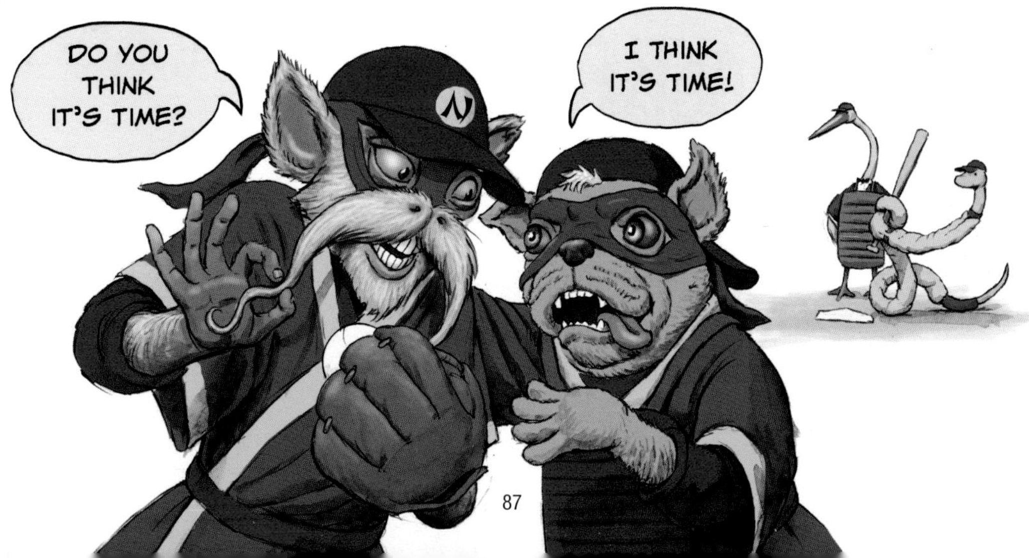
DO YOU THINK IT'S TIME?
I THINK IT'S TIME!

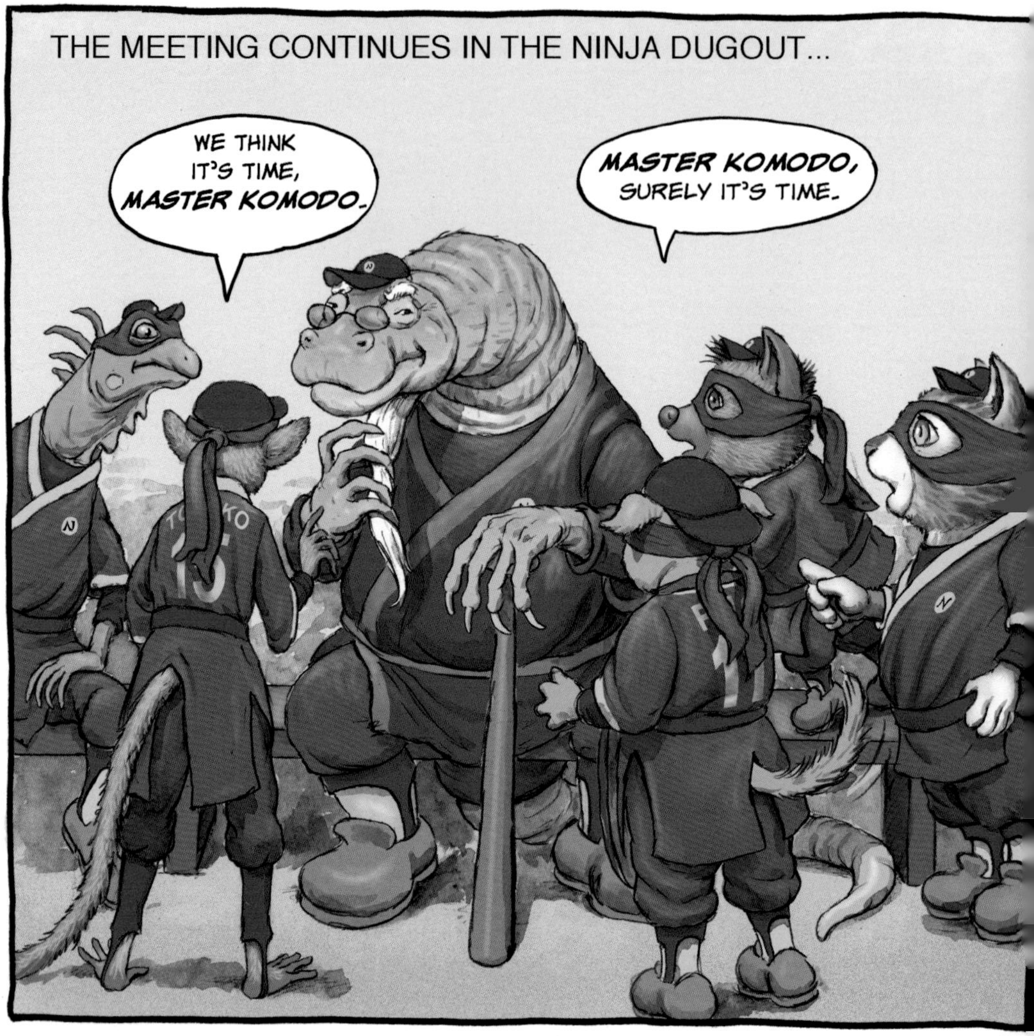
THE MEETING CONTINUES IN THE NINJA DUGOUT...
WE THINK IT'S TIME, MASTER KOMODO.
MASTER KOMODO, SURELY IT'S TIME.

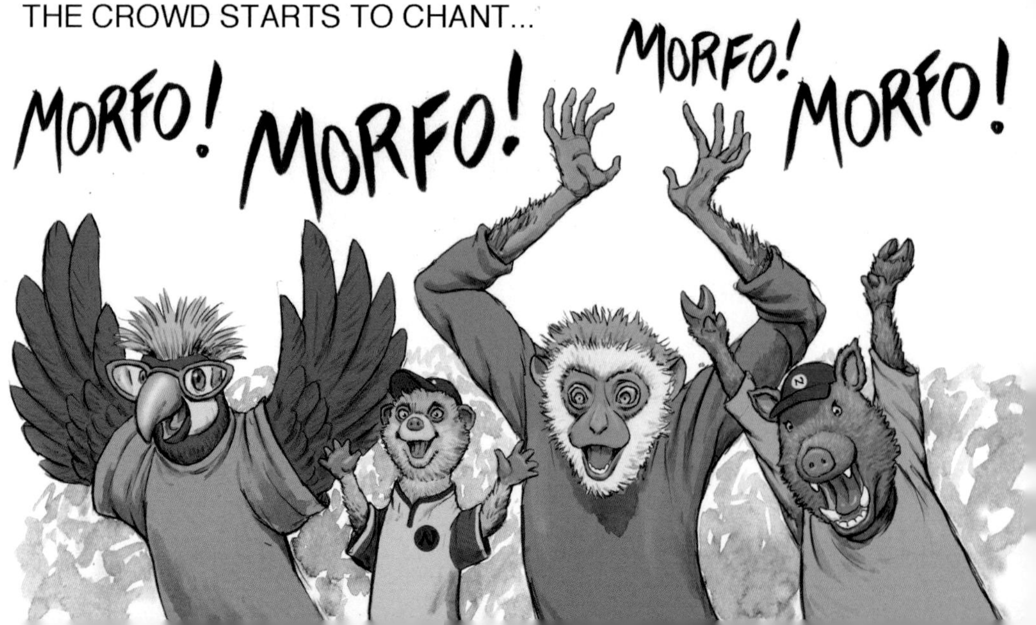
THE CROWD STARTS TO CHANT...
MORFO!
MORFO!
MORFO!
MORFO!

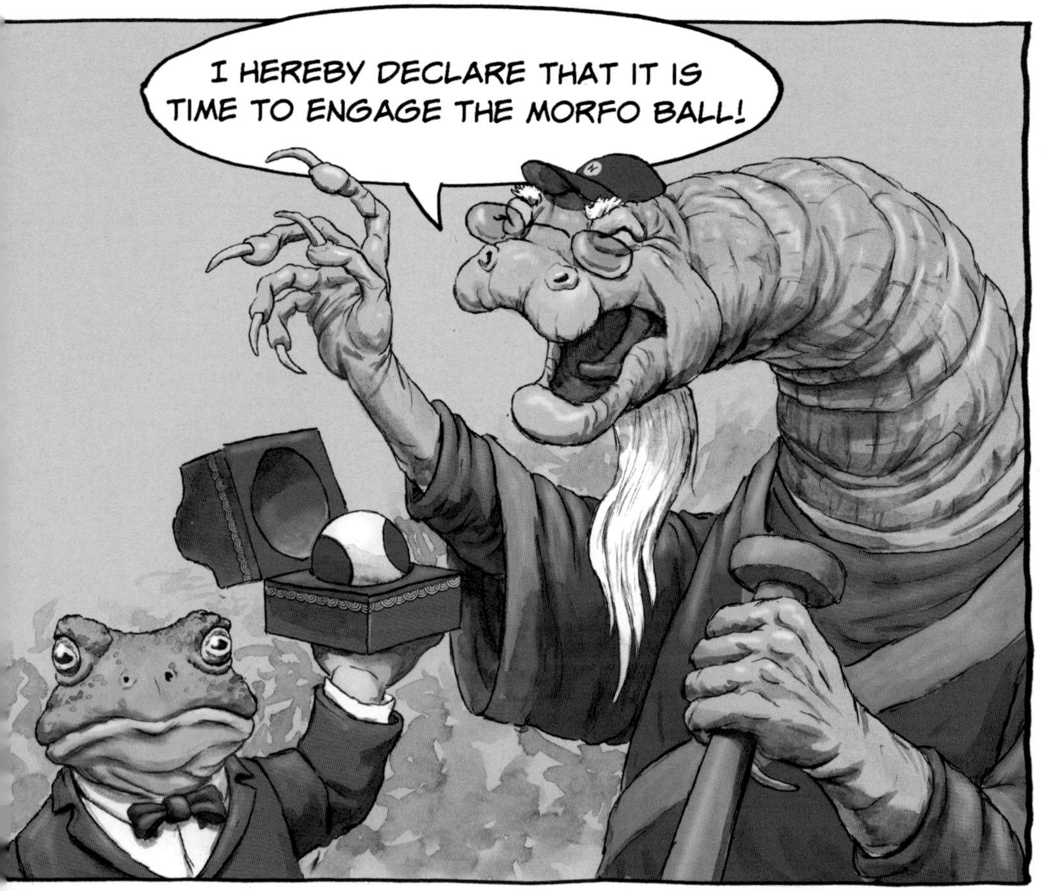
I HEREBY DECLARE THAT IT IS TIME TO ENGAGE THE MORFO BALL!

MASTER KOMODO PRESENTS THE MORFO BALL TO TOMIKO...

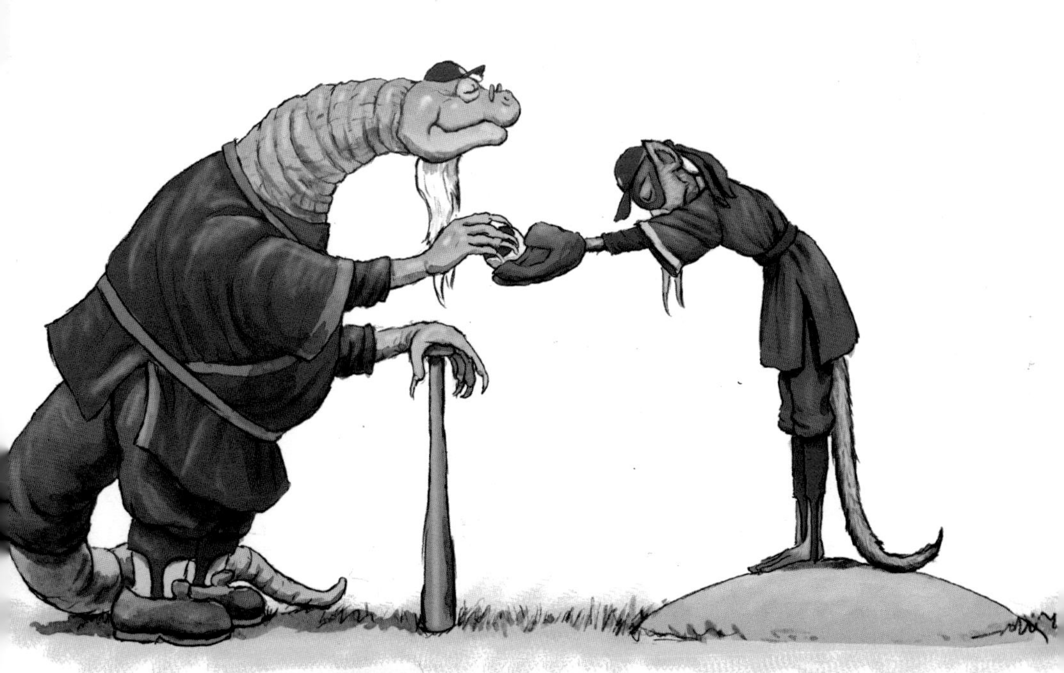

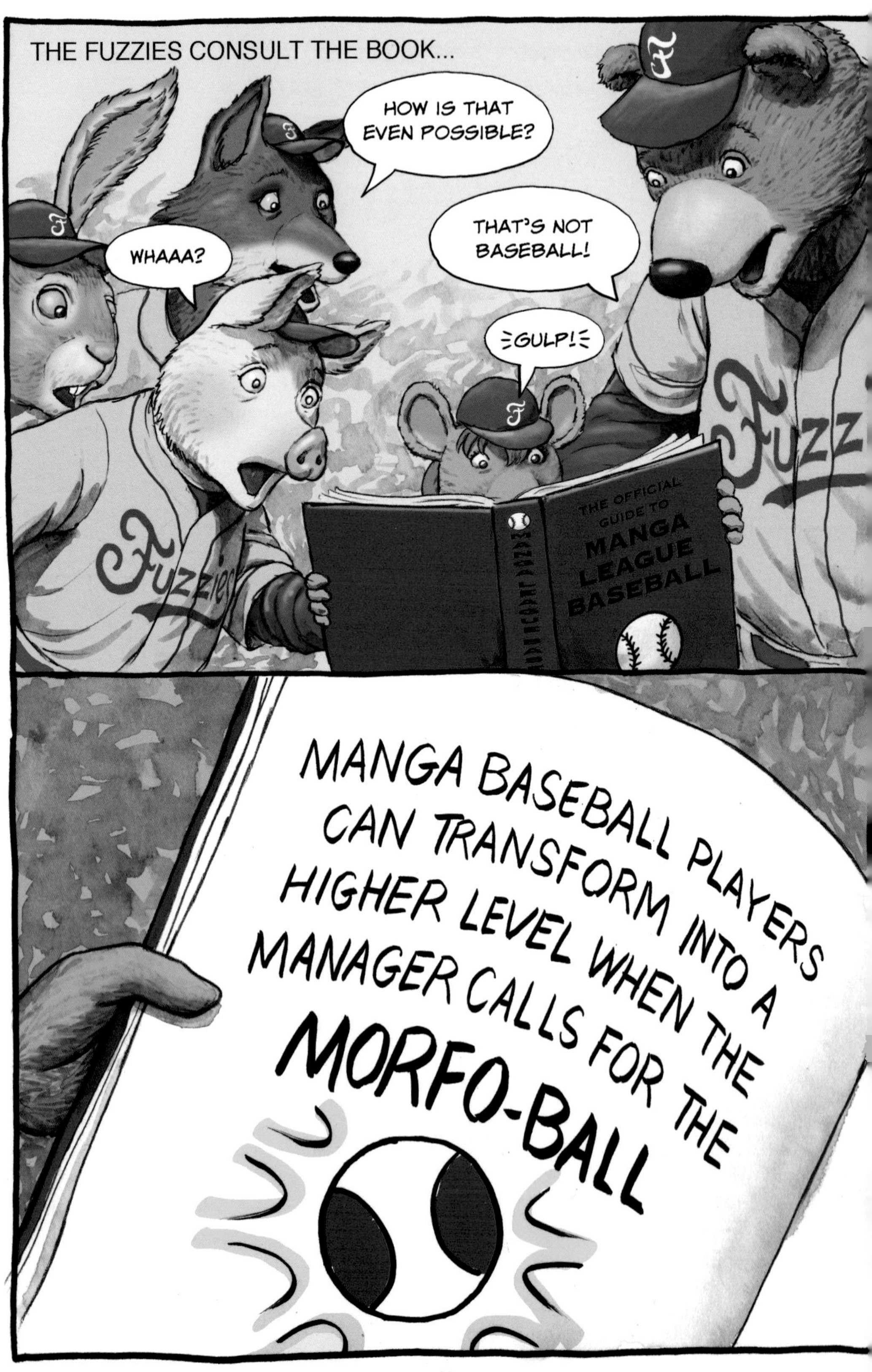
THE FUZZIES CONSULT THE BOOK...
WHAAA?
HOW IS THAT EVEN POSSIBLE?
THAT'S NOT BASEBALL!
GULP!
THE OFFICIAL GUIDE TO MANGA LEAGUE BASEBALL
MANGA BASEBALL PLAYERS CAN TRANSFORM INTO A HIGHER LEVEL WHEN THE MANAGER CALLS FOR THE MORFO-BALL

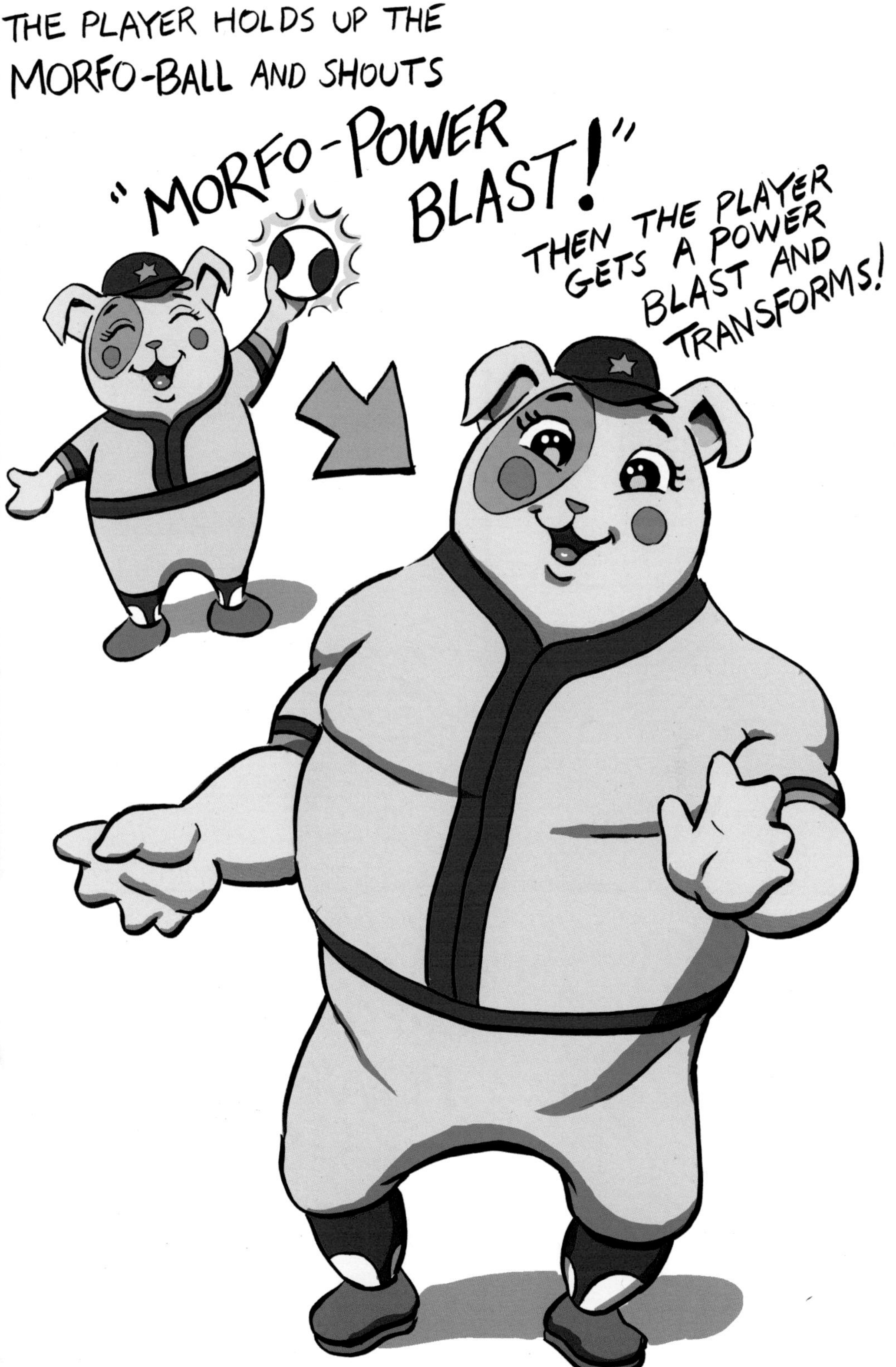
THE PLAYER HOLDS UP THE MORFO-BALL AND SHOUTS
"MORFO-POWER BLAST!"
THEN THE PLAYER GETS A POWER BLAST AND TRANSFORMS!

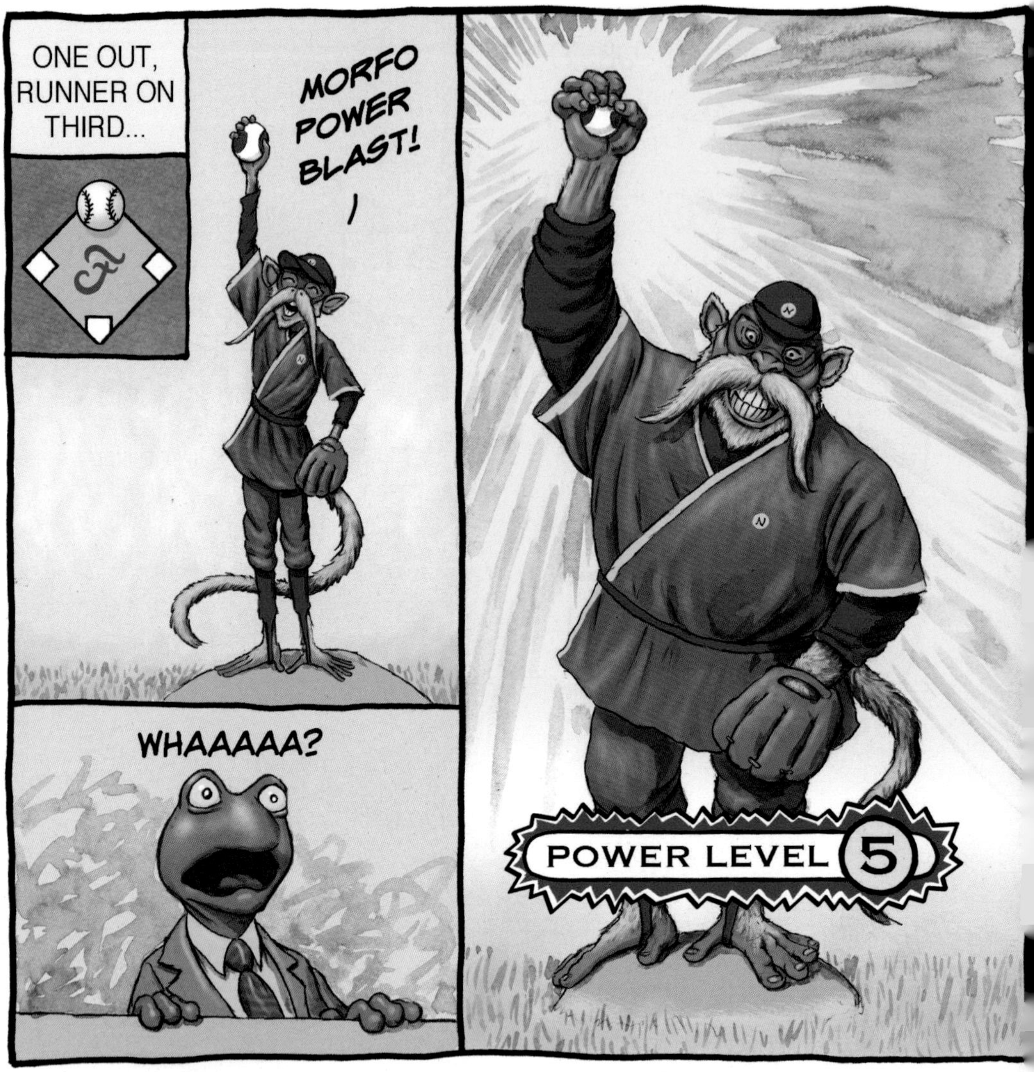
ONE OUT, RUNNER ON THIRD...
MORFO POWER BLAST!
WHAAAAA?
POWER LEVEL 5

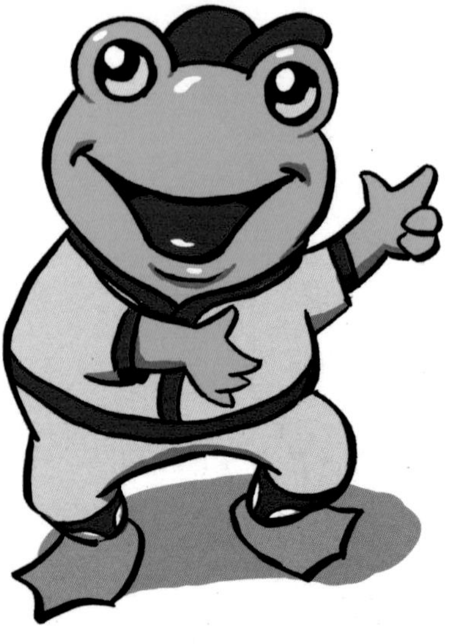

IN MANGA-BASEBALL YOUR MORFO-POWER BLAST POWER LEVEL IS BASED ON YOUR PASSION FOR BASEBALL!

LARRY AND THE NEXT BATTER STRIKE OUT TO END THE TOP OF THE SECOND INNING...

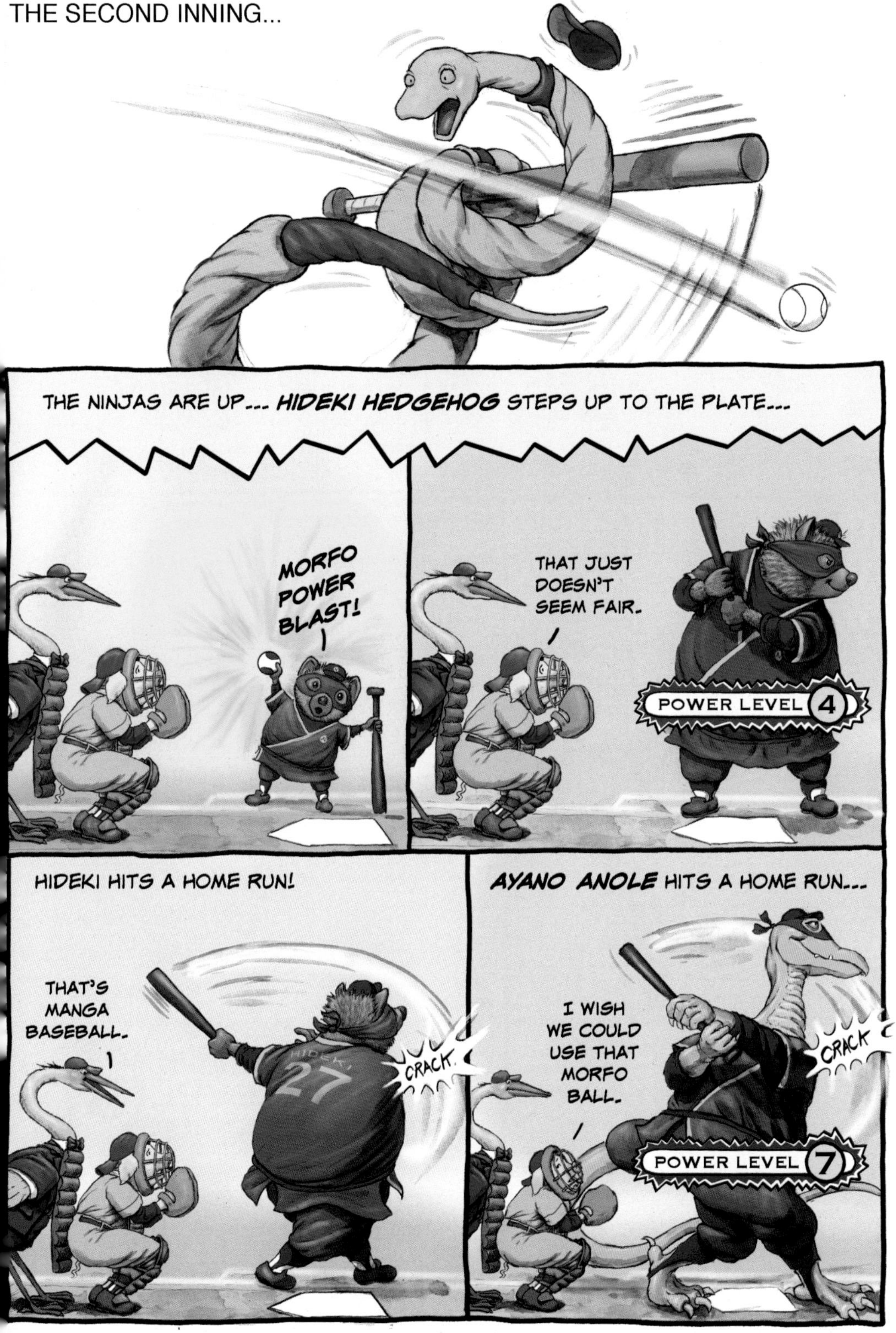
THE NINJAS ARE UP... HIDEKI HEDGEHOG STEPS UP TO THE PLATE...
MORFO POWER BLAST!
THAT JUST DOESN'T SEEM FAIR.
POWER LEVEL 4
HIDEKI HITS A HOME RUN!
THAT'S MANGA BASEBALL.
HIDEKI 27
CRACK
AYANO ANOLE HITS A HOME RUN...
I WISH WE COULD USE THAT MORFO BALL.
CRACK
POWER LEVEL 7

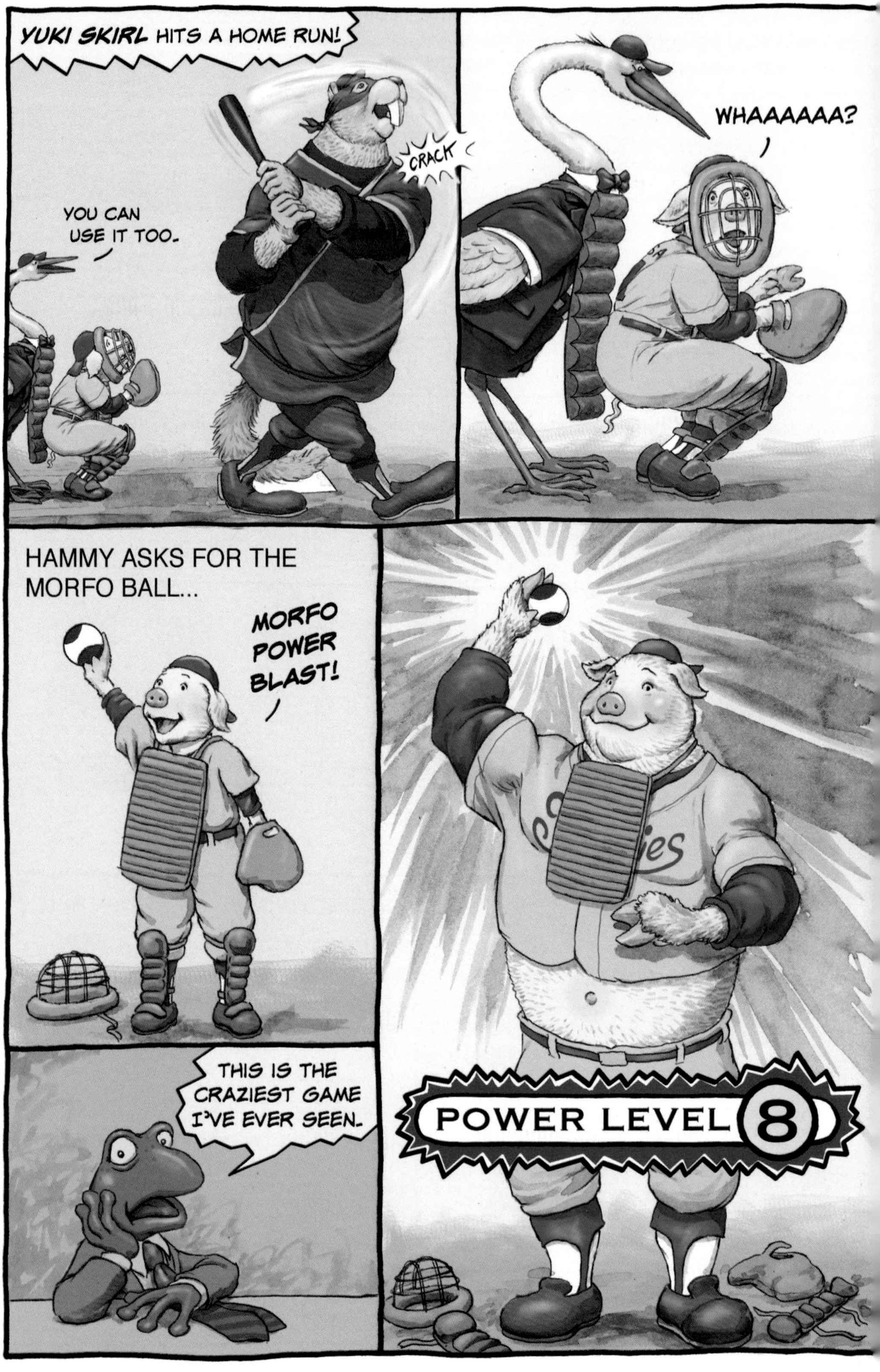
YUKI SKIRL HITS A HOME RUN!
CRACK
YOU CAN USE IT TOO.
WHAAAAAAA?
HAMMY ASKS FOR THE MORFO BALL...
MORFO POWER BLAST!
THIS IS THE CRAZIEST GAME I'VE EVER SEEN.
POWER LEVEL 8

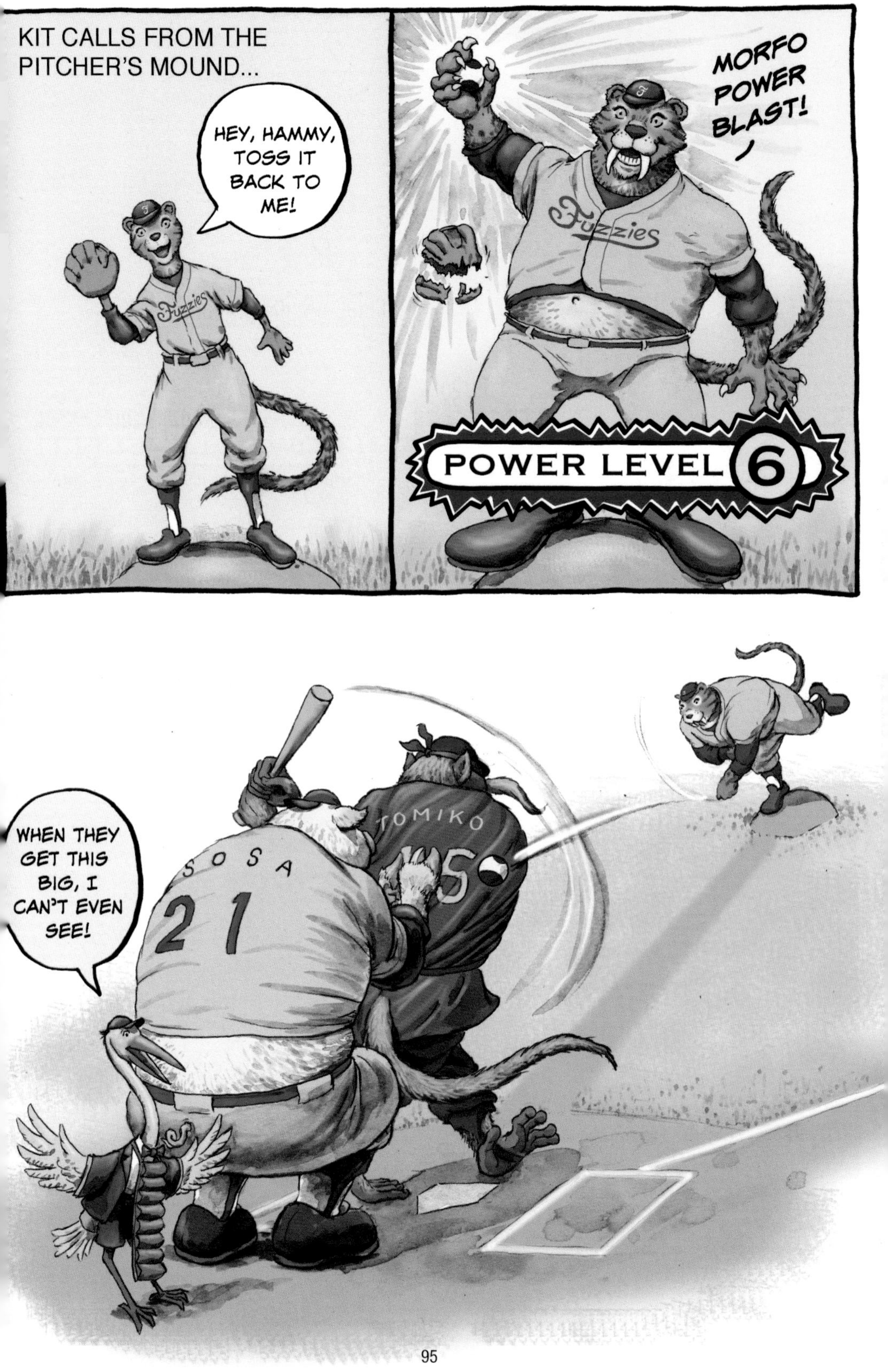

KIT CALLS FROM THE PITCHER'S MOUND...
HEY, HAMMY, TOSS IT BACK TO ME!
MORFO POWER BLAST!
POWER LEVEL 6
SOSA 21
TOMIKO
WHEN THEY GET THIS BIG, I CAN'T EVEN SEE!

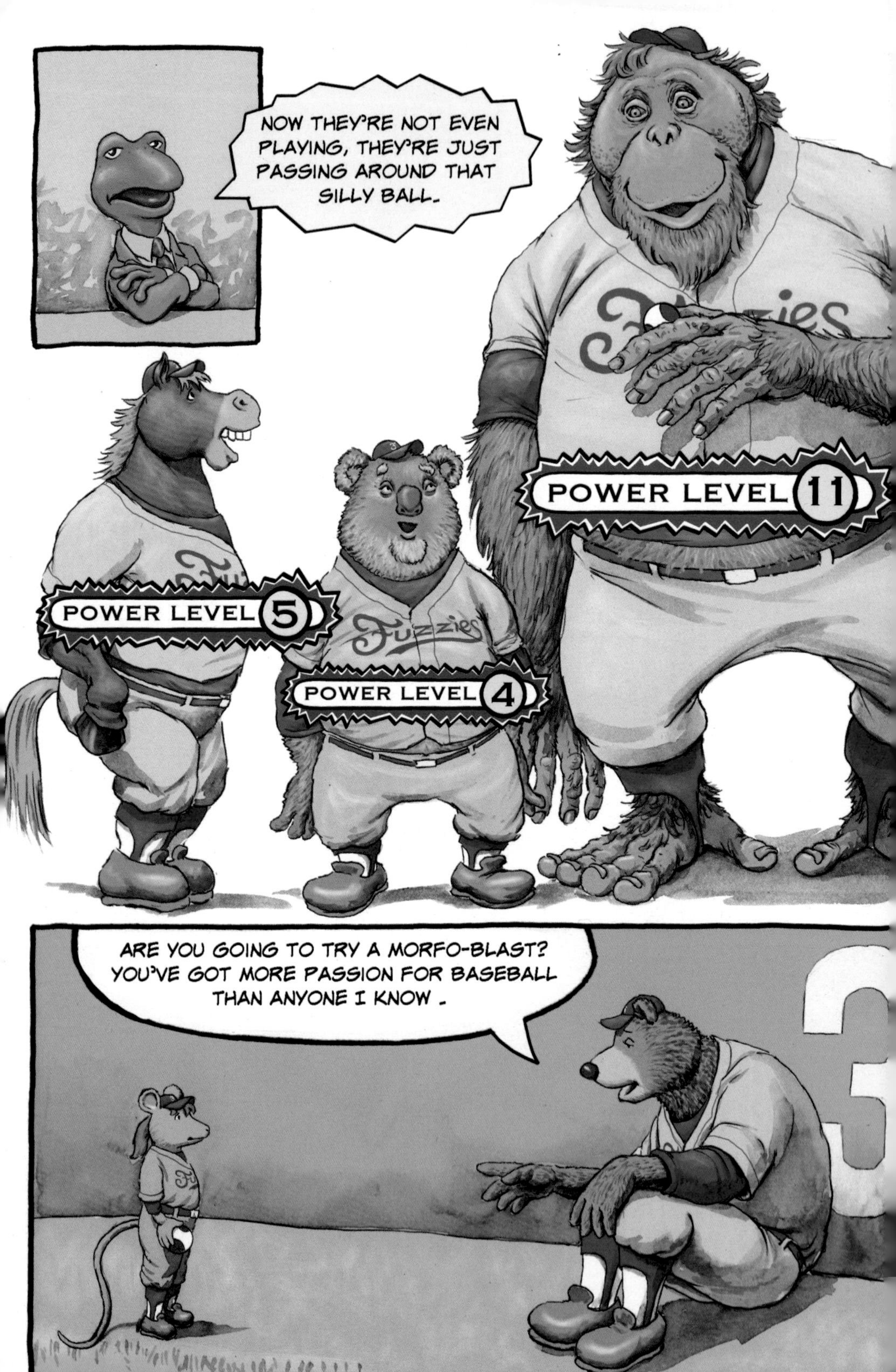
NOW THEY'RE NOT EVEN PLAYING, THEY'RE JUST PASSING AROUND THAT SILLY BALL.
POWER LEVEL 5
POWER LEVEL 4
POWER LEVEL 11
Fuzzies
ARE YOU GOING TO TRY A MORFO-BLAST? YOU'VE GOT MORE PASSION FOR BASEBALL THAN ANYONE I KNOW.

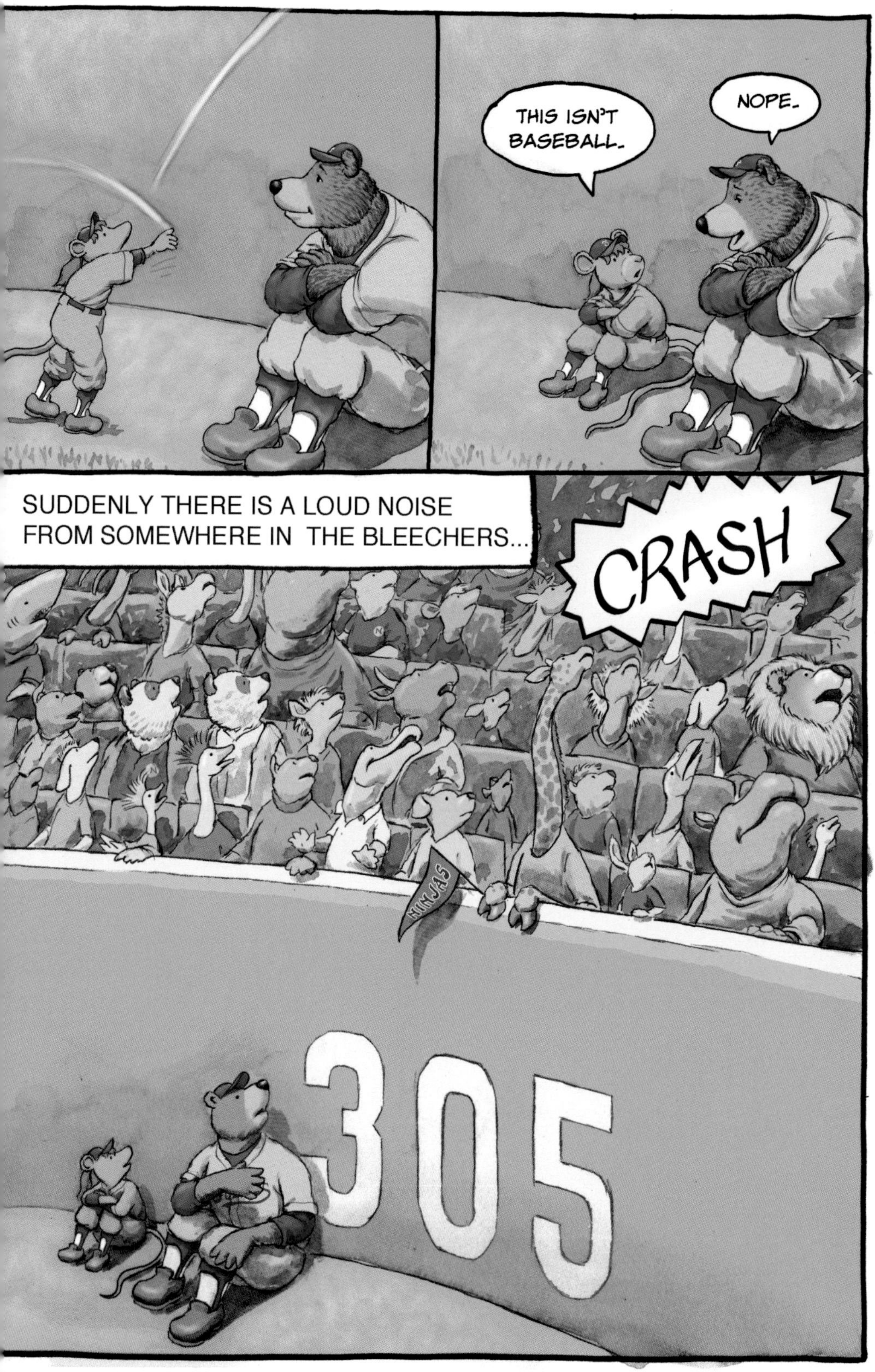
THIS ISN'T BASEBALL.
NOPE.
SUDDENLY THERE IS A LOUD NOISE FROM SOMEWHERE IN THE BLEECHERS...
CRASH
NINJAS
305

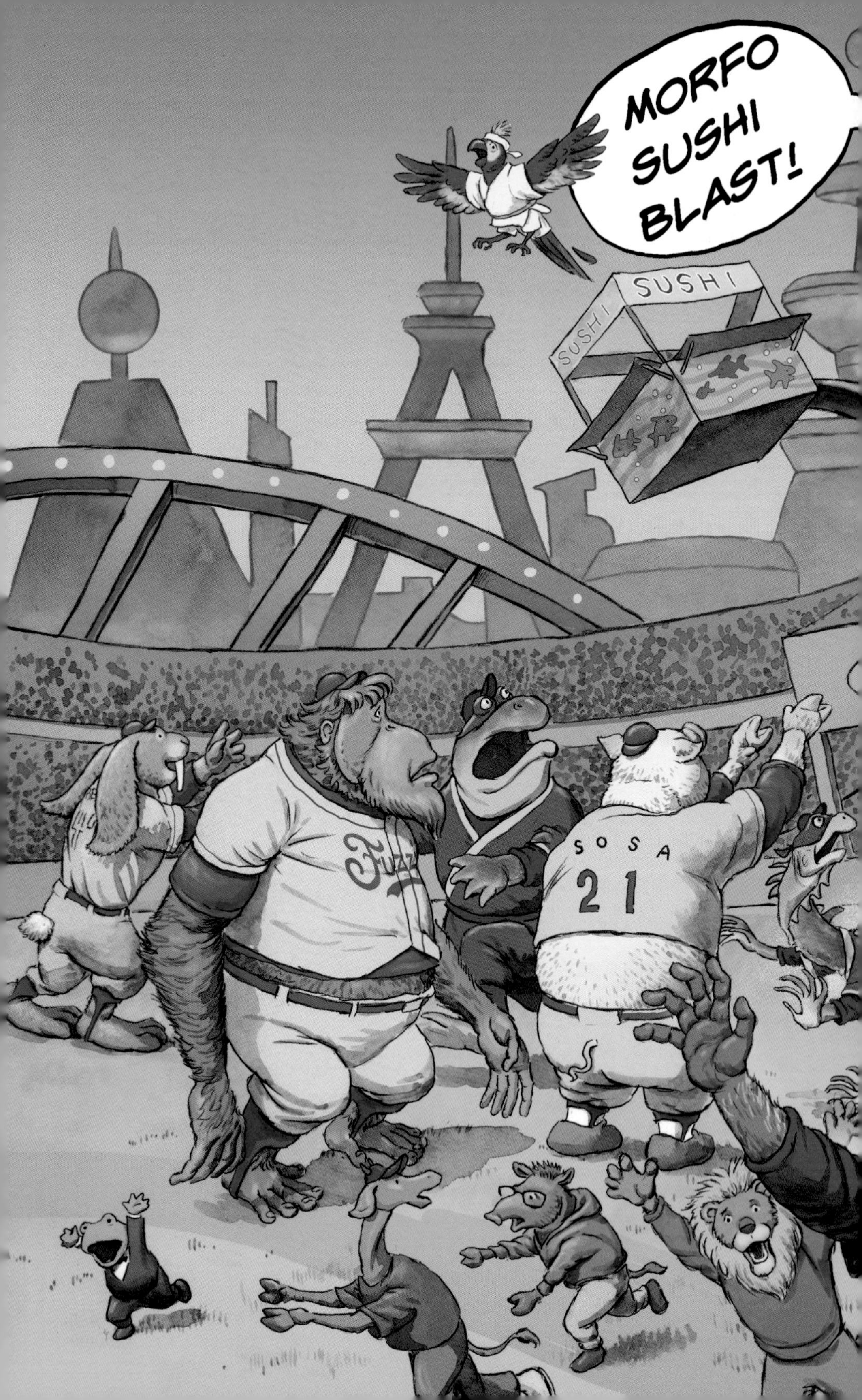
MORFO SUSHI BLAST!
SUSHI
SUSHI
SOSA
21

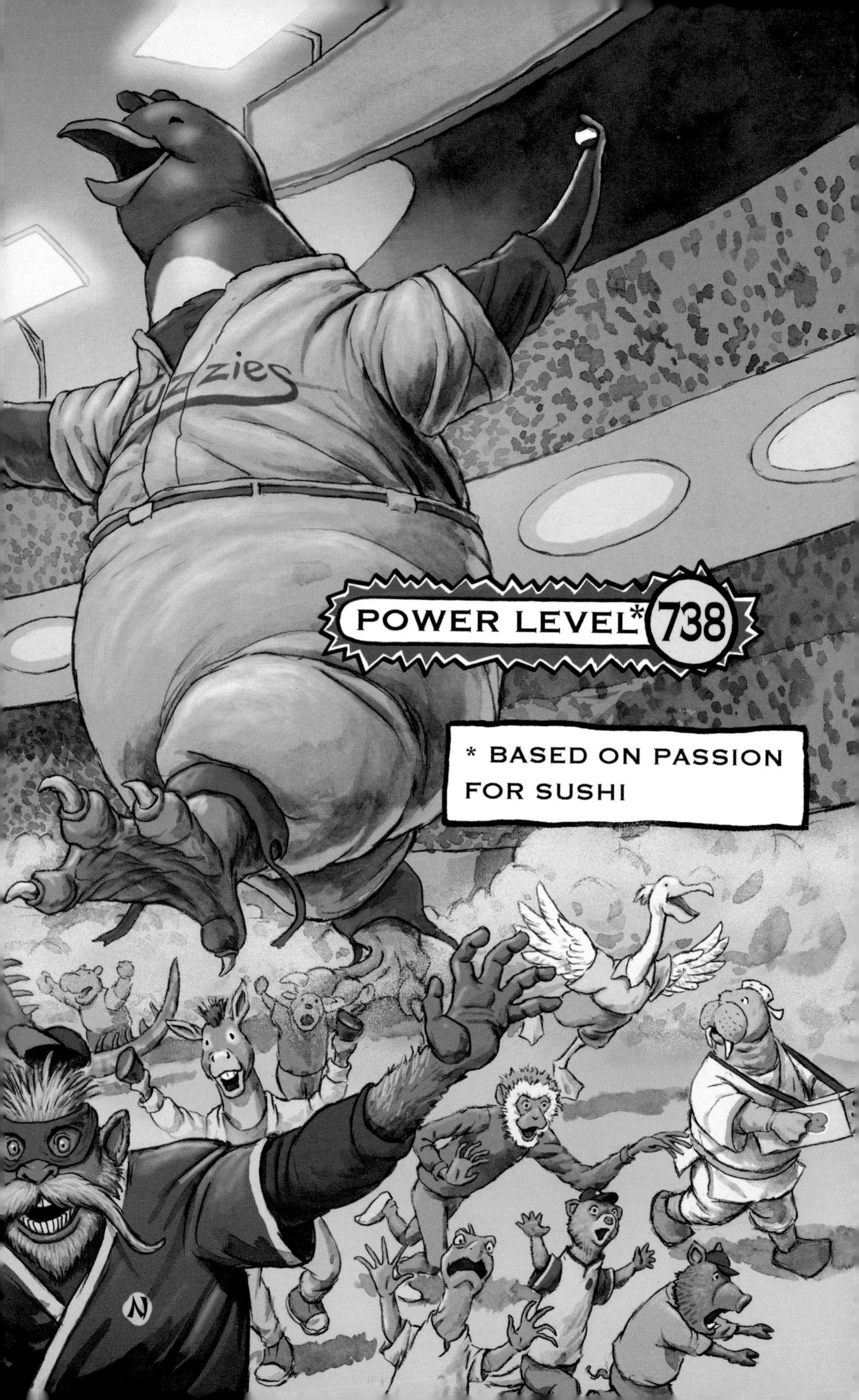
POWER LEVEL* 738
* BASED ON PASSION FOR SUSHI

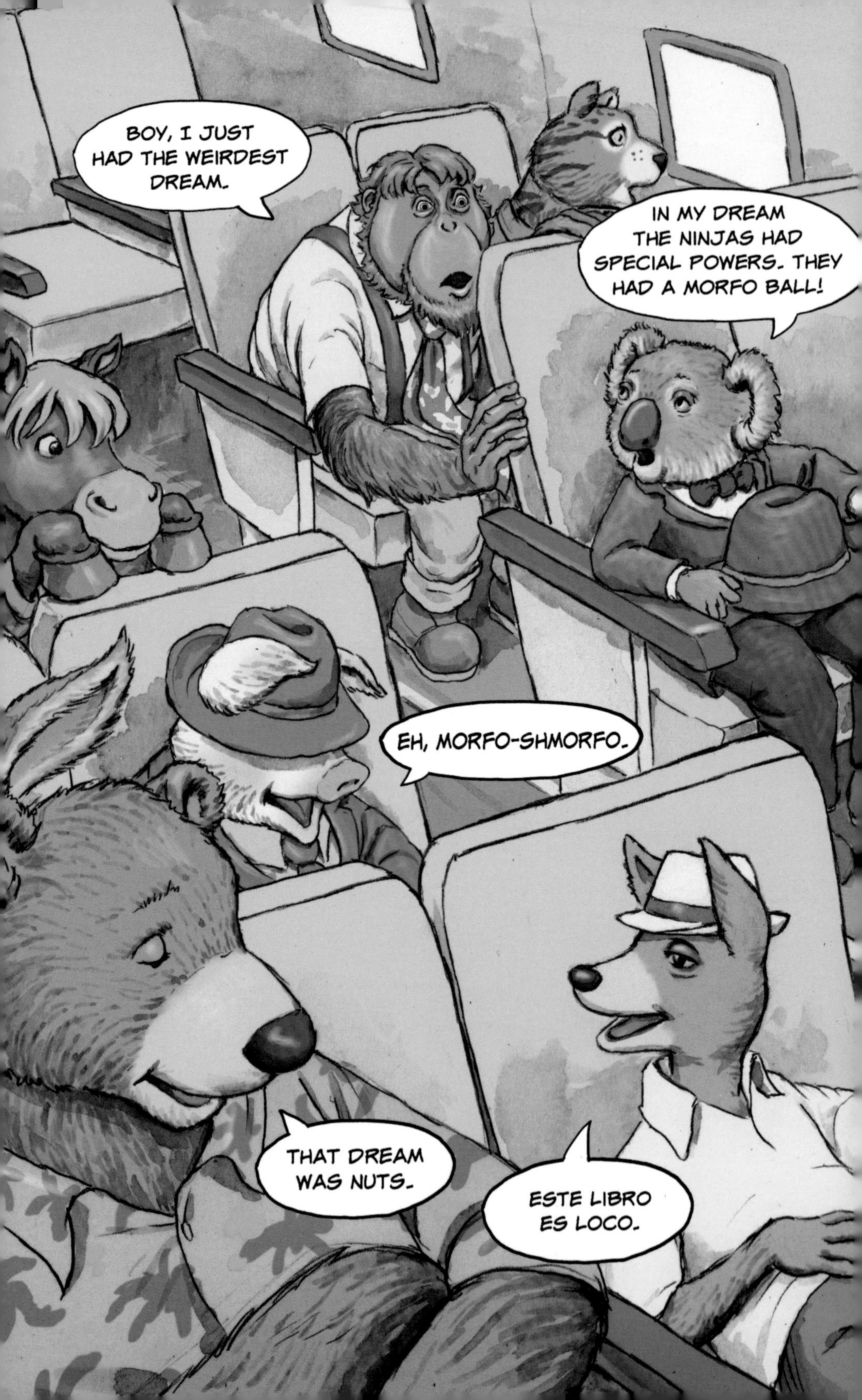
BOY, I JUST HAD THE WEIRDEST DREAM.
IN MY DREAM THE NINJAS HAD SPECIAL POWERS. THEY HAD A MORFO BALL!
EH, MORFO-SHMORFO.
THAT DREAM WAS NUTS.
ESTE LIBRO ES LOCO.

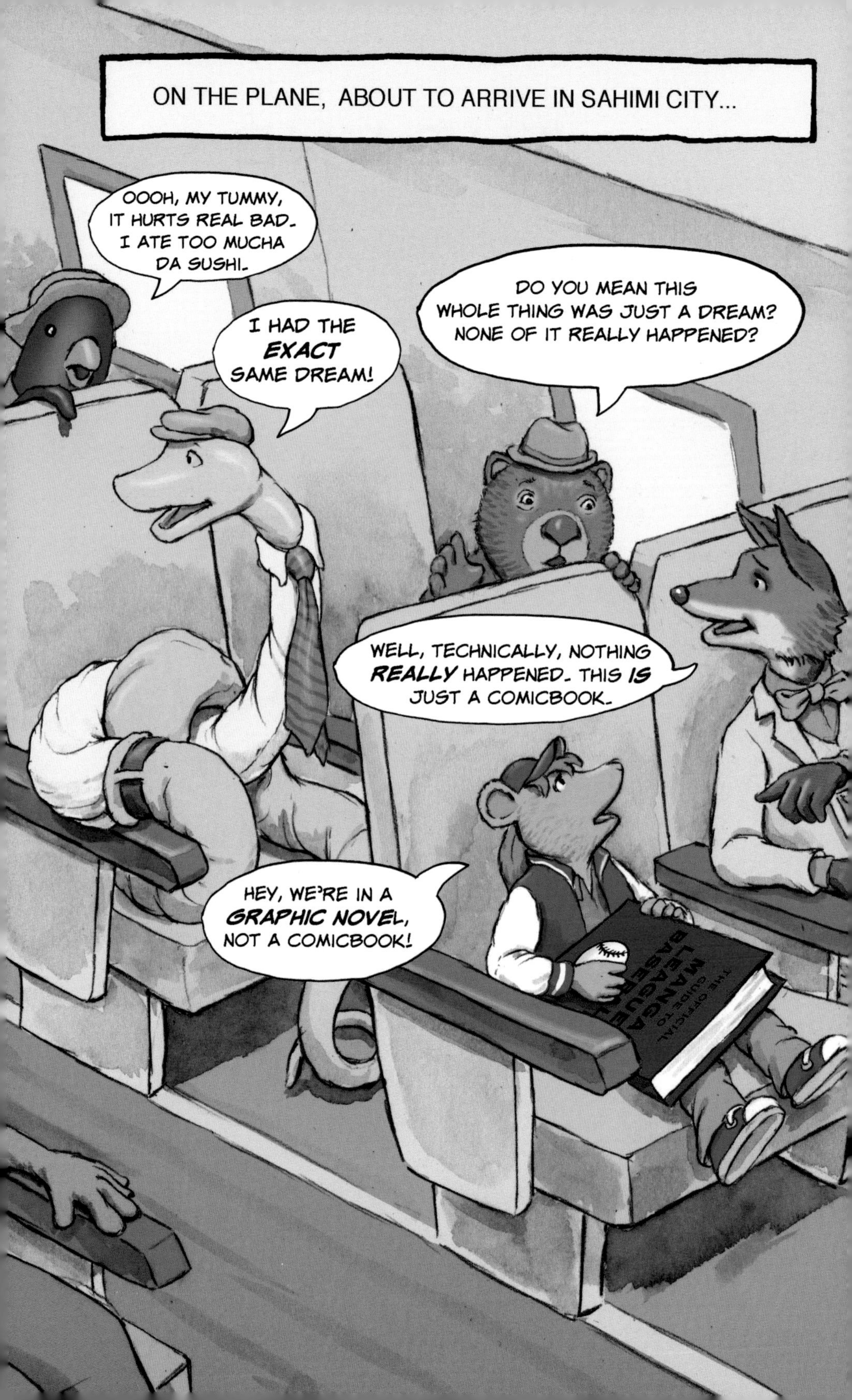
ON THE PLANE, ABOUT TO ARRIVE IN SAHIMI CITY...
OOOH, MY TUMMY, IT HURTS REAL BAD. I ATE TOO MUCHA DA SUSHI.
I HAD THE EXACT SAME DREAM!
DO YOU MEAN THIS WHOLE THING WAS JUST A DREAM? NONE OF IT REALLY HAPPENED?
WELL, TECHNICALLY, NOTHING REALLY HAPPENED. THIS IS JUST A COMICBOOK.
HEY, WE'RE IN A GRAPHIC NOVEL, NOT A COMICBOOK!
THE OFFICIAL GUIDE TO MANGA LEAGUE

THE END

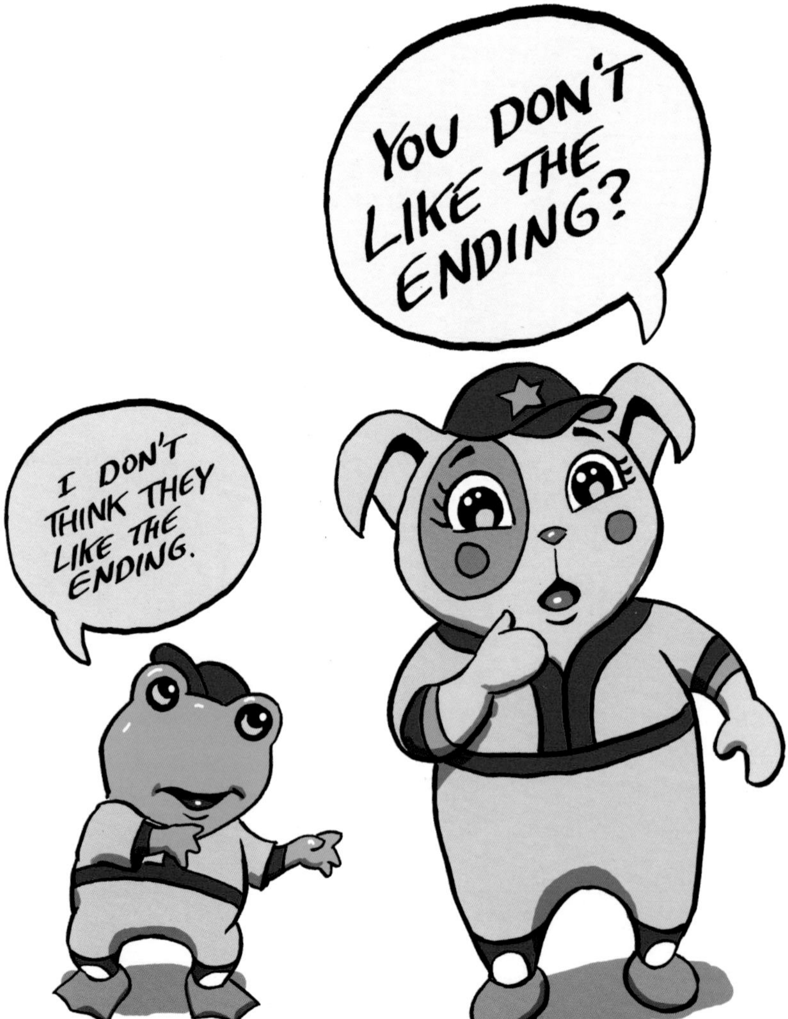
YOU DON'T LIKE THE ENDING?
I DON'T THINK THEY LIKE THE ENDING.

INSTANT REPLAY

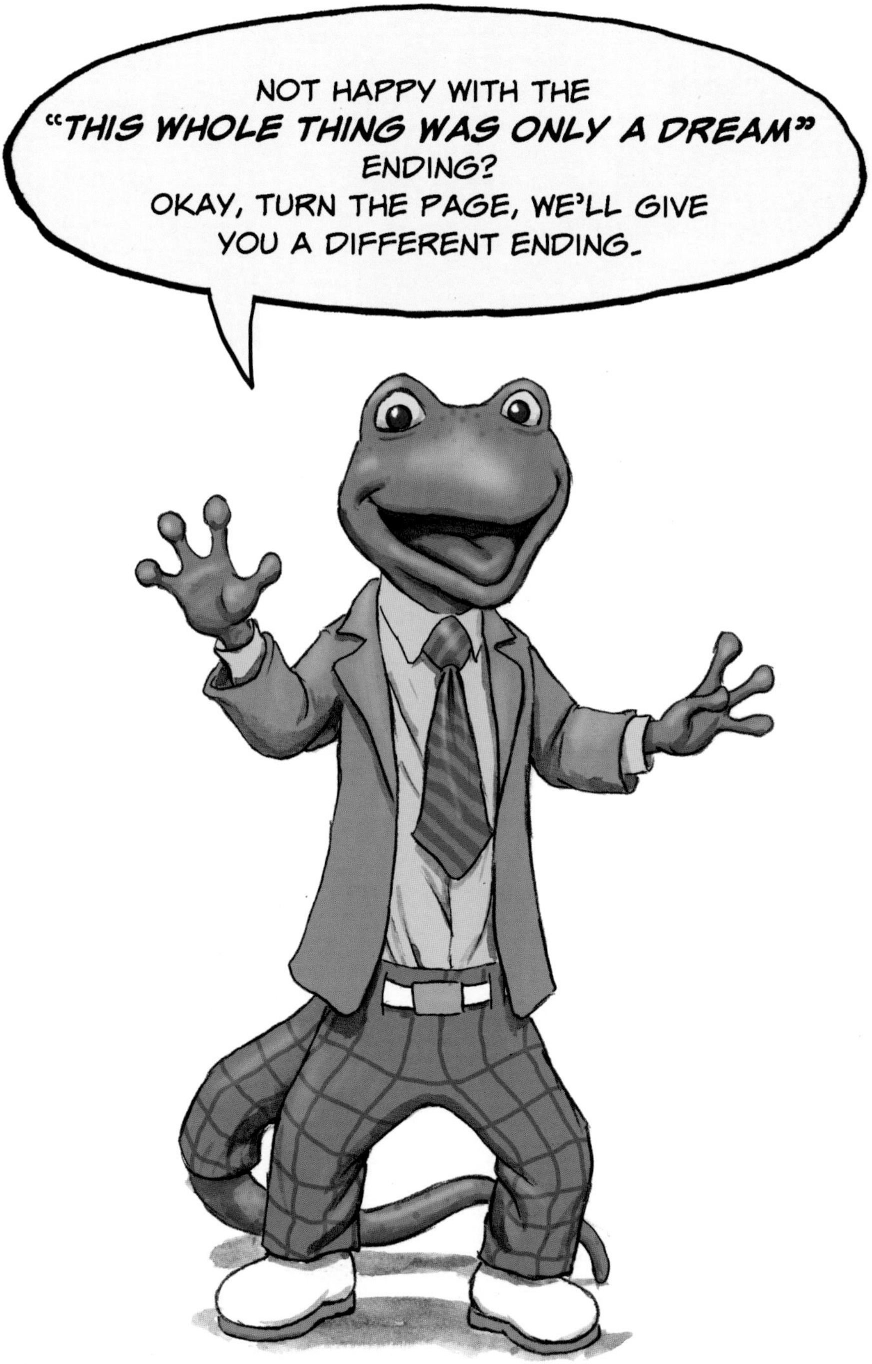
NOT HAPPY WITH THE
"THIS WHOLE THING WAS ONLY A DREAM"
ENDING?
OKAY, TURN THE PAGE, WE'LL GIVE
YOU A DIFFERENT ENDING.

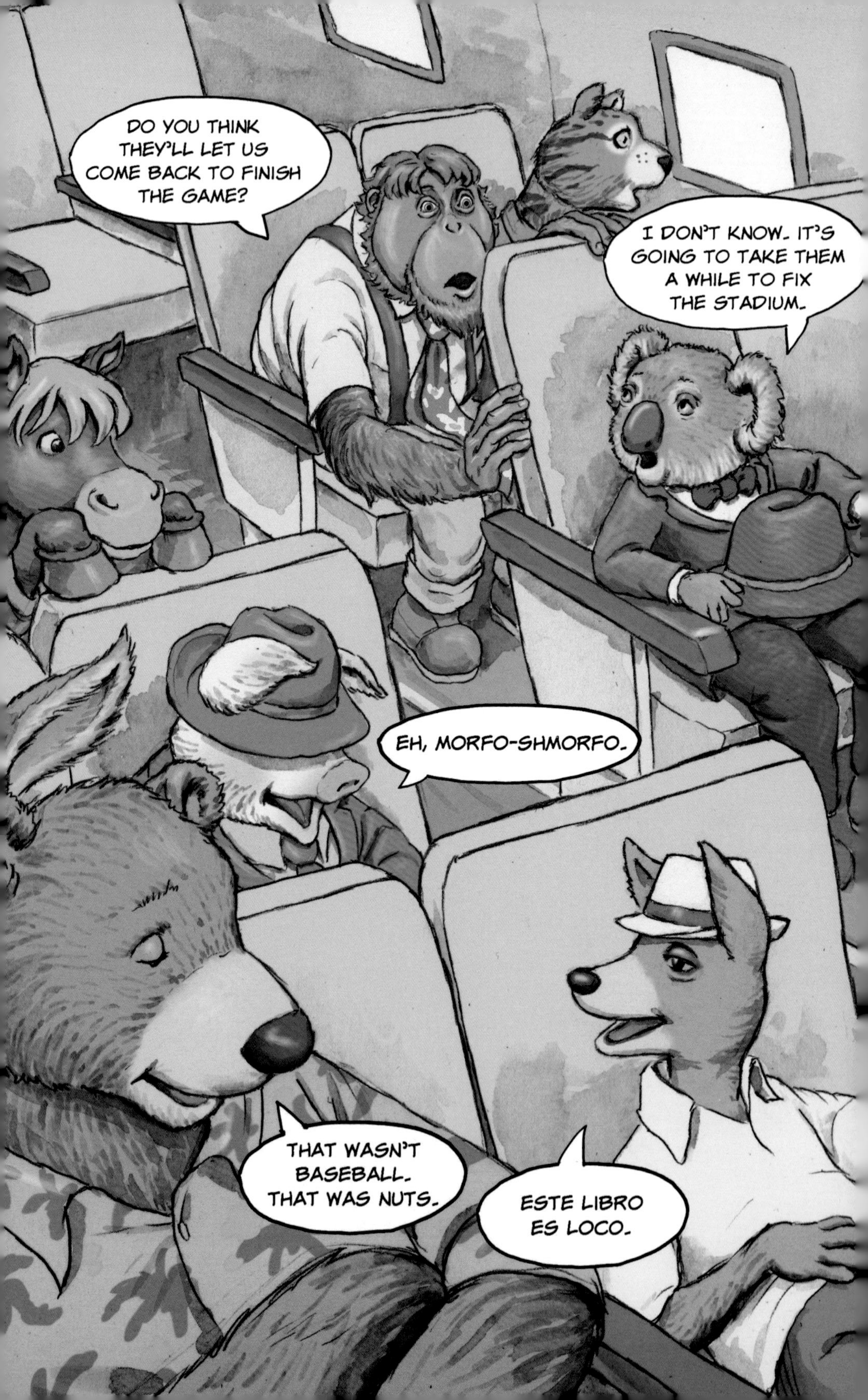
DO YOU THINK THEY'LL LET US COME BACK TO FINISH THE GAME?
I DON'T KNOW. IT'S GOING TO TAKE THEM A WHILE TO FIX THE STADIUM.
EH, MORFO-SHMORFO.
THAT WASN'T BASEBALL. THAT WAS NUTS.
ESTE LIBRO ES LOCO.

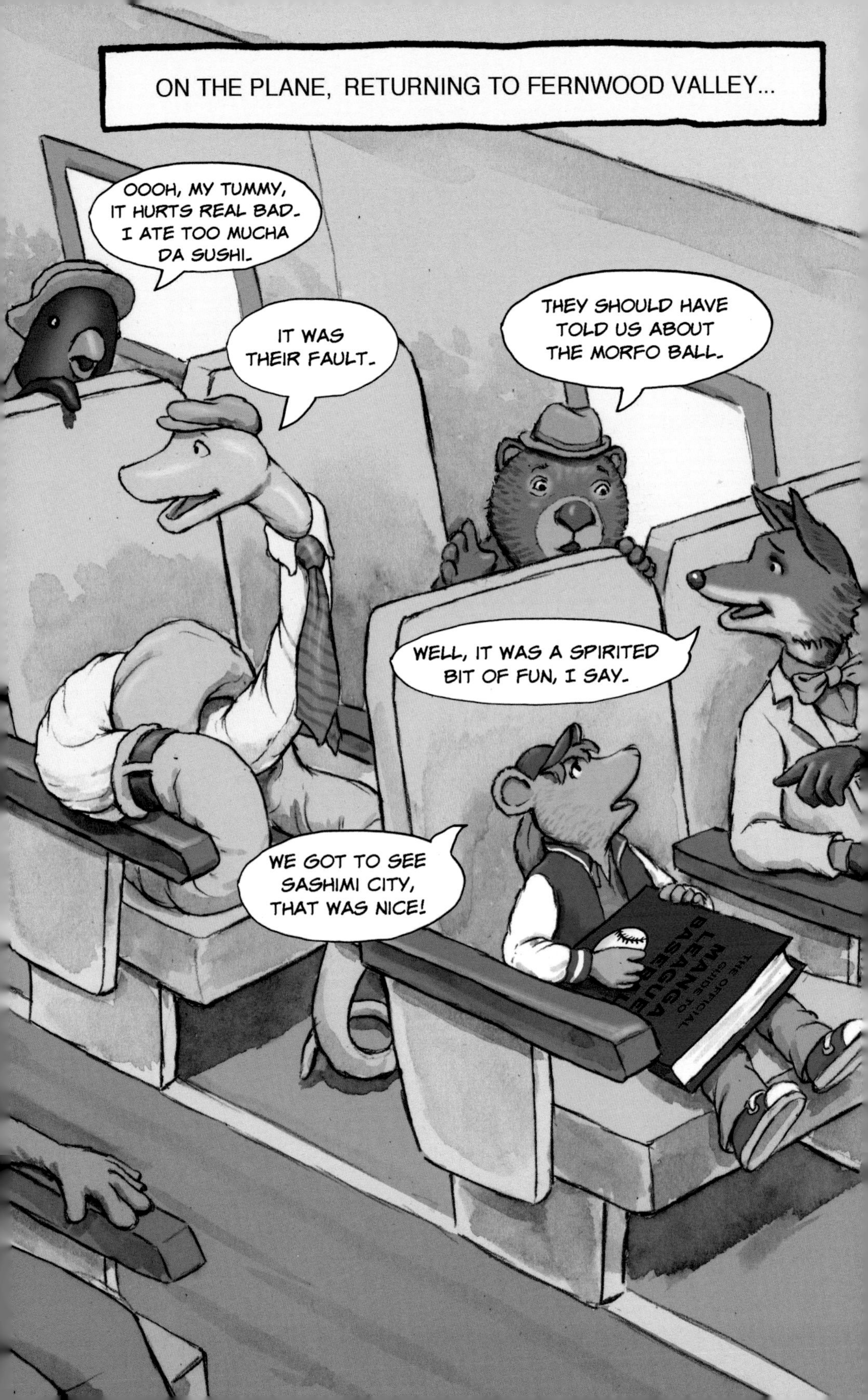
ON THE PLANE, RETURNING TO FERNWOOD VALLEY...
OOOH, MY TUMMY, IT HURTS REAL BAD. I ATE TOO MUCHA DA SUSHI.
IT WAS THEIR FAULT.
THEY SHOULD HAVE TOLD US ABOUT THE MORFO BALL.
WELL, IT WAS A SPIRITED BIT OF FUN, I SAY.
WE GOT TO SEE SASHIMI CITY, THAT WAS NICE!

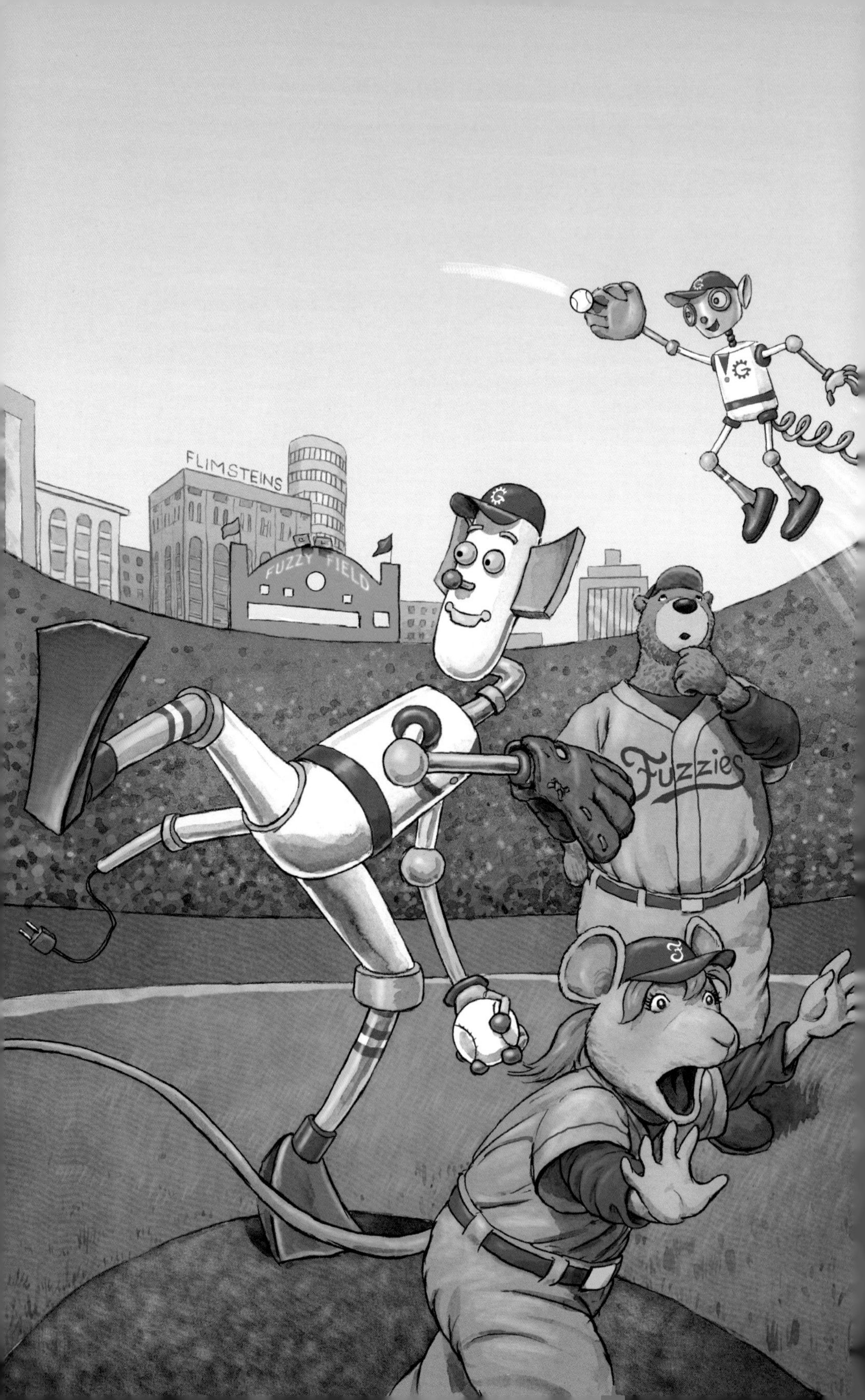
FLIMSTEINS
FUZZY FIELD
Fuzzies

Fuzzy Baseball

RBI robots

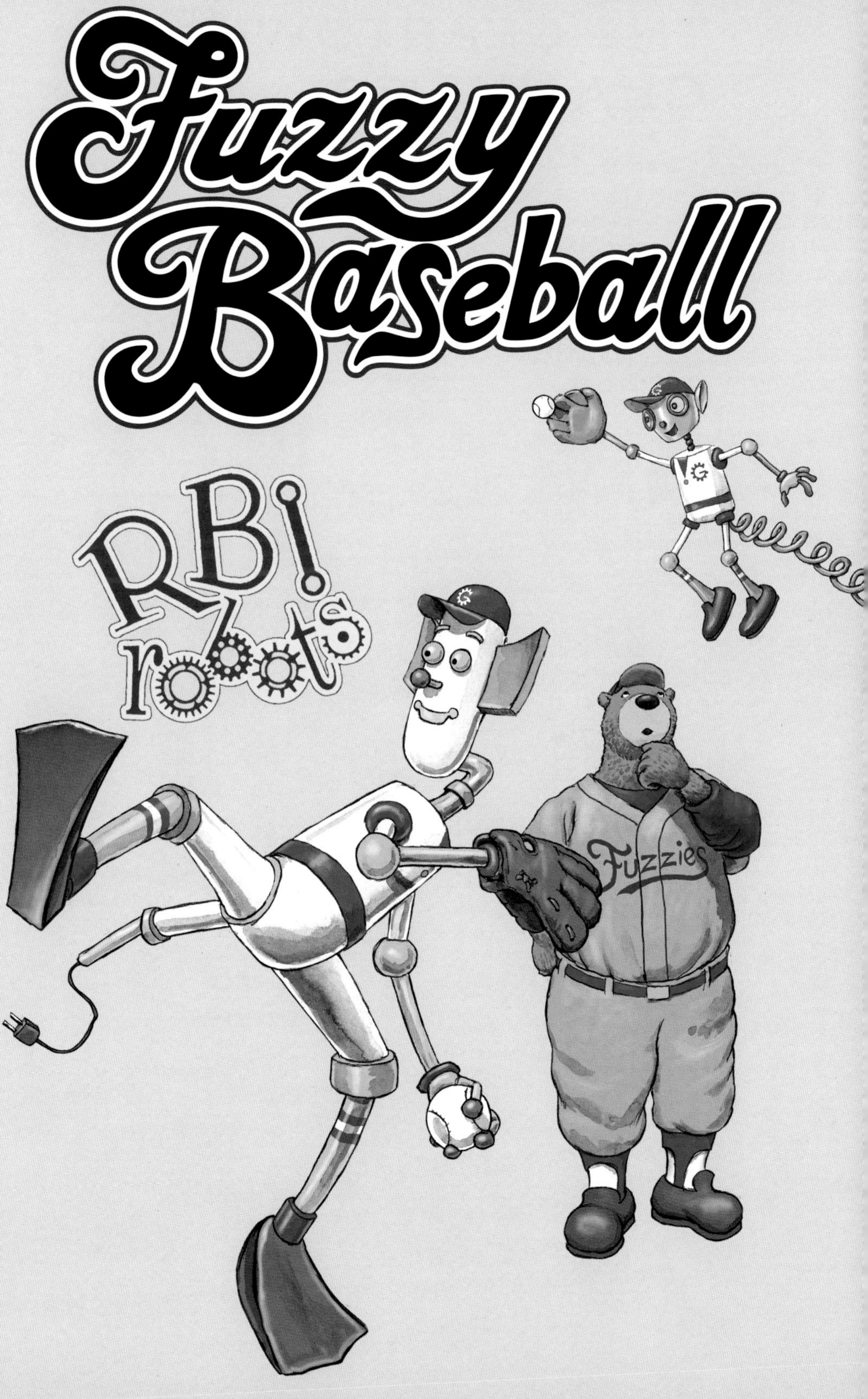
Fuzzies

THE GEARTOWN CLANKEES

#3 Harmon Kilowatt, third base
#4 Lou Gearig, right field
#5 Johnny Wrench, catcher
#9 Rotor Hornsby, pitcher
#10 Crusty Fob, left field
#13 Axel Rod Regrease, shortstop
#15 Ty Cog, left field
#19 Greg Pluginsky, second base
#20 Clunky Dent, Manager
#24 Cyborg Young, pitcher
#25 Spark McPlyer, first base
#33 Honus Wingnut, right field
#34 Kirby Sprocket, pitcher
#44 Crank Aaron, center field
#55 Techy Matsui, third base

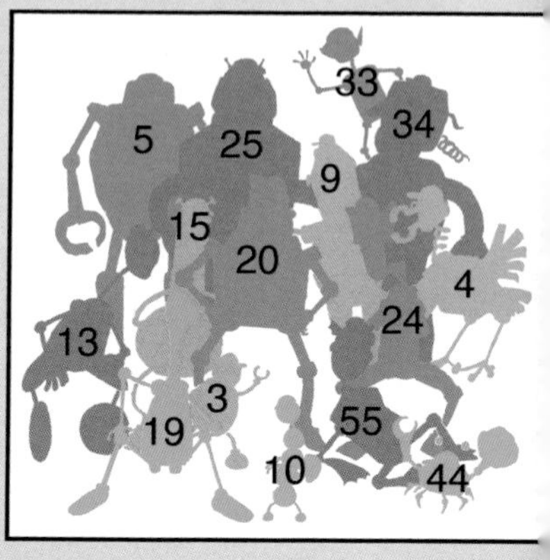
33
34
5
25
9
15
20
4
24
13
3
19
55
10
44

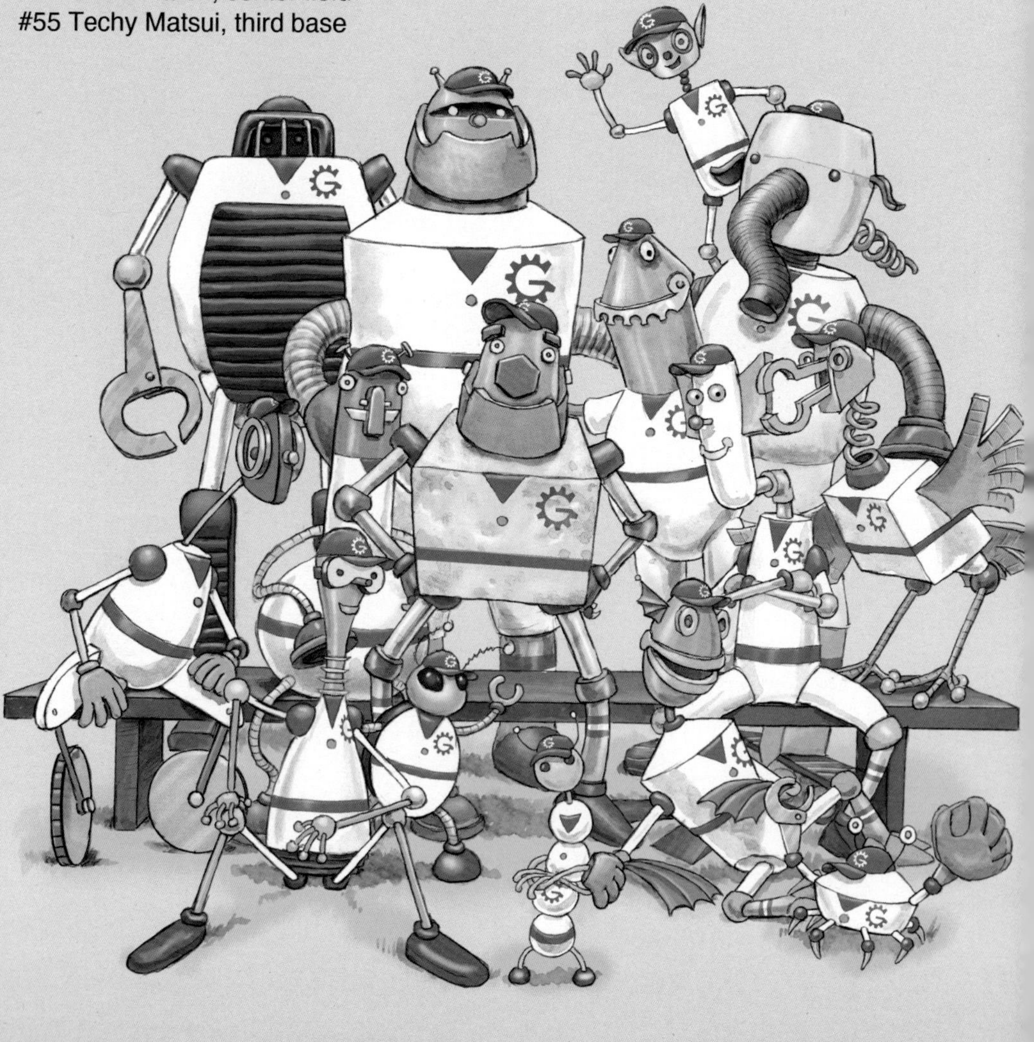

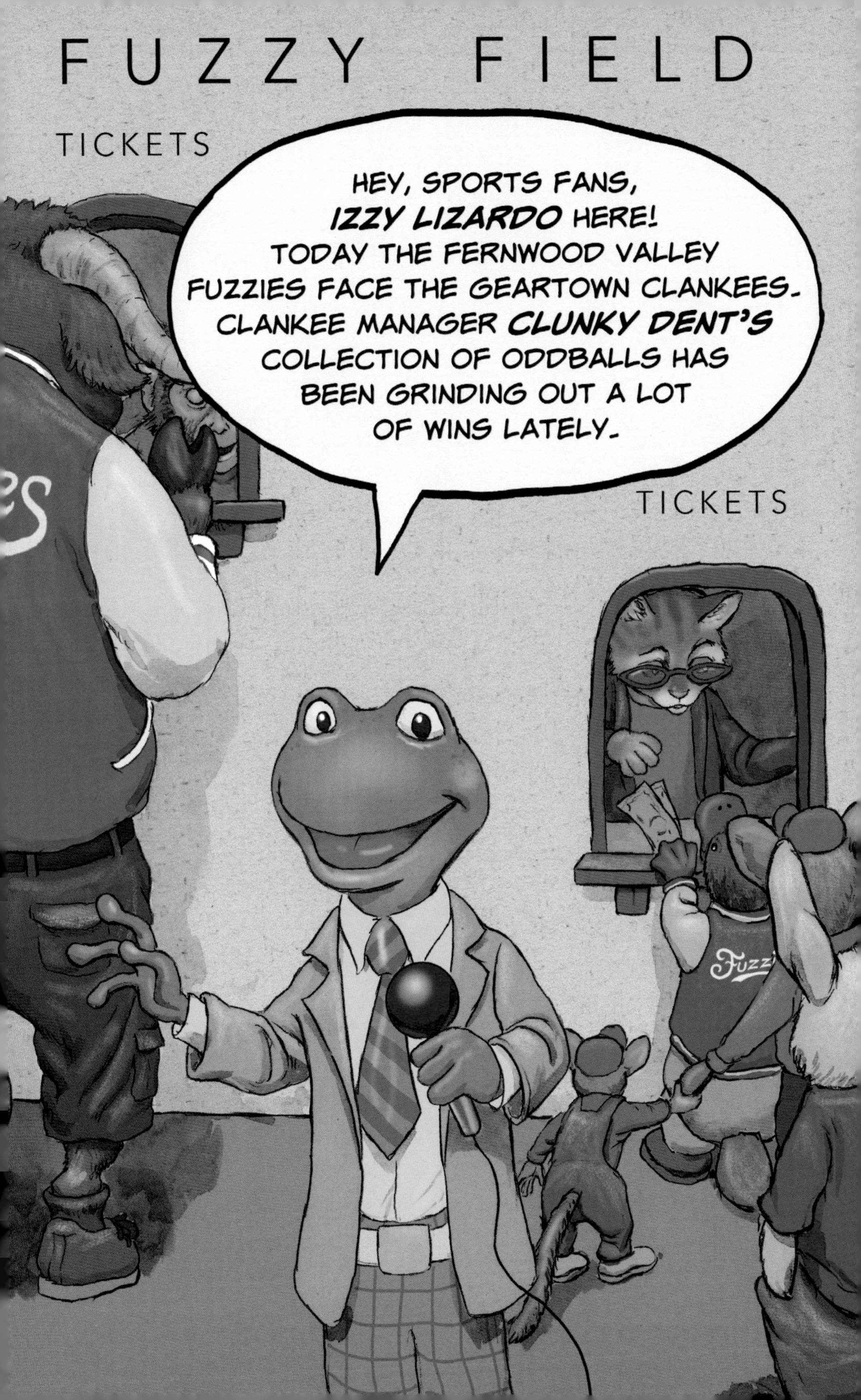
FUZZY FIELD
TICKETS
HEY, SPORTS FANS, IZZY LIZARDO HERE! TODAY THE FERNWOOD VALLEY FUZZIES FACE THE GEARTOWN CLANKEES. CLANKEE MANAGER CLUNKY DENT'S COLLECTION OF ODDBALLS HAS BEEN GRINDING OUT A LOT OF WINS LATELY.
TICKETS

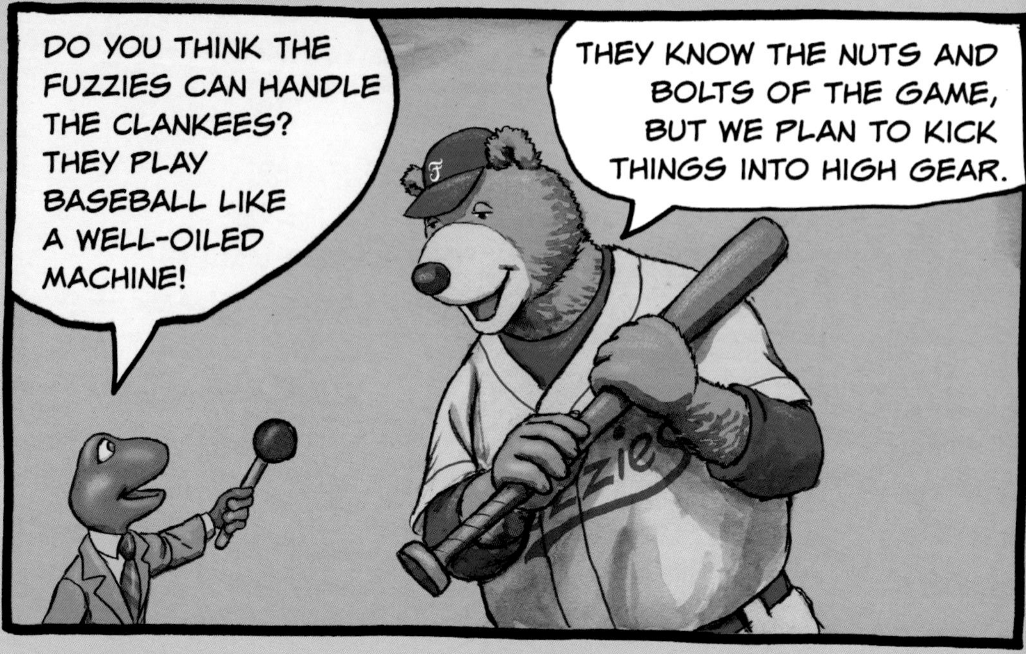
DO YOU THINK THE FUZZIES CAN HANDLE THE CLANKEES? THEY PLAY BASEBALL LIKE A WELL-OILED MACHINE!
THEY KNOW THE NUTS AND BOLTS OF THE GAME, BUT WE PLAN TO KICK THINGS INTO HIGH GEAR.

INTRODUCING THE GEARTOWN CLANKEES...

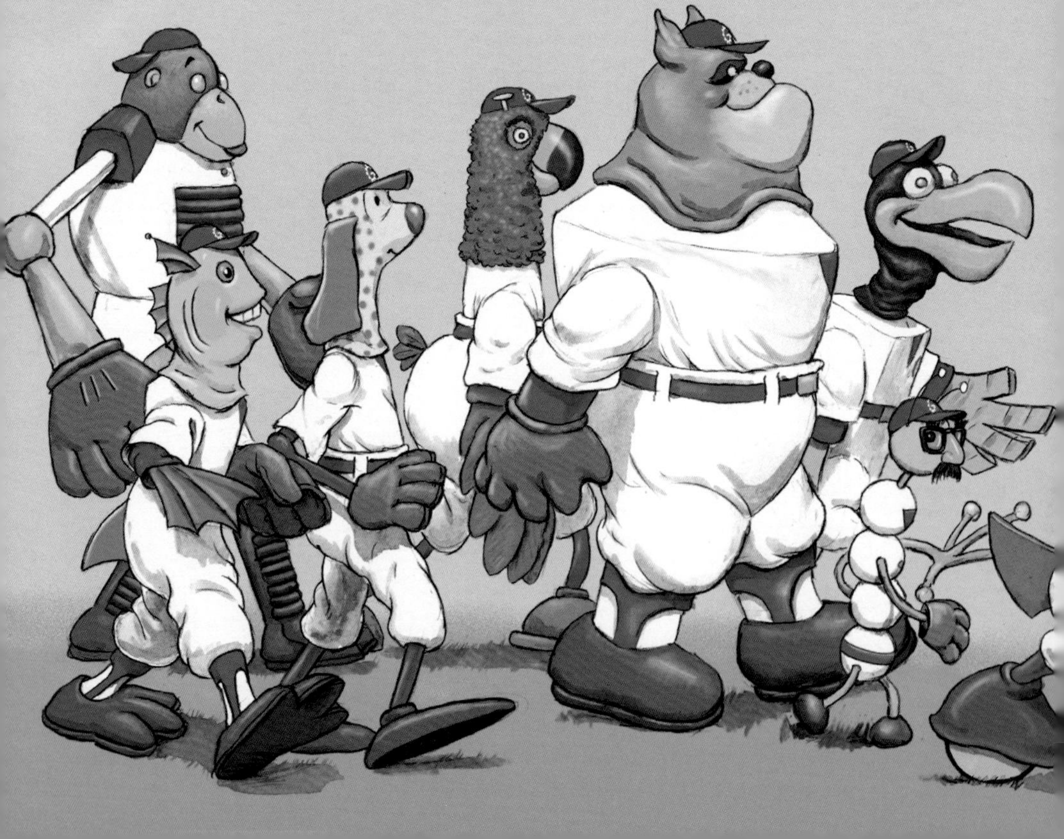

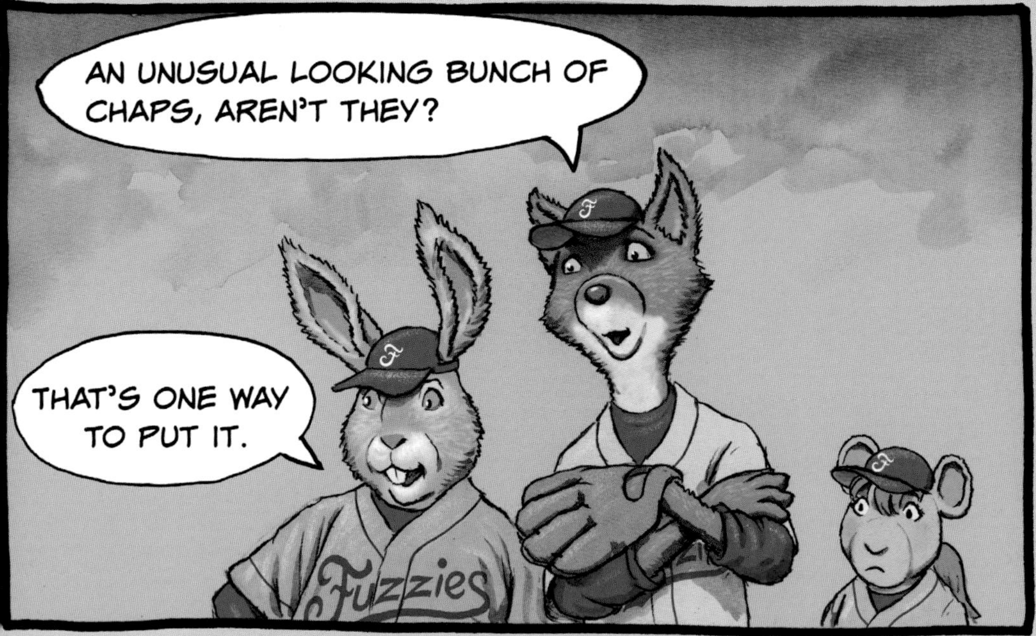
AN UNUSUAL LOOKING BUNCH OF CHAPS, AREN'T THEY?
THAT'S ONE WAY TO PUT IT.
Fuzzies

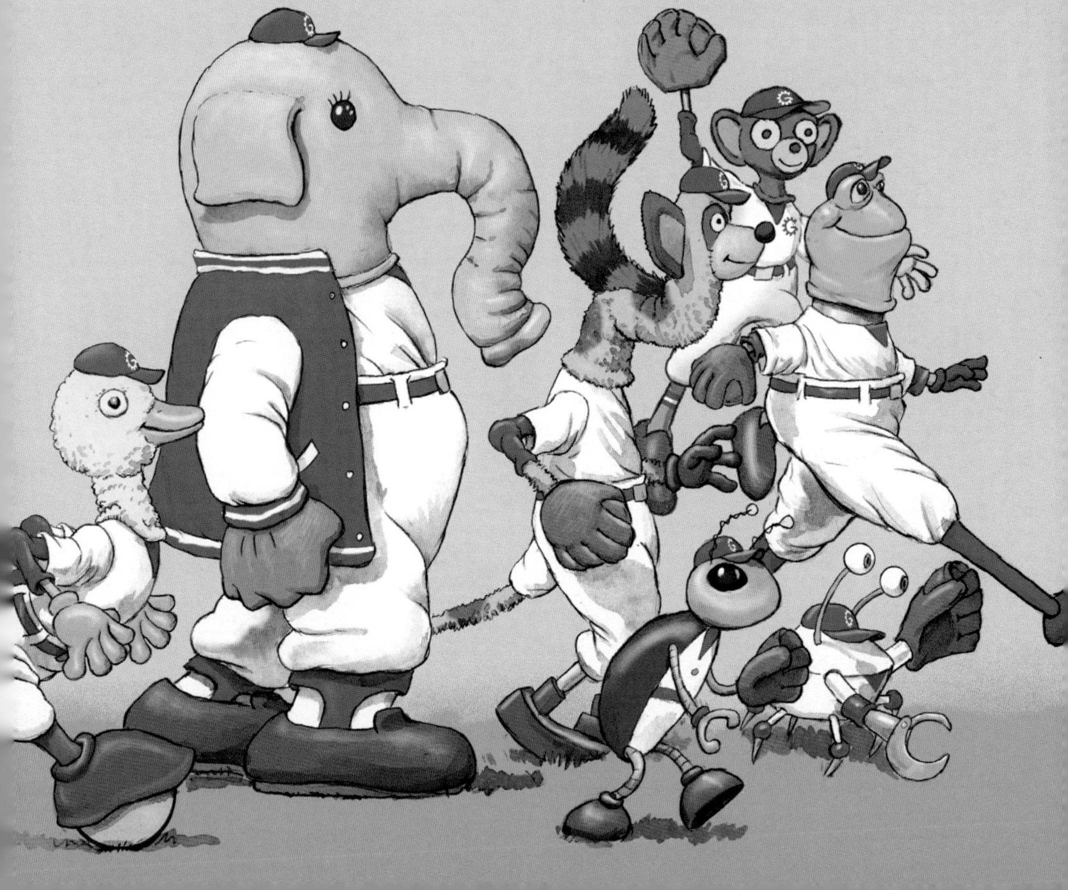

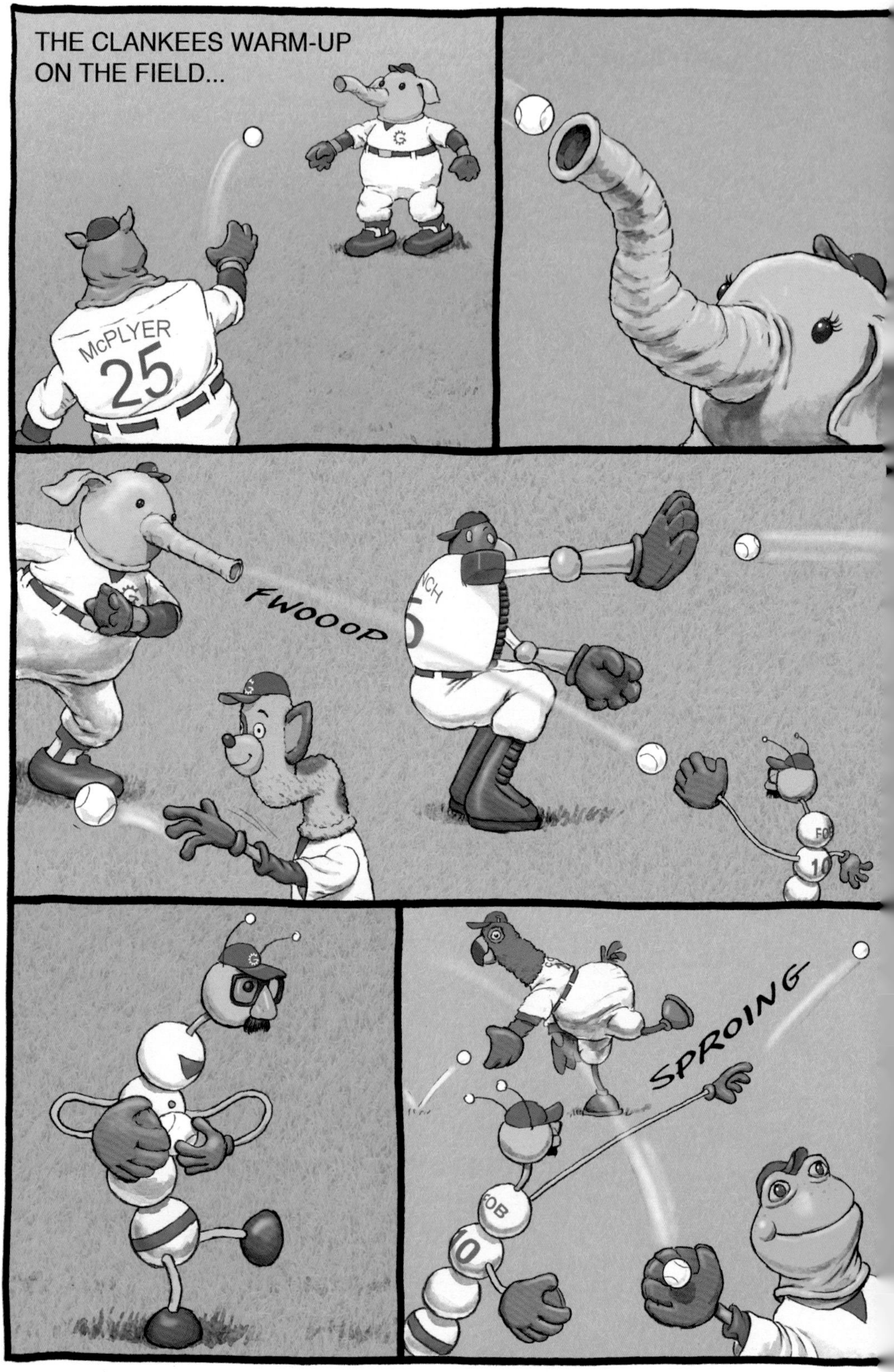
THE CLANKEES WARM-UP ON THE FIELD...
McPLYER
25
FWOOOP
SPROING

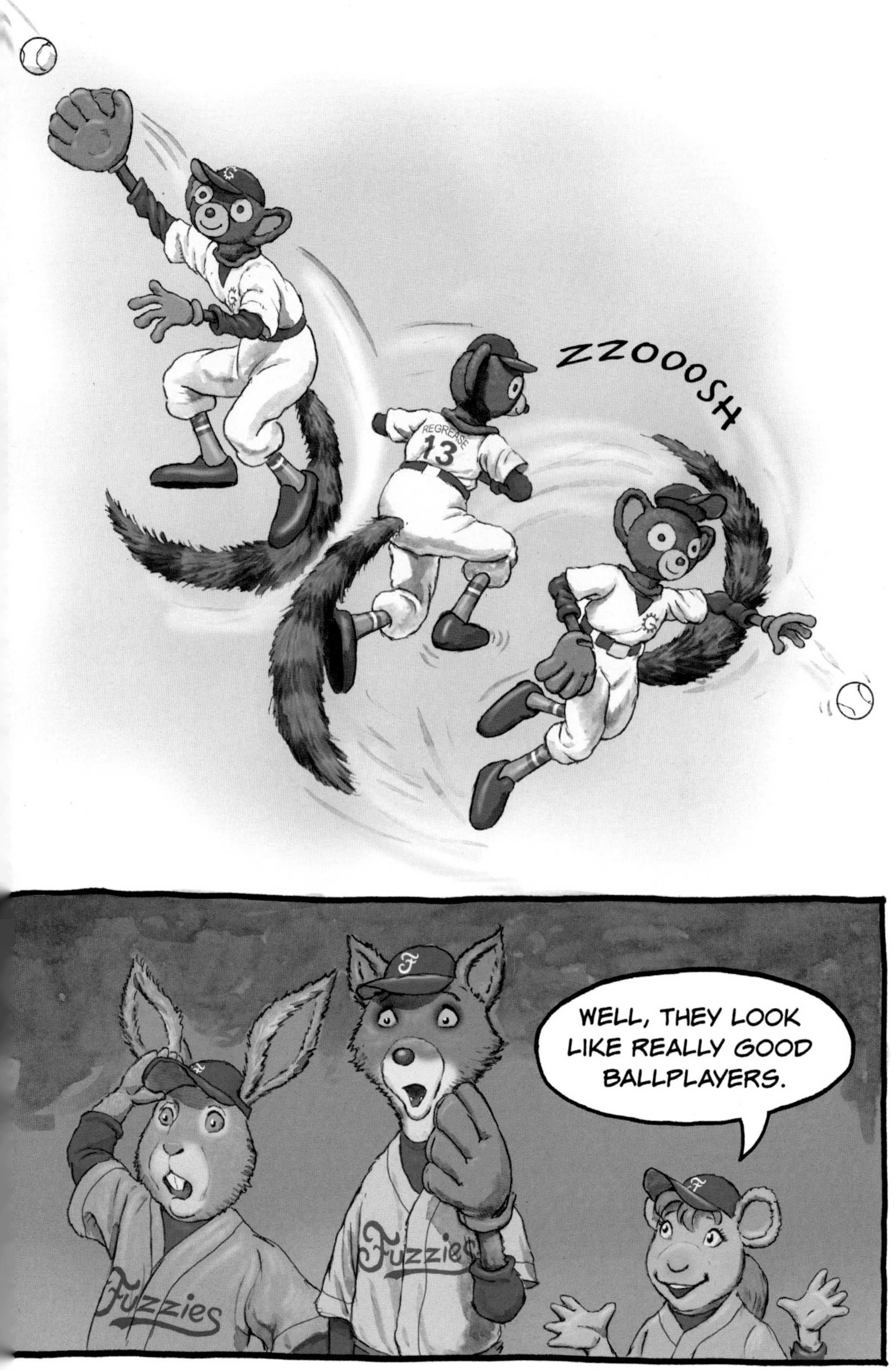
ZZOOOOSH
REGREASE
13
Fuzzies
Fuzzies
WELL, THEY LOOK LIKE REALLY GOOD BALLPLAYERS.

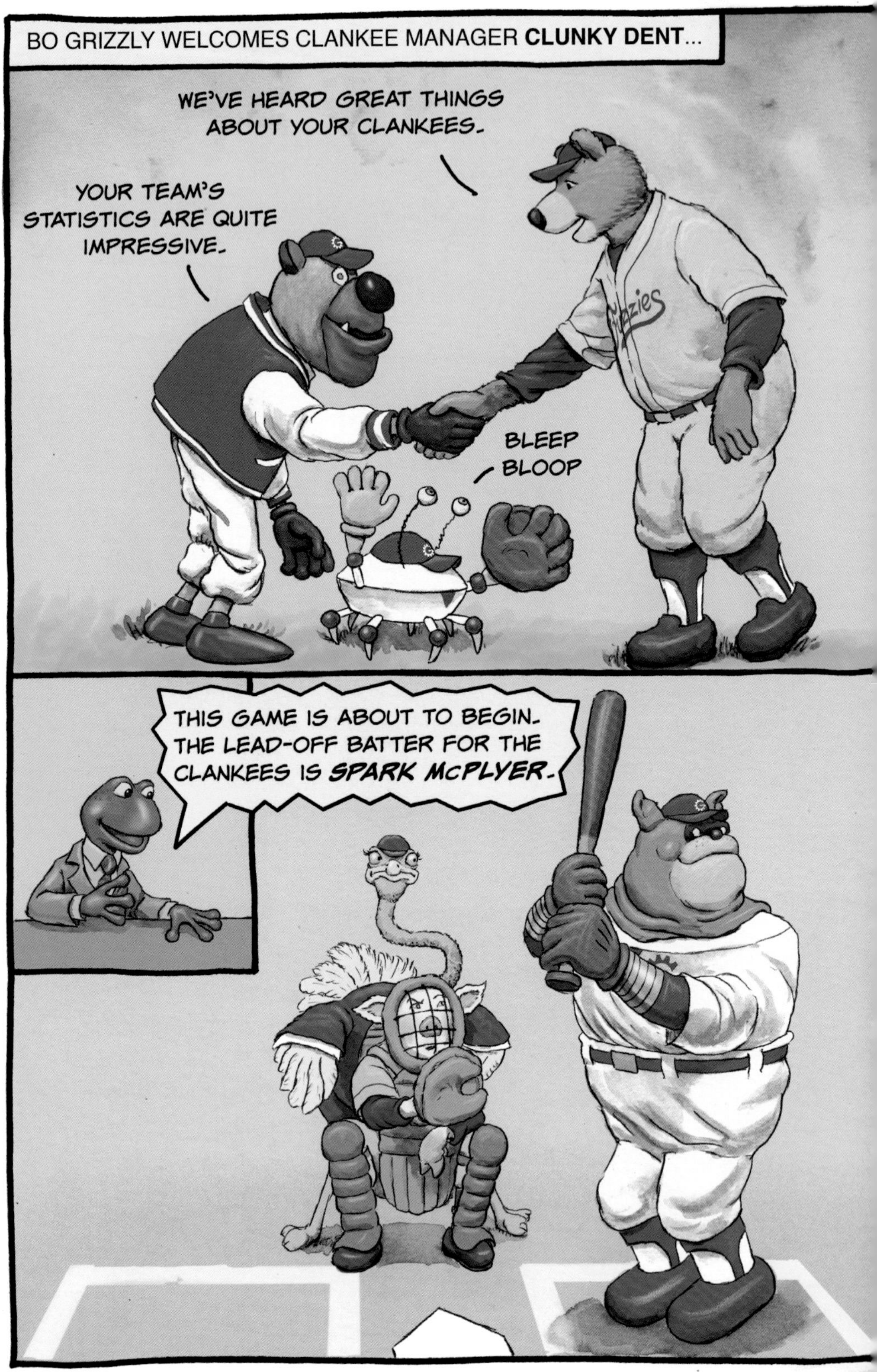

BO GRIZZLY WELCOMES CLANKEE MANAGER **CLUNKY DENT**...
WE'VE HEARD GREAT THINGS ABOUT YOUR CLANKEES.
YOUR TEAM'S STATISTICS ARE QUITE IMPRESSIVE.
BLEEP BLOOP
THIS GAME IS ABOUT TO BEGIN. THE LEAD-OFF BATTER FOR THE CLANKEES IS *SPARK McPLYER*.

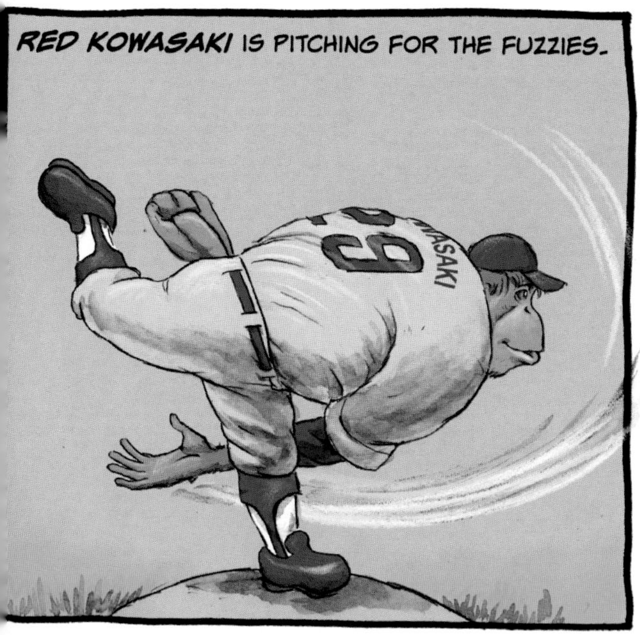
RED KOWASAKI IS PITCHING FOR THE FUZZIES.
KOWASAKI
69

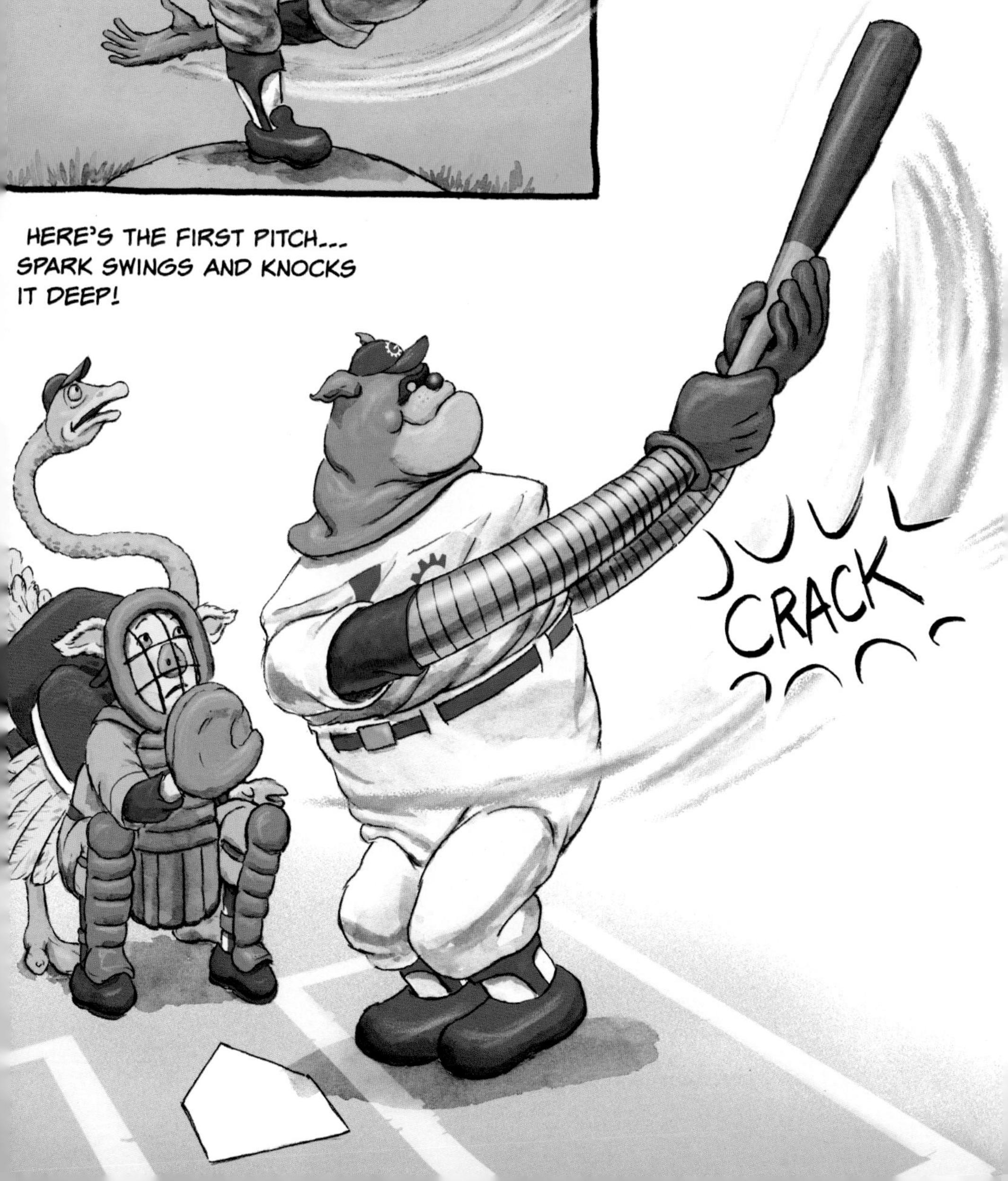
HERE'S THE FIRST PITCH... SPARK SWINGS AND KNOCKS IT DEEP!
CRACK

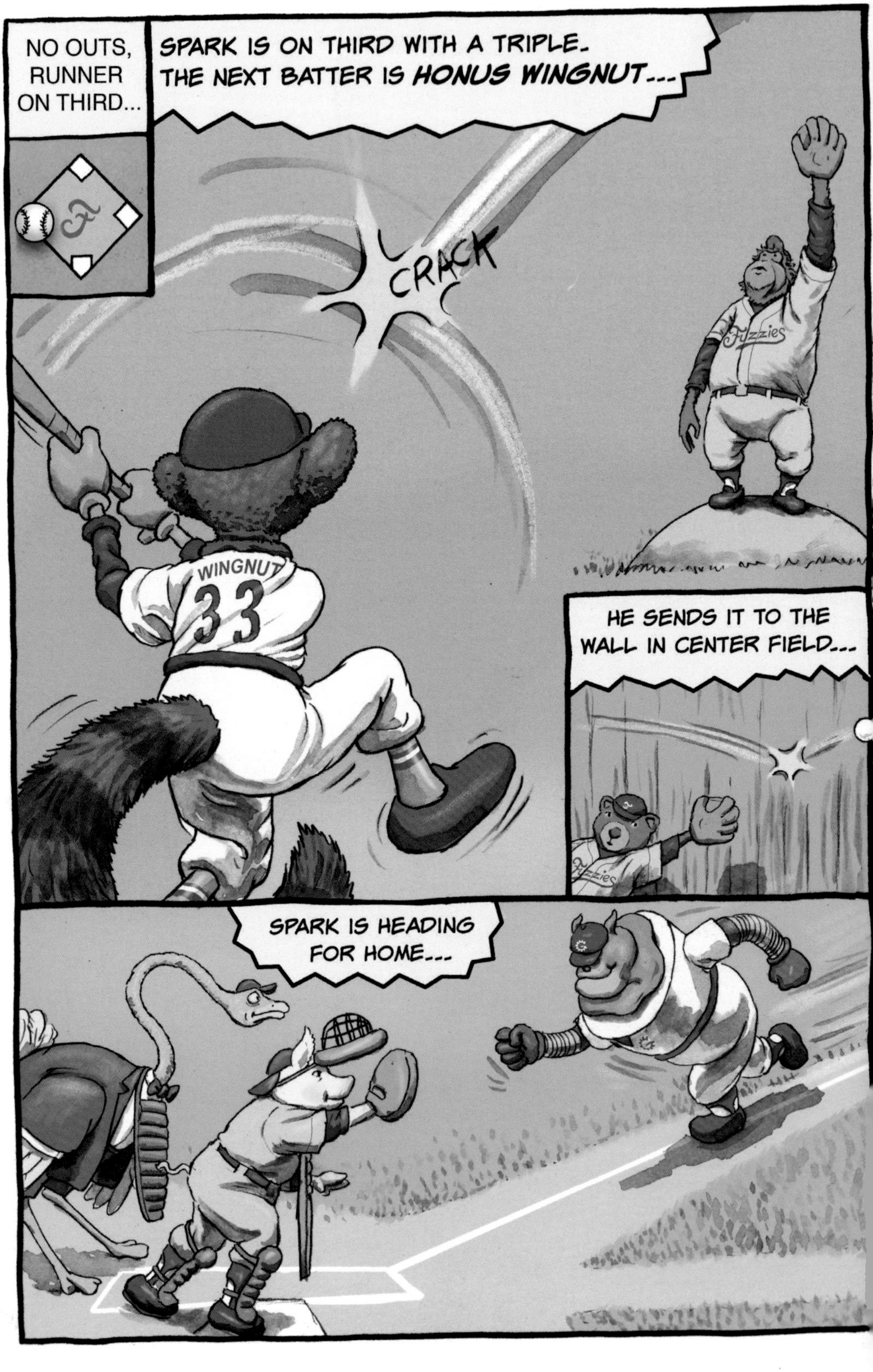
NO OUTS, RUNNER ON THIRD...
SPARK IS ON THIRD WITH A TRIPLE. THE NEXT BATTER IS HONUS WINGNUT...
CRACK
Fuzzies
WINGNUT
33
HE SENDS IT TO THE WALL IN CENTER FIELD...
Fuzzies
SPARK IS HEADING FOR HOME...

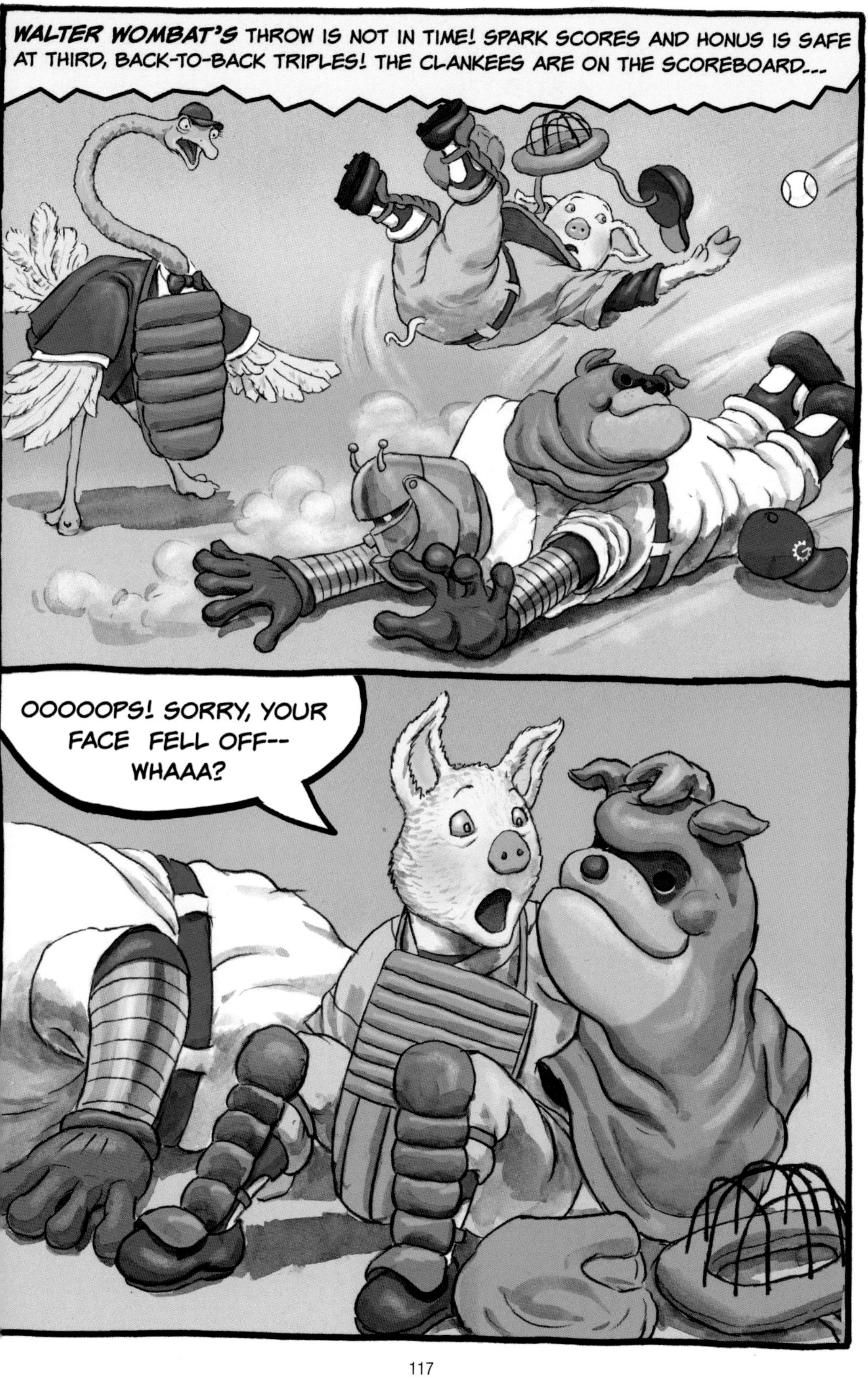
WALTER WOMBAT'S THROW IS NOT IN TIME! SPARK SCORES AND HONUS IS SAFE AT THIRD, BACK-TO-BACK TRIPLES! THE CLANKEES ARE ON THE SCOREBOARD...
OOOOOPS! SORRY, YOUR FACE FELL OFF-- WHAAA?

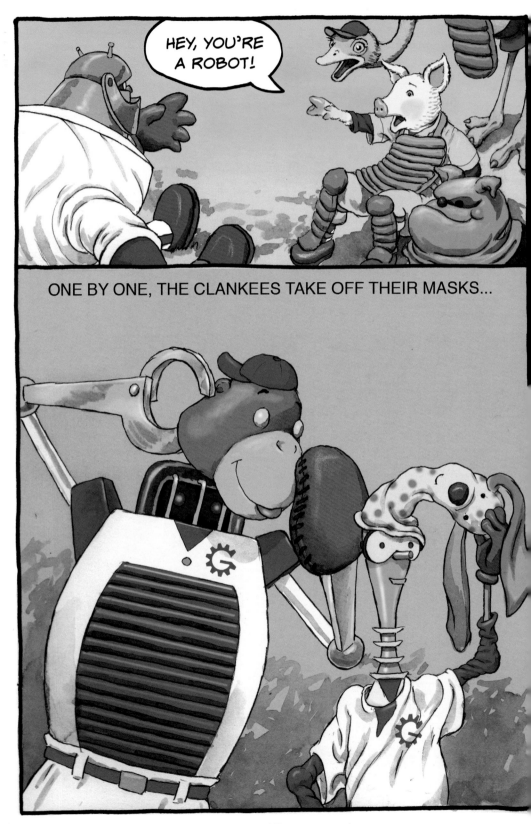

ONE BY ONE, THE CLANKEES TAKE OFF THEIR MASKS...

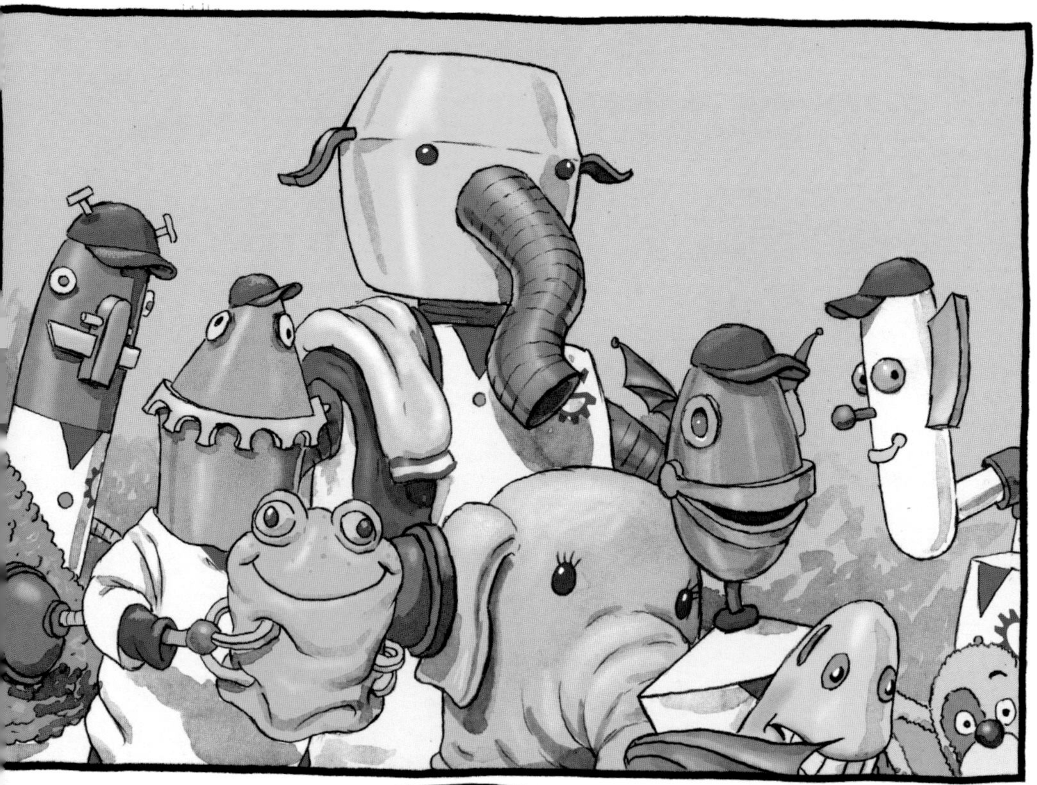

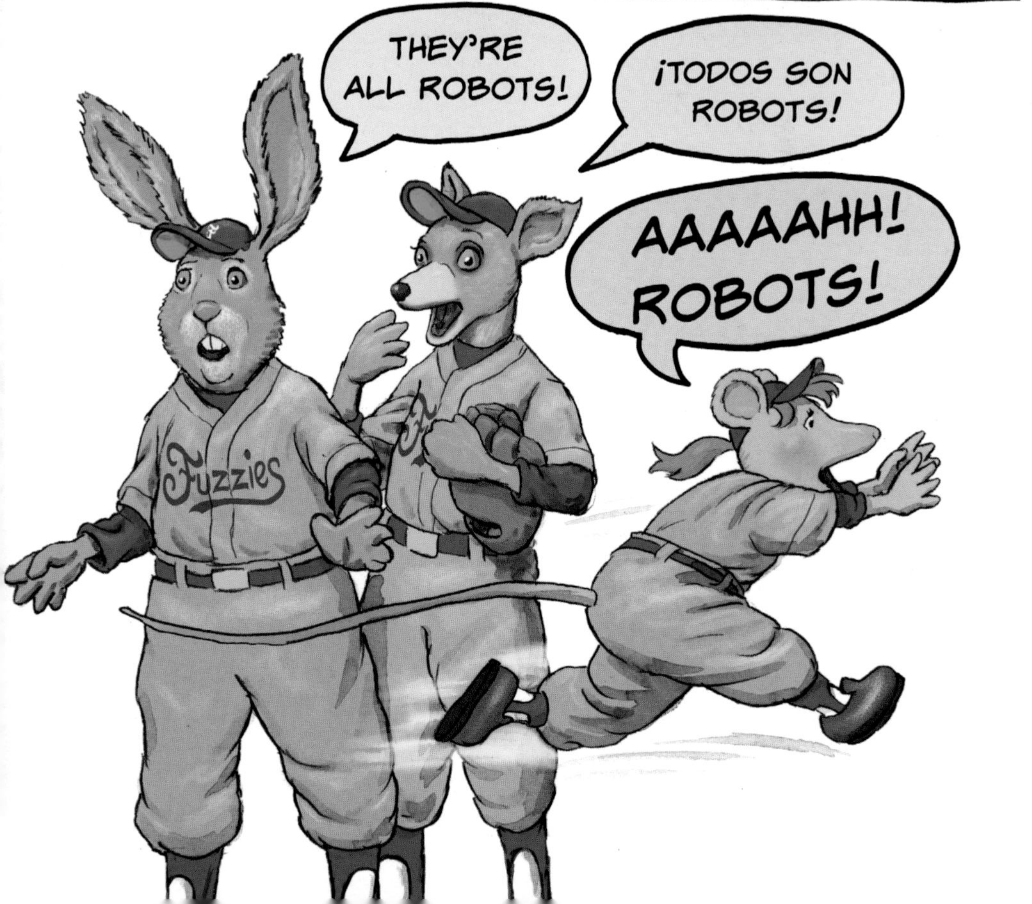
THEY'RE ALL ROBOTS!
¡TODOS SON ROBOTS!
AAAAAHH! ROBOTS!
Fuzzies

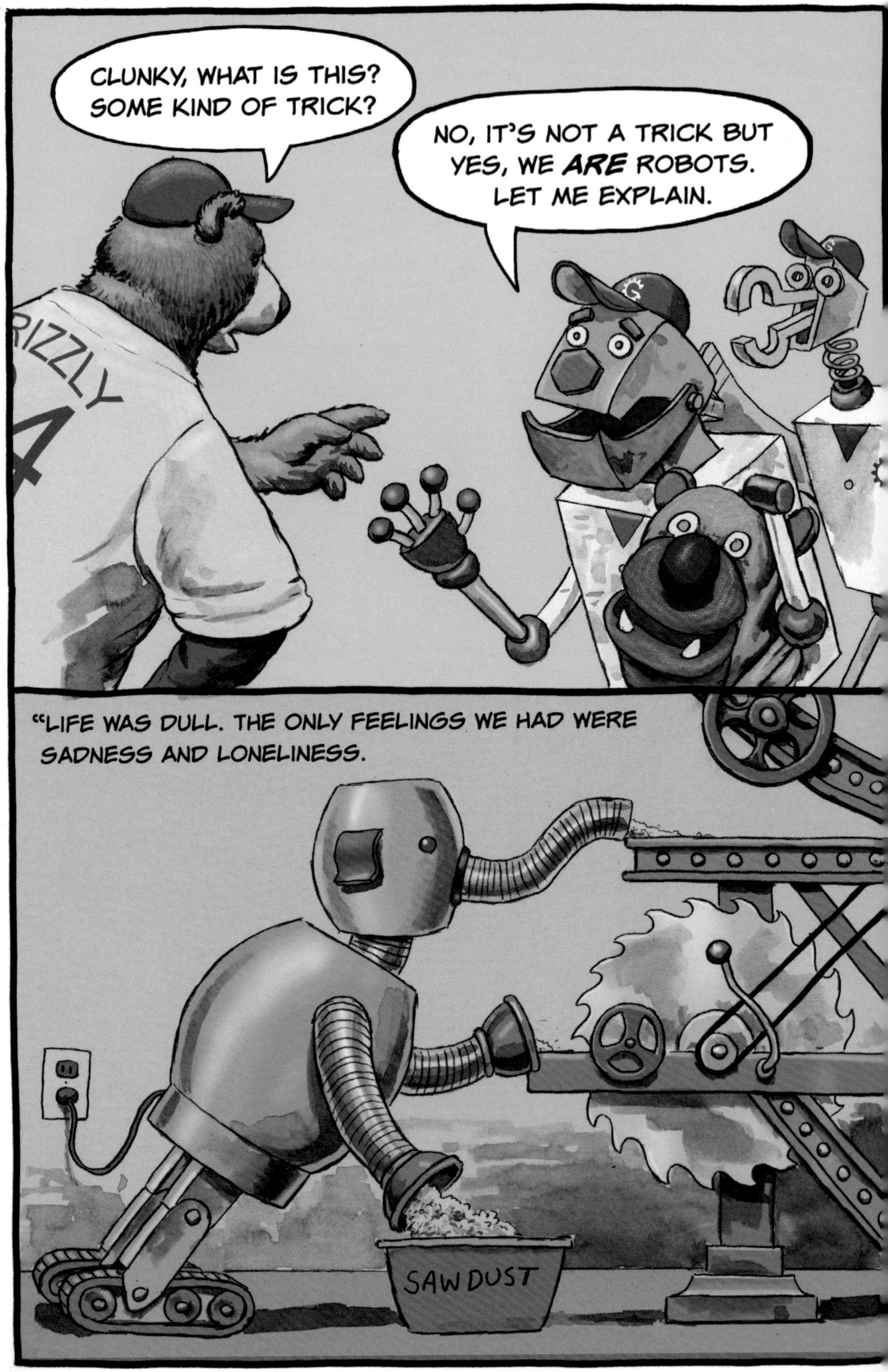
CLUNKY, WHAT IS THIS? SOME KIND OF TRICK?
NO, IT'S NOT A TRICK BUT YES, WE **ARE** ROBOTS. LET ME EXPLAIN.
RIZZLY
4
"LIFE WAS DULL. THE ONLY FEELINGS WE HAD WERE SADNESS AND LONELINESS.
SAWDUST

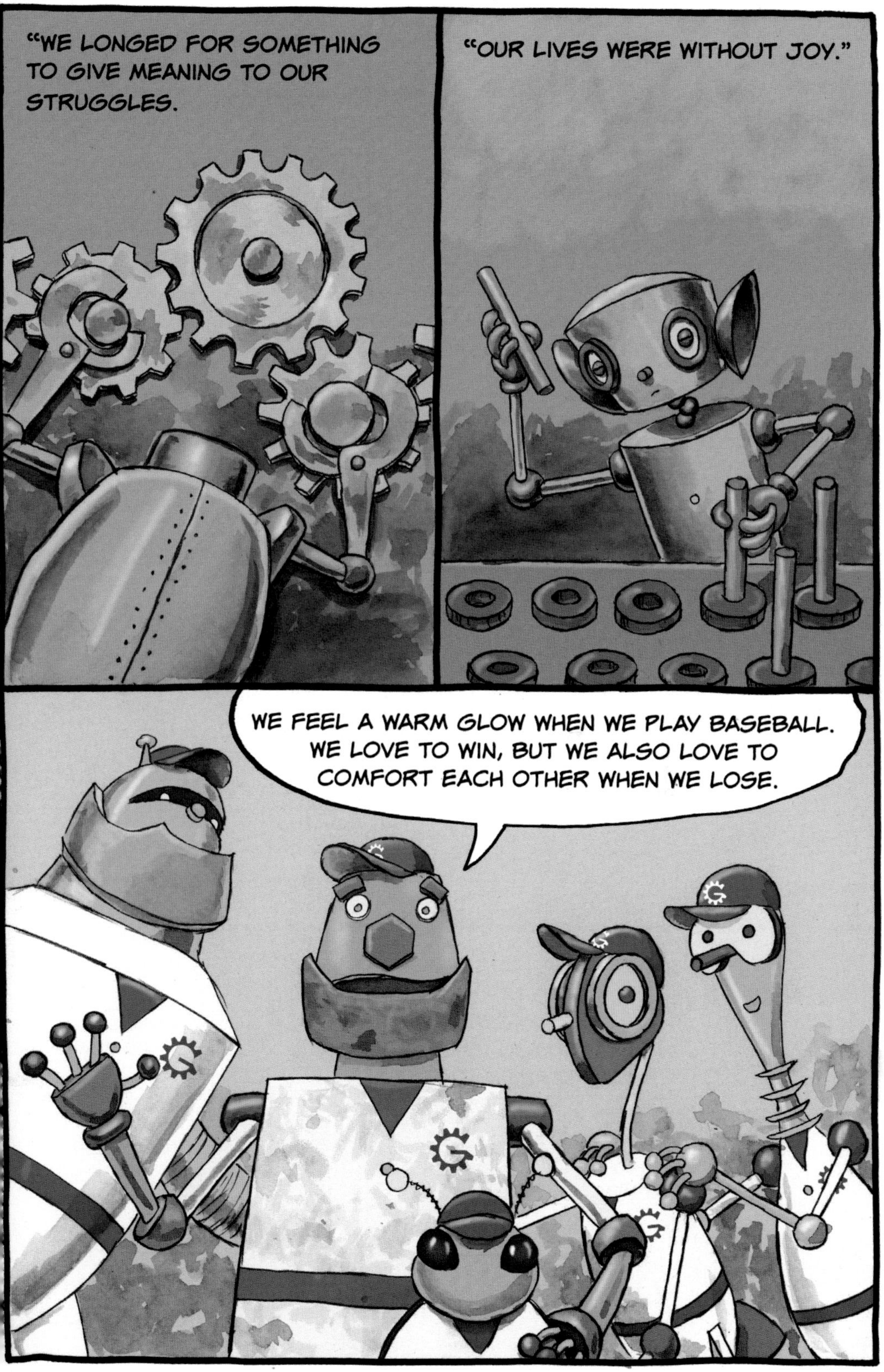
"WE LONGED FOR SOMETHING TO GIVE MEANING TO OUR STRUGGLES.
"OUR LIVES WERE WITHOUT JOY."
WE FEEL A WARM GLOW WHEN WE PLAY BASEBALL. WE LOVE TO WIN, BUT WE ALSO LOVE TO COMFORT EACH OTHER WHEN WE LOSE.

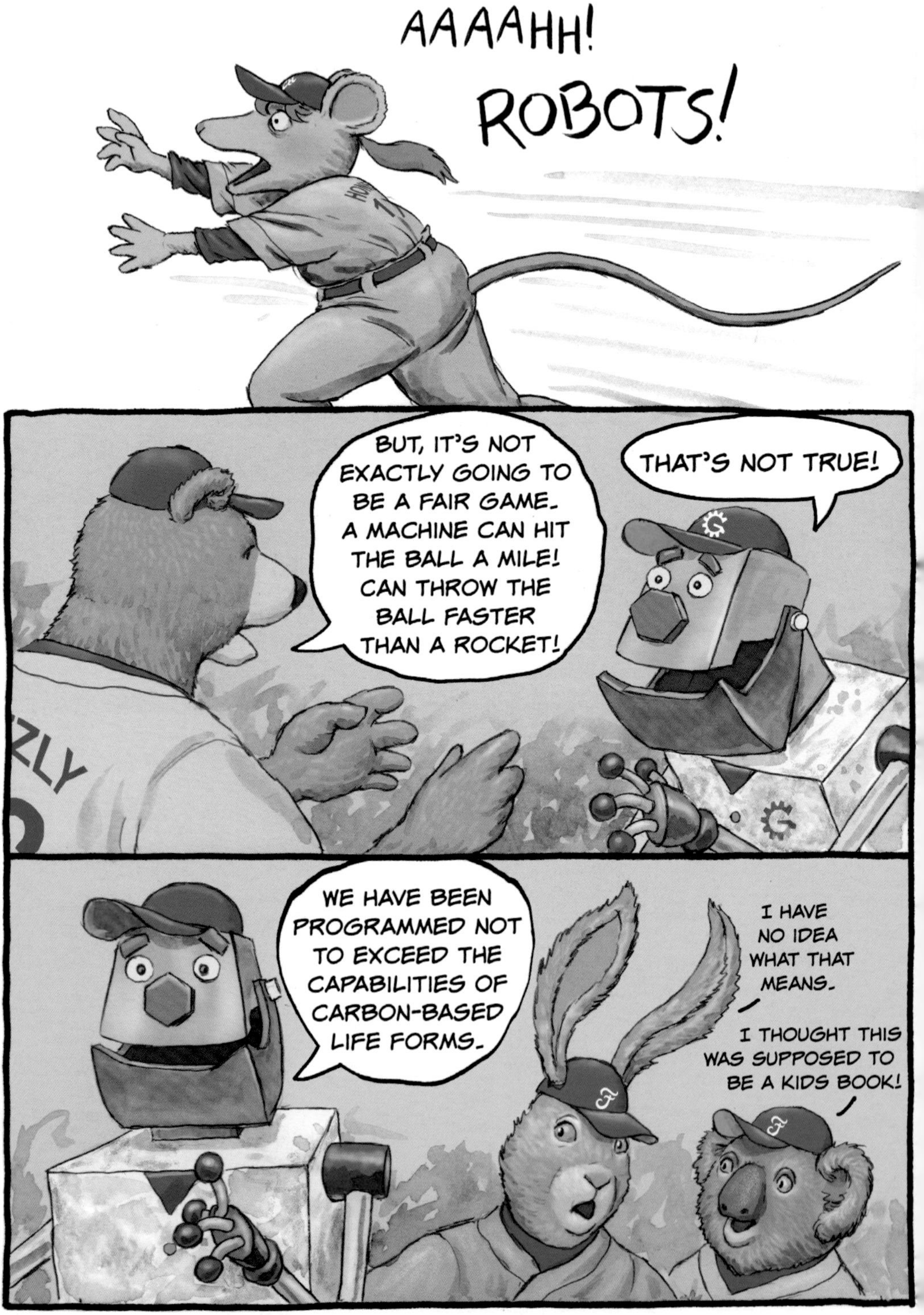
AAAAHH!
ROBOTS!
BUT, IT'S NOT EXACTLY GOING TO BE A FAIR GAME. A MACHINE CAN HIT THE BALL A MILE! CAN THROW THE BALL FASTER THAN A ROCKET!
THAT'S NOT TRUE!
WE HAVE BEEN PROGRAMMED NOT TO EXCEED THE CAPABILITIES OF CARBON-BASED LIFE FORMS.
I HAVE NO IDEA WHAT THAT MEANS.
I THOUGHT THIS WAS SUPPOSED TO BE A KIDS BOOK!

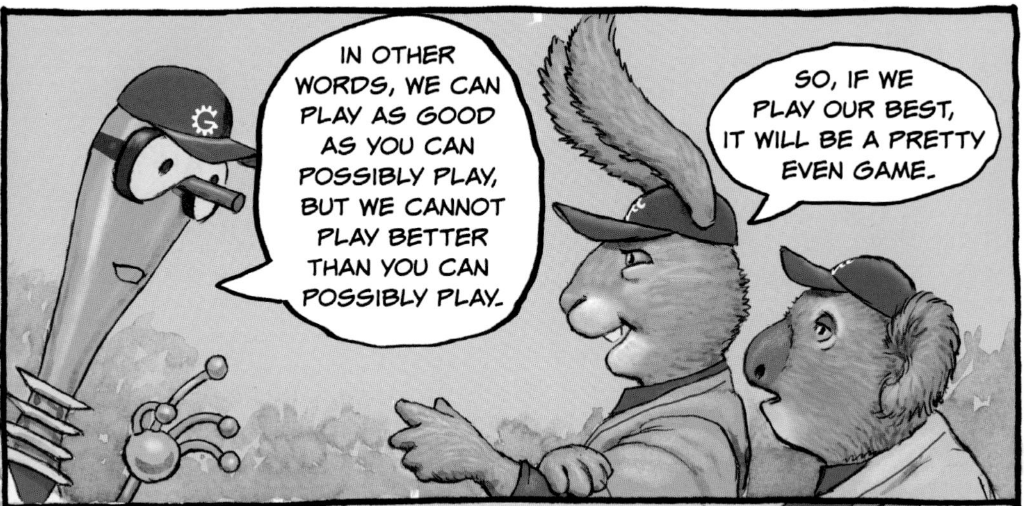
IN OTHER WORDS, WE CAN PLAY AS GOOD AS YOU CAN POSSIBLY PLAY, BUT WE CANNOT PLAY BETTER THAN YOU CAN POSSIBLY PLAY.
SO, IF WE PLAY OUR BEST, IT WILL BE A PRETTY EVEN GAME.

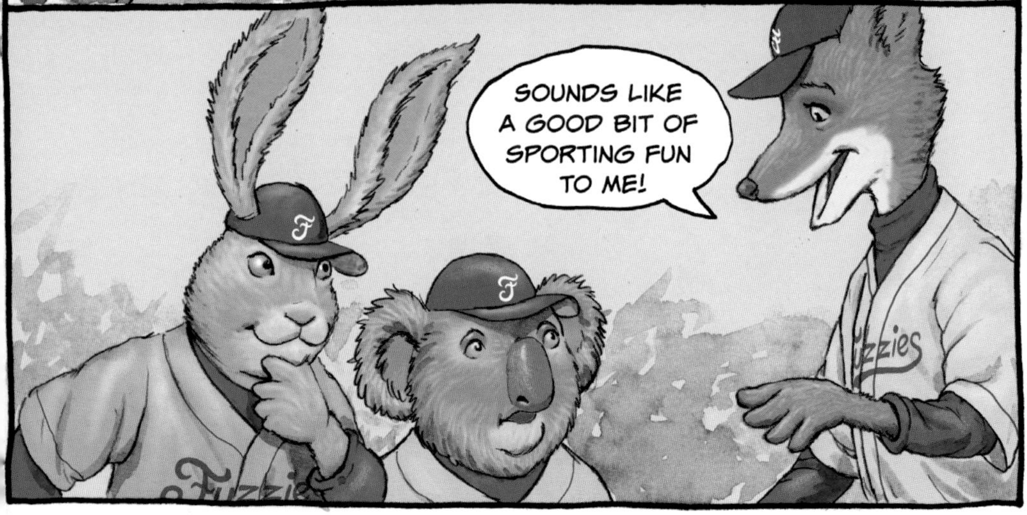
SOUNDS LIKE A GOOD BIT OF SPORTING FUN TO ME!
Fuzzies

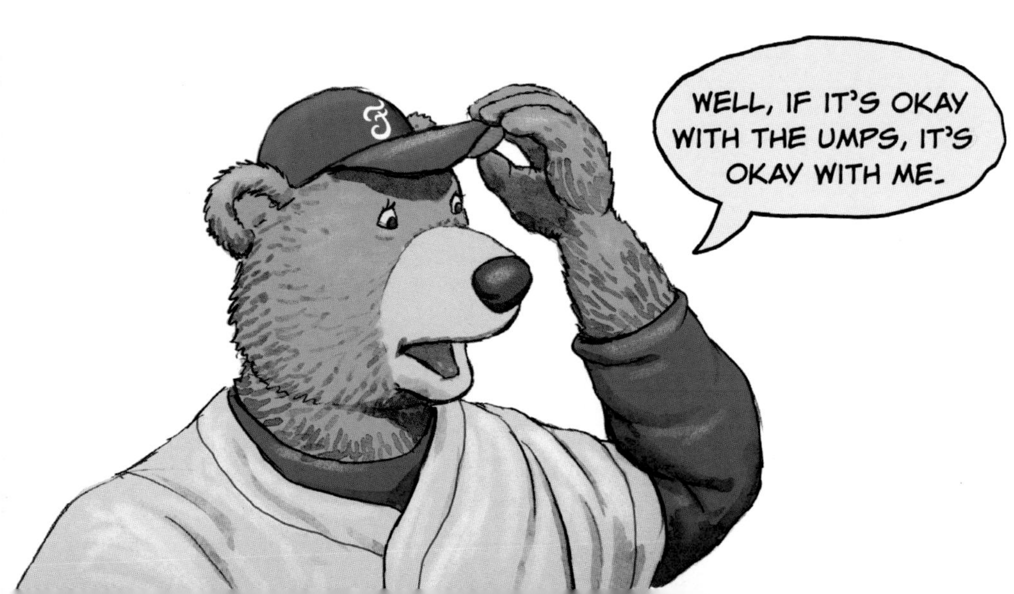
WELL, IF IT'S OKAY WITH THE UMPS, IT'S OKAY WITH ME.

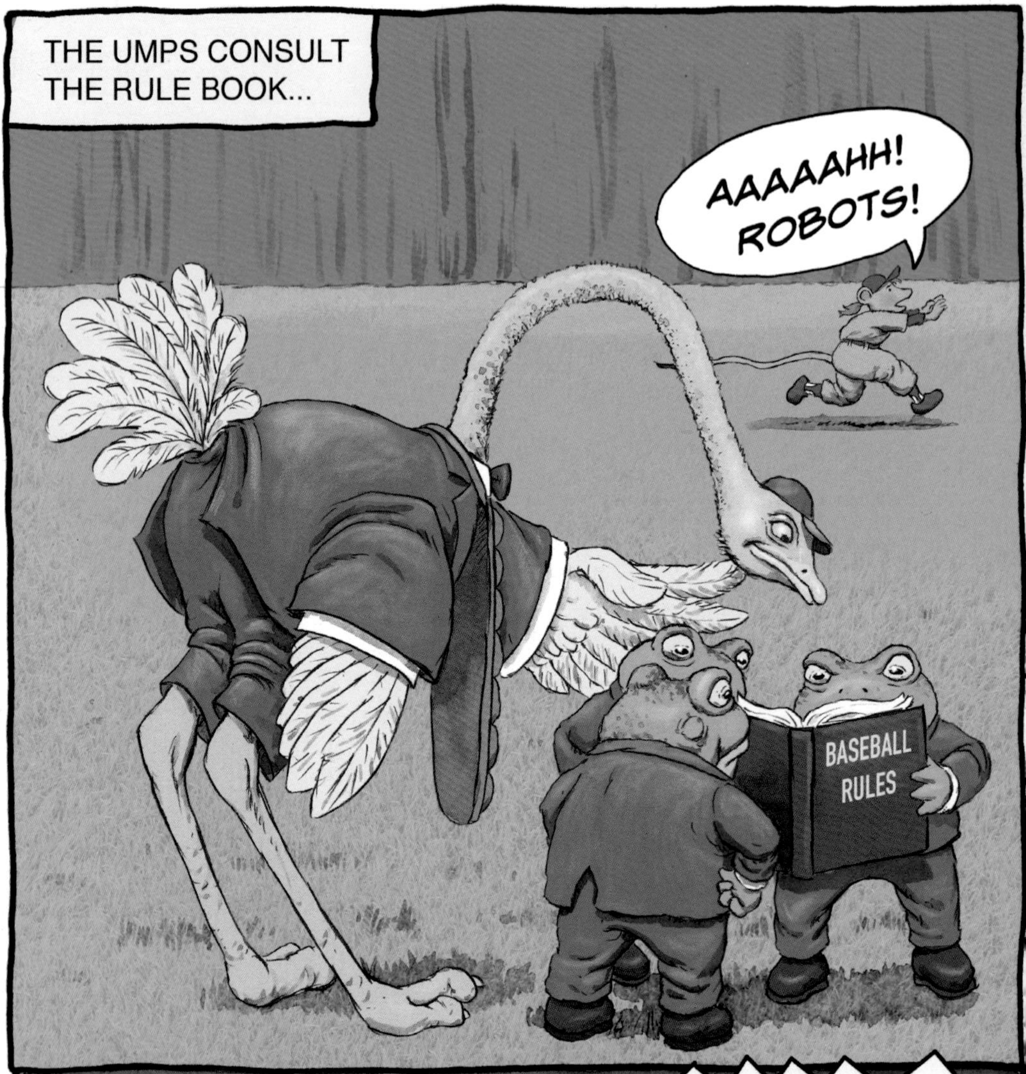
THE UMPS CONSULT THE RULE BOOK...
AAAAAHH! ROBOTS!
BASEBALL RULES

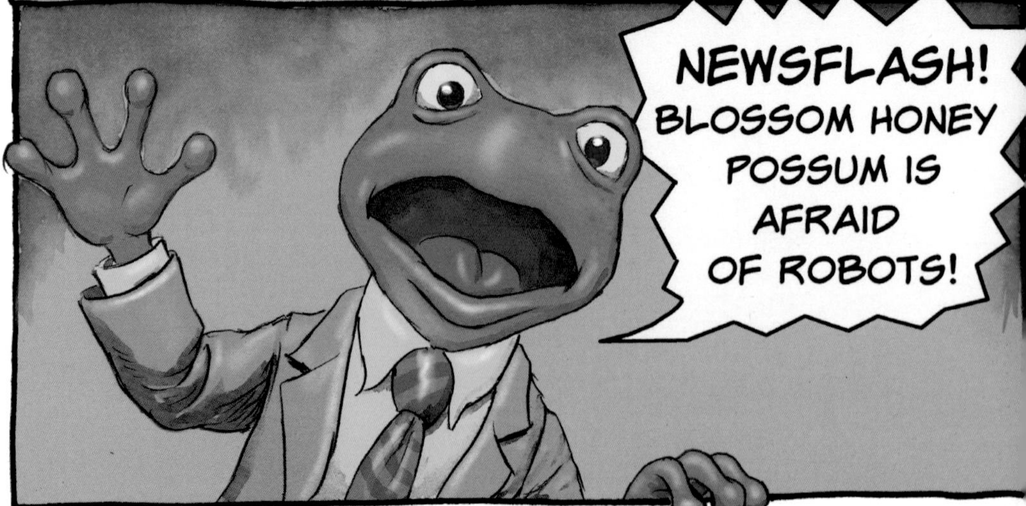
NEWSFLASH! BLOSSOM HONEY POSSUM IS AFRAID OF ROBOTS!

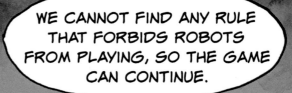

WE CANNOT FIND ANY RULE THAT FORBIDS ROBOTS FROM PLAYING, SO THE GAME CAN CONTINUE.

HOWEVER, THE ROBOTS ARE *NOT* ALLOWED TO PLUG IN AND RECHARGE DURING THE GAME.

OOPS!

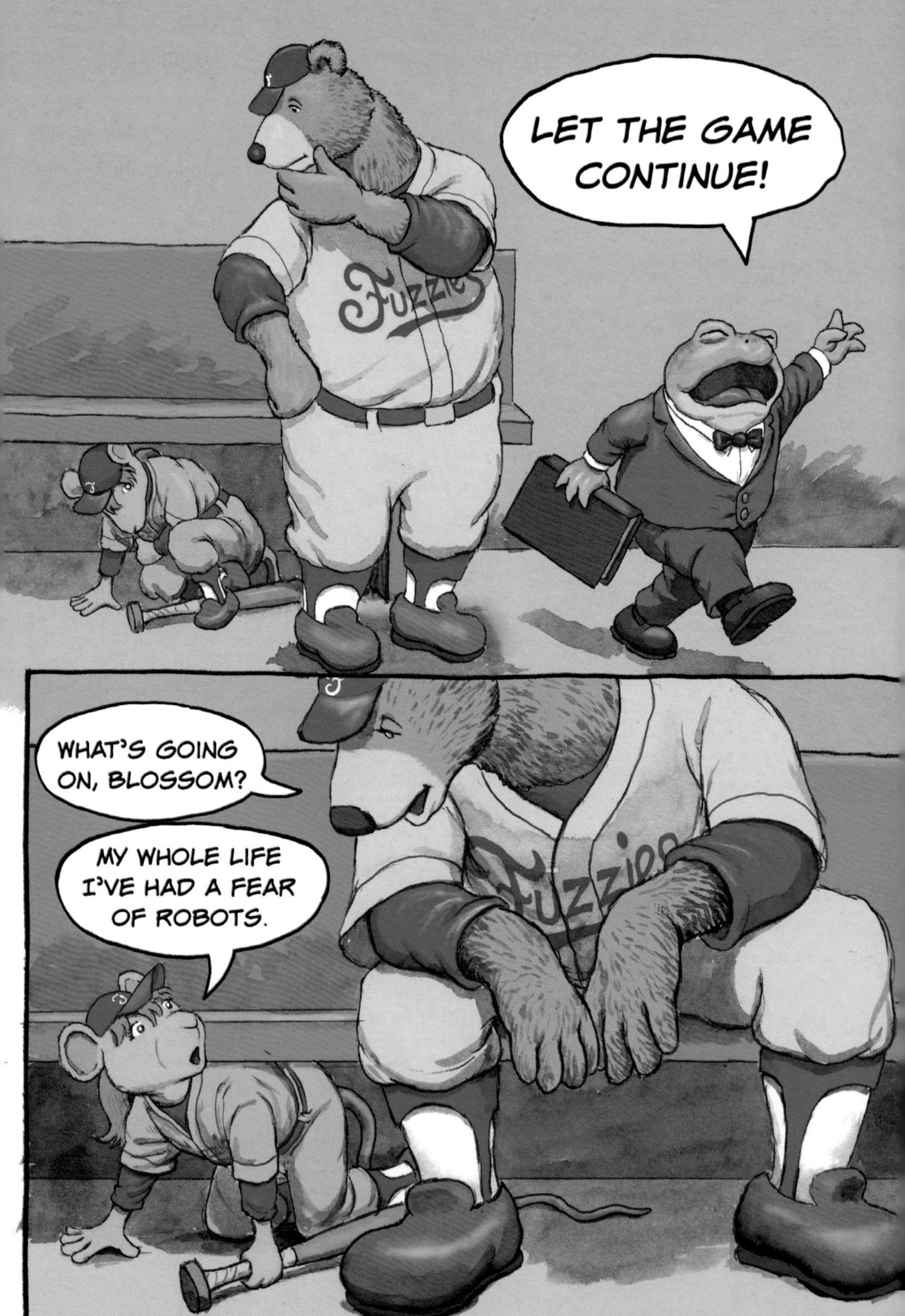
LET THE GAME CONTINUE!
FUZZIES
WHAT'S GOING ON, BLOSSOM?
MY WHOLE LIFE I'VE HAD A FEAR OF ROBOTS.
FUZZIES

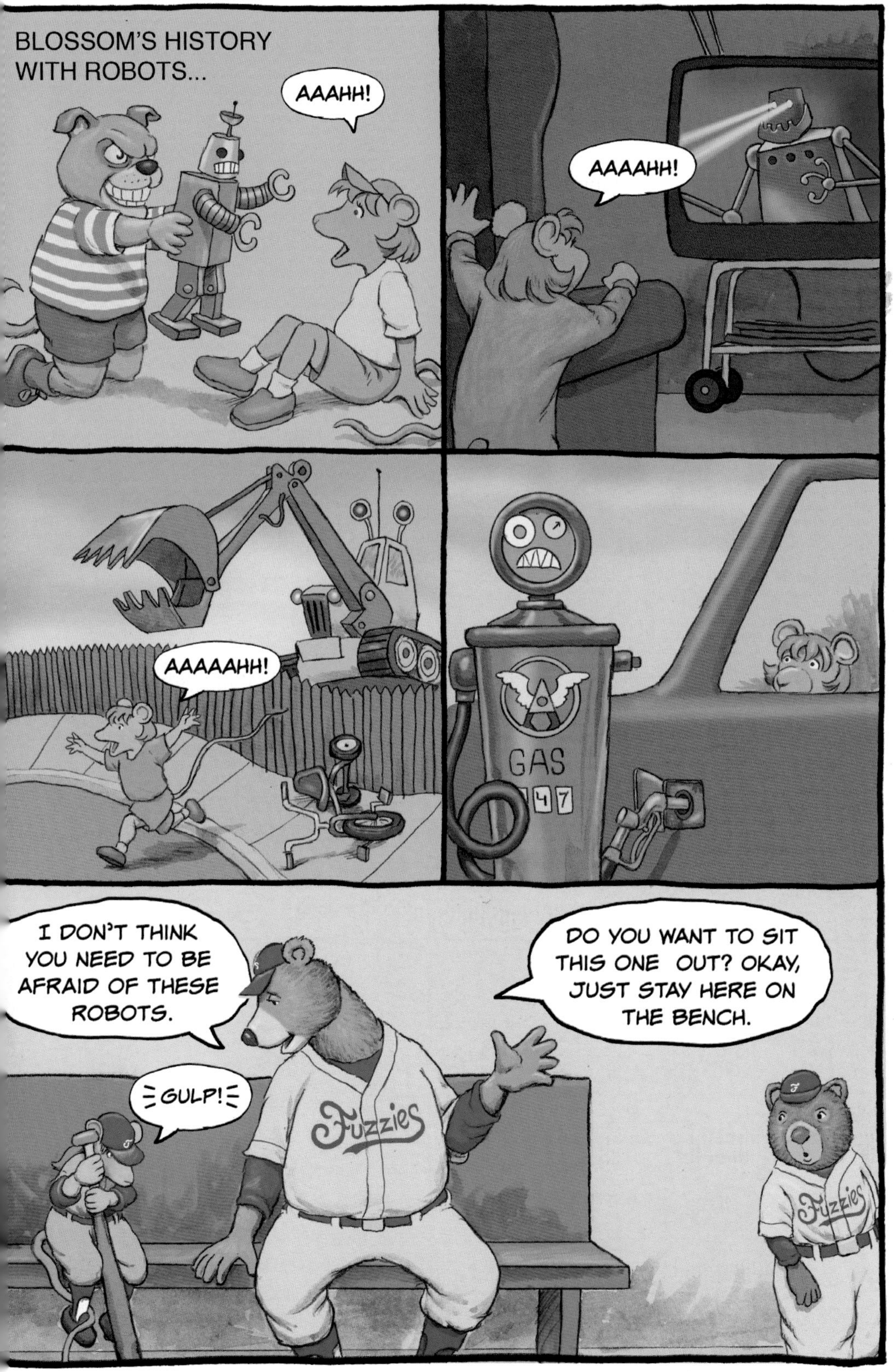
BLOSSOM'S HISTORY WITH ROBOTS...
AAAHH!
AAAAHH!
AAAAAHH!
GAS
I DON'T THINK YOU NEED TO BE AFRAID OF THESE ROBOTS.
DO YOU WANT TO SIT THIS ONE OUT? OKAY, JUST STAY HERE ON THE BENCH.
GULP!
Fuzzies

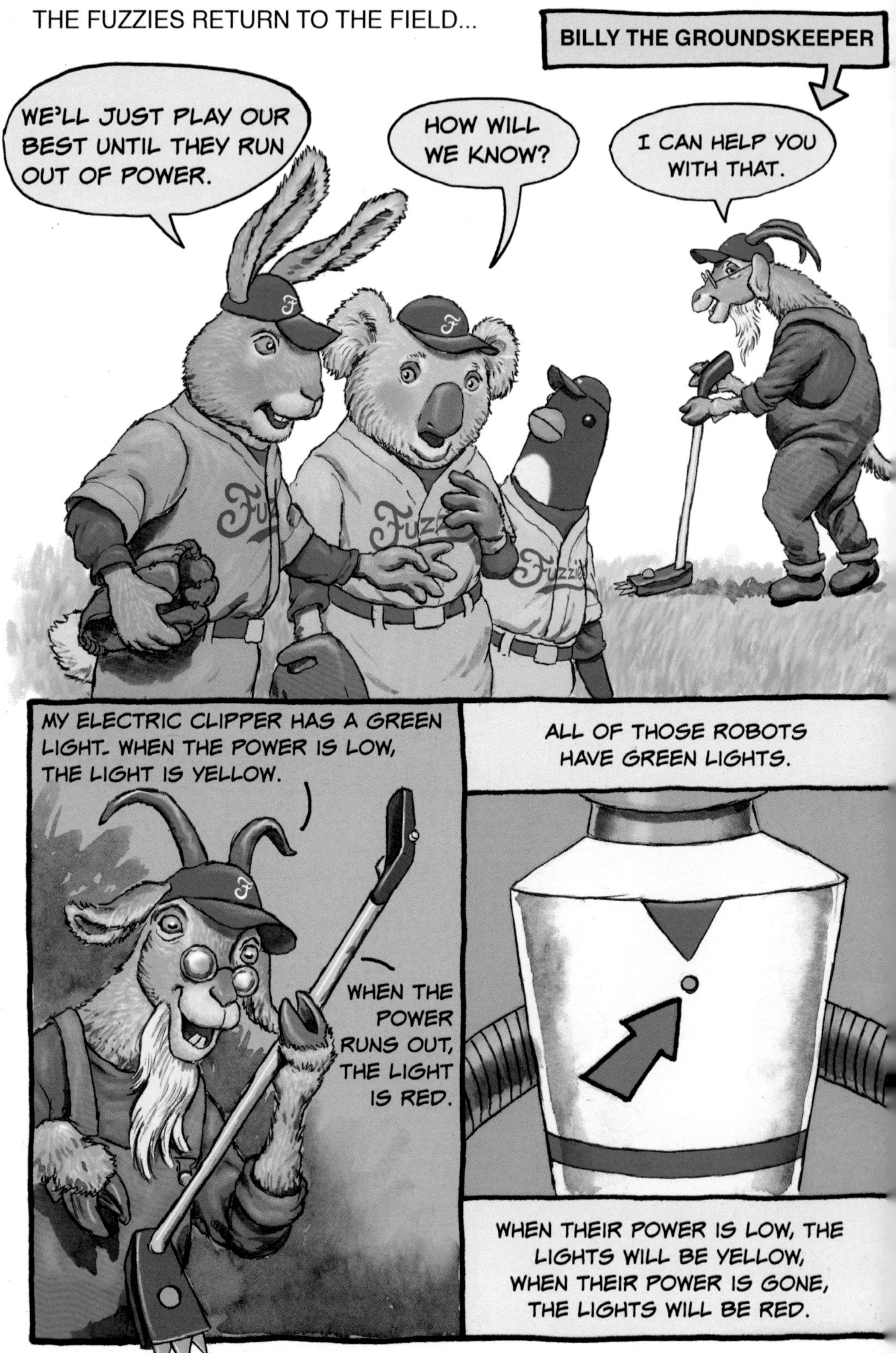
THE FUZZIES RETURN TO THE FIELD...
BILLY THE GROUNDSKEEPER
WE'LL JUST PLAY OUR BEST UNTIL THEY RUN OUT OF POWER.
HOW WILL WE KNOW?
I CAN HELP YOU WITH THAT.
MY ELECTRIC CLIPPER HAS A GREEN LIGHT. WHEN THE POWER IS LOW, THE LIGHT IS YELLOW.
WHEN THE POWER RUNS OUT, THE LIGHT IS RED.
ALL OF THOSE ROBOTS HAVE GREEN LIGHTS.
WHEN THEIR POWER IS LOW, THE LIGHTS WILL BE YELLOW, WHEN THEIR POWER IS GONE, THE LIGHTS WILL BE RED.

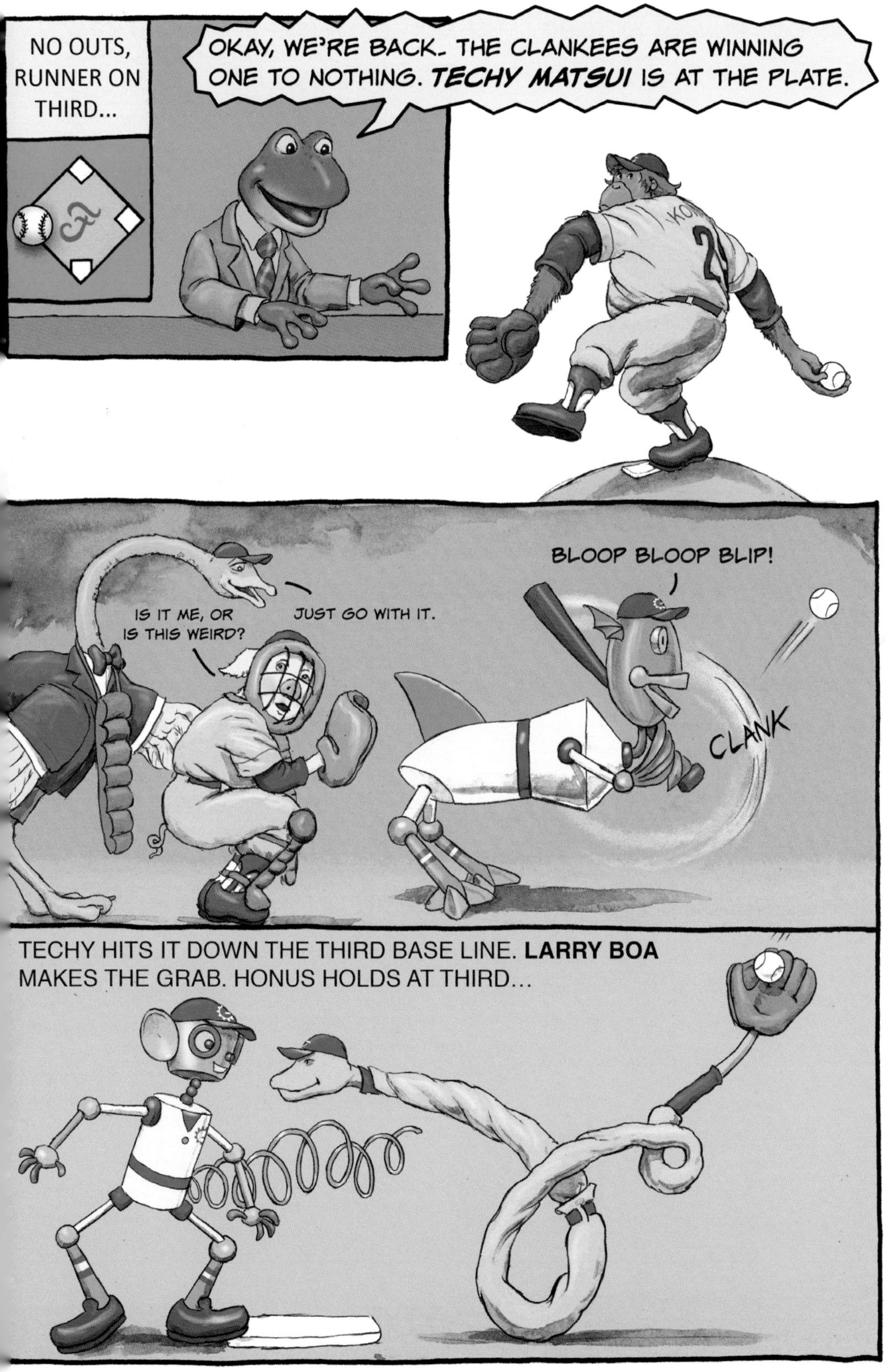
NO OUTS, RUNNER ON THIRD...
OKAY, WE'RE BACK. THE CLANKEES ARE WINNING ONE TO NOTHING. ***TECHY MATSUI*** IS AT THE PLATE.
IS IT ME, OR IS THIS WEIRD?
JUST GO WITH IT.
BLOOP BLOOP BLIP!
CLANK
TECHY HITS IT DOWN THE THIRD BASE LINE. **LARRY BOA** MAKES THE GRAB. HONUS HOLDS AT THIRD...

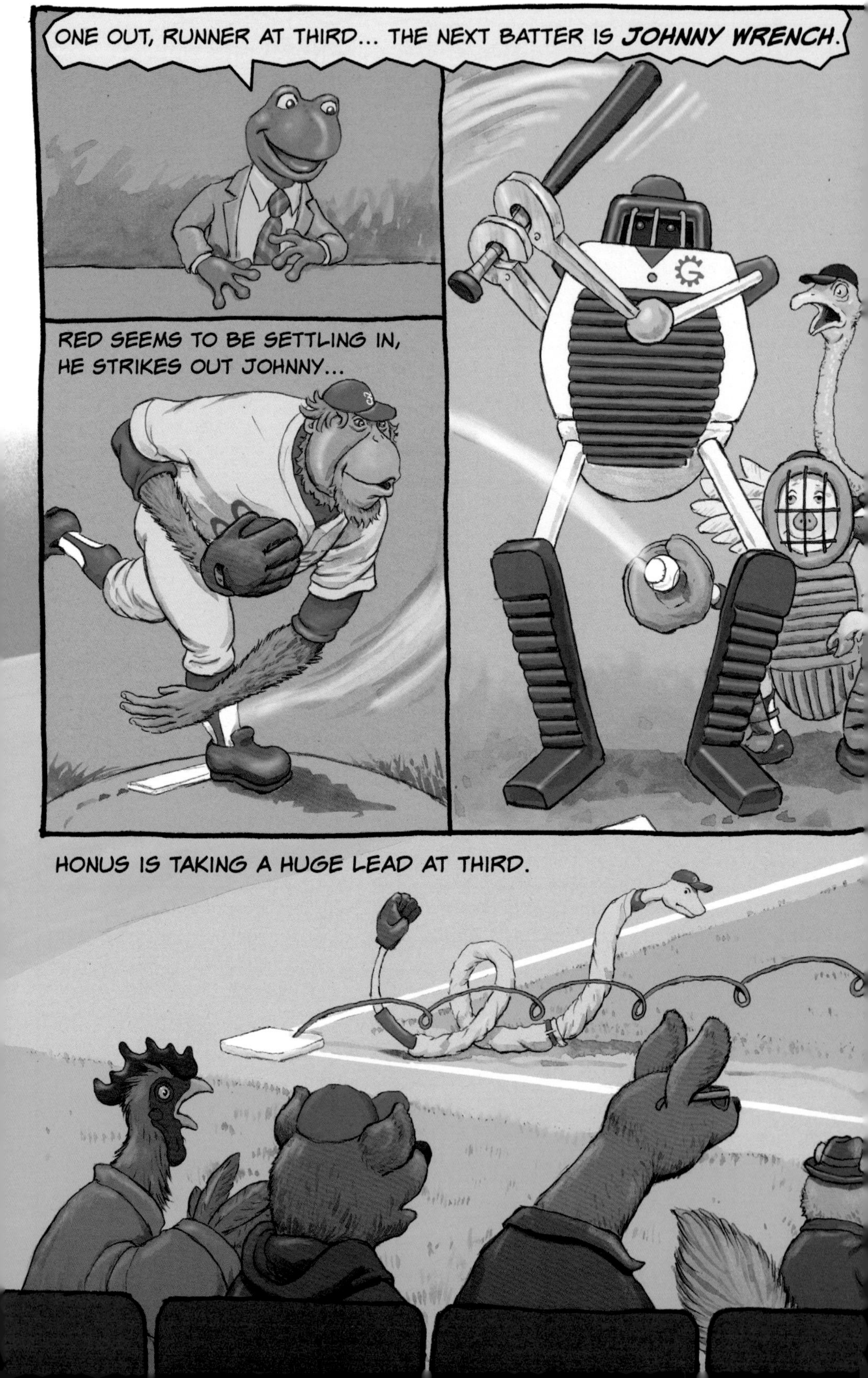
ONE OUT, RUNNER AT THIRD... THE NEXT BATTER IS *JOHNNY WRENCH*.
RED SEEMS TO BE SETTLING IN, HE STRIKES OUT JOHNNY...
HONUS IS TAKING A HUGE LEAD AT THIRD.

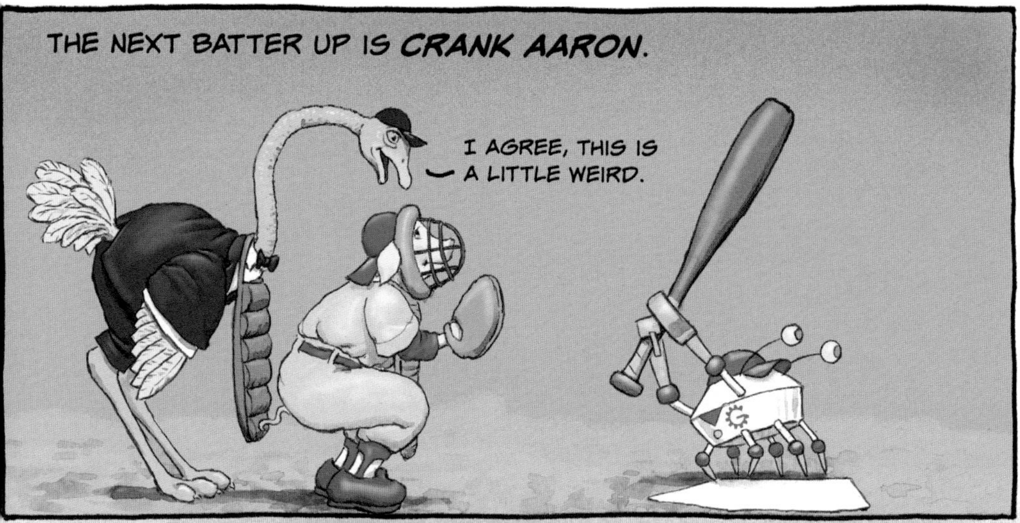
THE NEXT BATTER UP IS CRANK AARON.
I AGREE, THIS IS A LITTLE WEIRD.

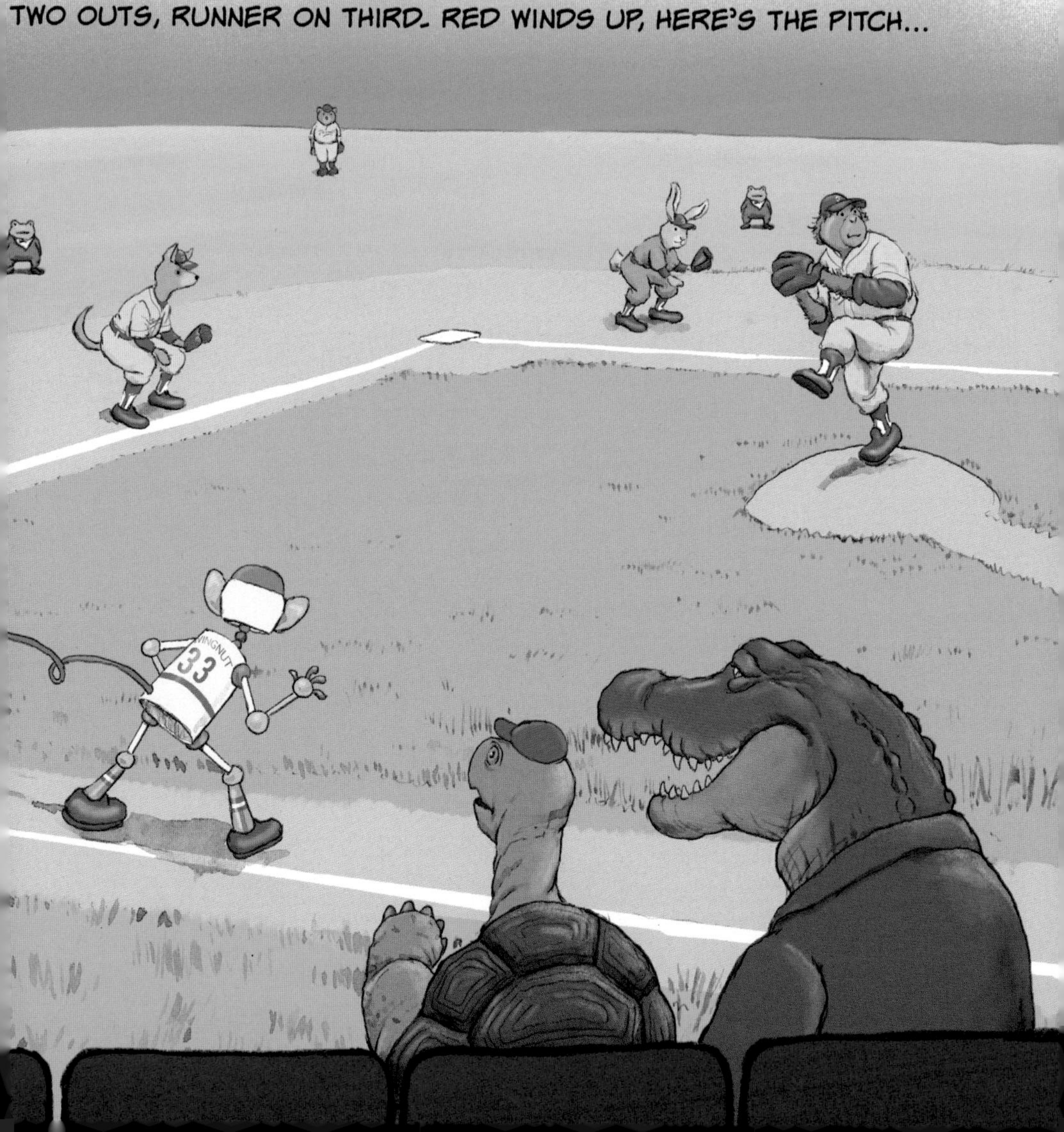
TWO OUTS, RUNNER ON THIRD. RED WINDS UP, HERE'S THE PITCH...

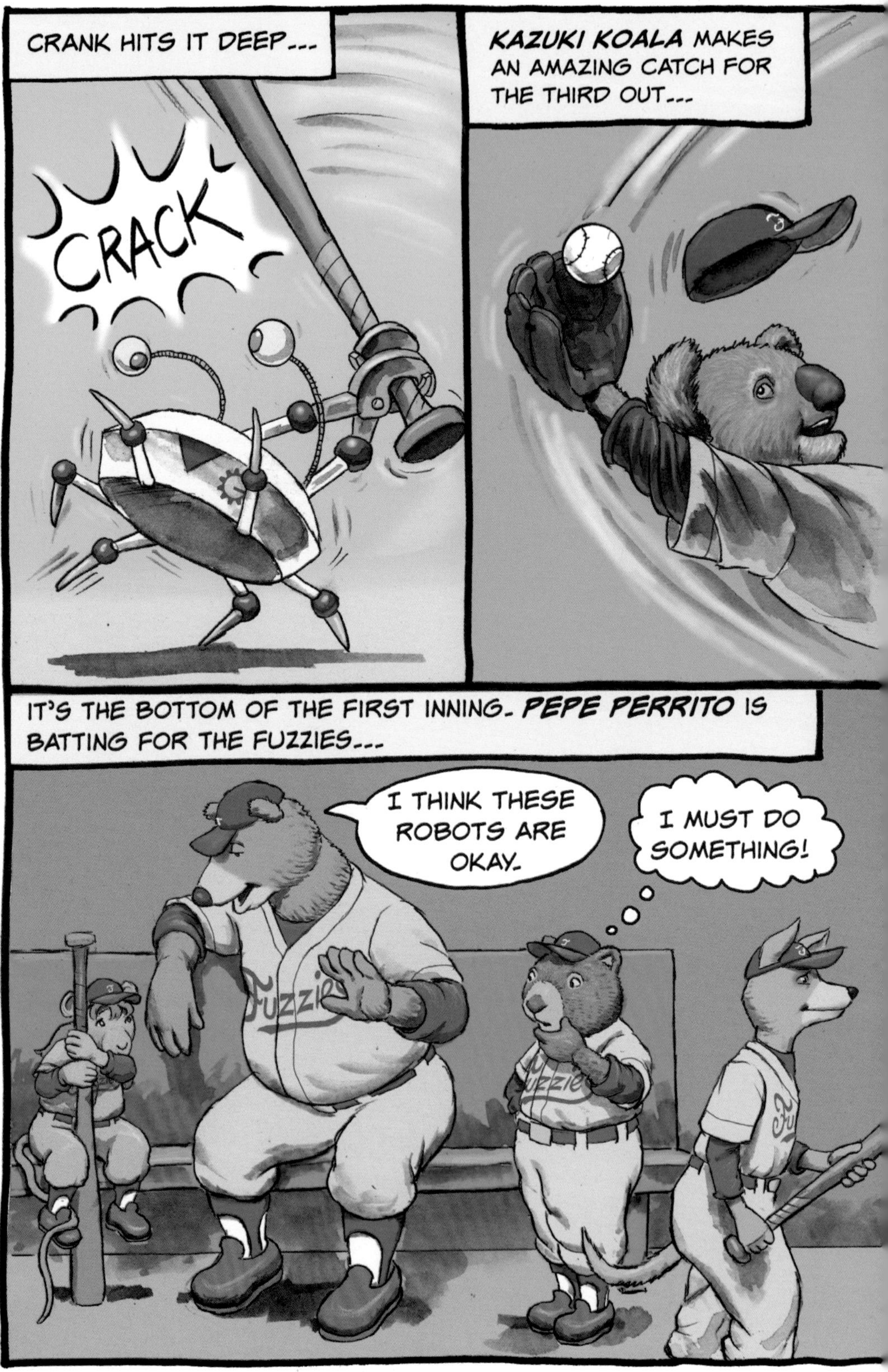
CRANK HITS IT DEEP...
CRACK
KAZUKI KOALA MAKES AN AMAZING CATCH FOR THE THIRD OUT...
IT'S THE BOTTOM OF THE FIRST INNING. *PEPE PERRITO* IS BATTING FOR THE FUZZIES...
I THINK THESE ROBOTS ARE OKAY.
I MUST DO SOMETHING!

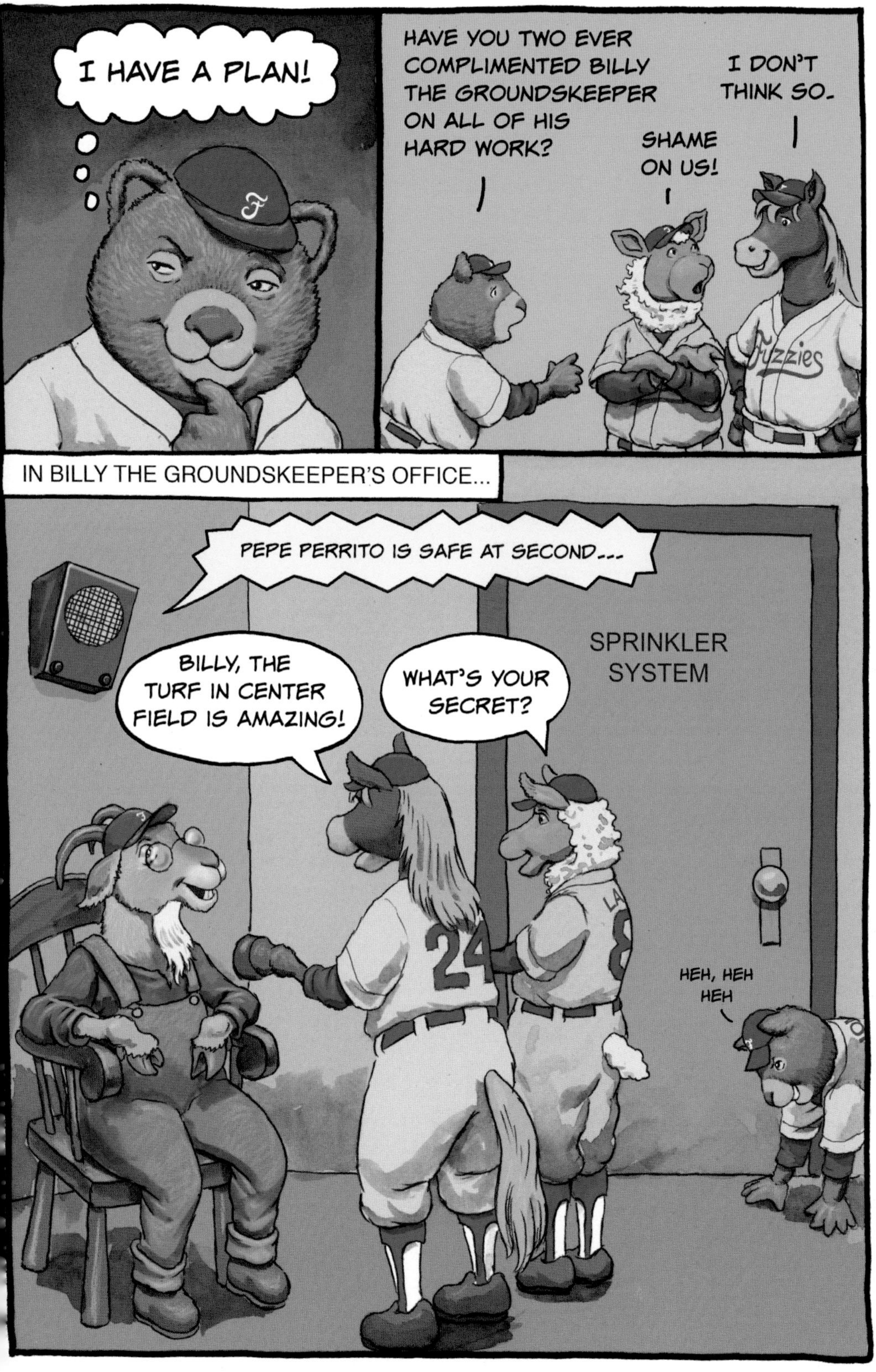
I HAVE A PLAN!
HAVE YOU TWO EVER COMPLIMENTED BILLY THE GROUNDSKEEPER ON ALL OF HIS HARD WORK?
SHAME ON US!
I DON'T THINK SO.
IN BILLY THE GROUNDSKEEPER'S OFFICE...
PEPE PERRITO IS SAFE AT SECOND...
SPRINKLER SYSTEM
BILLY, THE TURF IN CENTER FIELD IS AMAZING!
WHAT'S YOUR SECRET?
HEH, HEH HEH

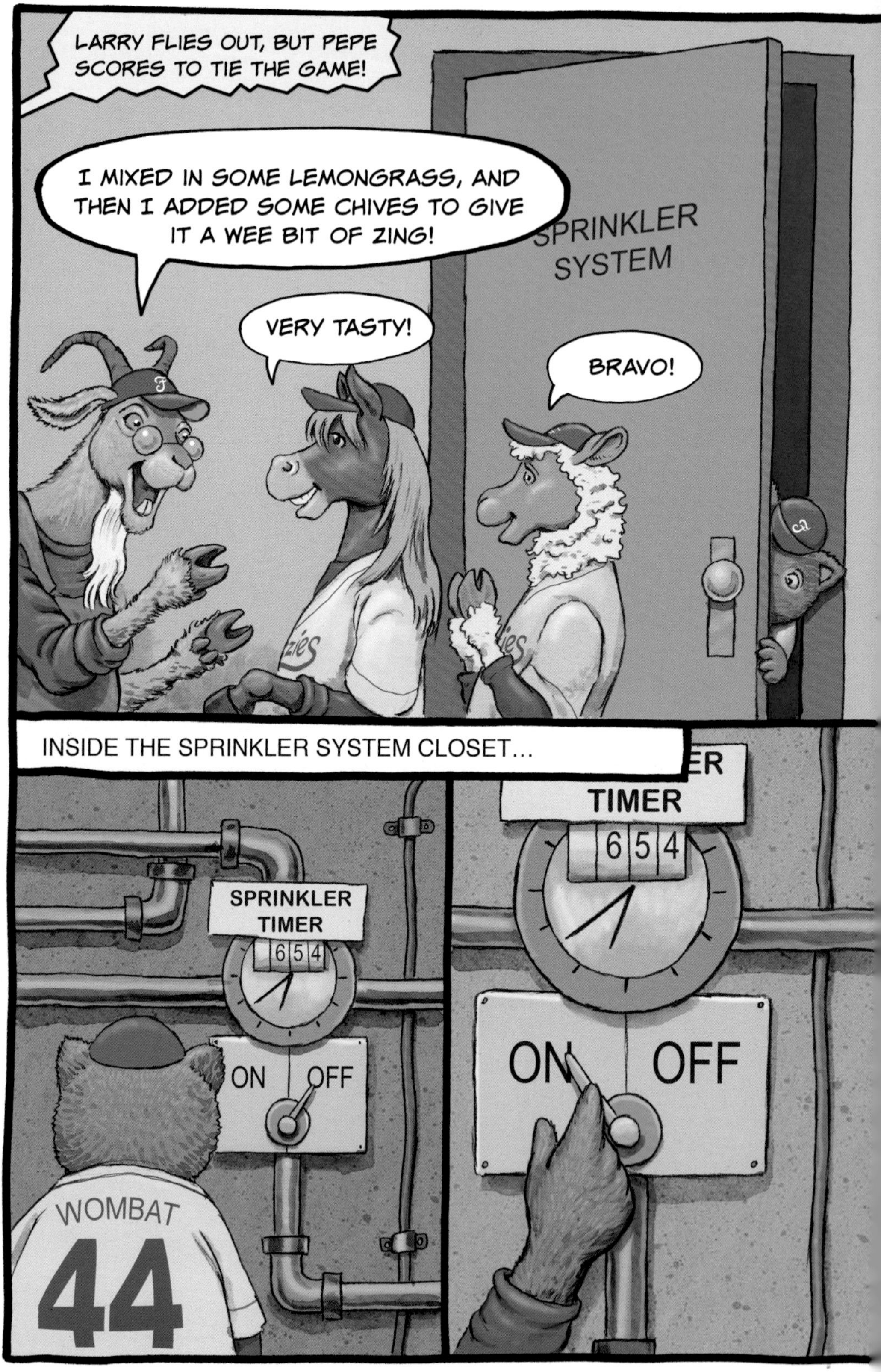
LARRY FLIES OUT, BUT PEPE SCORES TO TIE THE GAME!
I MIXED IN SOME LEMONGRASS, AND THEN I ADDED SOME CHIVES TO GIVE IT A WEE BIT OF ZING!
SPRINKLER SYSTEM
VERY TASTY!
BRAVO!
INSIDE THE SPRINKLER SYSTEM CLOSET…
SPRINKLER TIMER
654
ON
OFF
WOMBAT
44
ER
TIMER
654
ON
OFF

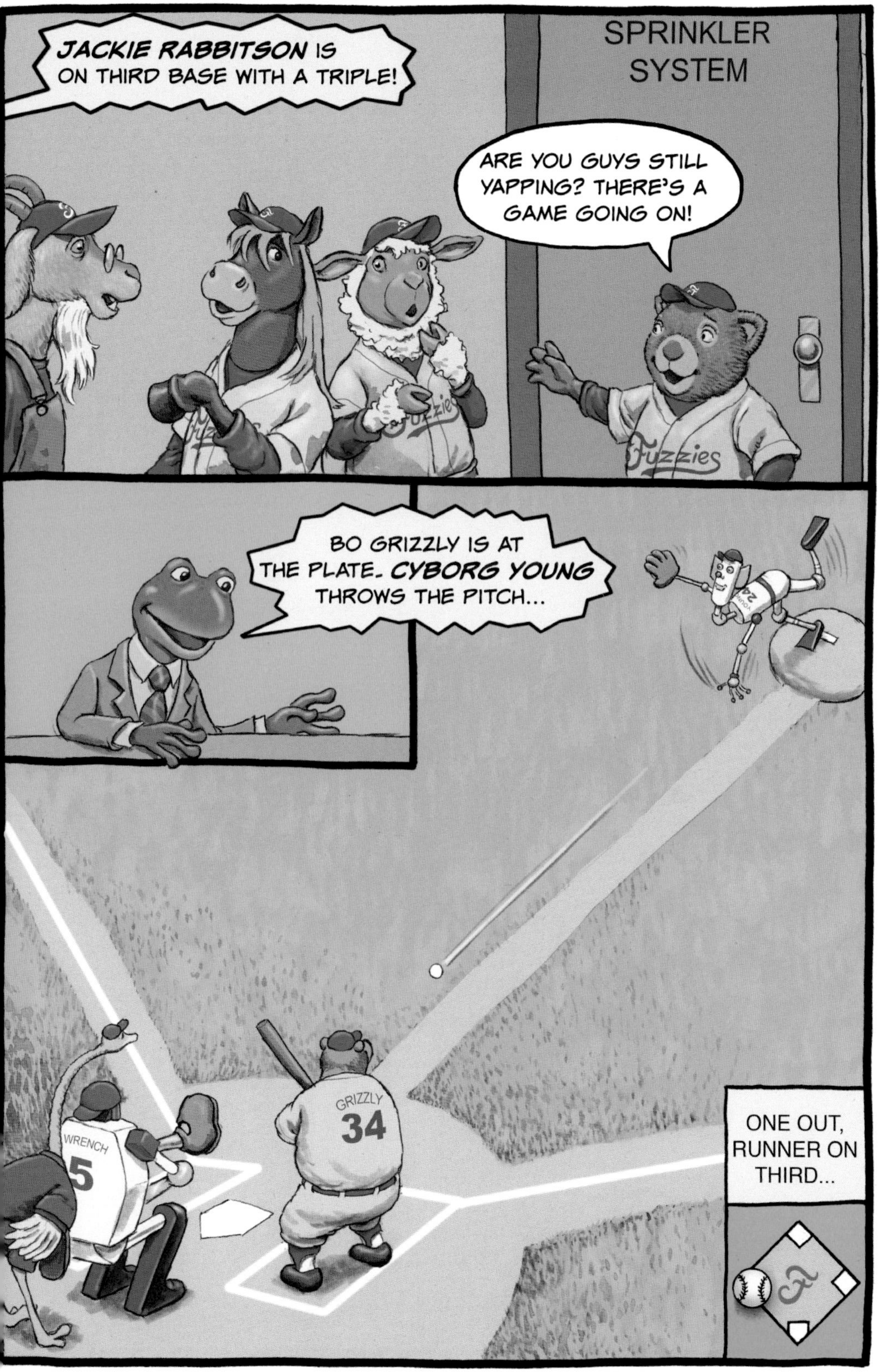
JACKIE RABBITSON IS ON THIRD BASE WITH A TRIPLE!
SPRINKLER SYSTEM
ARE YOU GUYS STILL YAPPING? THERE'S A GAME GOING ON!
Fuzzies
BO GRIZZLY IS AT THE PLATE. CYBORG YOUNG THROWS THE PITCH...
YOUNG 24
GRIZZLY 34
WRENCH 5
ONE OUT, RUNNER ON THIRD...

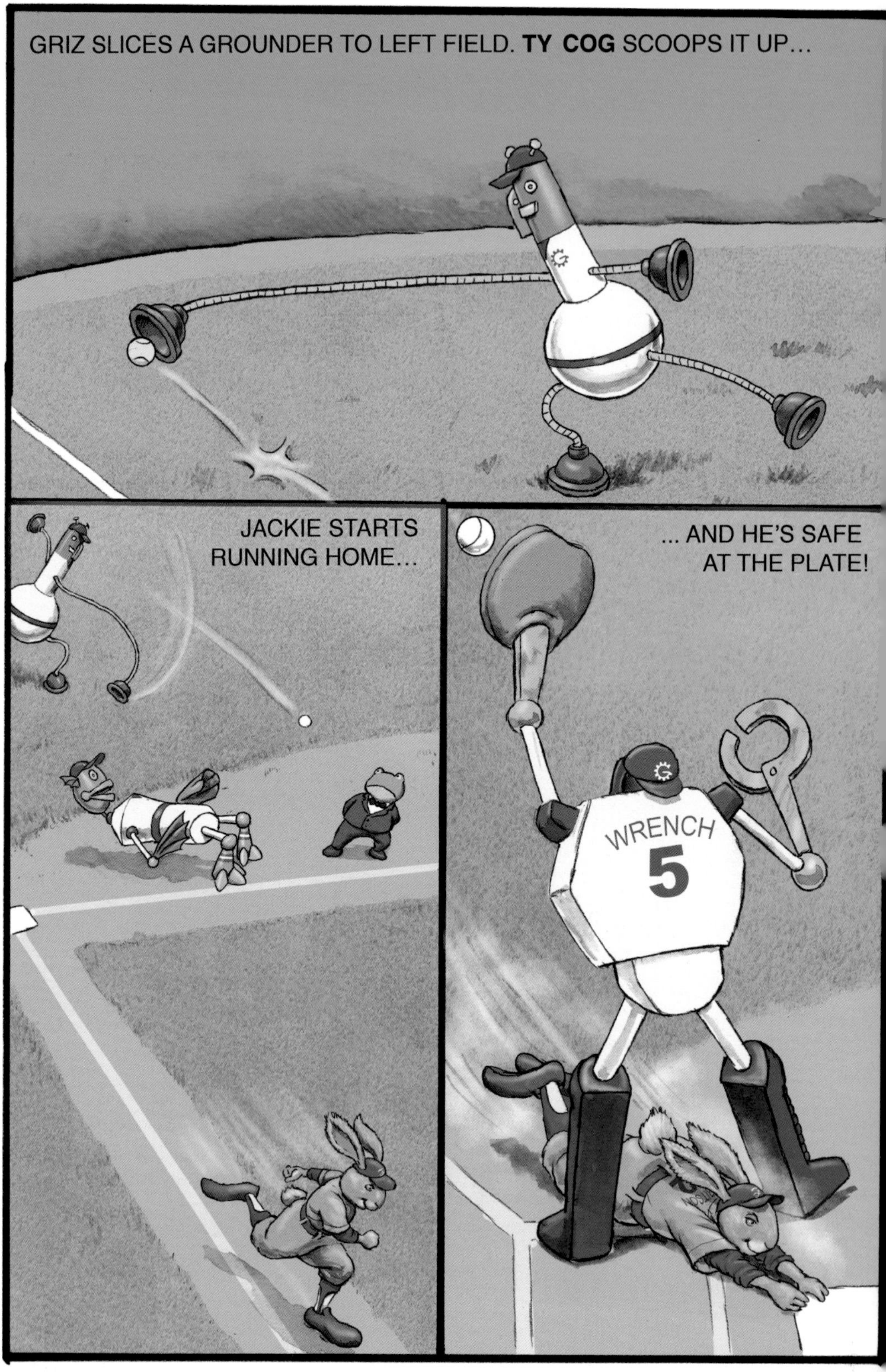
GRIZ SLICES A GROUNDER TO LEFT FIELD. TY COG SCOOPS IT UP…
JACKIE STARTS RUNNING HOME…
... AND HE'S SAFE AT THE PLATE!
WRENCH
5

..AND GRIZ IS SAFE AT SECOND.

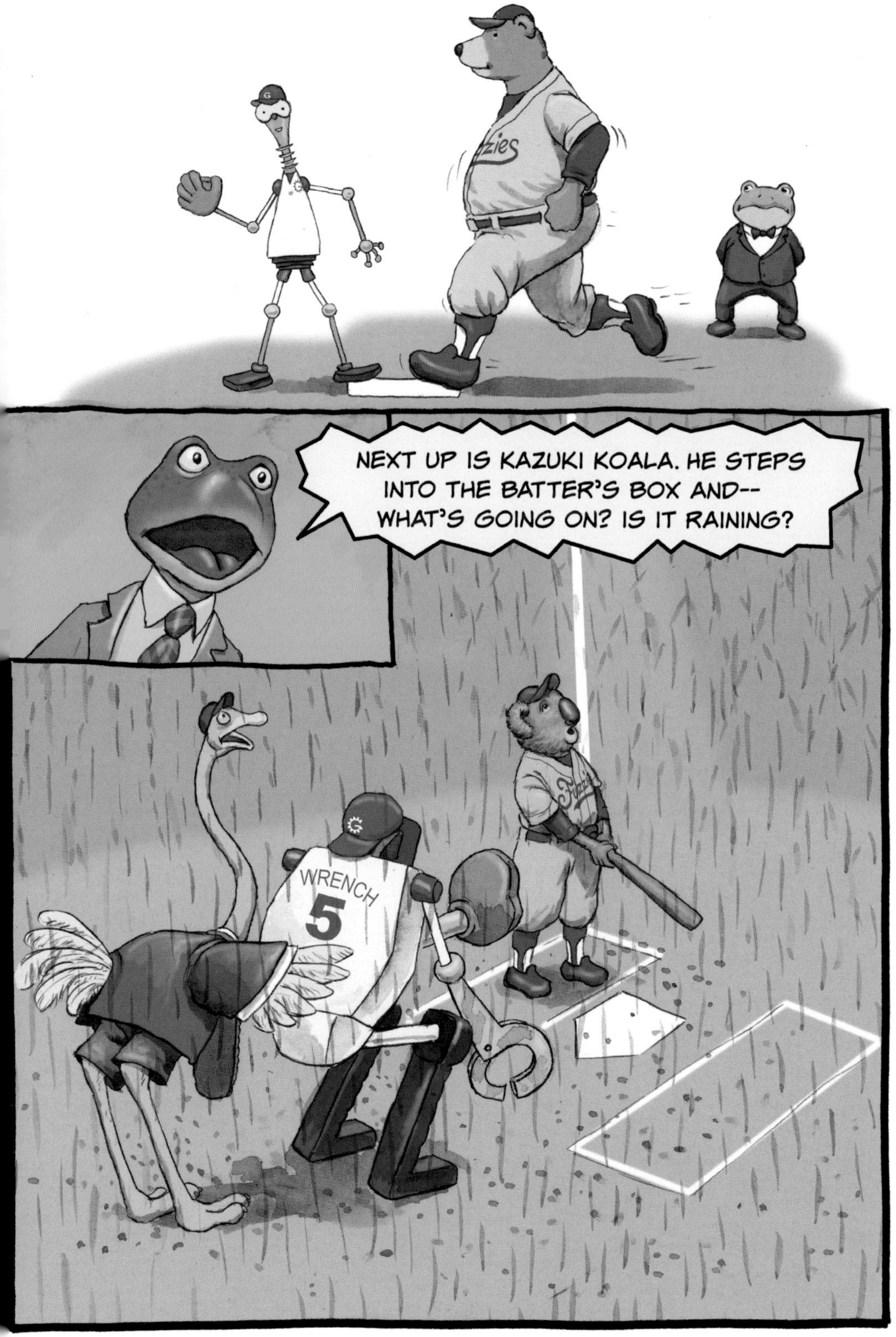
NEXT UP IS KAZUKI KOALA. HE STEPS INTO THE BATTER'S BOX AND-- WHAT'S GOING ON? IS IT RAINING?
WRENCH
5

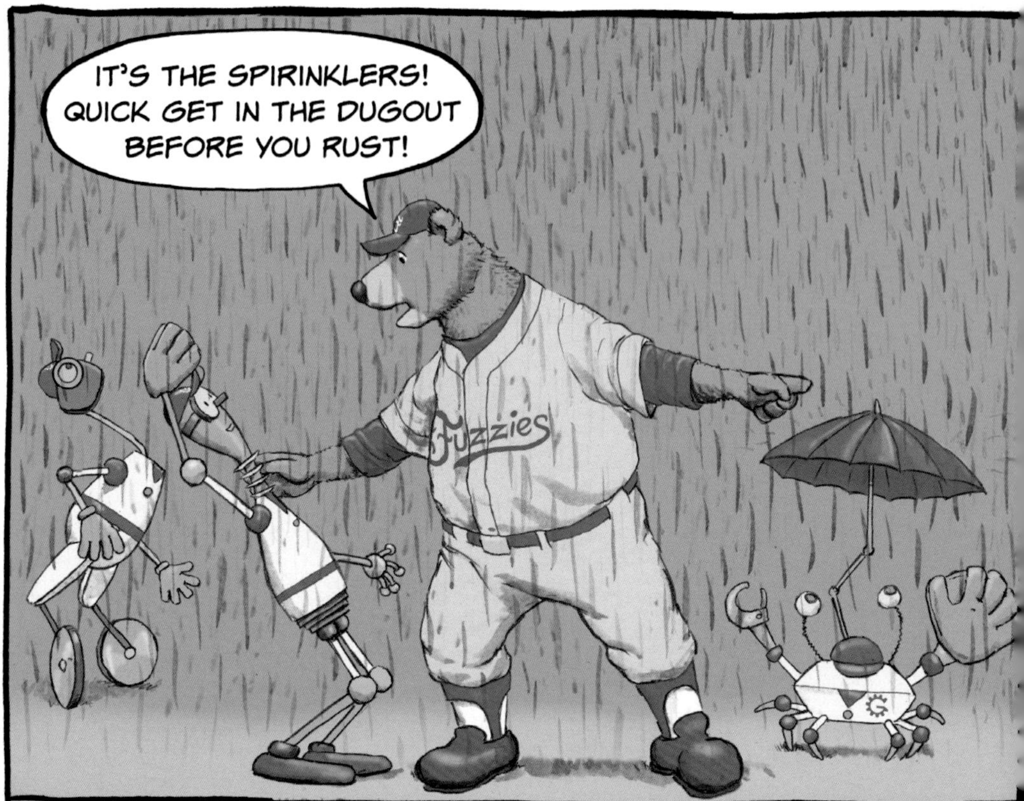
IT'S THE SPIRINKLERS! QUICK GET IN THE DUGOUT BEFORE YOU RUST!
Fuzzies

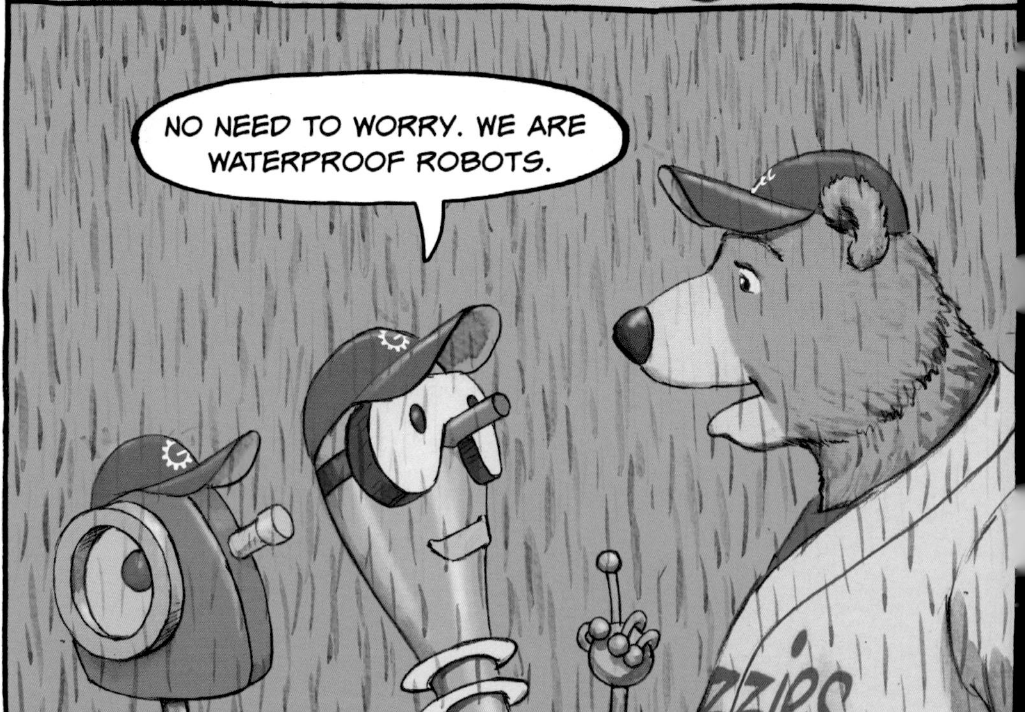
NO NEED TO WORRY. WE ARE WATERPROOF ROBOTS.

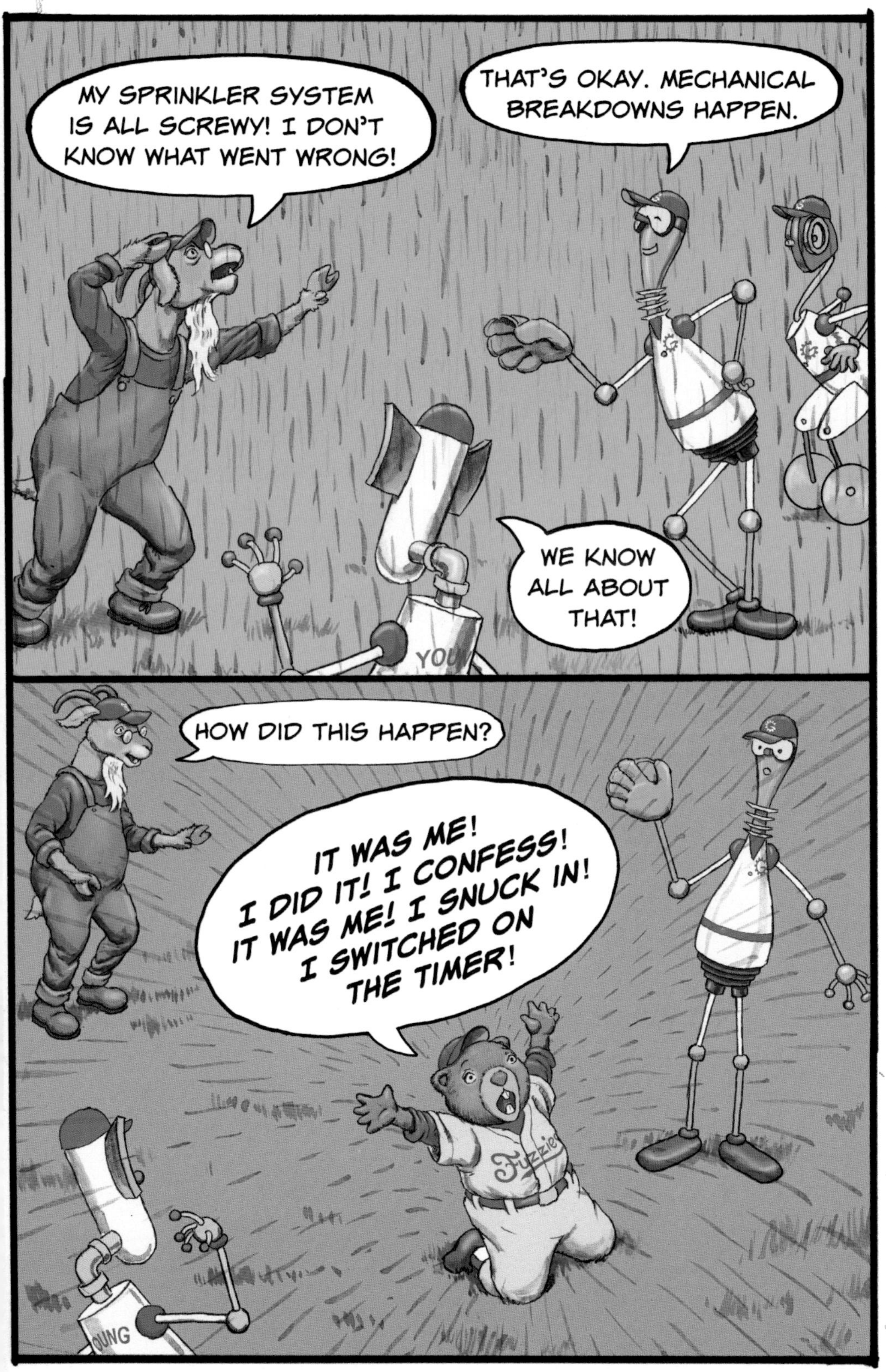
MY SPRINKLER SYSTEM IS ALL SCREWY! I DON'T KNOW WHAT WENT WRONG!
THAT'S OKAY. MECHANICAL BREAKDOWNS HAPPEN.
WE KNOW ALL ABOUT THAT!
YOU
HOW DID THIS HAPPEN?
IT WAS ME! I DID IT! I CONFESS! IT WAS ME! I SNUCK IN! I SWITCHED ON THE TIMER!
Fuzzies
OUNG

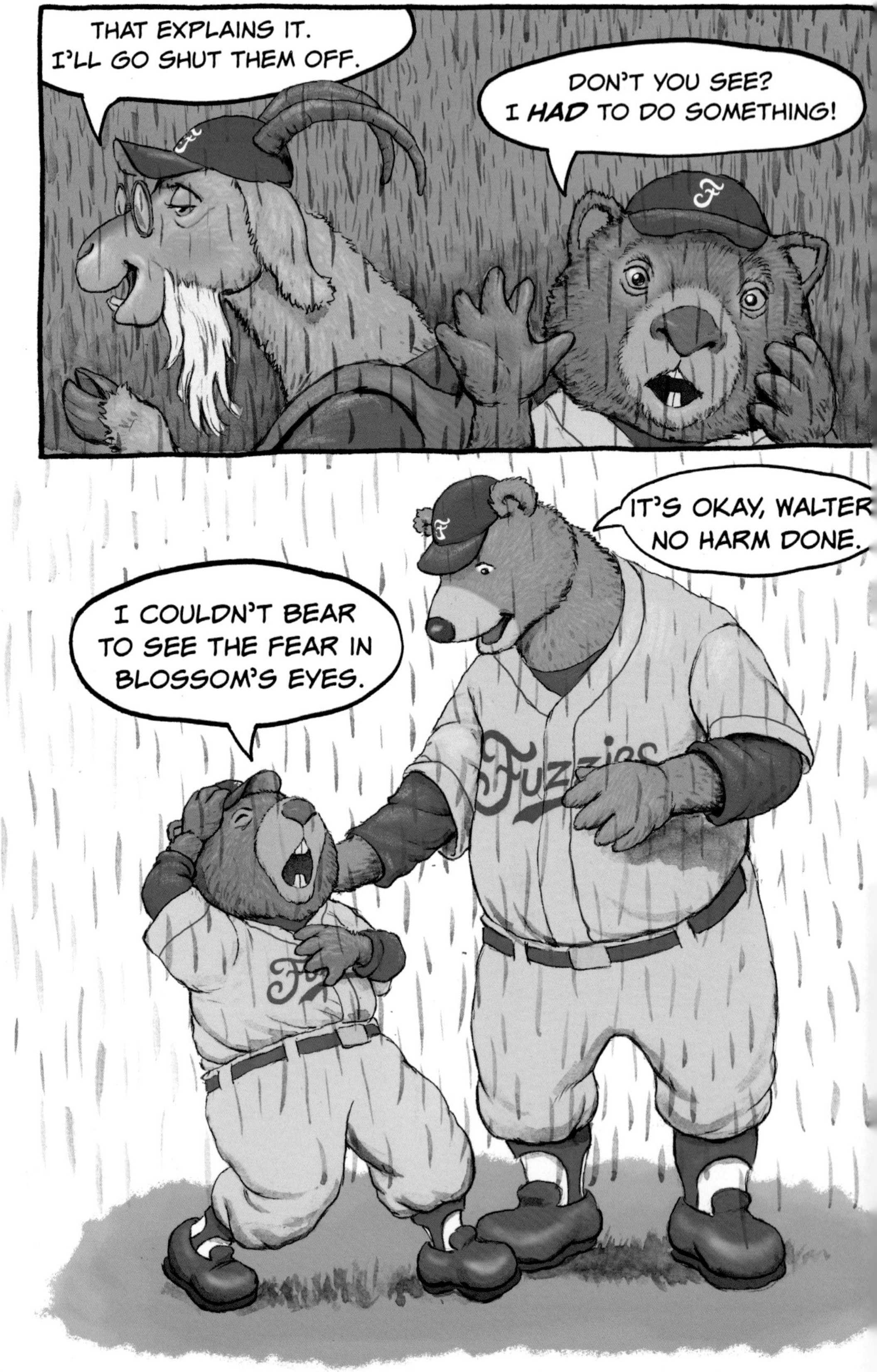
THAT EXPLAINS IT. I'LL GO SHUT THEM OFF.
DON'T YOU SEE? I *HAD* TO DO SOMETHING!
I COULDN'T BEAR TO SEE THE FEAR IN BLOSSOM'S EYES.
IT'S OKAY, WALTER NO HARM DONE.

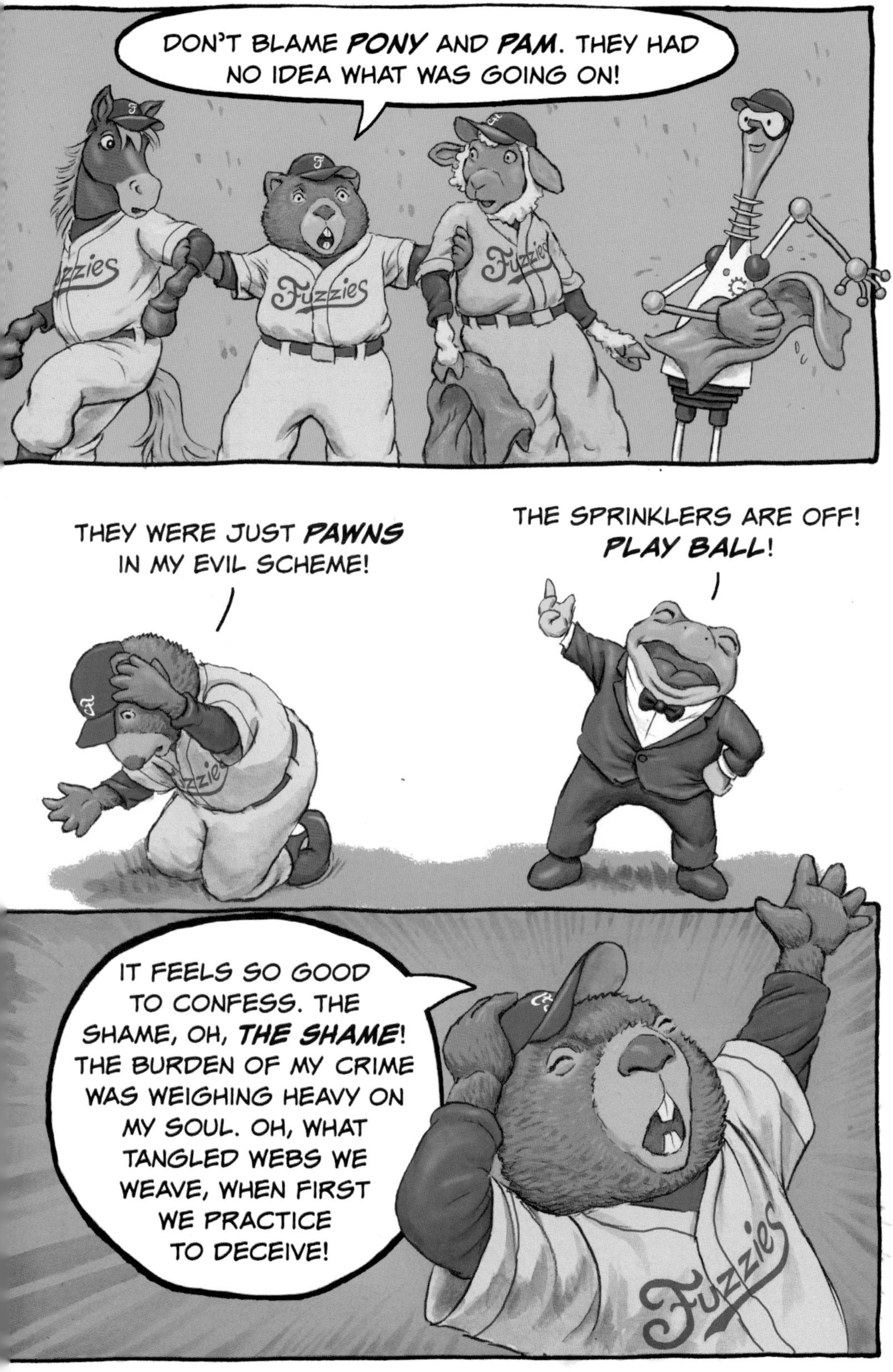
DON'T BLAME PONY AND PAM. THEY HAD NO IDEA WHAT WAS GOING ON!
THEY WERE JUST PAWNS IN MY EVIL SCHEME!
THE SPRINKLERS ARE OFF! PLAY BALL!
IT FEELS SO GOOD TO CONFESS. THE SHAME, OH, THE SHAME! THE BURDEN OF MY CRIME WAS WEIGHING HEAVY ON MY SOUL. OH, WHAT TANGLED WEBS WE WEAVE, WHEN FIRST WE PRACTICE TO DECEIVE!

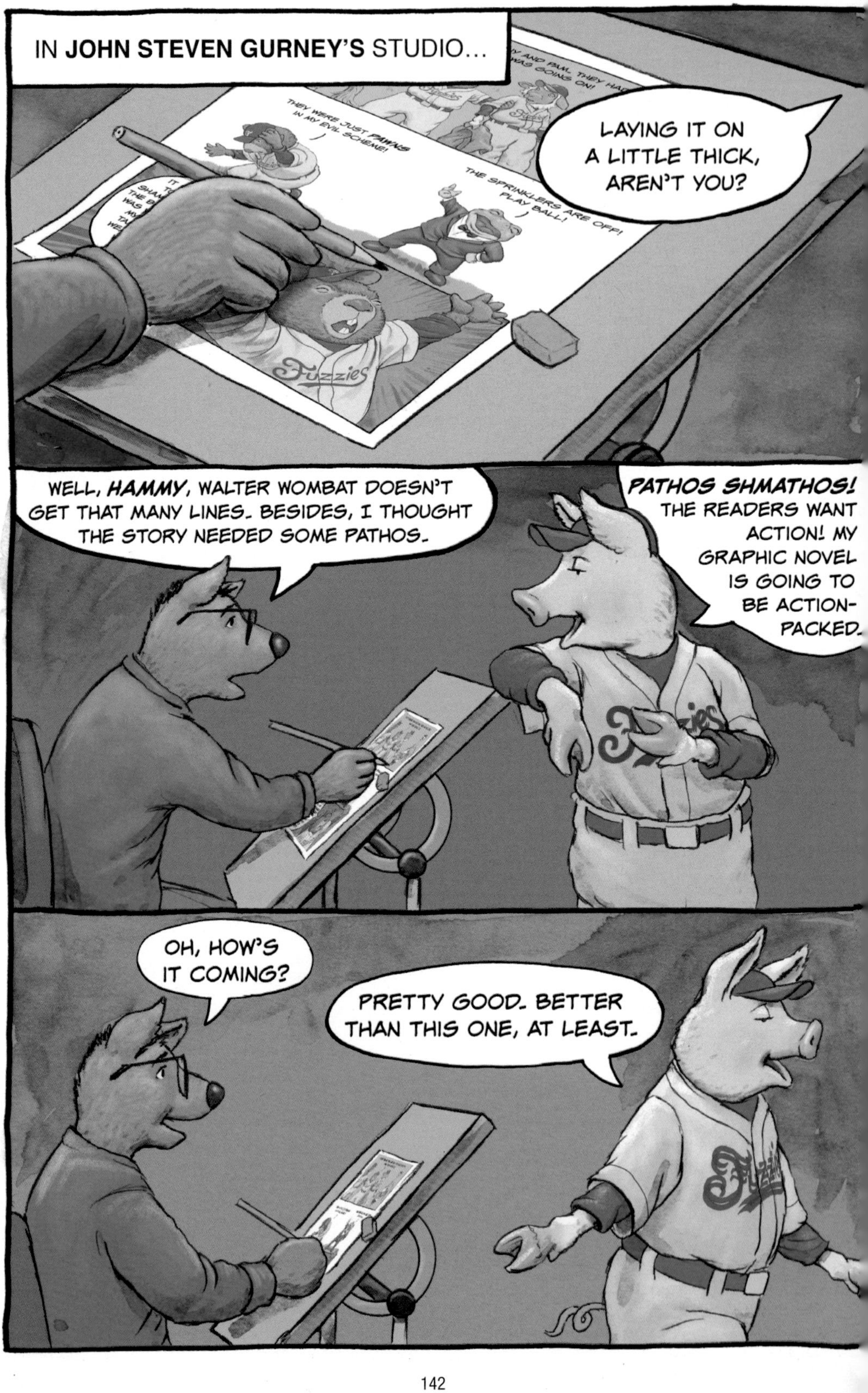
IN JOHN STEVEN GURNEY'S STUDIO...
THEY WERE JUST PAWNS IN MY EVIL SCHEME!
THE SPRINKLERS ARE OFF! PLAY BALL!
LAYING IT ON A LITTLE THICK, AREN'T YOU?
WELL, HAMMY, WALTER WOMBAT DOESN'T GET THAT MANY LINES. BESIDES, I THOUGHT THE STORY NEEDED SOME PATHOS.
PATHOS SHMATHOS! THE READERS WANT ACTION! MY GRAPHIC NOVEL IS GOING TO BE ACTION-PACKED.
OH, HOW'S IT COMING?
PRETTY GOOD. BETTER THAN THIS ONE, AT LEAST.

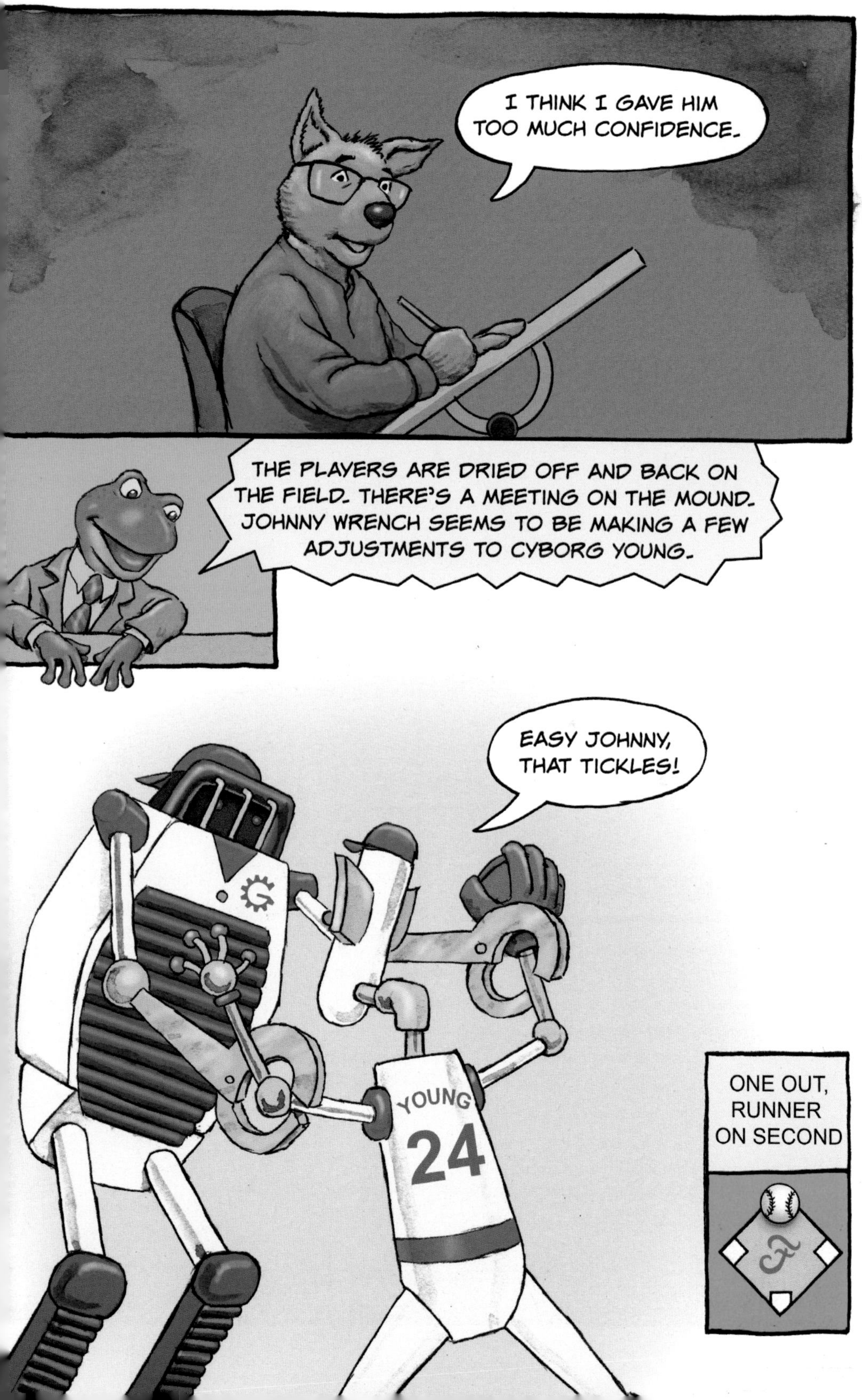
I THINK I GAVE HIM TOO MUCH CONFIDENCE.
THE PLAYERS ARE DRIED OFF AND BACK ON THE FIELD. THERE'S A MEETING ON THE MOUND. JOHNNY WRENCH SEEMS TO BE MAKING A FEW ADJUSTMENTS TO CYBORG YOUNG.
EASY JOHNNY, THAT TICKLES!
YOUNG
24
ONE OUT, RUNNER ON SECOND

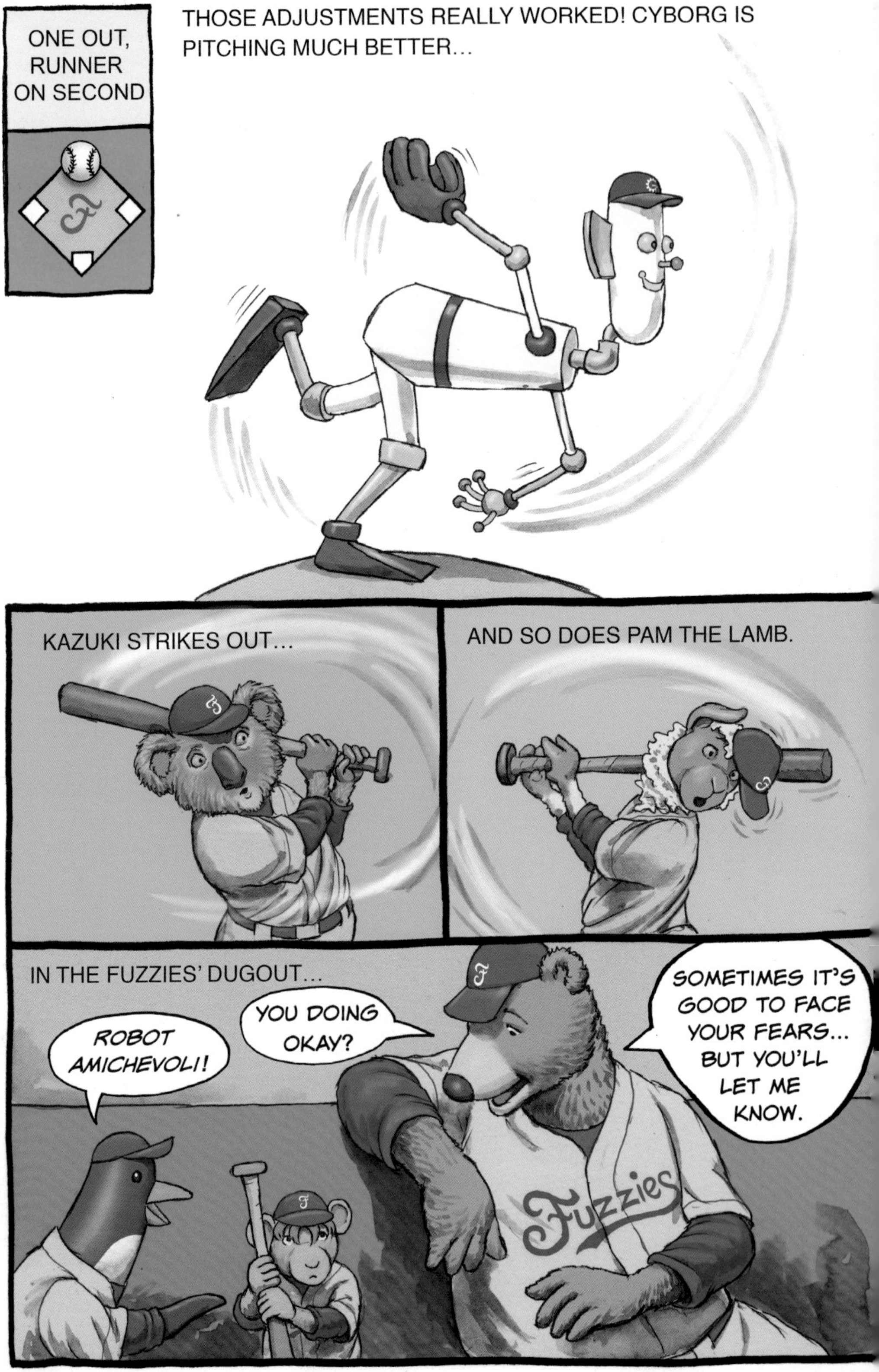
ONE OUT, RUNNER ON SECOND
THOSE ADJUSTMENTS REALLY WORKED! CYBORG IS PITCHING MUCH BETTER…
KAZUKI STRIKES OUT…
AND SO DOES PAM THE LAMB.
IN THE FUZZIES' DUGOUT…
ROBOT AMICHEVOLI!
YOU DOING OKAY?
SOMETIMES IT'S GOOD TO FACE YOUR FEARS… BUT YOU'LL LET ME KNOW.
Fuzzies

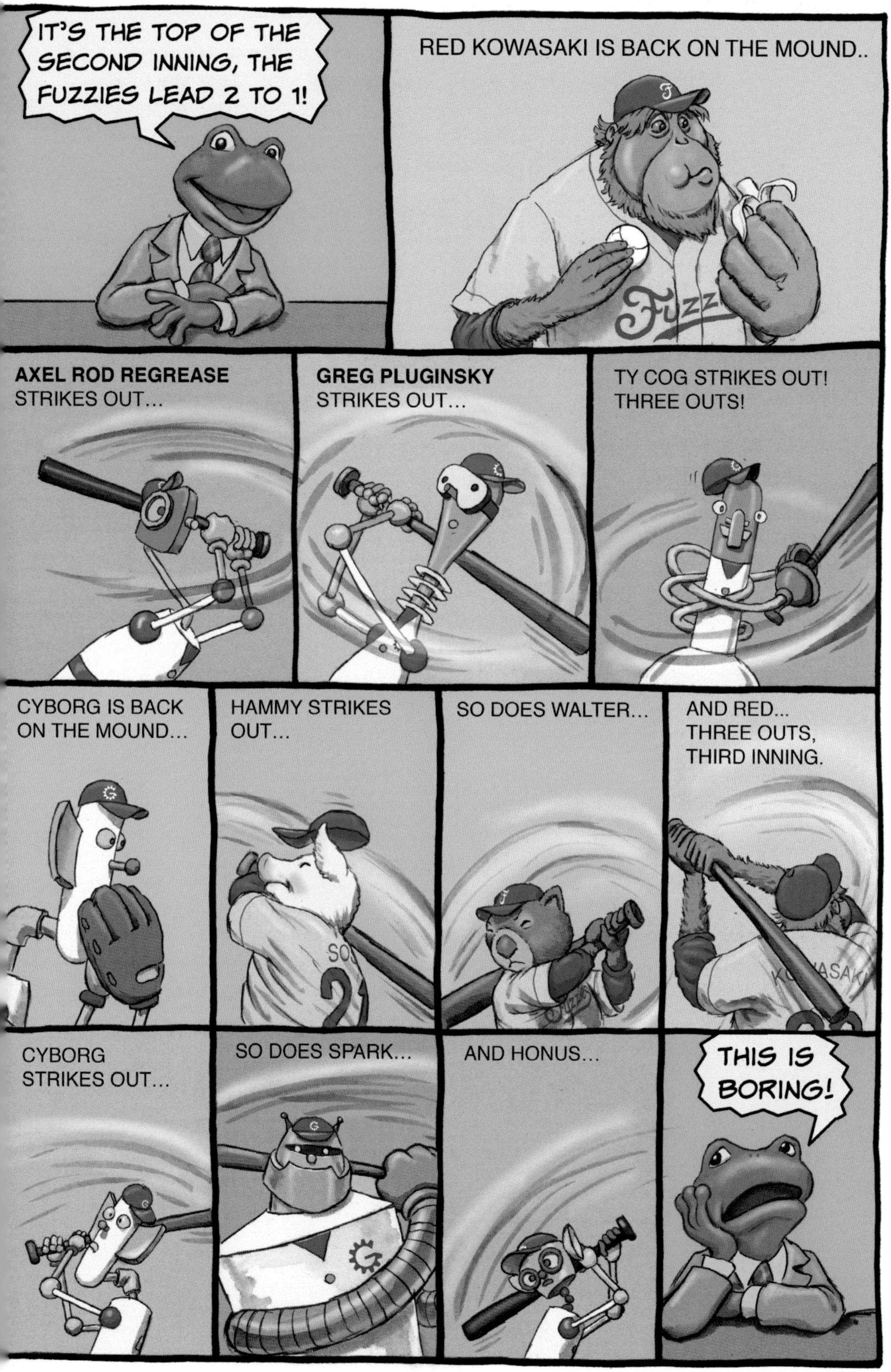
IT'S THE TOP OF THE SECOND INNING, THE FUZZIES LEAD 2 TO 1!
RED KOWASAKI IS BACK ON THE MOUND..
AXEL ROD REGREASE STRIKES OUT…
GREG PLUGINSKY STRIKES OUT…
TY COG STRIKES OUT! THREE OUTS!
CYBORG IS BACK ON THE MOUND…
HAMMY STRIKES OUT…
SO DOES WALTER…
AND RED… THREE OUTS, THIRD INNING.
CYBORG STRIKES OUT…
SO DOES SPARK…
AND HONUS…
THIS IS BORING!

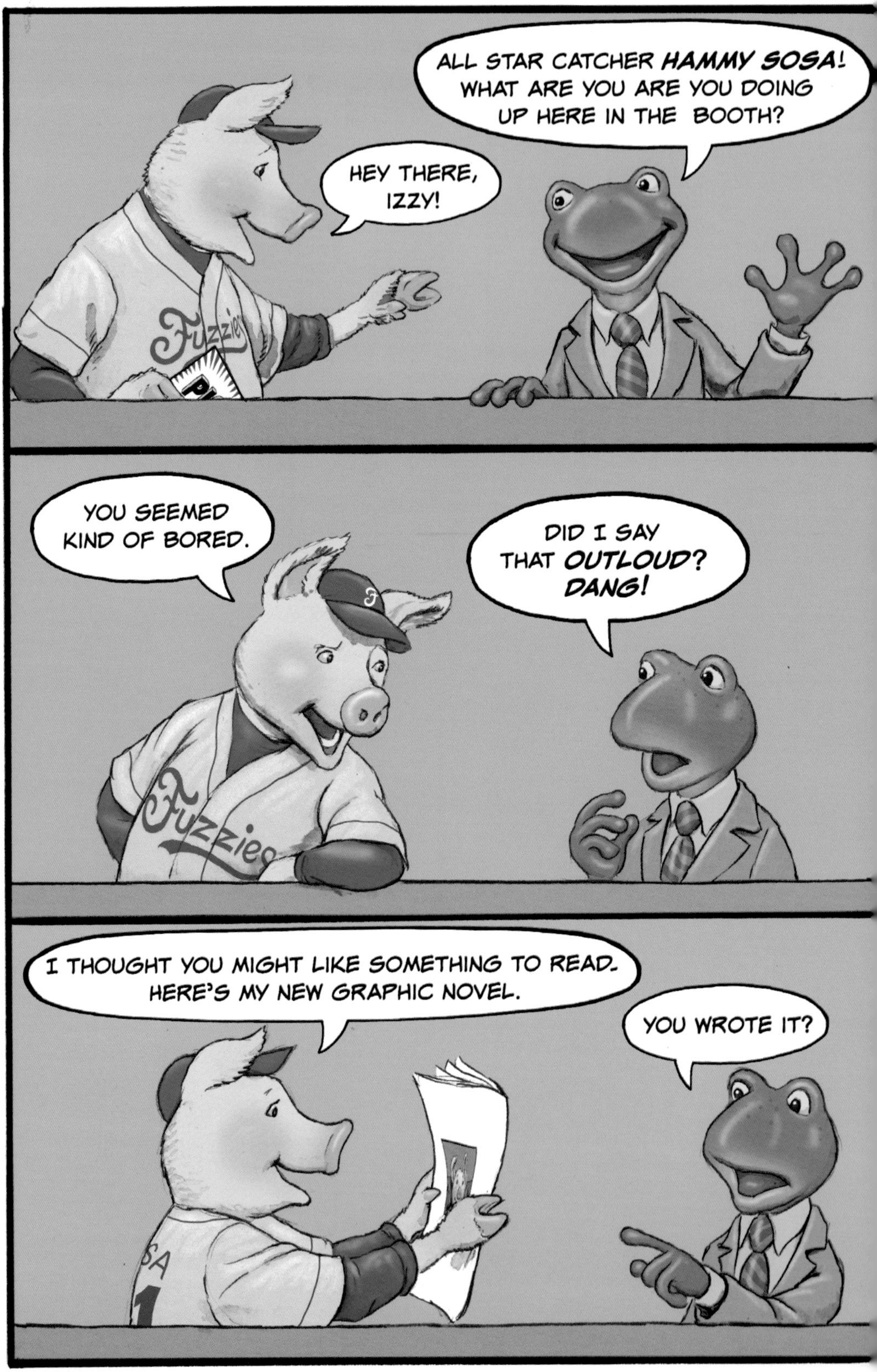
ALL STAR CATCHER HAMMY SOSA! WHAT ARE YOU ARE YOU DOING UP HERE IN THE BOOTH?
HEY THERE, IZZY!
YOU SEEMED KIND OF BORED.
DID I SAY THAT OUTLOUD? DANG!
I THOUGHT YOU MIGHT LIKE SOMETHING TO READ. HERE'S MY NEW GRAPHIC NOVEL.
YOU WROTE IT?

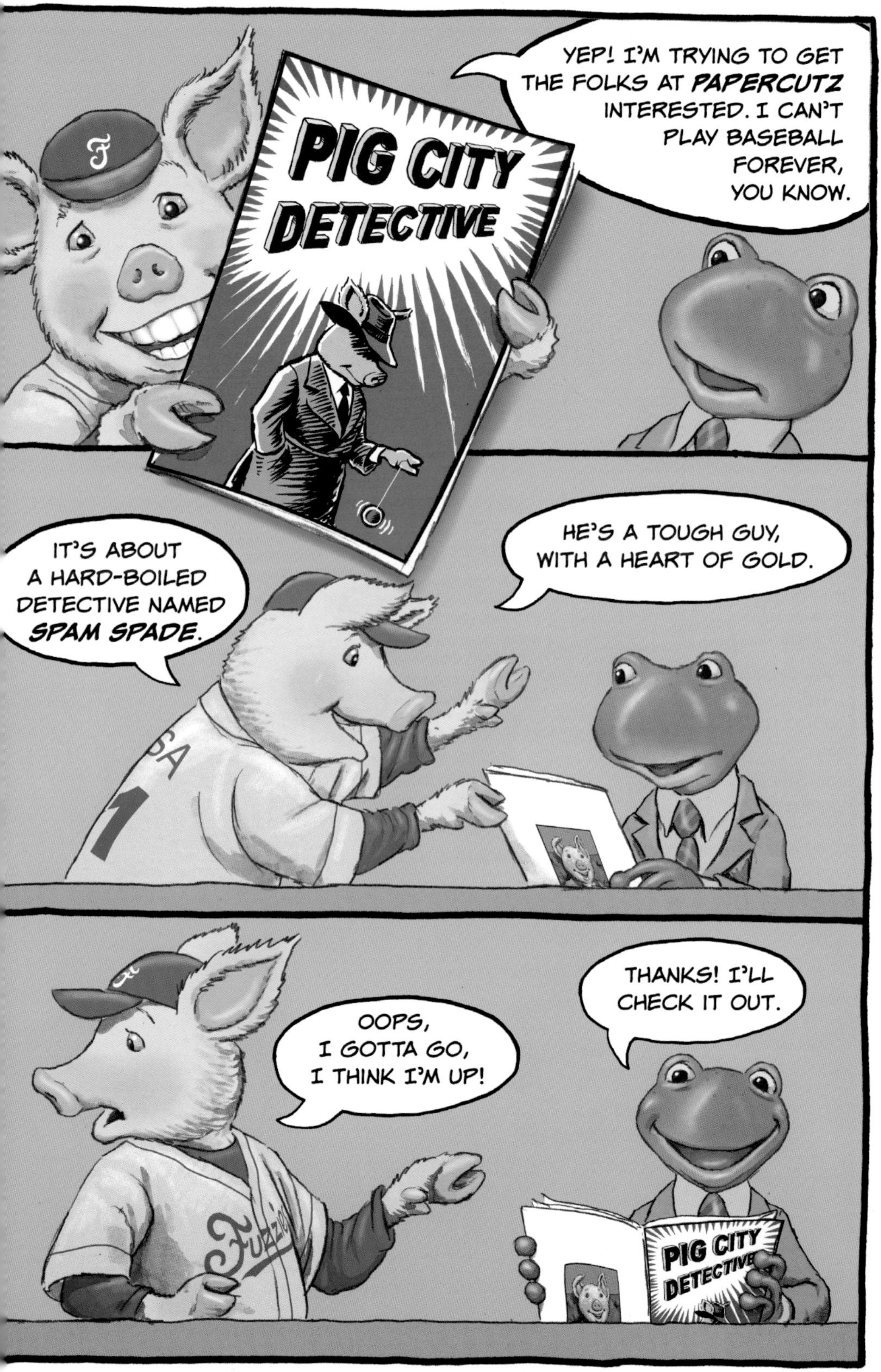
PIG CITY DETECTIVE
YEP! I'M TRYING TO GET THE FOLKS AT PAPERCUTZ INTERESTED. I CAN'T PLAY BASEBALL FOREVER, YOU KNOW.
IT'S ABOUT A HARD-BOILED DETECTIVE NAMED SPAM SPADE.
HE'S A TOUGH GUY, WITH A HEART OF GOLD.
OOPS, I GOTTA GO, I THINK I'M UP!
THANKS! I'LL CHECK IT OUT.
PIG CITY DETECTIVE

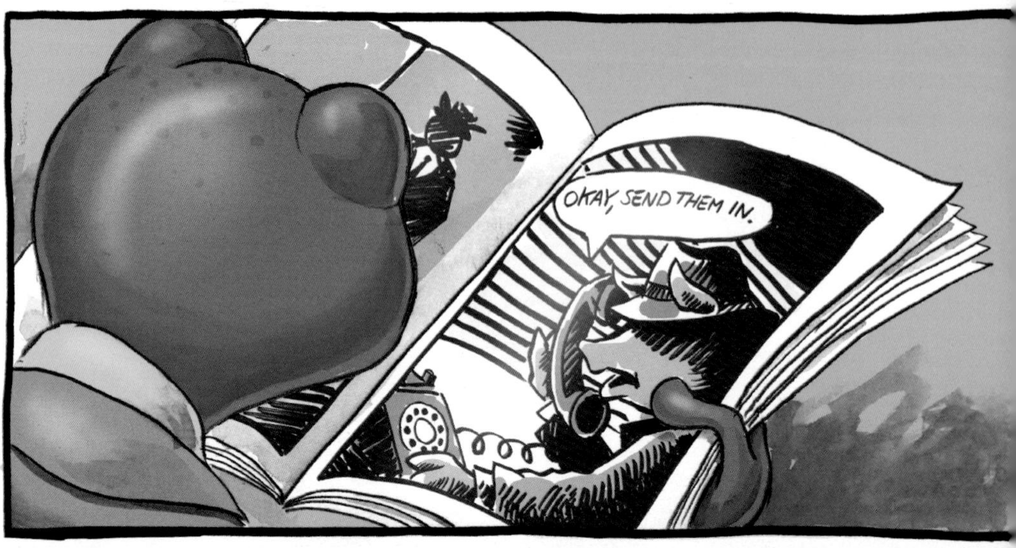
OKAY, SEND THEM IN.

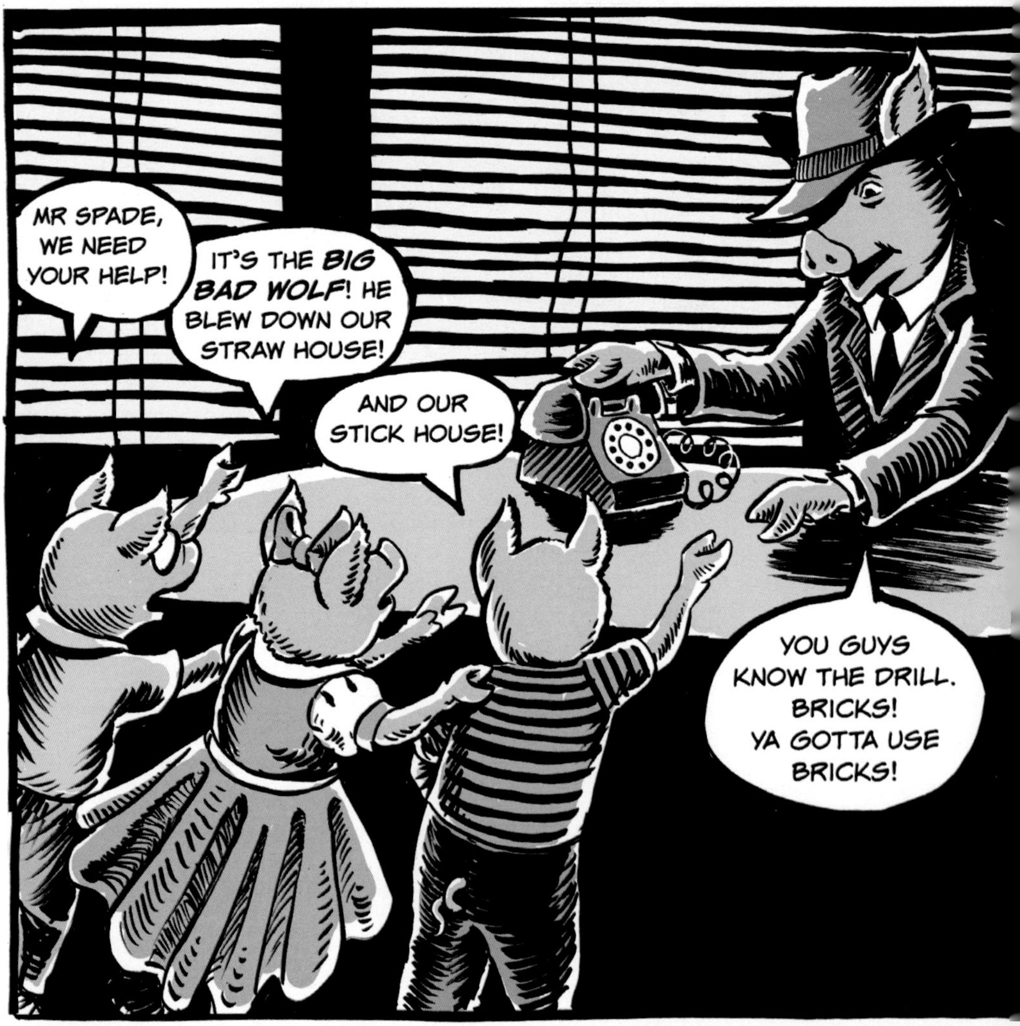
MR SPADE, WE NEED YOUR HELP!
IT'S THE *BIG BAD WOLF*! HE BLEW DOWN OUR STRAW HOUSE!
AND OUR STICK HOUSE!
YOU GUYS KNOW THE DRILL. BRICKS! YA GOTTA USE BRICKS!

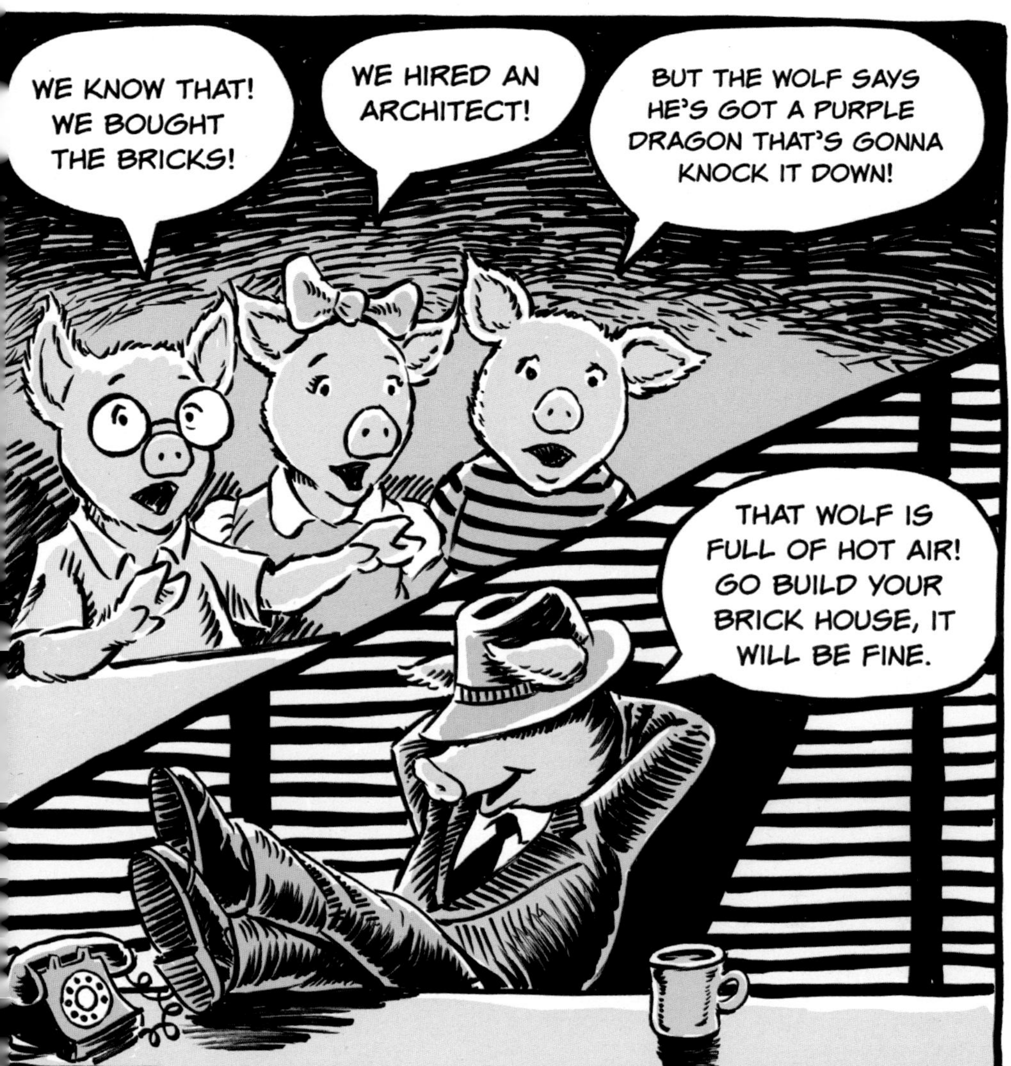
WE KNOW THAT! WE BOUGHT THE BRICKS!
WE HIRED AN ARCHITECT!
BUT THE WOLF SAYS HE'S GOT A PURPLE DRAGON THAT'S GONNA KNOCK IT DOWN!
THAT WOLF IS FULL OF HOT AIR! GO BUILD YOUR BRICK HOUSE, IT WILL BE FINE.

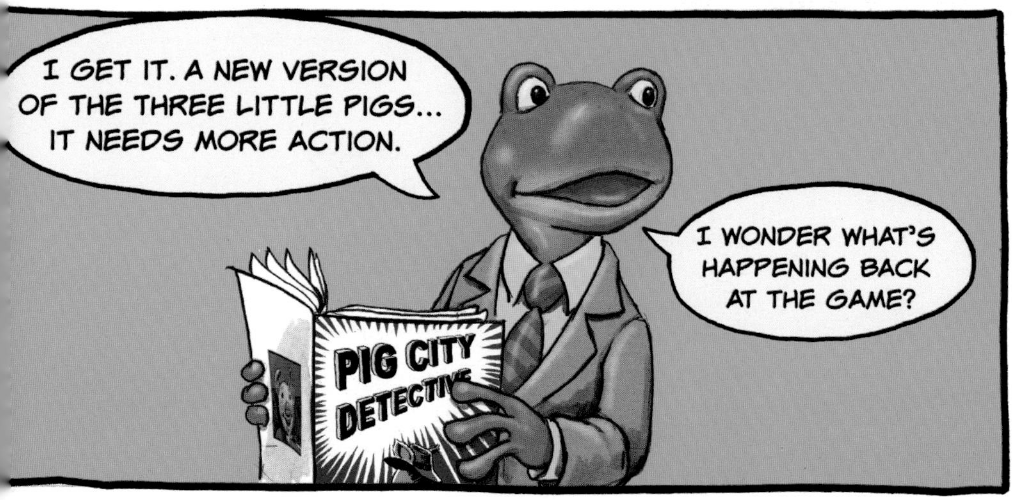
I GET IT. A NEW VERSION OF THE THREE LITTLE PIGS... IT NEEDS MORE ACTION.
I WONDER WHAT'S HAPPENING BACK AT THE GAME?
PIG CITY DETECTIVE

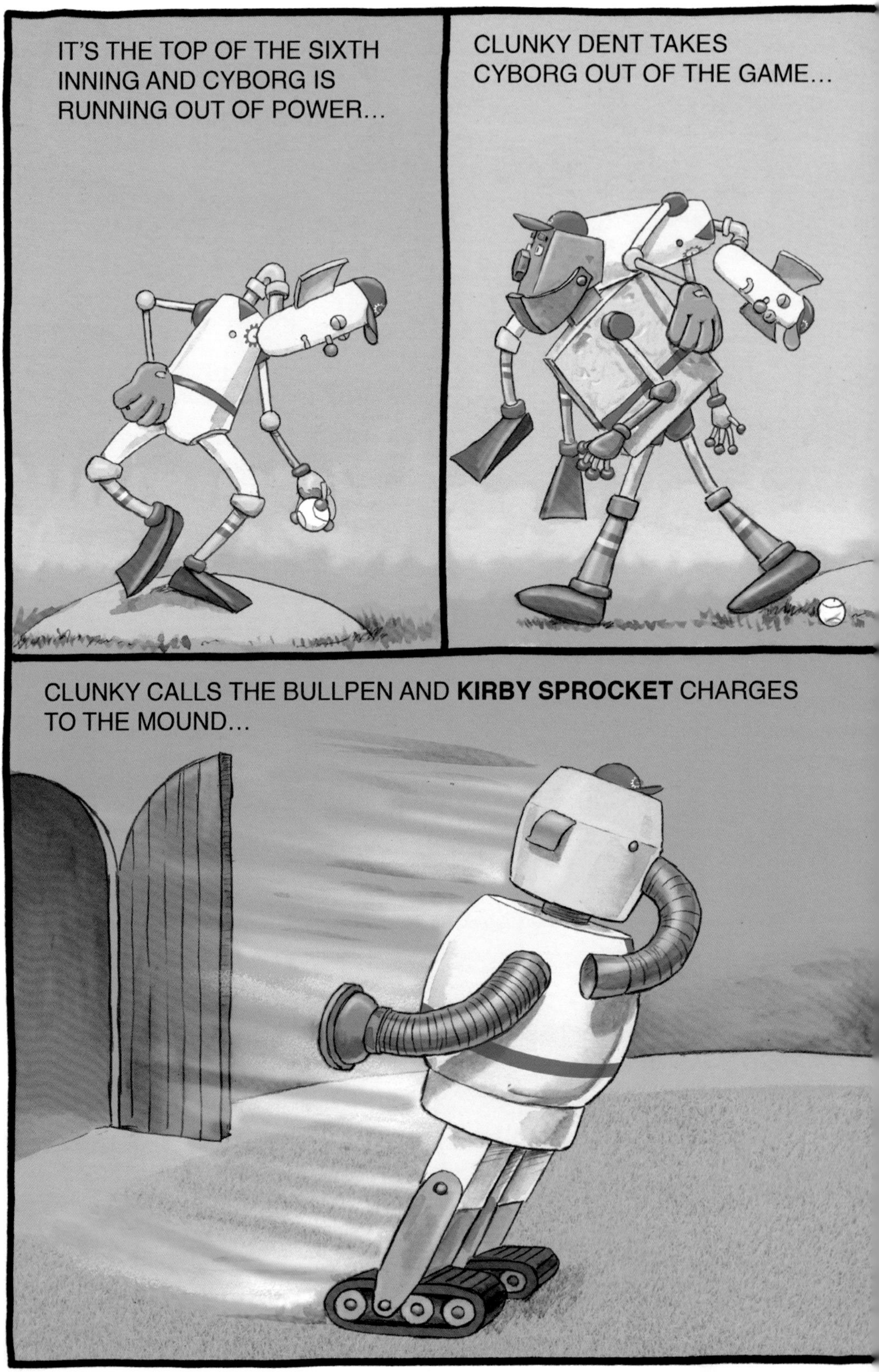
IT'S THE TOP OF THE SIXTH INNING AND CYBORG IS RUNNING OUT OF POWER...
CLUNKY DENT TAKES CYBORG OUT OF THE GAME...
CLUNKY CALLS THE BULLPEN AND **KIRBY SPROCKET** CHARGES TO THE MOUND...

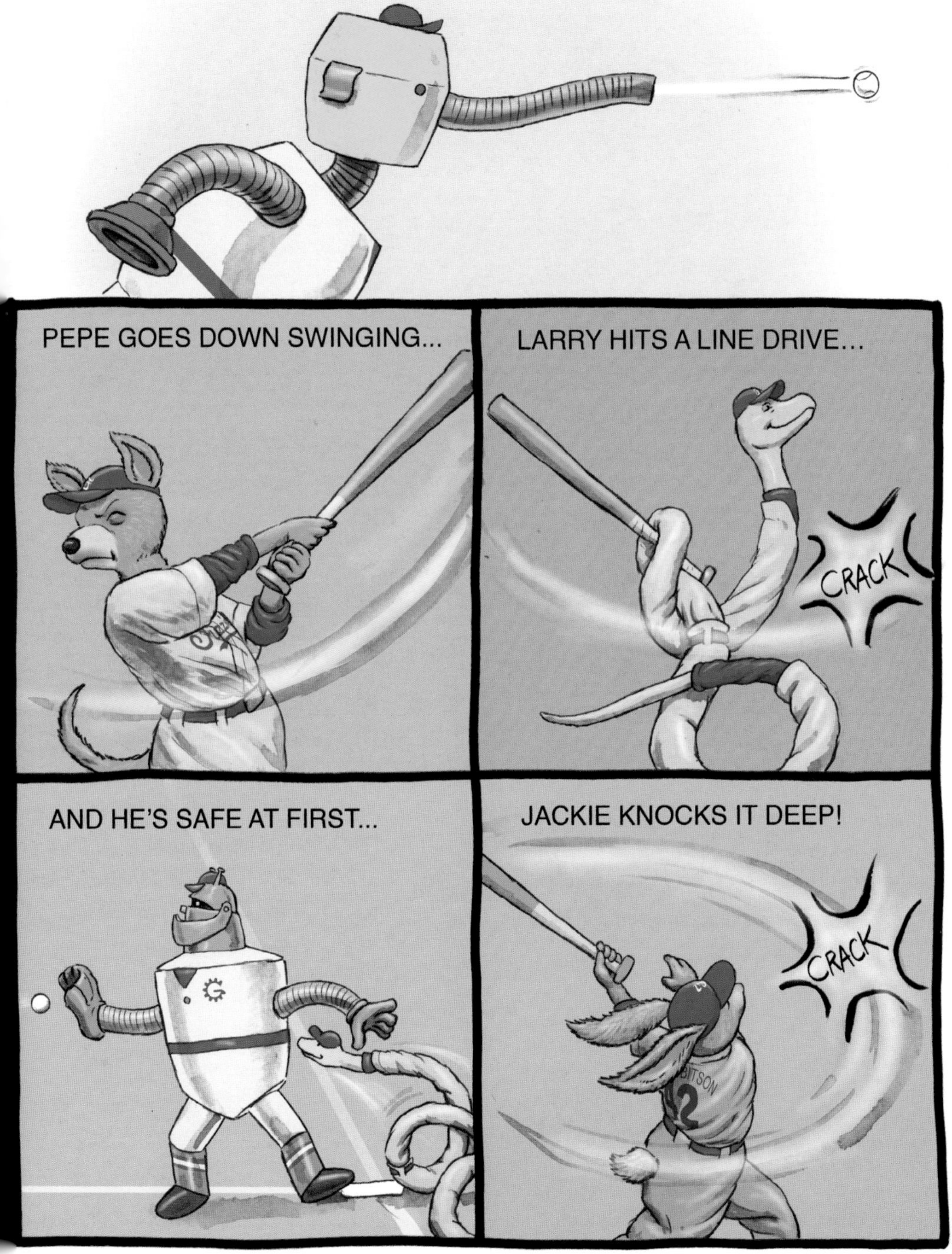
PEPE GOES DOWN SWINGING...
LARRY HITS A LINE DRIVE...
CRACK
AND HE'S SAFE AT FIRST...
JACKIE KNOCKS IT DEEP!
CRACK

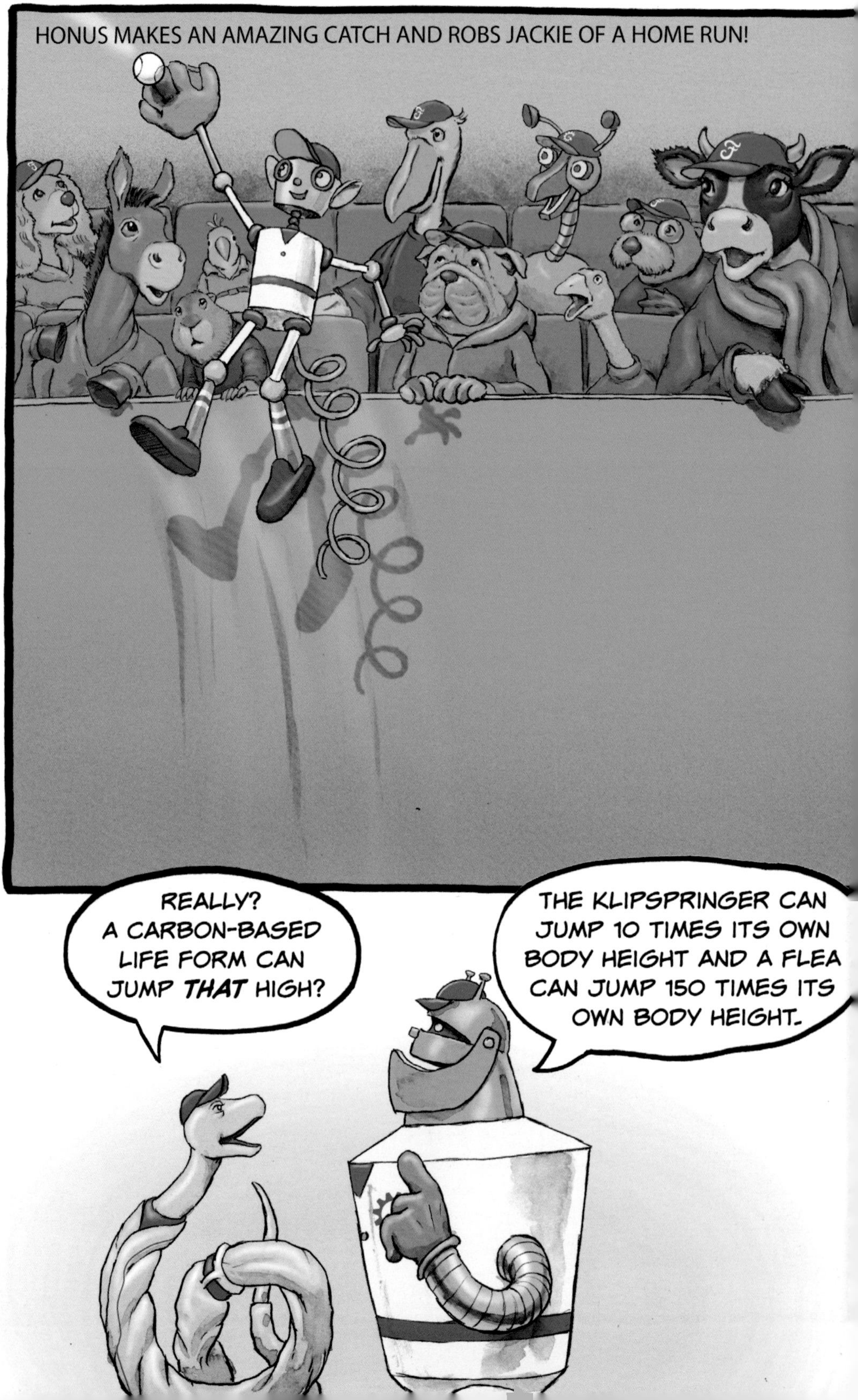
HONUS MAKES AN AMAZING CATCH AND ROBS JACKIE OF A HOME RUN!
REALLY? A CARBON-BASED LIFE FORM CAN JUMP THAT HIGH?
THE KLIPSPRINGER CAN JUMP 10 TIMES ITS OWN BODY HEIGHT AND A FLEA CAN JUMP 150 TIMES ITS OWN BODY HEIGHT.

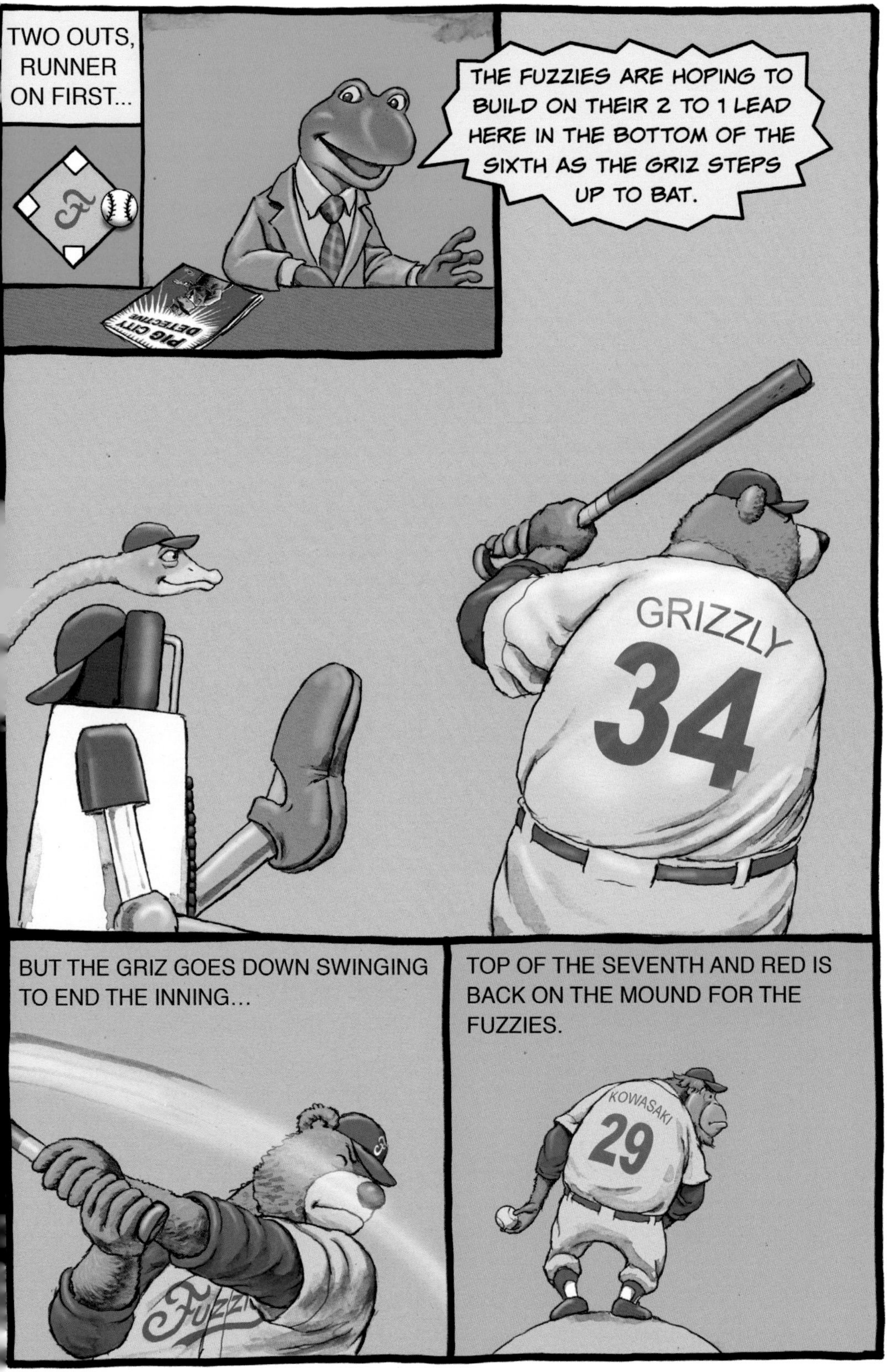
TWO OUTS, RUNNER ON FIRST...
THE FUZZIES ARE HOPING TO BUILD ON THEIR 2 TO 1 LEAD HERE IN THE BOTTOM OF THE SIXTH AS THE GRIZ STEPS UP TO BAT.
PIG CITY DETECTIVE
GRIZZLY
34
BUT THE GRIZ GOES DOWN SWINGING TO END THE INNING...
TOP OF THE SEVENTH AND RED IS BACK ON THE MOUND FOR THE FUZZIES.
KOWASAKI
29

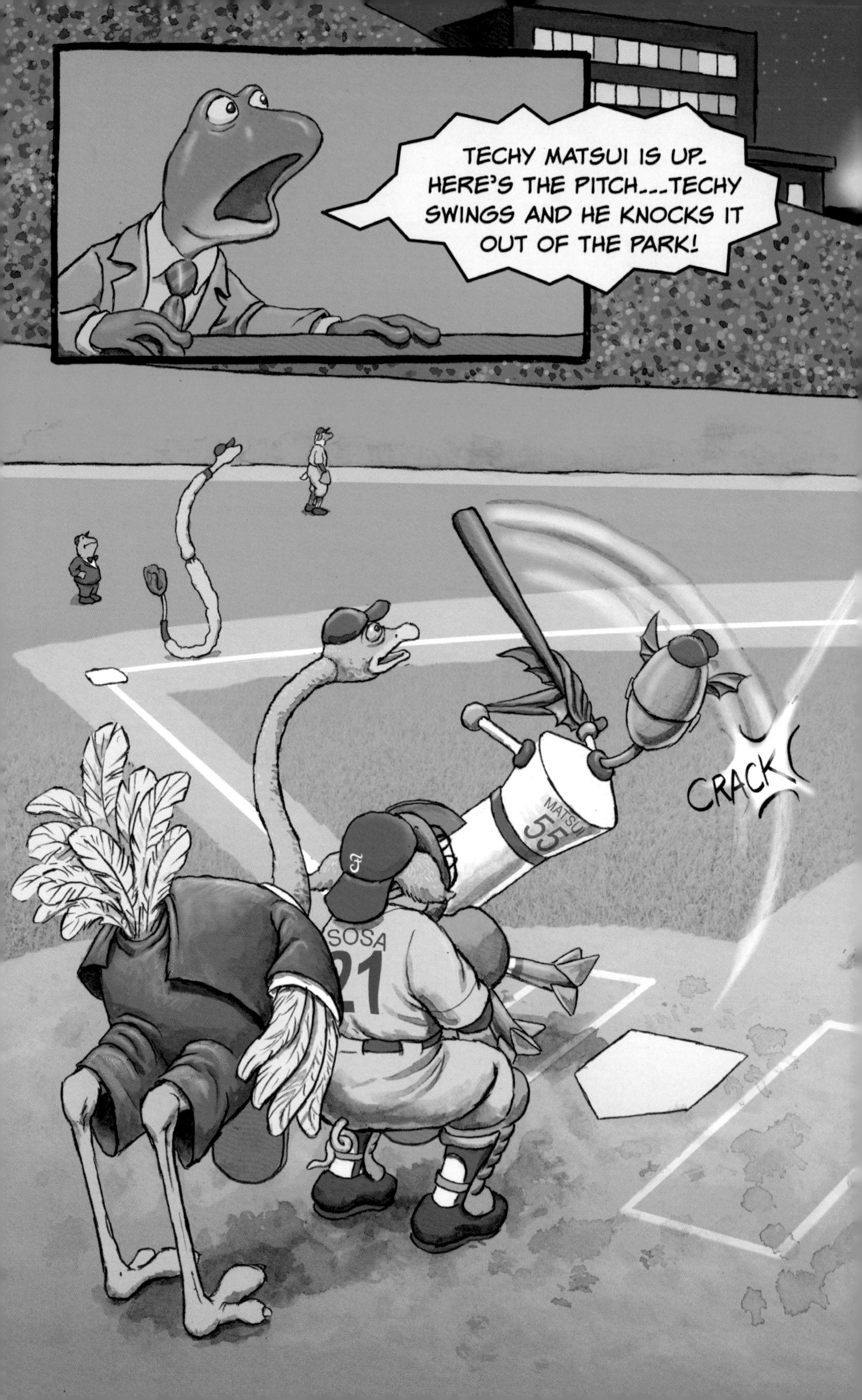
TECHY MATSUI IS UP. HERE'S THE PITCH...TECHY SWINGS AND HE KNOCKS IT OUT OF THE PARK!
MATSUI 55
SOSA 21
CRACK

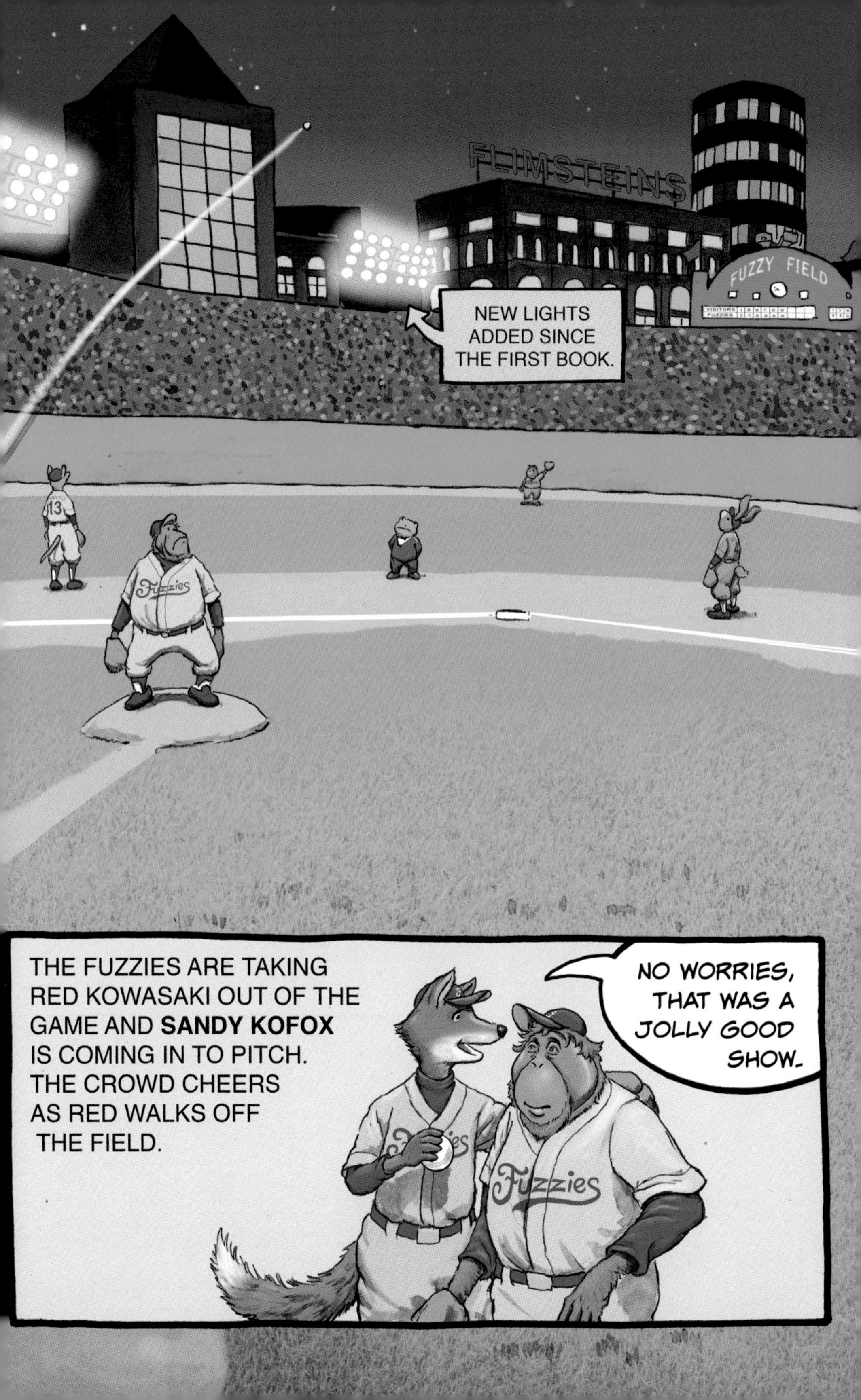
FLIMSTEINS
FUZZY FIELD
NEW LIGHTS ADDED SINCE THE FIRST BOOK.
Fuzzies
THE FUZZIES ARE TAKING RED KOWASAKI OUT OF THE GAME AND **SANDY KOFOX** IS COMING IN TO PITCH. THE CROWD CHEERS AS RED WALKS OFF THE FIELD.
NO WORRIES, THAT WAS A JOLLY GOOD SHOW.
Fuzzies

SEVENTH INNING AND THE SCORE IS TIED AT 2 TO 2.
NO OUTS, AND THE CLANKEES ARE UP...

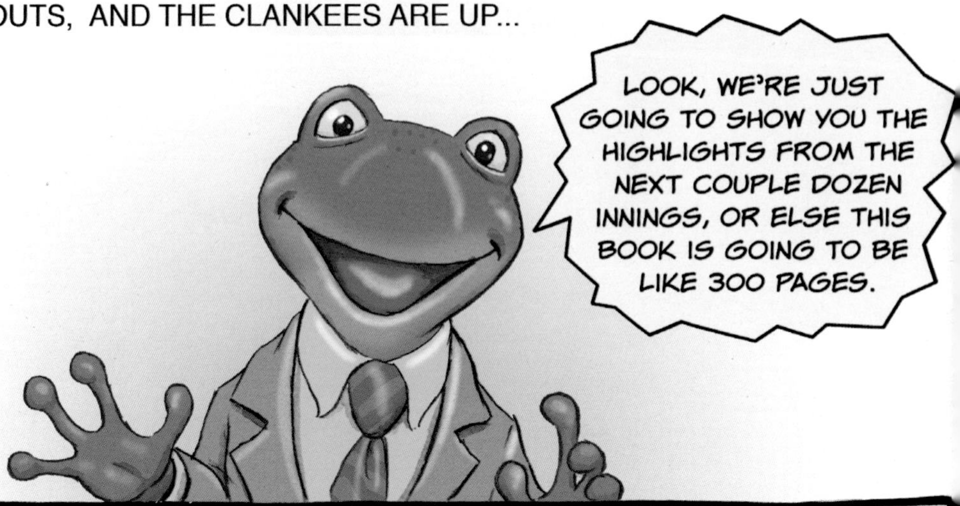
LOOK, WE'RE JUST GOING TO SHOW YOU THE HIGHLIGHTS FROM THE NEXT COUPLE DOZEN INNINGS, OR ELSE THIS BOOK IS GOING TO BE LIKE 300 PAGES.

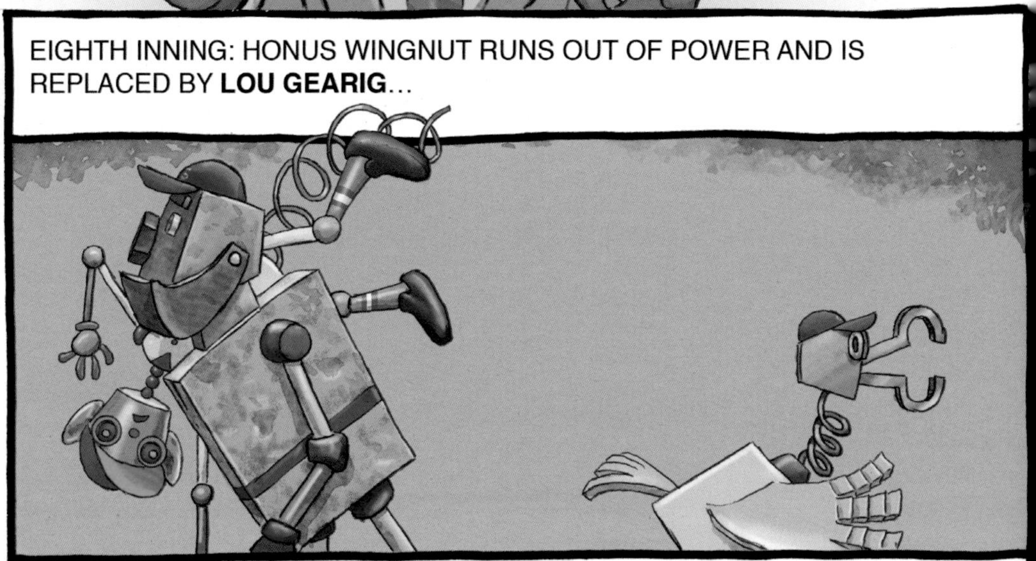
EIGHTH INNING: HONUS WINGNUT RUNS OUT OF POWER AND IS REPLACED BY **LOU GEARIG**...

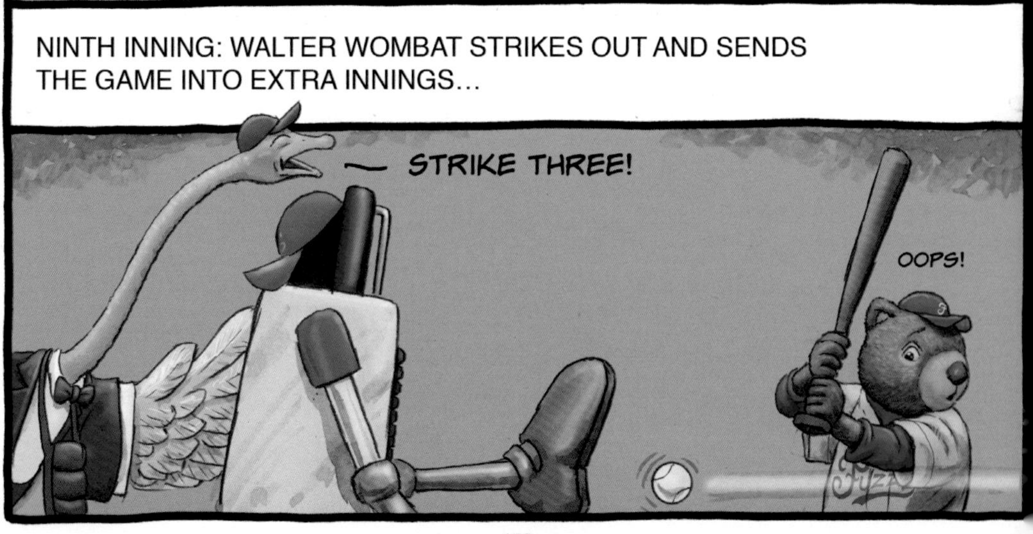
NINTH INNING: WALTER WOMBAT STRIKES OUT AND SENDS THE GAME INTO EXTRA INNINGS...
— STRIKE THREE!
OOPS!

TWELFTH INNING: PERCIVALE PENGUINO GOES IN FOR KAZUKI KOALA...
NAP TIME!
POSSO GIOCARE!
FIFTEENTH INNING: TECHY MATSUI RUNS OUT OF POWER AND IS REPLACED BY HARMON KILOWATT...
BLEEEP!
EIGHTEENTH INNING: PITCHING CHANGE, KIT OCELOT COMES IN FOR THE FUZZIES...
THEY'LL FADE SOON.
TWENTY-FIRST INNING: PITCHING CHANGE, ROTOR HORNSBY COMES IN FOR THE CLANKEES...
TWENTY-THIRD INNING: THE GAME IS STILL TIED AT 2...
MIND IF I REST MY HEAD?
GO FOR IT.
TWENTY-SIXTH INNING: CRUSTY FOB GOES IN FOR TY COG...

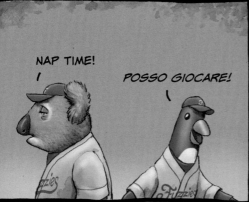

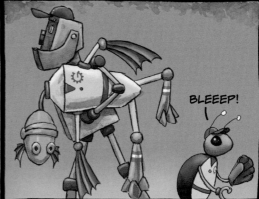

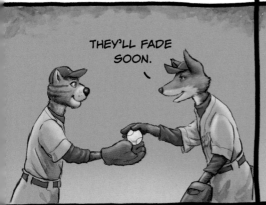

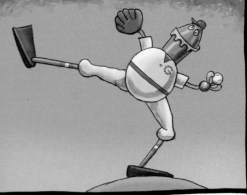

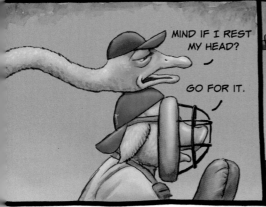

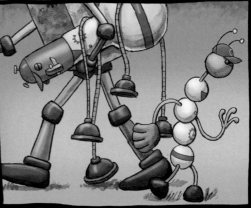

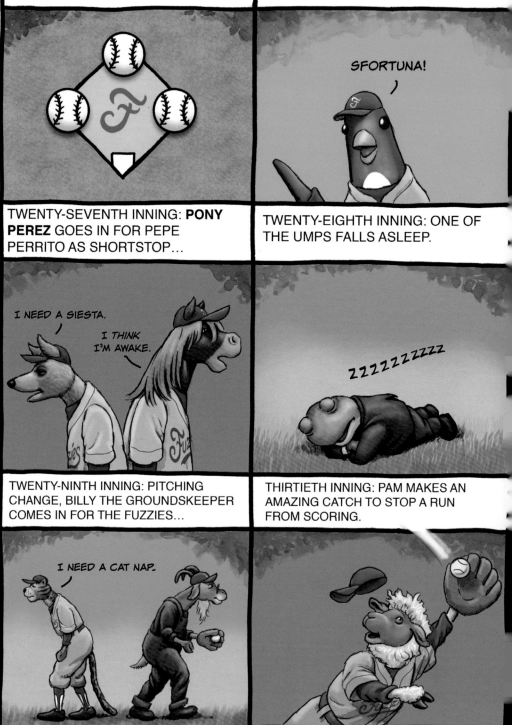

TWENTY-FOURTH INNING: THE FUZZIES LOAD THE BASES WITH NO OUTS!

BUT THE NEXT BATTER STRIKES OUT, AND THEN THERE'S A DOUBLE PLAY...

SFORTUNA!

TWENTY-SEVENTH INNING: **PONY PEREZ** GOES IN FOR PEPE PERRITO AS SHORTSTOP...

TWENTY-EIGHTH INNING: ONE OF THE UMPS FALLS ASLEEP.

I NEED A SIESTA.

I THINK I'M AWAKE.

ZZZZZZZZZZ

TWENTY-NINTH INNING: PITCHING CHANGE, BILLY THE GROUNDSKEEPER COMES IN FOR THE FUZZIES...

THIRTIETH INNING: PAM MAKES AN AMAZING CATCH TO STOP A RUN FROM SCORING.

I NEED A CAT NAP.

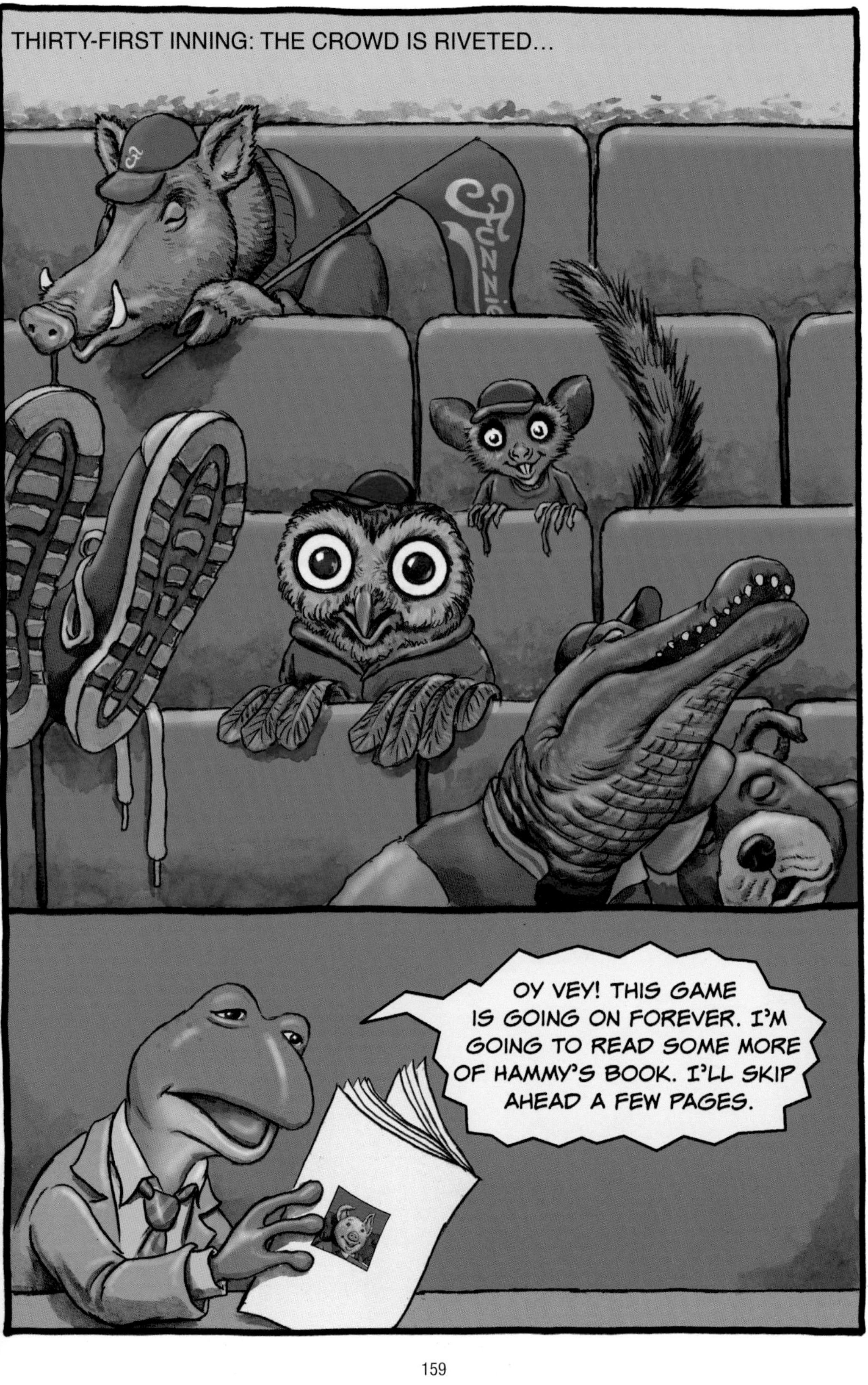
THIRTY-FIRST INNING: THE CROWD IS RIVETED…
OY VEY! THIS GAME IS GOING ON FOREVER. I'M GOING TO READ SOME MORE OF HAMMY'S BOOK. I'LL SKIP AHEAD A FEW PAGES.

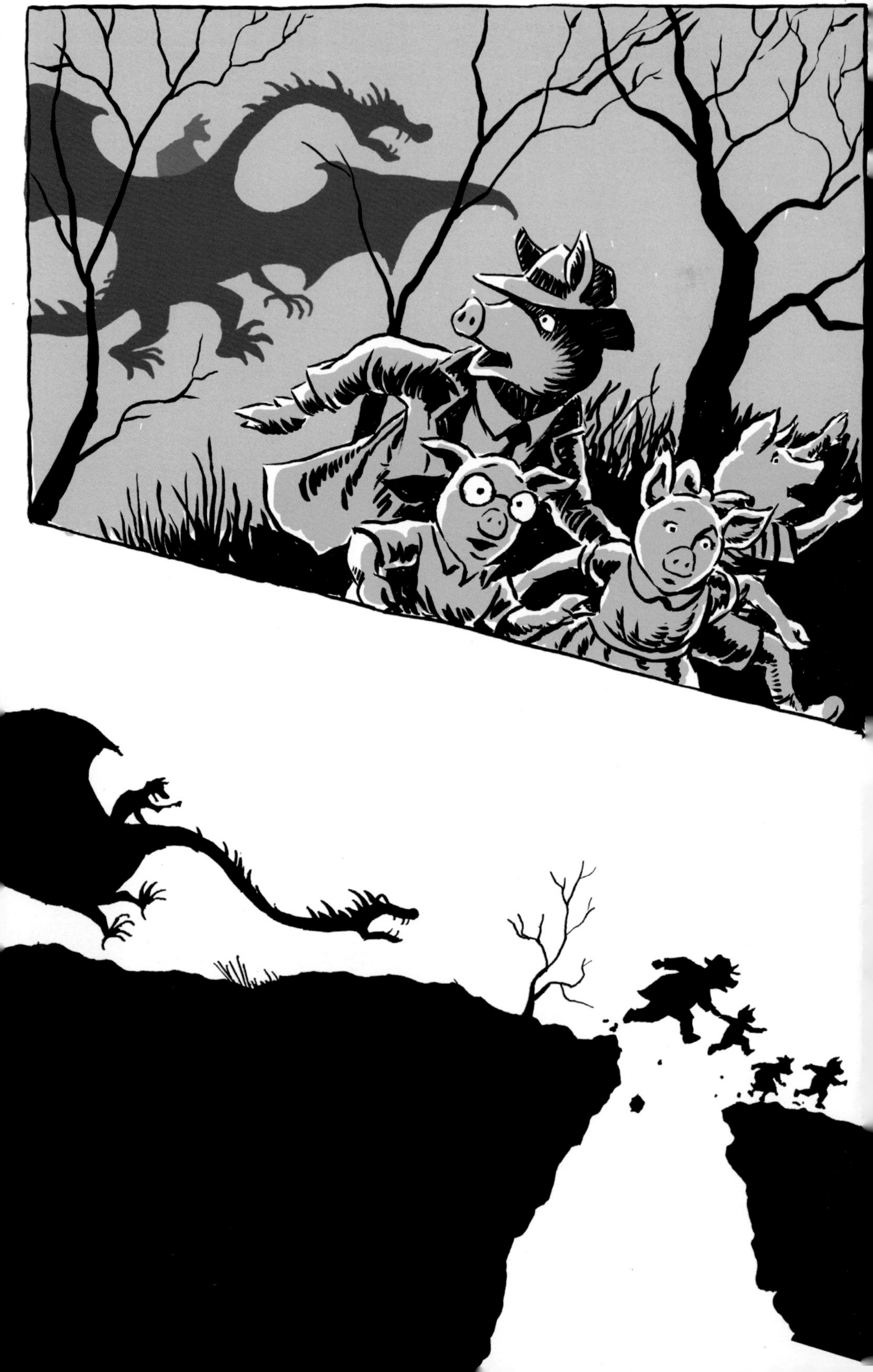

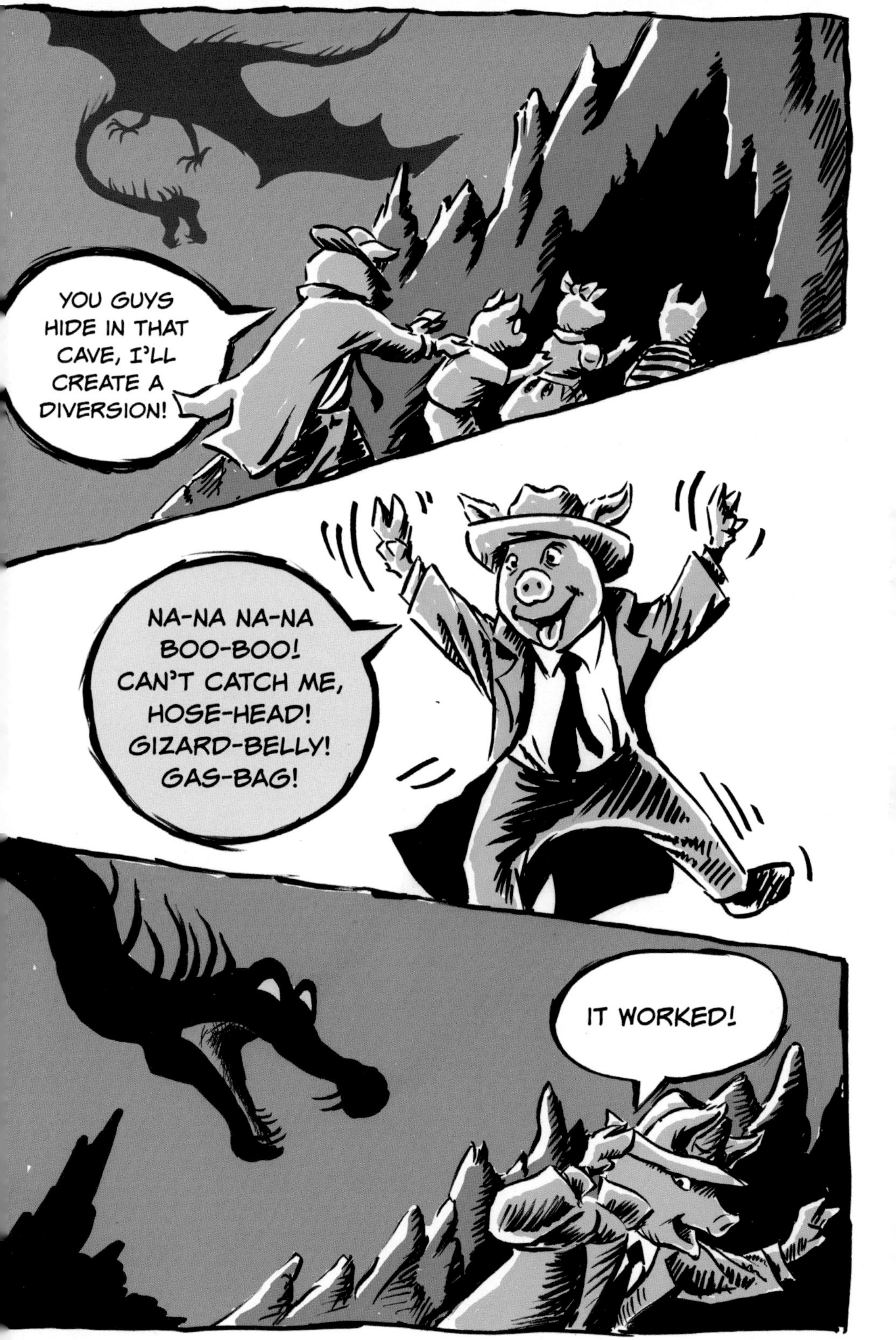
YOU GUYS HIDE IN THAT CAVE, I'LL CREATE A DIVERSION!
NA-NA NA-NA BOO-BOO! CAN'T CATCH ME, HOSE-HEAD! GIZARD-BELLY! GAS-BAG!
IT WORKED!

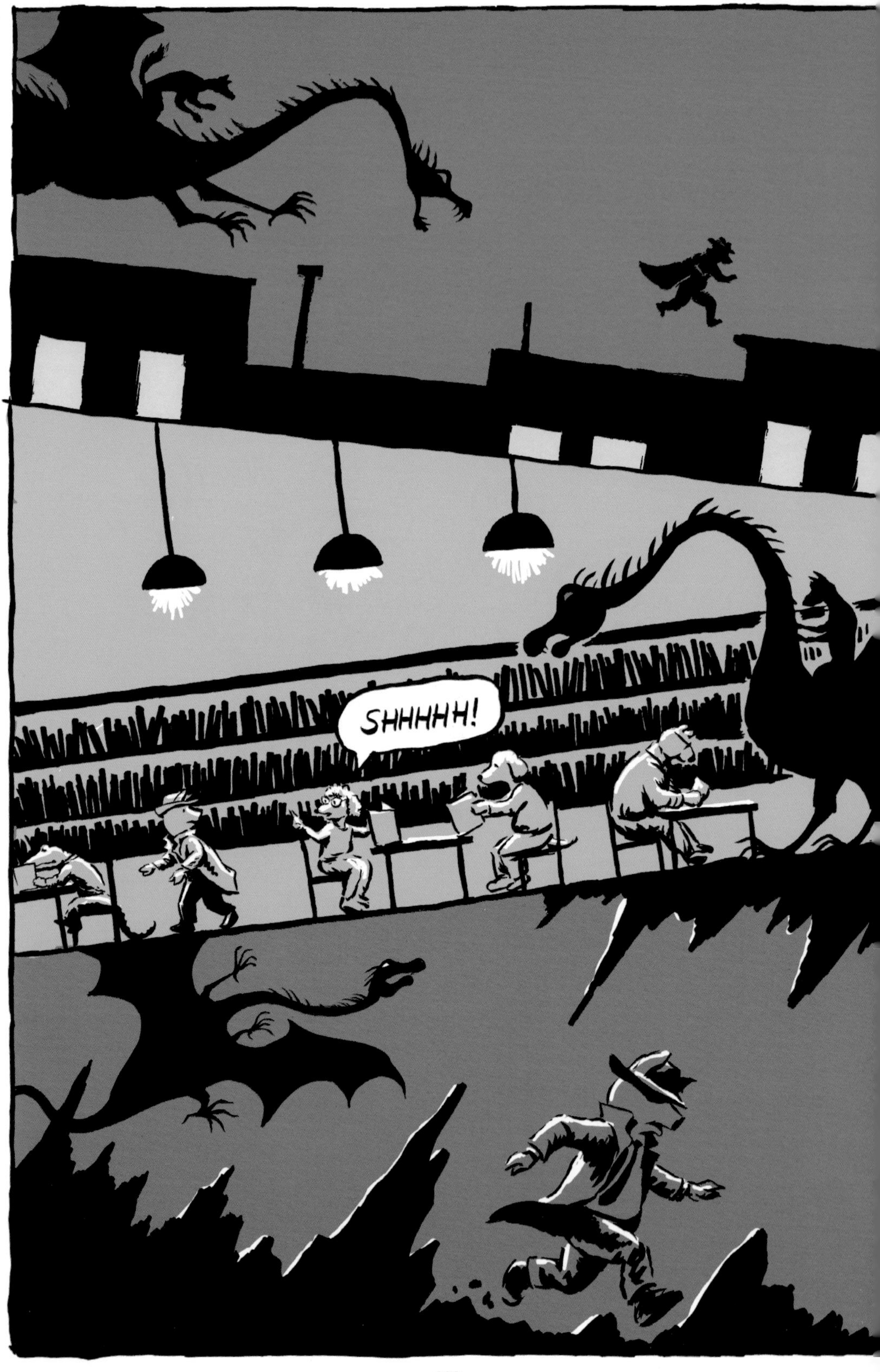
SHHHHH!

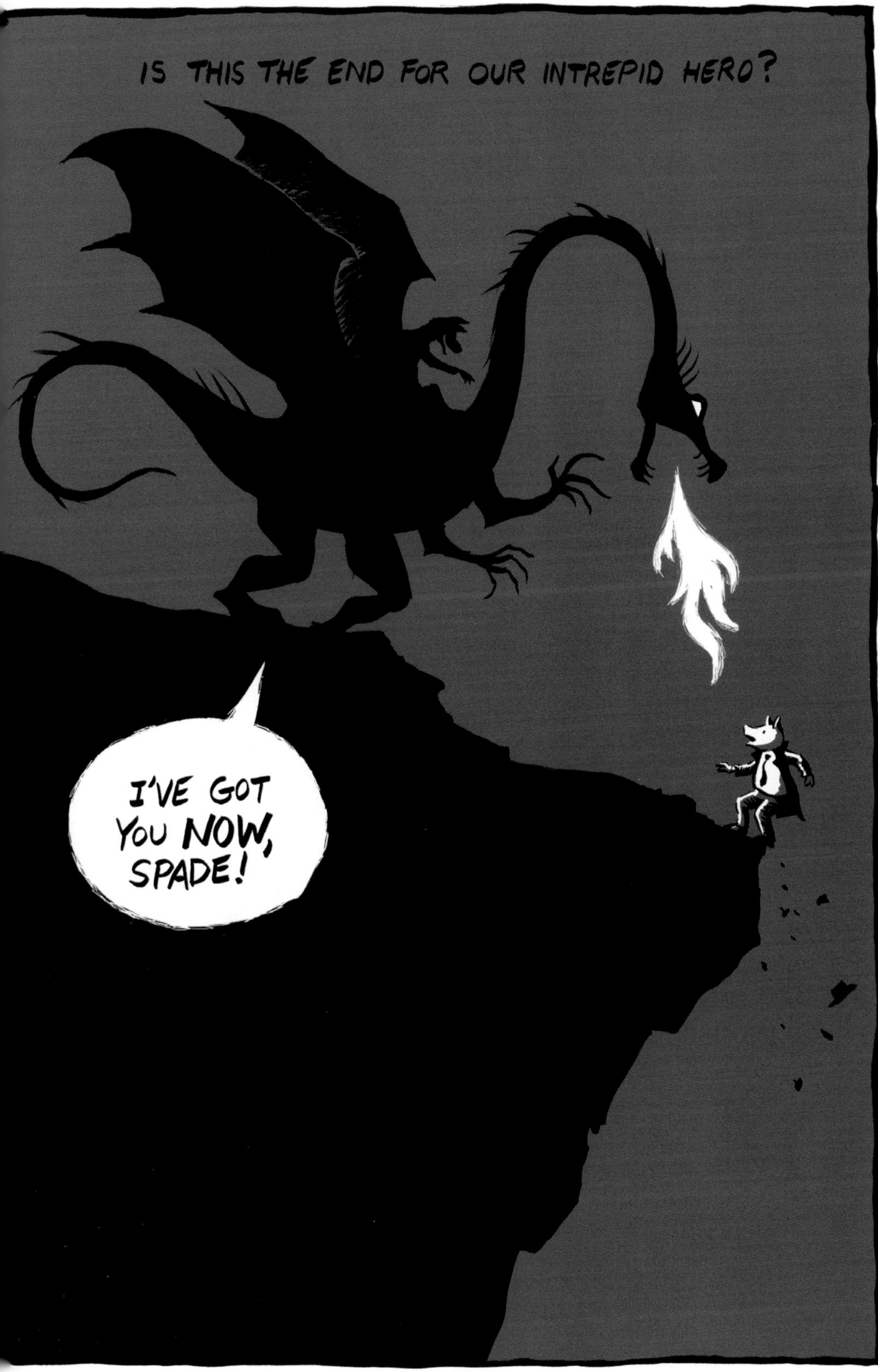
IS THIS THE END FOR OUR INTREPID HERO?
I'VE GOT YOU NOW, SPADE!

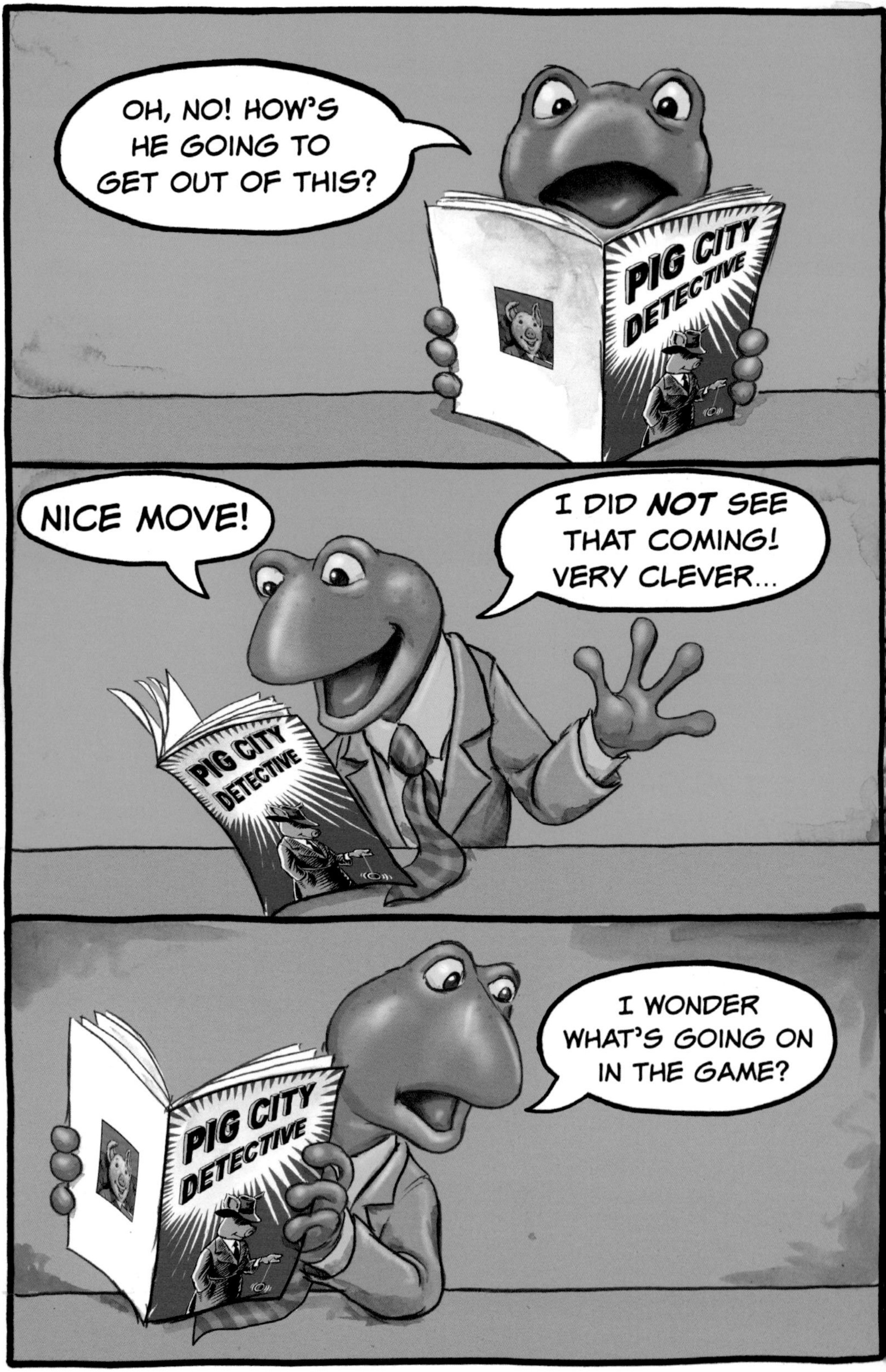
OH, NO! HOW'S HE GOING TO GET OUT OF THIS?
PIG CITY DETECTIVE
NICE MOVE!
I DID **NOT** SEE THAT COMING! VERY CLEVER...
PIG CITY DETECTIVE
I WONDER WHAT'S GOING ON IN THE GAME?
PIG CITY DETECTIVE

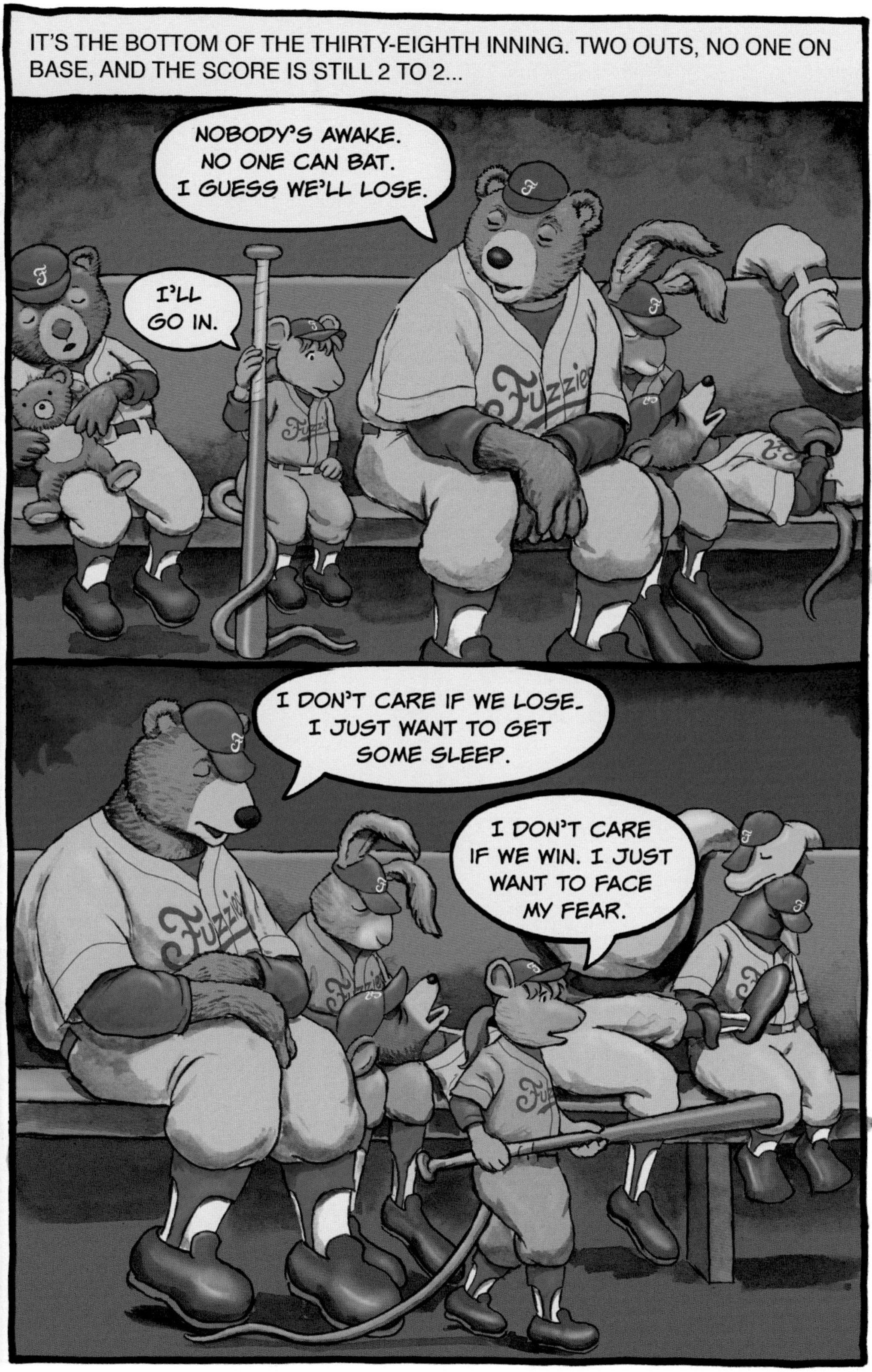
IT'S THE BOTTOM OF THE THIRTY-EIGHTH INNING. TWO OUTS, NO ONE ON BASE, AND THE SCORE IS STILL 2 TO 2...
NOBODY'S AWAKE. NO ONE CAN BAT. I GUESS WE'LL LOSE.
I'LL GO IN.
I DON'T CARE IF WE LOSE. I JUST WANT TO GET SOME SLEEP.
I DON'T CARE IF WE WIN. I JUST WANT TO FACE MY FEAR.

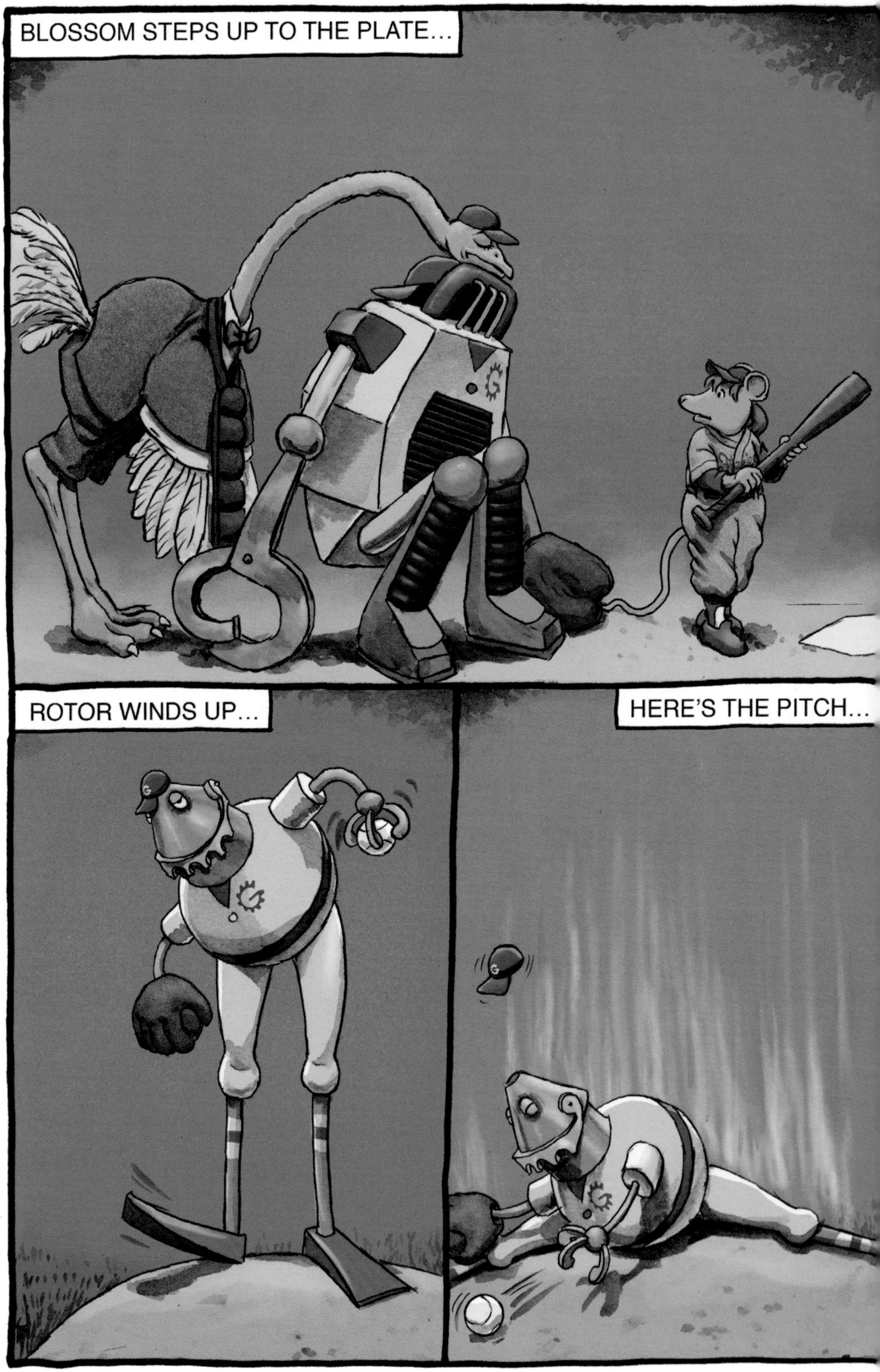
BLOSSOM STEPS UP TO THE PLATE...
ROTOR WINDS UP...
HERE'S THE PITCH...

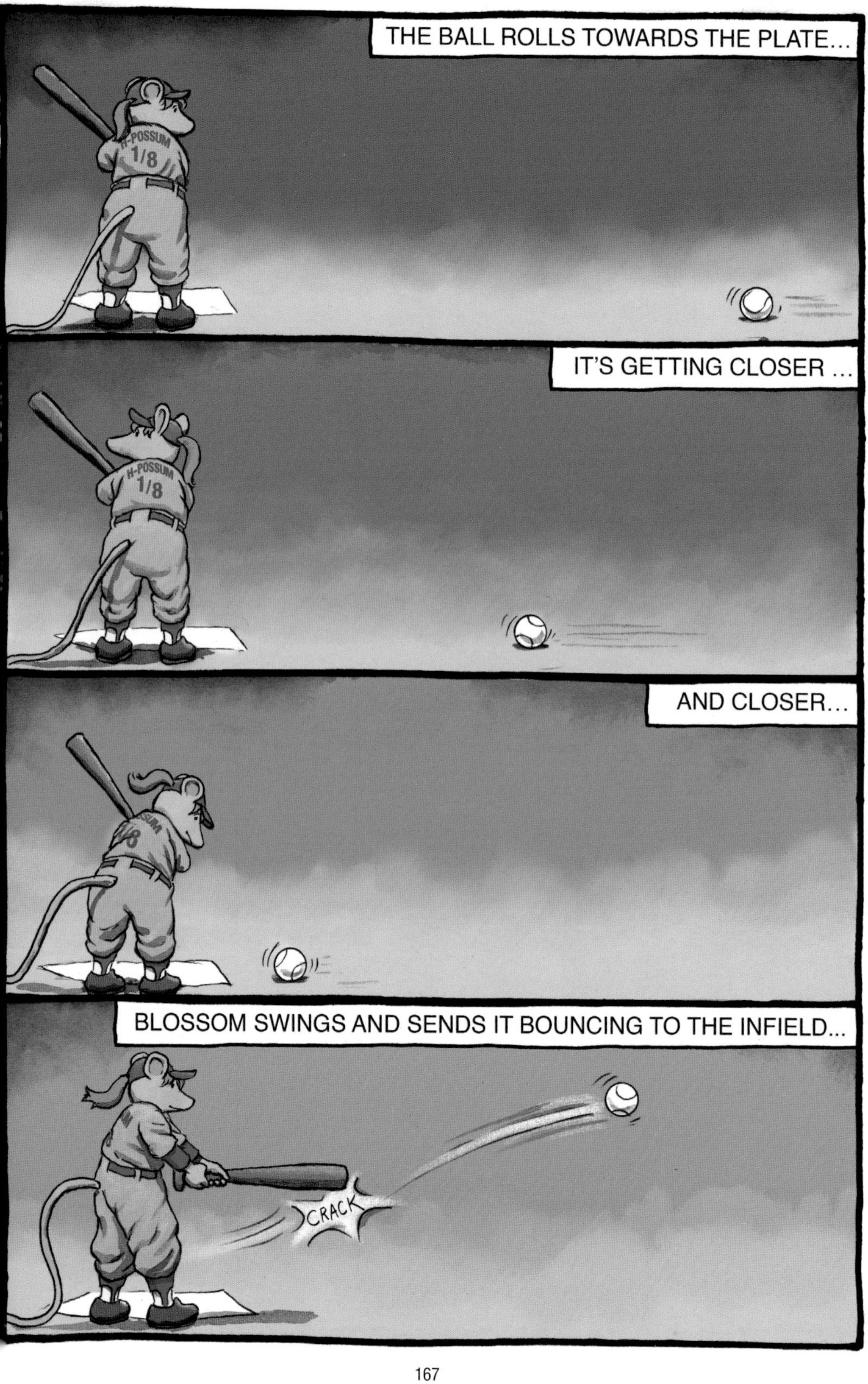
THE BALL ROLLS TOWARDS THE PLATE...
H-POSSUM
1/8
IT'S GETTING CLOSER ...
H-POSSUM
1/8
AND CLOSER...
BLOSSOM SWINGS AND SENDS IT BOUNCING TO THE INFIELD...
CRACK

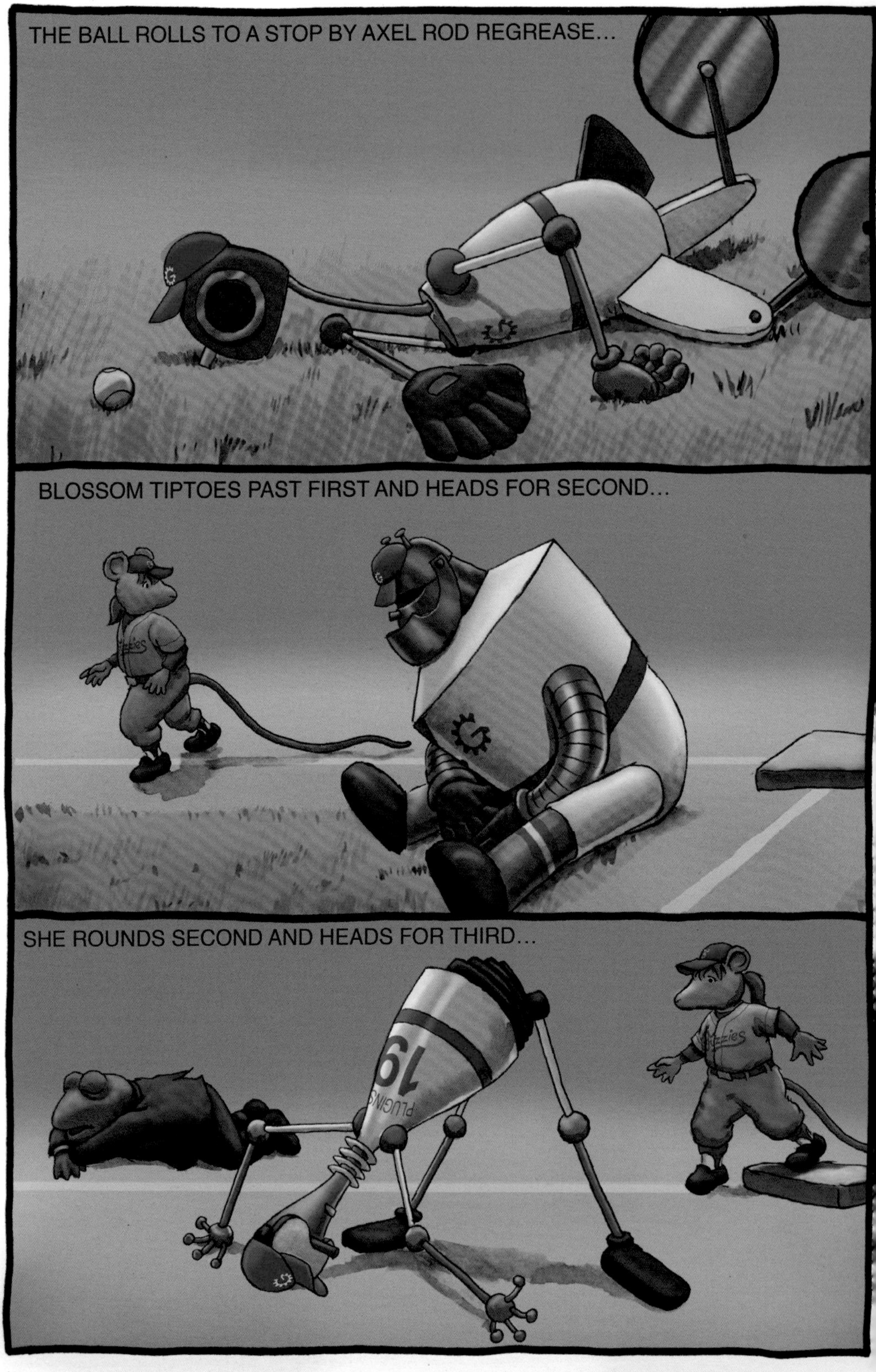
THE BALL ROLLS TO A STOP BY AXEL ROD REGREASE…
BLOSSOM TIPTOES PAST FIRST AND HEADS FOR SECOND…
SHE ROUNDS SECOND AND HEADS FOR THIRD…
19
PLUGINS

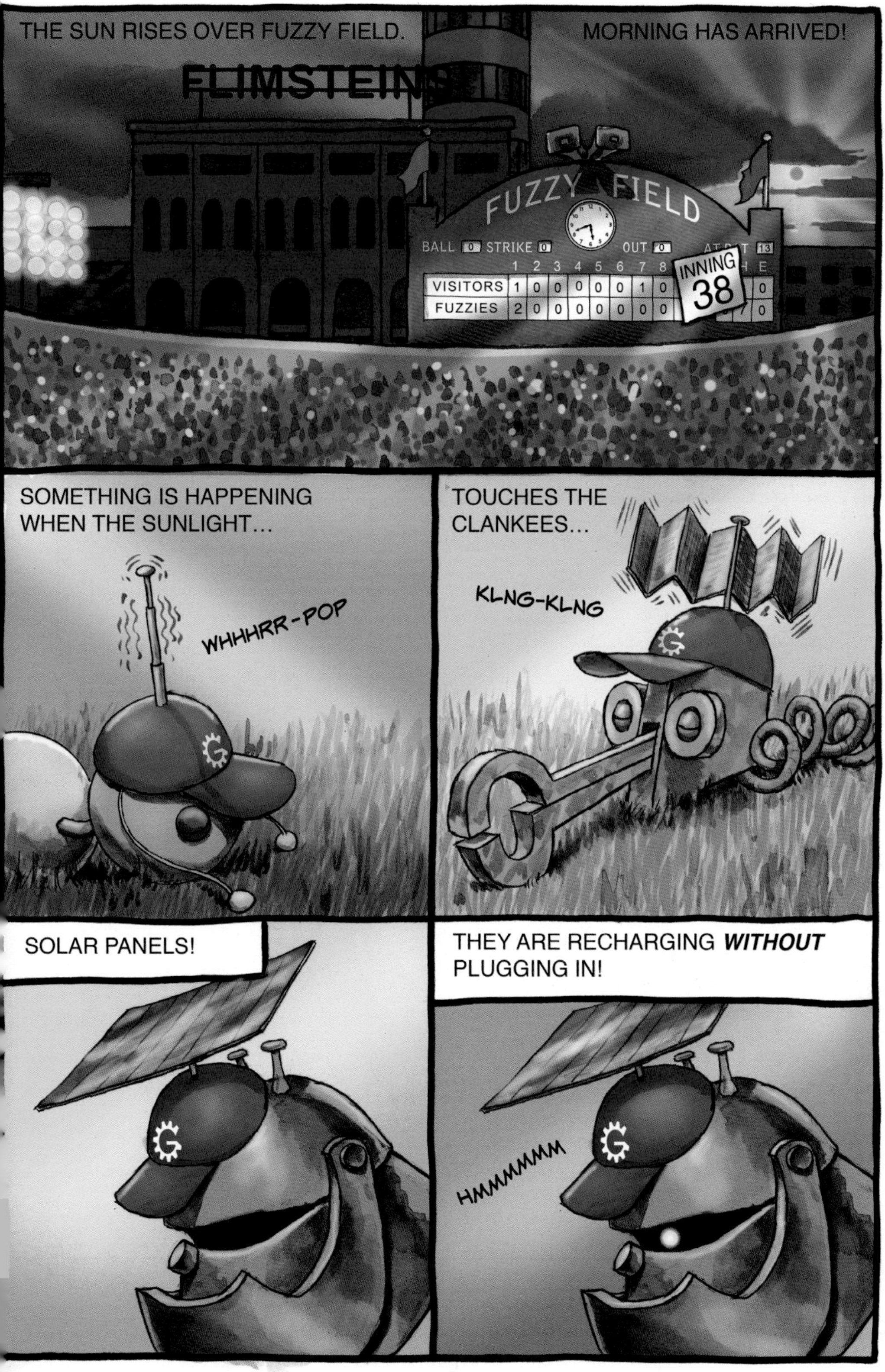
THE SUN RISES OVER FUZZY FIELD.
MORNING HAS ARRIVED!
FLIMSTEINS
FUZZY FIELD
INNING 38
VISITORS
FUZZIES
SOMETHING IS HAPPENING WHEN THE SUNLIGHT…
WHHHRR-POP
TOUCHES THE CLANKEES…
KLNG-KLNG
SOLAR PANELS!
THEY ARE RECHARGING ***WITHOUT*** PLUGGING IN!
HMMMMMM

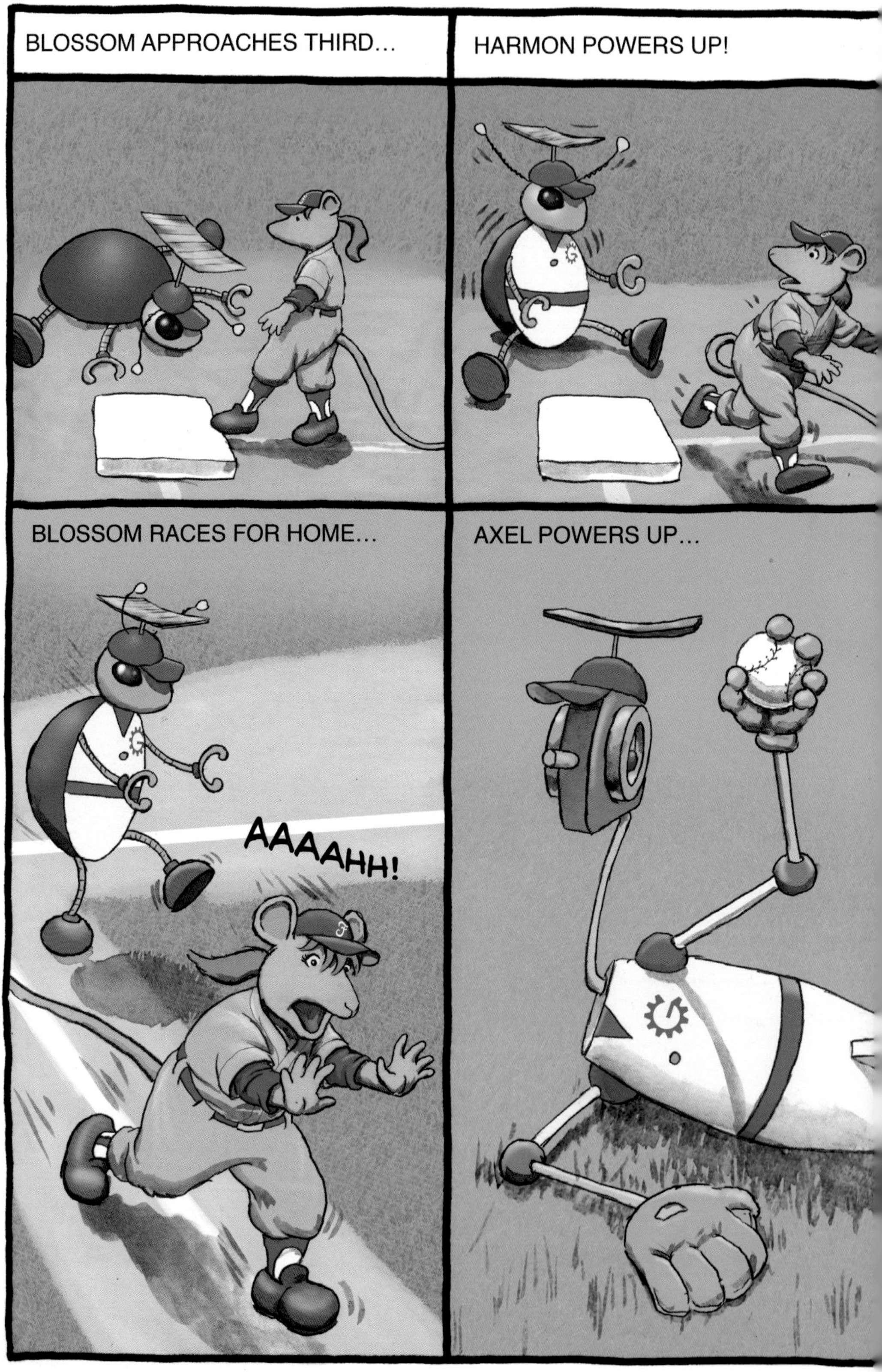
BLOSSOM APPROACHES THIRD...
HARMON POWERS UP!
BLOSSOM RACES FOR HOME...
AAAAHH!
AXEL POWERS UP...

THERE'S GOING TO BE A PLAY AT THE PLATE...

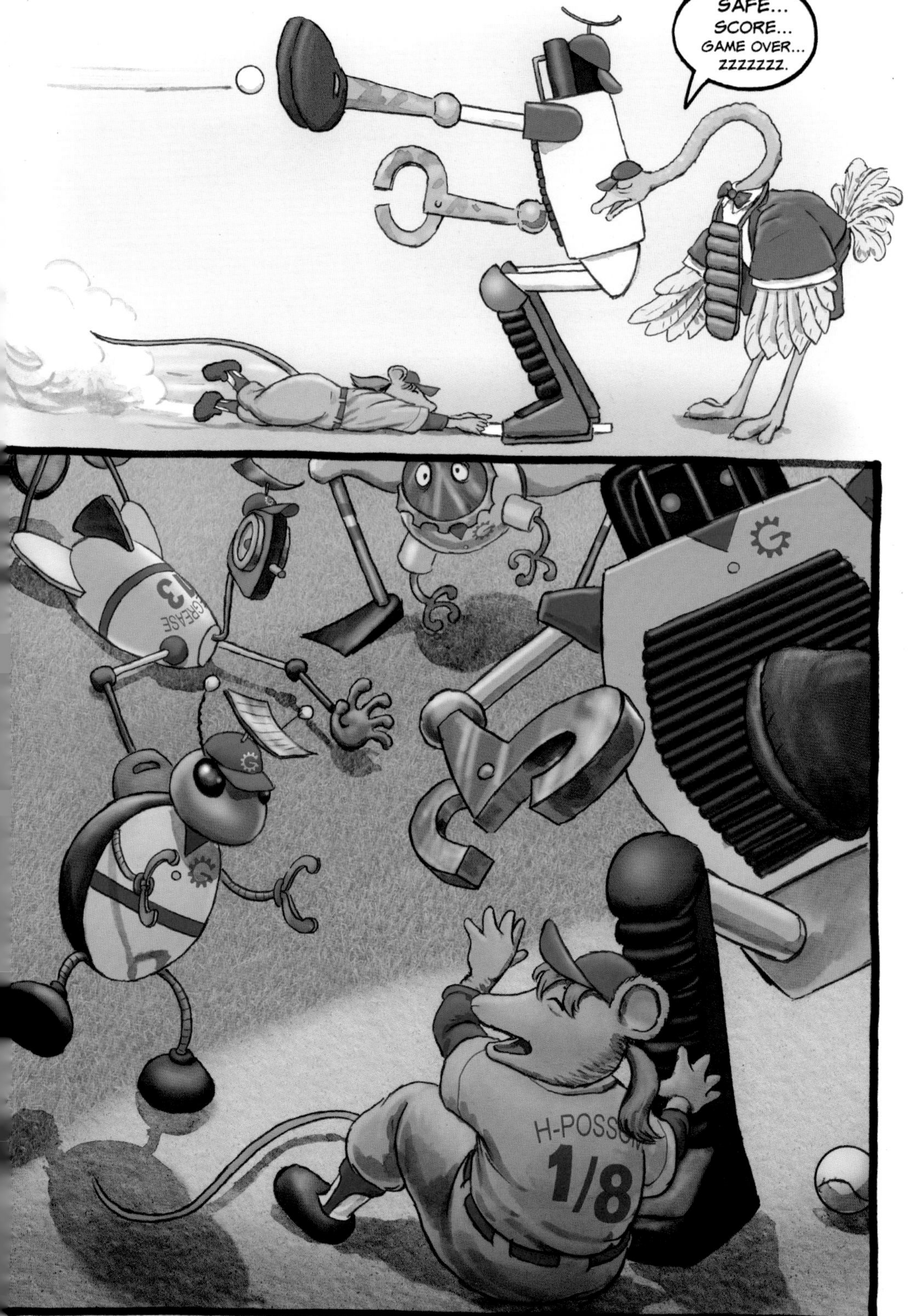
SAFE...
SCORE...
GAME OVER...
ZZZZZZZ.
GREASE
1/8

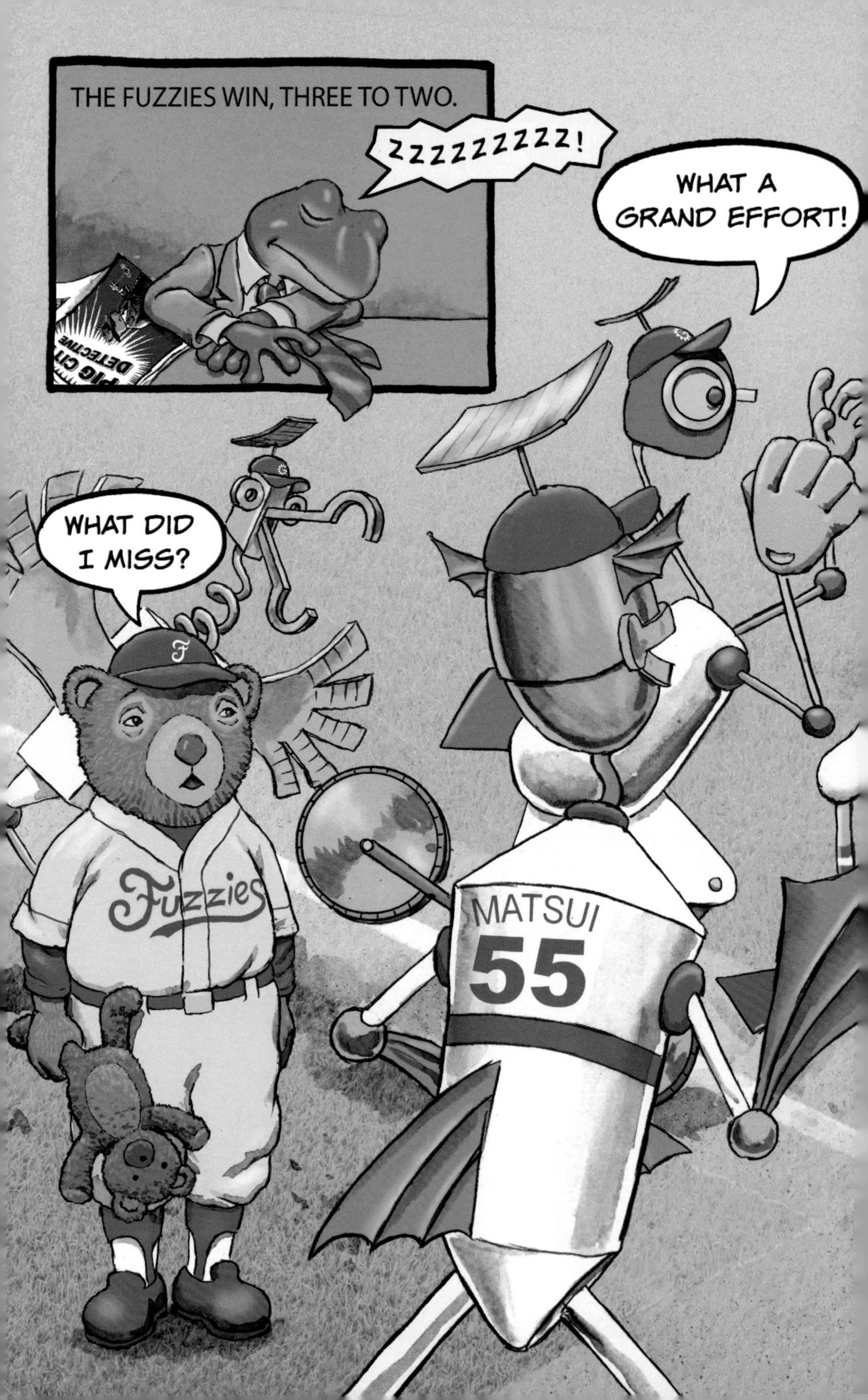
THE FUZZIES WIN, THREE TO TWO.
ZZZZZZZZZZ!
WHAT A GRAND EFFORT!
WHAT DID I MISS?
MATSUI
55
Fuzzies

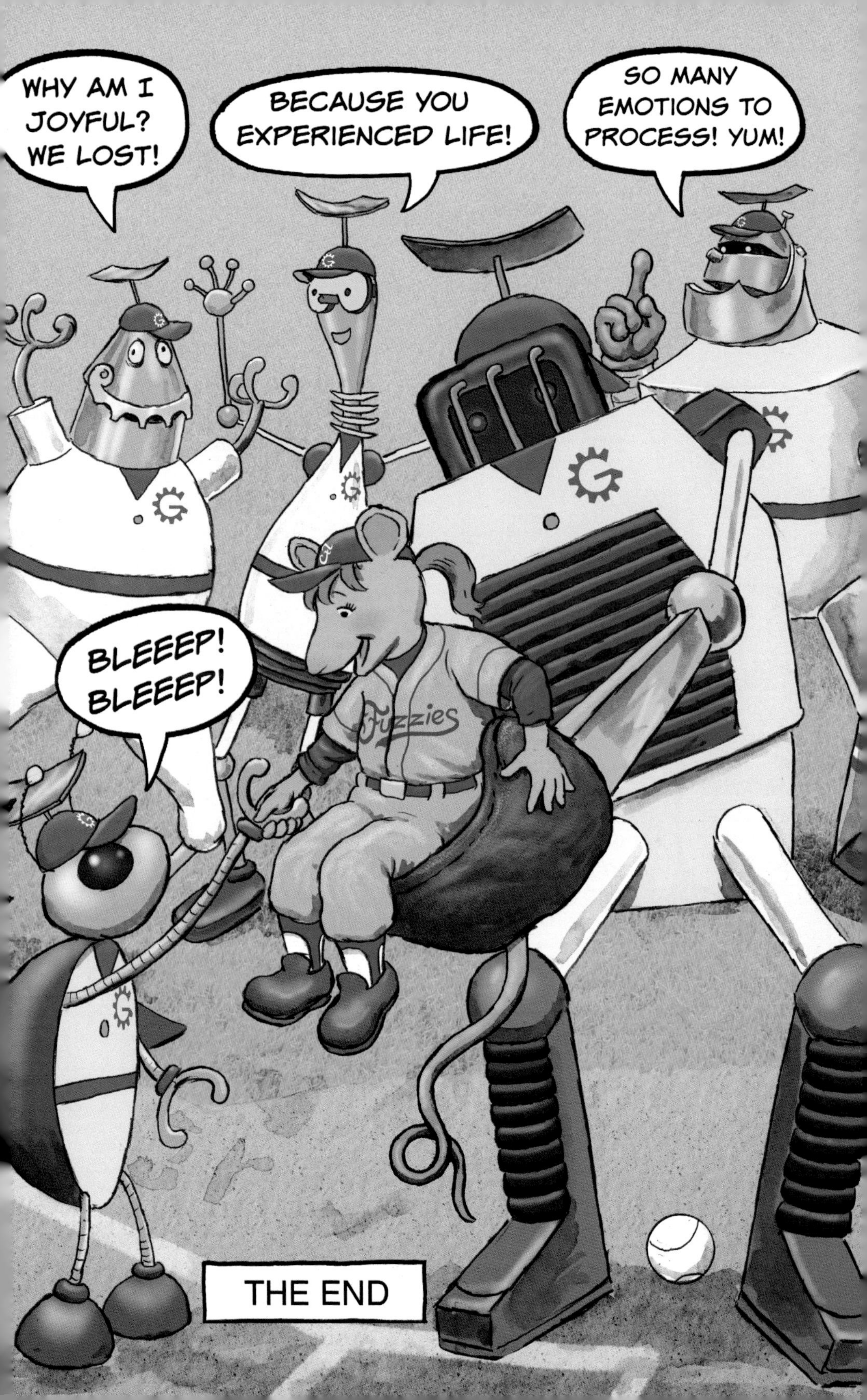
WHY AM I JOYFUL? WE LOST!
BECAUSE YOU EXPERIENCED LIFE!
SO MANY EMOTIONS TO PROCESS! YUM!
BLEEEP! BLEEEP!
Fuzzies
THE END

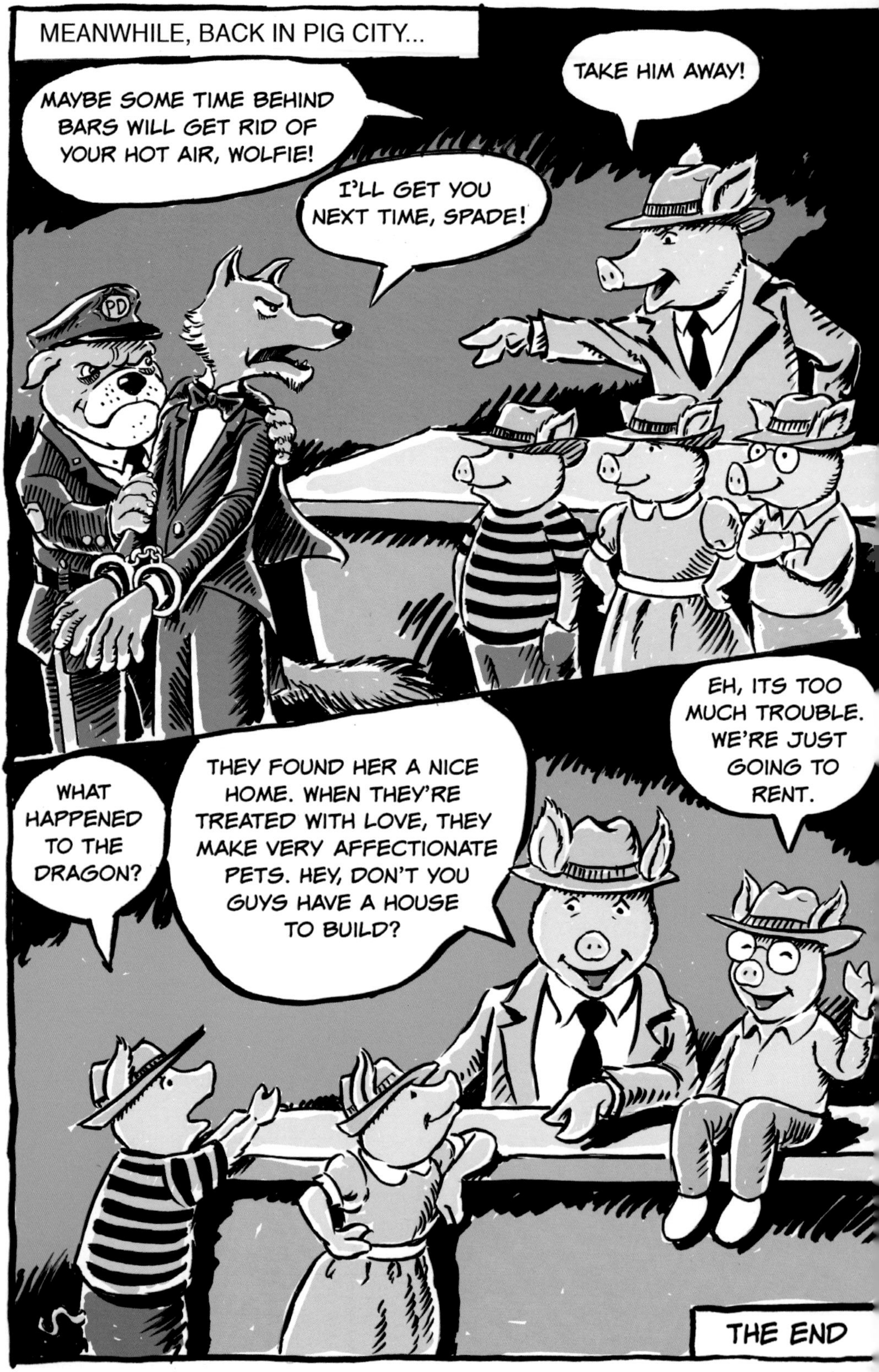
MEANWHILE, BACK IN PIG CITY...
MAYBE SOME TIME BEHIND BARS WILL GET RID OF YOUR HOT AIR, WOLFIE!
I'LL GET YOU NEXT TIME, SPADE!
TAKE HIM AWAY!
WHAT HAPPENED TO THE DRAGON?
THEY FOUND HER A NICE HOME. WHEN THEY'RE TREATED WITH LOVE, THEY MAKE VERY AFFECTIONATE PETS. HEY, DON'T YOU GUYS HAVE A HOUSE TO BUILD?
EH, ITS TOO MUCH TROUBLE. WE'RE JUST GOING TO RENT.
PD
THE END

A MEMO FROM THE COMMISIONER

As I was writing this book I had a lot of fun coming up with the names for the Geartown Clankees. Although some of the Fuzzies are named after actual players (Jackie Robinson and Sammy Sosa) every one of the Clankees are named after players from baseball history. The challenge was to find names that I could blend with words associated with engines, robots, or anything mechanical. I imagine that adults will groan as they read my puns, but I hope young readers will be curious enough to look up some of these baseball greats. I should add that the positions the characters play in this book do not necessarily correspond with the positions that they played in real life.
Here is a list of the actual players:

Harmon Killebrew   Lou Gehrig   Johnny Bench   Rogers Hornsby
Rusty Staub   Alex Rodriguez   Ty Cobb   Greg Luzinski
Bucky Dent   Cy Young
Mark McGwire   Honus Wagner
Kirby Puckett   Hank Aaron
Hideki Matsui

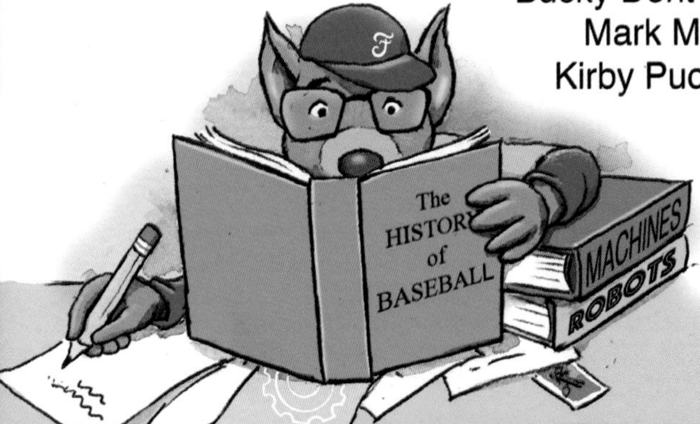
The
HISTOR
of
BASEBALL
MACHINES
ROBOTS

LEARN TO SPEAK ITALIAN WITH PERCIVALE PENGUINO

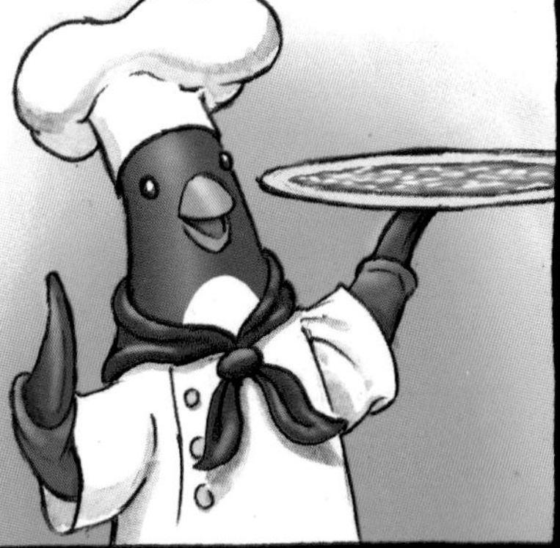

robot amichevoli – friendy robots

sfortuna – bad luck

posso giocare – I can play

WATCH OUT FOR PAPERCUTZ™

Welcome to FUZZY BASEBALL TRIPLE PLAY, collecting the first three FUZZY BASEBALL graphic novels by "The Commissioner" John Steven Gurney, brought to you by Papercutz, those editorial all-stars dedicated to publishing great graphic novels for all ages. I'm Jim Salicrup, Editor-in-Chief and Baseball Errors Corrector, here to ruminate about my relationship with America's Favorite Pastime...

It seems impossible to be born in the USA and not be aware of the sport of Baseball. In my case, I grew up in the Bronx, home of the World-Champion Yankees, and it was automatically assumed that I was a fan of the home team. Yet, the truth is I was never really a serious sports fan. The closest I came to ever playing baseball was playing with Baseball cards as a kid—we played "colors." The game had virtually nothing to do with the sport and was just a simpler version of the card game war. (Little did I realize that one day, before coming to Papercutz, I'd be editing a line of comics for The Topps Company, the folks who made those baseball cards I played with.)

But despite my not participating in the game, I still enjoyed watching movies and TV shows about baseball, everything from the *Bad News Bears to Field of Dreams* to *A League of Their Own*. One of my favorite poems is about baseball, "Casey at the Bat" by Ernest Lawrence Thayer (1863-1940). It's a truly wonderful poem that captures the drama of the sport. Allow me share a little bit of it with you. *SPOILER ALERT* Forgive me, but here's how the poem ends: With the bases loaded, Casey, Mudville's favorite player, lets two pitches go unanswered ("That ain't my style," said Casey explaining why he didn't swing at them) and then, after the third pitch...

Oh, somewhere in this favored land the sun is shining bright,
The band is playing somewhere, and somewhere hearts are light;
And somewhere men are laughing, and somewhere children shout,
But there is no joy in Mudville—mighty Casey has struck out.

I've loved comedy all my life, and as a kid loved this classic comedy routine based on baseball performed by Abbott and Costello. When Costello wants to find out the names of the players of the team Abbott is coaching, Abbott explains that the players have peculiar, funny names...

Bud Abbott: Well, let's see, we have on the bags, Who's on first, What's on second, and I Don't Know's on third.
Lou Costello: That's what I want to find out.
Bud Abbott: I say Who's on first, What's on second, I Don't Know's on third.
Lou Costello: Are you the manager?
Bud Abbott: Yes.
Lou Costello: You gonna be the coach too?
Bud Abbott: Yes.
Lou Costello: And you don't know the fellows' names?
Bud Abbott: Well, I should.
Lou Costello: Well, then who's on first?
Bud Abbott: Yes.
Lou Costello: I mean the fellow's name.
Bud Abbott: Who.
Lou Costello: The guy on first.
Bud Abbott: Who.

Well, you get the idea. Anyway, I also loved an old cartoon, "Baseball Bugs," that had Bugs Bunny playing baseball, long before he discovered basketball. Bugs single-handedly defeats the *Gashouse Gorillas*, who unfortunately were just a bunch of thugs and not really gorillas. Which finally brings me to why I love FUZZY BASEBALL. John Steven Gurney's wonderful creation combines so many things that I love—comics, comedy, cartoons, funny animals—that I don't have to be a baseball fan to totally enjoy it. I enjoy his cartooning, his characters, his puns, and the silly situations that he comes up with so much, that I can't help being a FUZZY BASEBALL fan. And if, like me, you enjoyed the stories collected in this special volume, you'll be happy to know that John's busy creating even more FUZZY BASEBALL graphic novels to further delight us all. Just keep your eye on the ball and on our wonderful website for all the latest FUZZY BASEBALL news.

Thanks,

Jim

STAY IN TOUCH!

EMAIL: salicrup@papercutz.com
WEB: www.papercutz.com
TWITTER: @papercutzgn
FACEBOOK: PAPERCUTZGRAPHICNOVELS
REGULAR MAIL: Papercutz, 160 Broadway, Suite 700, East Wing, New York, NY 10038

Go to papercutz.com and sign up for the free Papercutz e-newsletter!